THE SHADOW OF THE SOUL

Also by Sarah Pinborough from Gollancz:

A Matter of Blood

THE SHADOW OF THE SOUL

The Dog-Faced Gods

BOOK TWO

SARAH PINBOROUGH

GOLLANCZ

LONDON

Copyright © Sarah Pinborough 2011
All rights reserved

The right of Sarah Pinborough to be identified as the author
of this work has been asserted by her in accordance
with the Copyright, Designs and Patents Act 1988.

First published in Great Britain in 2011
by Gollancz
An imprint of the Orion Publishing Group
Orion House, 5 Upper St Martin's Lane,
London WC2H 9EA
An Hachette UK Company

A CIP catalogue record for this book
is available from the British Library

ISBN 978 0 575 08949 5 (Cased)
ISBN 978 0 575 08950 1 (Trade Paperback)

1 3 5 7 9 10 8 6 4 2

Typeset by Input Data Services Ltd,
Bridgwater, Somerset

Printed in Great Britain by
Clays Ltd, St Ives plc

The Orion Publishing Group's policy is to use papers
that are natural, renewable and recyclable products and
made from wood grown in sustainable forests. The logging
and manufacturing processes are expected to conform to
the environmental regulations of the country of origin.

www.sarahpinborough.com
www.orionbooks.co.uk

For Beth,
Good friends and great times are hard to come by. Go and
rock LA, you star, and get the spare room ready.

'If you were only given one choice: to choose or not to choose, which would you choose?'

Dr Shad Helmstetter, *Choices*

Prologue

The vast office was cool, but as the man stared out at the bright, sandy streets of Marrakesh sweat prickled under his linen shirt. It had nothing to do with the temperature. He looked down once again at the faxed sheet of paper that confirmed clinically what he had been told on the telephone a mere ten minutes before. His fingers felt clammy. His stomach churned. A strange taste filled his mouth. He knew this emotion: it had been creeping up on him for years, since the first signs that things were going wrong. He'd thought he'd understood the feeling then, but he'd been wrong. Had he truly felt it before? Ever? This terrible, terrible fear? Not like this, he concluded. Not like this at all. He shivered.

His slim, manicured fingers undid the locks and he pushed open the doors to the verandah. The smell of orange blossom and heat filled his nostrils and rushed past him to flood into the corners of his achingly stylish work space. He stepped out onto the warm tiles. Noise rushed upwards from the busy streets beyond the garden and guarded gates that separated him from the earthy, dirty life outside. Car horns screeched and curses flew; the men leading donkeys laden with goats' milk ignored them.

From one of the minarets that reached high above the uneven skyline of buildings that made up the swarming city, a muezzin began the call to prayer. Gone were the days when the simple power of the human voice reached out over the population. The modern world was too noisy: now the callers were projected through microphones and loudspeakers, each voice battling with those others to get their holy message across.

In the old days, he'd always enjoyed this human ritual of subservience. To watch people whose lives were filled with grief and pain and hardship, and which were ultimately so very, very short, commit so fully to a belief that this was the work of a loving God, filled him with mild amusement. The Network had sown the seeds for these religions so long ago, and then watched them grow like aggressive weeds: part truth, part fiction, part something entirely human.

For a while he'd felt affection for them, in the way a child does with some small, helpless animal whose life could be squeezed away in one unfortunate clumsy moment. Not any more.

He looked down at the piece of paper in his hand. In the bright sunlight the whiteness glared back at him, the black letters shimmering as if floating on its surface. Now the call to prayer filled him with something else – bitterness, perhaps. A sense of being cheated. He felt a sudden urge to go to Damascus, as if by returning to the place that had been his home for so very long he could somehow avoid the blunt facts on the printed sheet. They were wrong, those facts. They had to be. Things like this had never been part of the plan. What were they – a last laugh?

The muezzin was in full flow: Allah Akbar. God is the greatest. There is no deity except Allah. Come to the true success. Allah Akbar.

God is the greatest. He couldn't help but smile, even with the stale tang of fear on his tongue. If only these people really understood their own history. If only they knew how truly *glorious and terrible it was;* then *they should bow down in prayer.*

The phone behind him had been ringing for several seconds before he noticed it. He was lost in the heat and the life outside and the fear within and wondering how all these millions lived with it every day. The answerphone didn't cut in and eventually the peal of the bell summoned him from his reverie and he turned back to his office. He closed the doors on the world outside and sat in his expensive leather chair, enjoying the familiar feel of its cool surface as it took his weight. He placed the sheet of paper on the blotting pad beside him before reaching for the handset. A single red light flashed along with each trill of the bell and he knew what that meant. He breathed ... regained his composure ... and then answered.

'Yes?'

'Monmir?'

'Who else would it be?' He kept the irritation at the edge of his voice. His eyes were drawn to the sheet of paper beside him. One phone call ago. Fifteen minutes ago. A world ago.

'The Architect has called a meeting.'

'Since when did the Architect have the power to do that?' Monmir liked the idle tone of his own voice. It had the echo of arrogance in it, despite the fear gnawing at him.

'He comes with a majority.' There was a pause. 'And he's the Architect.'

'Yes, I suppose he is.' The Architect had always been different. Monmir wasn't even sure he'd ever particularly liked him. 'When?'

'There's a jet on its way to you.'

'Of course there is.' Monmir was about to hang up when he glanced at the paper again. 'One more thing,' he said softly. 'You can tell him I apparently have pancreatic cancer. It's aggressive. And terminal.'

3

There was a long silence at the other end. Monmir wasn't surprised. Fear was catching. Eventually the phone clicked off in his ear.

After replacing the handset, he stared at the faxed copy of his results for several long moments before carefully screwing it up into a tight ball and dropping it into the bin beside him. He just wished his hands hadn't been shaking so much as he did it.

Chapter One

Hell came to earth.

As fire raged, black smoke choked the clear blue skies, its pall gloating over the devastation that littered the ground beneath. Glass shattered as the heat broke its will. Bodies lay quiet in the wreckage, legs and arms spread wide at strange, inhuman angles, their dignity stripped. Others wandered, lost, no longer recognising their surroundings, pale shadows of themselves, caked in grime with red streaks cutting through the dirt from injuries that might or might not yet prove fatal.

A bland man in his forties – not too tall, not too short, not too much of anything but a little bit of everything – staggered into view, and his eyes were wide as he fell to his knees. Blood pumped onto the filthy pavement from the crater at his shoulder where his arm had so recently been attached. He looked down at his ruined suit, and his mouth dropped open. For a moment the chaos around him stilled before he tumbled sideways. *Should have taken the next bus. Should have chosen to work from home today.* His eyes were still in denial just before the light went out of them. No one rushed over to him. Sirens wailed quietly in the background and more screams erupted; in the distance a woman called plaintively for help, her voice mono amidst the stereo of death. She clutched the body of an unmoving child, trapped half in and half out of some twisted metal debris that might once have been a car, or maybe part of a bus. It was hard to tell.

The screen displaying the images went ignored by the small group of men and women studying laptops and taking phone calls.

'Mobile phone networks shut down.'

'All of them?'

'Done.'

'Good.'

'If that's how they're triggering.'

'Fuck me, the LRT have put out there've been power surges on several lines.'

'Does anyone still believe that bullshit?'

'No one that's near a TV. The PM's message is about to broadcast.'

'Get people off the buses.'

'Which buses?'

'All of them. Anything moving with people on it. Off, now.'

More phones rang and bodies moved in flashes of suits and sweat around the small underground room. Abigail Porter watched from the corner. Her own shirt was dry, despite the muggy warmth of the COBR office.

More movement; more snapped sentences.

'Keep talking to me, people. Who reported this as a major incident?'

'Ambulance Service.'

'Other ES have universally confirmed.'

'Silver Command?'

'All in situ at the JESCC.'

'Only life-threatening injuries to hospitals for now.'

'Passing it on.'

'You won't fucking believe this! Russians had intel on potential attacks on London today.'

'What?'

'I know, I'm on it. Where were the ATD on this?'

'Blame later, people. Manage now.'

'PM's pre-record is going out.'

'Fuck, the streets are going to be a mess.'

'Reports of fires coming in.'

'Let's keep the info stream clean.'

'Chemicals?'

'Nothing confirmed.'

'ChemTeams on their way to sites.'

'Then let's worry about that when we have to.'

'Jesus.'

Abigail figured she was the only person who'd realised the Prime Minister had entered the room until she spoke.

'Is this Ealing Broadway?' Alison McDonnell's heavyset face was pale, and she hadn't taken her gaze from the unfolding news as she waited for one of the gathered aides to answer.

Abigail stayed quiet, and leaned against the desk. Her heart thumped with the adrenalin surge, but it was an empty beat. She felt distanced from the dying and injured displayed across the screen. To be honest, most days she felt distanced from everything.

'Yes,' Andrew Dunne, head of Special Branch, answered quietly as the devastation on screen was replaced with the PM's own face for a few minutes, her mouth moving, silent and serious, as she instructed people to stay calm, to get off whatever public transport they were on and walk home.

'From what we gather, there were three explosions in close proximity to each other that went off eighteen minutes ago. We need to get into the site to know for sure but it looks like one detonated in a bus, one in a car and one in a clothes shop. All three occurred within a ninety-second period: people fleeing from one blast got caught in the next, and so on. This was very well planned.'

There was a pause, and Abigail felt the tension tighten in the air around her. The stillness that filled the room in Downing Street was in stark contrast to the frantic activity on the screen as the pre-record finished and journalists scrambled to each of the sites, filling the gaps around the incoming footage with their jabber. From her corner, Abigail thought she could see a distinct glint of satisfaction in their eyes.

'Jesus,' Alison McDonnell repeated, 'it's *Saturday lunchtime* – that street would be crowded.' She paused. 'And in the Underground?'

'We've not got any footage yet, but we can confirm a large explosion on the Northern Line at Tottenham Court Road fourteen minutes ago, and another on the District Line at Tower Hill. And we've got unconfirmed reports' – he cleared his throat a little, as if the words were sticking there – 'of a similar event at Liverpool Street, on the Central Line.'

'A similar event?' She turned a sharp eye on the policeman. 'These are bombs, man, not events. People are *dying*, Dunne. They deserve more than your euphemisms.'

The phone on the desk rang and Abigail noticed the flinch that shuddered through the room, as if somehow the line were causing the terror rather than just reporting it. Dunne lifted the receiver and listened quietly before lowering it back.

'Hampstead. Two explosions.'

'Dear God, let that be it.' She looked like she had aged years in the fifteen minutes since chaos took London's reins, and as she rubbed her face, the skin moved like slack putty. 'In the name of all that's holy, let that be it.'

'Emergency services are flat-out, and the hospitals are as ready as they can be. We're already pulling in more resources from wherever can spare them.' Dunne paused. 'But, ma'am, there are going to be a large number of casualties. There's no avoiding that.'

Alison McDonnell's sigh came from a place inside her the public rarely saw: the softer side. The feminine side that was hidden under her butch, no-nonsense exterior. Very few people, even those in her Cabinet, got to see that part of their leader, but Abigail Porter recognised it. She understood her boss. In the game of personal protection, understanding the client was imperative.

The PM slowly straightened up, her broad shoulders squaring. 'I know it's early, but has anyone claimed responsibility yet? Where the hell is Fletcher? Shouldn't he be here?'

'He's on his way over,' Lucius Dawson, the Home Secretary, cut in. 'Although I recommend you send him back to the CNS. There's nothing he or his men can do from here except watch the television with us. He'll be on the other end of the phone.'

The PM gave him a slight nod of acknowledgement.

There was a long pause, then she said, 'I suppose we'd better prepare a statement and get ready to face the press.'

'Tony Barker's on it already. He'll be ready for you in about fifteen.'

The room hummed with activity as now there was something to do, but Abigail felt her eyes drawn back to the screen, where the screaming and moaning and dying continued. 'Ma'am,' she said, quietly, 'tonight's dinner?'

'Will be going ahead. The peace talks might be a farce

behind closed doors, but I'll be damned if these bastards stop what is at least an attempt at sanity.'

Abigail wasn't surprised. Alison McDonnell was not a woman who was easily bullied. Her opponents snarkily put it down to her sexual tendencies, calling her more man than woman, but such comments just made the Prime Minister smile. Abigail understood why: men never really got women: when they were tough, they were terrifying. She knew that because she knew herself, and the coldness that lived at the core of her. If her job required it, she'd shoot a child, and she doubted she'd hesitate for even a breath.

'I'll rework the arrangements,' she said, stepping away from the desk.

'Good,' the PM said, but she wasn't really listening; her eyes had returned to the screen.

Abigail gave it one last glance before leaving the stuffy heat of the busy room. She didn't see anything on it that touched her.

Chapter Two

Abigail Porter scanned the room as the PM and the foreign ministers from Chechnya and Russia respectively smiled and nodded at the flashing cameras and declared how happy they were with the peace talks. She didn't have to listen to know what was being said: *Although no final agreements have been reached we are confident that all parties are moving in the right direction to secure more friendly relations between these two proud nations* – some bullshit like that. She'd heard enough of these speeches from trips to the Middle East and China, about all those suicidal little countries that were eager to self-destruct, as long as they were taking someone else out with them.

The room was barely half-full after this afternoon's bombs, with only a select few journalists allowed access to the short post-dinner press conference. Security on the way in had been beyond tight. As Barker, Number 10's press officer, took to the microphone, the three politicians slipped into a side-room, Abigail falling in behind them. Her job was not the security of all; only the security of the stolid, serious woman who had been elected to run the country.

In the quiet office the smiles fell away from the Eastern Europeans as if their weight had been unbearable. The Prime Minister poured both men a brandy, and took one herself. For a moment none of them spoke.

'I'm sorry your visits couldn't have ended on a happier note,' Alison McDonnell said after swirling her brandy, sniffing it, then taking a sip, 'but after today's events the inability of your nations to get on with each other is no longer my immediate concern.'

Abigail could see that her boss was exhausted. Cracks were visible in her usually impeccable make-up, which sat uncomfortably on her drained face.

'Let me reassure you once again,' the Russian started, his thick accent sounding grumbling as he spoke, 'these terrible events had nothing to do with Russia. We have always considered the United Kingdom to be among our friends.'

'As have we.' The Chechen Foreign Minister glared at the Russian. 'But this you know. Chechnya does not have the capability to organise such attack on your capital.'

'Don't treat me like I'm naïve, Mr Maskadhov. Of course you do. Your people have survived through terrorism.'

The other man stood up abruptly, and she raised her hands. 'I'm sorry. That was harsh, perhaps, and poorly expressed – but you understand my concerns. Hundreds of British citizens died today, and I am quite sure you are aware it will not look good for any future talks if either of your nations is found to bear any responsibility.'

'You will have our full support in your investigation, and our own security forces will be on hand to assist, should you need them.'

She smiled at the Russian. 'How kind, *gaspadeen* Nemov. If only you'd been so generous and shared your intel earlier – I'm aware your agencies had knowledge of a potential attack. Perhaps next time you'll pass that on before it's too late?'

'Unfortunately,' Nemov replied smoothly, 'there are too many threats every day, and it is not always easy to know which are serious. And the one to which I think you are referring was not this kind of threat. It was . . .' he hesitated, then continued, 'more personal, shall we say.'

Ignoring the crackling voices in her ear alerting her to the dignitaries' cars arriving, cleared by security, Abigail homed in on his comment. *More personal?* So the intel the Russians had uncovered was for an attack on McDonnell herself. The news didn't surprise or overly concern her. The nation's security level had been rated critical ever since the Eurotunnel disaster, and no one was keen to lower it, not even down to severe. There were too many threats constantly flooding the system. Still, Russian intel was normally reliable; maybe they were just a little off with their interpretation of the target. London certainly got hit today.

'Perhaps whichever MI6 agents you have in our services' – Nemov smiled, before draining his brandy – 'should pay more attention to the detail.'

Abigail stepped forward and filled the space occupied by tense silence. 'Prime Minister, gentlemen, your cars are ready and your routes are secured.' As she spoke she saw the tiniest flicker of a smile on the PM's face. Abigail didn't blame her. This was a day that everyone wanted to be over.

By midnight her relief had arrived and within fifteen minutes Abigail had changed into her jogging suit and trainers and was running past the guards, who let her out of the small gate at the bottom of Downing Street. Her feet thumped out a steady beat as she ran around St James' Park and then headed along the Embankment and up into the old city towards her flat, just off Fleet Street. It wasn't a long or particularly taxing run, but it did help her unwind for the night. There had been a time when she would have used the clear air to calm down and sort the rush of thoughts that filled her head, but recently she found she simply switched it all off and let the physical take over.

Around her, London was deathly still, but already invisible people had stuck pictures of the missing up on lamp posts and the thick grey stone that lined the river, and paper flapped in the light breeze. She didn't pause. People died every day. She let the emptiness take her. There was a comfort in it.

She was nearly home when a figure caught her eye, a man on the other side of the road, in a dark suit. A very fat man in a dark suit.

She stopped, her heart still pounding from the exercise, and frowned. What was he doing out tonight? And at this time, after everything that had happened? Her skin tingled with something that wasn't fear or unease but something *other*, something indefinable at her very core. She didn't move. He was strange. A *stranger* – instinct told her that. Her thoughts had stilled, but her eyes continued with the tasks she had been so well trained in. She scanned his large body: the pale hands that hung straight at his sides held no posters or papers, so he wasn't looking for a missing loved one. The suit was tight against his round body, and although she couldn't be completely certain, there were no tell-tale breaks in the line hinting at a concealed weapon – plus the three buttons that ran down the middle were neatly done up, making it difficult for a quick attack.

She watched him while she consciously slowed her breathing, the only noise in the quiet night. He stood next to an old-fashioned red phone box, and for a moment they faced each other across the deserted tarmac. Despite his bulk he looked ill, or perhaps more as if sickness was his natural state. He was pale, his visible skin almost marbling in the streetlights. He didn't smile, and she was too far away to make out the expression in his dark eyes. Her feet shuffled, breaking the stillness.

'What do you want?' she called over to him. The words surprised her. She'd meant to ask if he was okay, or if he was lost, but somehow that wasn't the question that came out. Maybe it came from that *other* feeling, the one she couldn't put her finger on. He wanted something, this stranger, she was sure. And he wanted it specifically from her.

He raised one finger to his lips. The air around her softened and settled in her lungs. For a moment the emptiness was all, and then he walked away, his back stiff, his movements precise as he turned the corner and headed down a gloomy alleyway. As Abigail watched him go, part of her brain thought she should run after him, but her feet didn't move. *I'll see him again.* The thought anchored itself in her mind for a moment before drifting away.

She shook herself. She peered into the alleyway, but there was no one there. The weirdness of the moment slunk away into the night and she shivered a little as her running sweat dried. It had been a long day, that was all: just a long day filled with death. She needed to sleep. She walked the rest of the short way home and she didn't look back. Whoever the man was, he was gone.

Inside her practical, modern and impersonal flat she stretched for twenty minutes and then headed for a long shower. The water was almost hot enough to burn and her taut skin was pink when she stepped out. She wasn't sure she'd even really felt it.

It was two a.m. when she set her alarm for 6.30 and let her eyes close. She fell asleep quickly, her head uncluttered with any mundane trivia of emotion and reflection. At some point during the short course of her adult life she'd found that where others' lives were getting filled with more people, and families, and mortgages, hers was emptying. There had been no serious boyfriend in nearly five years, despite her sensual good looks. She had sex when the urge came on her, and she found that she didn't much mind whether it was with a man or woman, but male or female, she avoided any more than a second or third date. What was the point? They were all incidental; a virus spread across the earth. Nature's accident, that's all anyone was – herself included. There was neither logic nor rhyme nor reason to it.

She would live out her time alone. Her flat was rented so she could leave at a moment's notice, should she choose, and what possessions she had, though expensive, were all necessary. Life was fleeting. There was no point in trying to anchor yourself with things.

It was only just before unconsciousness claimed her that she realised she hadn't thought to check on Hayley today, to see if she had been affected by the attacks. The thought made her soul tremble. Even for her, there was too much that was wrong in that inaction. How could she not have checked? *How could she not have cared?* Her heart thumped loudly for a beat or two and then settled into its normal slow march. Their parents would have checked on her. If anything had happened to Hayley, they would have called. She let that thought calm her, even though she knew it didn't touch the problem. *She* was the problem.

When she slept, she dreamed of running through endless corridors of darkness chasing a strip of glowing gold light that was always out of reach. She wouldn't remember it in the morning. She never did.

Katie Dodds had turned the TV off an hour or so ago, and since then had just stared at the ceiling. She was barely aware of the sharp knife in her hand. The news had gone round in circles all night, and it had all become a blur. The news-readers talked too fast, and the images were confusing. With awkward fingers she pulled up her sleeves and then sighed, feeling the heaviness that sank back into her limbs. The bulb hanging from the ceiling reflected in the dark shine of her dulled eyes. She wasn't sure of the time. Four a.m. maybe? It was dark outside, but the thickness of night had faded. Her room was silent apart from her shallow breath, but despite the late hour there was still noise in the rest of the house. Laughter drifted under the bottom of her closed door, but she didn't recognise it. Her forehead tensed in a small frown. That wasn't quite true. She did know whose laugh it was, but she couldn't quite match it up with the faces of the other students in her house. It was dislocated. Just like her.

As she stared at the ceiling her mouth moved, though she emitted no sound. It had not been a good day. Her brain had felt wrong; not painful, but as if someone had been pulling down on one side of it. Her words hadn't come out right all afternoon. She'd been glad to get to the quiet of her room, away from everyone. She'd thought about going to the hospital – briefly – but she hadn't been in any pain outside of this weird confusion, and then with all the bombs going off there would have been no one to see her anyway, and after a while it had all been too much effort.

Her mind emptied. She tried to focus on something other than the buzz in her ears. Her heart raced and her eyes forced themselves inwards. She gasped. She didn't want to see. She'd never wanted to see. Her hand tightened around the knife. On the ceiling the bland paint swirled in a million colours, wanting to suck her in. For the briefest moment she thought she saw her own face staring back behind them.

After a while she became aware of coolness in her wrists.

She glanced down. Her left hand dropped the small, sharp knife, as if aware of guiltily being caught after the fact. She frowned again. Shouldn't it hurt? Shouldn't all this bleeding hurt? She looked from one slashed wrist to the other as her blood pumped out of her and onto the covers below. She sighed. It took all her effort to dip one finger in the soaking mess and write on the wall beside her the only sentence that would stay in her head.

When she was done she closed her eyes and died. It came as a relief.

Chapter Three

Cass Jones took the stairs up through the untidy student house two at a time, ignoring the faces that peered nervously out from their bedroom doors. He was tired. He was always fucking tired, and in the chaos of the past two weeks since the bombings, the rest of the force might have caught up with him, but he'd had a bloody good head-start. For Cass, the past six months had dragged on forever, in a constant round of interviews, arrests, statements, and of course the backlash that comes with uncovering corruption among your own. The resentment was far from behind him as the overloaded justice system slowly trundled towards court dates. Still, it wasn't like he really gave a shit what the rest of the force thought of him. He only had to remember Clare May's broken body lying at the bottom of the stairs of Paddington Green nick to feel good about the number of careers that were now well and truly over. They'd done it to themselves.

'The constable downstairs says it's suicide.'

Cass paused as he took in the scene in the room. 'So what the fuck have you called me up at stupid o'clock in the morning for?' He finished the sentence more quietly than he'd started. The dead girl was kneeling in a pool of her own blood. Her arms were thrust into the glass screen of the TV, and her wrists were slashed on the jagged glass edges. There was still a sour tang of electricity in the air. Cass didn't know how she'd looked alive, but there was nothing pretty about her dead.

'I can think of better ways to kill myself,' Cass muttered.

'Great, isn't it?' Josh Eagleton, the assistant ME, straightened up from where he'd been crouched by the body and smiled at Cass. 'Morning. Glad you could make it.'

'At least one of us is.'

Eagleton's cheeky grin didn't fade, and despite his own frown, Cass was glad to see that easy cheer. Eagleton might have been left with a slight limp, but the young pathologist was lucky to be alive after being run down and left for dead. If he was still smiling, despite whatever nightmares Cass was sure he must have, then Eagleton was going to be okay in the long run.

'I think you'll like this. It's a curious one.'

'Is it murder?' Cass looked at the girl again. Her head had lolled forward as her body slumped into the TV, and her hair now hid her face. He didn't want to disturb the scene just to see her expression. Novels and films overrated the death stare. You couldn't read much from a dying face – everyone died scared, whether it was suicide, murder or natural causes. All he ever saw on a corpse's face was the ghost of that fear.

'Not murder in any ordinary sense, I don't think. But there's definitely something weird going on here.'

'Spit it out, Josh. I've got a busy day ahead.'

'Tell me about it. Everyone who's breathing in my job is still spending all their spare time in some hospital somewhere, putting together pieces of the dead. Most of the time it's just a lucky dip: if the limb fits, use it. This girl's lucky she got anyone at all.'

The young man had a point. Dr Marsden, the new ME

for Paddington and Chelsea, had pulled triple shifts in one of the central hospitals in the aftermath of what was already known only by its date: 26/09, and the gruesome task was still ongoing. Even for people who worked with the dead on a daily basis, the mangled wreckage of bodies from the explosion sites was disturbing. He looked at the doctor's assistant more closely. Judging by the bags under Eagleton's eyes, he'd put in plenty of hours himself.

'Point taken,' Cass said. 'But what's so interesting about this one? Apart from her imaginative choice of exit?' He glanced around the rest of the room. Textbooks lay sprawled open across the floor beside the bed, with half a joint and the rest of the contents of a fallen ashtray sprinkled across them. Some hippy jewellery shit hung over the corners of the mirror, and photos and posters covered the cheap wallpaper. The room could have belonged to pretty much any female student in the country.

'Her boyfriend was here when she did it. They'd been watching some movie. He'd fallen asleep and woke up to see her crawling across the floor to the TV.'

'Is the boyfriend still here?'

'Yeah, downstairs. Shaken up, not least by the electric shock he got trying to pull her out.' Eagleton paused. 'Don't think I'll tell him that his pulling her backwards only made her bleed out quicker.' He held up his own slim wrists where the blue veins stood out against the skin. 'He tugged, she tore.' He mimicked the movement.

'You were born for this job, Eagleton, you know that, don't you?'

'There's something to be said for spending your days with the dead.' Eagleton pulled his gloves off. 'They don't interrupt me, or complain about my singing. And I get to be surrounded by nudity.'

21

'You're going to have to learn some new jokes if you're ever going to get promoted. That kind of comment is so old it should be on a slab itself.'

'Haha! You're funny, Jones, very funny.'

'And back to the point?'

'It's what the boyfriend said. He told me he woke up and tried to talk to her, and all she said was this one sentence. She said it three times, once just before she did this.'

'What pearl of wisdom was that, then?'

'She said, "Chaos in the darkness" and that was all.'

'What?'

'"Chaos in the darkness." He heard her pretty clearly, and it's not the kind of thing you'd make up.'

'She was stoned.' Cass pointed to the joint. 'She was probably just talking shit.'

'Yeah, and I'd probably have thought that too, if it was the first time I'd come across the phrase.'

'What do you mean?'

'I've seen it before – two weeks ago. Another student topped herself, this one from Chelsea Art College. She slit her own wrists – admittedly in a more traditional way – but she wrote the same sentence on the wall, in her own blood, probably as she was dying. "Chaos in the darkness."'

Cass looked down at the dead girl. Her blood would be settling quickly into her lower limbs, and soon her skin would turn bluey-purple. Hopefully Eagleton would get her out quickly, before her body distorted too much. At some point her parents were going to want to take her home.

'Are you sure it was the same sentence? She said the same thing the other girl wrote? Not your memory playing tricks?'

'No,' Eagleton said positively, 'I was called to the other one the morning after the bombs – had to go straight to Chelsea from St Mary's. I haven't forgotten anything about that particular twenty-four hours. And apart from that, there are photos in the file.'

Cass didn't speak. *Chaos in the darkness.* What did it mean? He fought a yawn. Maybe it didn't mean anything at all. He looked at the girl again and felt the familiar twinge that came with the job: the wanting to know *why*. It was a strange sentence for last words: it was a declaration of fact, not an explanation of her actions. Nor a suicide note. Or maybe in some way it was all three. His brain ticked and whirred, turning the words around this way and that.

'You on a good case at the moment?' Eagleton asked, breaking into Cass's reverie.

'You know the answer to that – until all that other shit is done and dusted I'm getting the dross. I'm spending too much time retelling the same story to different lawyers for them to trust me with a decent murder. You know how it is.'

'Oh yeah. I love those lawyers.'

For a moment the two men said nothing. The weight of the black mark they shared had formed a bond between them. Eagleton's evidence had been more than enough to get the old ME, Mark Farmer – his boss – charged, and Cass's information had led to the arrest of too many of Paddington Green's officers. Some had been quietly let off the hook in an effort to stop the press realising how far the corruption in the system had spread; in exchange they in turn fingered the ringleaders. But all of those involved in the conspiracy, not just to take money from criminals in exchange for looking the other way, but actually getting in on the criminal action themselves, had friends, and there were plenty among them who believed no one had really been doing any harm; it wasn't as if they were letting *murderers* off the hook, after all.

Cass looked again at the younger man. Eagleton didn't really look like a kid any more. He'd done a lot of growing up fast.

'You're right,' Cass said. 'This could be worth a quick check, as long as no one gets on my back over it. What was the other suicide's name, can you remember?'

'Yep. Katie Dodds. Just turned twenty-one. I'll get the file over to you. Someone's already taken an official statement from the boyfriend here. When I'm done here I'll get you a copy of the report. Can't see anyone else being interested.'

'Thanks. It's probably nothing, but I'll take a look.'

'Good,' Josh Eagleton said. 'They're only young. They deserve someone to know why.'

Cass headed back down the stairs. Eagleton was already well ahead of his old boss, in Cass's opinion. Cass knew all about how the fingers of the dead could grip you; looked like the lab rat was fast learning that too.

It was still early, and as he'd not showered or shaved before heading out to meet Eagleton, Cass headed home before going to the nick. He had plenty of time before he had to be in, and he wasn't ready for anyone at Paddington Green to see him looking anything less than professional. Sometimes appearances really were everything; he knew that better than most. He flicked on the kettle in the small kitchen before heading into the shower. His new flat in St John's Wood was small but functional, and it suited Cass, probably better than the big house in Muswell Hill ever had.

He stepped under the shower. He'd be glad when the house sale finally completed. He'd sold at a ridiculously low price, the only way to shift it in the dead housing market, but it was worth it, just to draw a line under some of the memories. And it wasn't as if he was short of cash: The

Bank had cleared his brother's mortgage once he'd proved Christian had been murdered, and that house was now rented out, while the life insurance pay-out was sitting as yet untouched in Cass's own bank account.

He let the hot water run over him. Every life could be accounted for by a cash sum. If the world had taught him anything it was that. From betrayal for thirty pieces of silver to Claire May tumbling to her death to protect illegal earnings, to family life insurance, life and death all came down to currency. It left a bad taste in his mouth ... he had a bad taste in his mouth and the healthiest bank balance he'd had in years. And on top of all that, his pay packet was going to be substantially bigger, as he was due a whole load of official bonuses after the arrests and convictions of his fellow officers. That was another reason why there weren't too many people at the station – and in nicks across London – keen to stand by Cass; there was a distinct feeling that he was profiteering from the force.

He turned up the heat, sending a cloud of steam billowing out through the shower curtain. He could live with all that shit. After all, he'd been through worse. As he scrubbed at his skin he started wishing it was as easy to clean off the memories of the past and the ghosts of the dead: Claire May, his wife Kate, Christian and his family, the lost child Luke ... and over everything loomed the dark shadow of The Bank, and the mysterious Mr Bright. He shut it out. *There is no glow* – the thought beat at his skull every morning, and though he knew it was a lie, he didn't care; he intended to try and live by that lie. Cass had no intention of taking part in whatever games Mr Bright and Solomon had wanted to play with him and his family. The gritty, real world of crime was all that interested him. They could find another family for their experiments.

Out of the shower, he quickly towelled himself dry.

There is no glow. That sentence was replaced with another, equally strange, if less familiar: *Chaos in the darkness.* Eagleton had been right: he was intrigued. Two girls at two separate universities, both using the same phrase while killing themselves – coincidence? A man had told him recently that there were no coincidences. Cass was inclined to agree with him.

He drank a quick cup of coffee as he dressed and headed for the door, until the answerphone's flashing light caught his eye. Two messages had been left while he'd been in the bathroom. The world might be dead on its feet, but it still started work early.

'Mr Jones? This is Edgar Marlowe, from Marlowe and Beale solicitors' office? It's really rather important that you call me back on—'

Cass didn't give the man a chance to finish his sentence before he hit delete. Another fucking lawyer. The voice sounded familiar, and Cass wondered if he had called before. More than likely; Bowman and Blackmore's trials were coming up soon, and most of the calls put through to his office were something to do with the fucking case. This one pissed him off though: this was his home number. Who the hell had given them that?

The next message clicked in: 'Wondered if you were up for a pint tonight?'

The very English sentence sounded strange in DI Ramsey's US drawl, but it made Cass smile.

'Meeting up with someone you'd probably like to see. We'll be at the Fox and Garter on Marylebone High Street at eight.'

At least Cass knew he still had some friends left on the force, and Charles Ramsey was top of that list. The irritating lawyer forgotten, Cass picked up his keys and headed out into the wreckage of London to face the day.

'Coffee, sir?' Toby Armstrong stood in the doorway with a mug already in hand.

'Thanks.'

Cass waved his new sergeant in and took the drink, and for a second there was an awkward silence. Armstrong was, by all accounts, a likeable character and a good policeman, and although Cass didn't doubt either, he hadn't yet seen much evidence of the first. At best they had a polite working relationship. They didn't go to the pub together. They didn't discuss their personal lives.

Cass wasn't bothered by the coolness between them. He was happy as long as the sergeant got on with his job; he could understand why being allocated to the DI who was almost single-handedly bringing down the Met might not be Armstrong's idea of a great partnership. The sergeant might not have said anything, but it was obvious he didn't want to get tarred by the Cass Jones brush.

'The Mitchell death?'

Cass looked up. 'What about it?' Barbara Mitchell had been clubbed to death with a tyre-iron in her kitchen a few days before. It was the closest Cass had come to a real case in six months, but it had proved depressingly lacking in anything remotely brain-taxing.

'I did what you said, brought the husband's secretary in and let her sweat overnight. She broke at four this morning. She started banging on the cell door, desperate to talk. Said he wasn't with her after all.'

'Got someone picking him up?'

'Already done,' Armstrong said, 'and he's cracked. His confession's being typed up now.'

'Good work.' Cass attempted a smile but it was empty. The Mitchell case had been blindingly obvious from the moment he'd first walked into that house and seen the husband's scrubbed pink hands and spotless clothes as he stood shaking beside her battered and bleeding body, stammering as he claimed he'd found her that way. It had only ever been a matter of time before they had their confession.

A small huddle of officers gathered in the corner of the Incident Room outside caught his eye, and he frowned.

'What's going on with them?'

'They're watching the news,' Armstrong said. 'A couple of bombs went off in the Moscow Underground during rush hour.'

'Like ours?'

'Looks that way.'

'Poor bastards.' He meant it too. For a moment he was tempted to go and join the group and watch the disaster unfold in all its glorious televisual Technicolor, but he shook the thought away. The bombings were someone else's problem, part of the bigger picture that made up the slowly rotting world. For Cass, all that mattered now were the small tragedies, the tiny deaths – the ones he could actually do something about.

'I've got a job for you.'

'Sir?'

'Student suicides. I want to know how many there have been in the past month – no, in fact, maybe go back three months. Get me whatever files we've got.'

'London, or nationwide?'

'London for now.'

'Can I ask why?'

Cass looked up. Claire could have asked why, and he'd probably have told her, but not this career copper who was

28

too worried about his own fledgling reputation to relax. 'No, Armstrong,' Cass said quietly, 'you can't.'

There was the slightest twitch in the other man's jaw and then the sergeant turned and left. Cass watched him. If only the stupid boy would see that someone among the headshed must think highly of him to have teamed him up with Cass in the middle of this shitstorm, then maybe he'd start to be half the copper he possibly could be.

He closed the door.

By lunchtime Cass had finished his own bland report on the Mitchell case and Armstrong had printed out all the information he'd requested. He'd had a message from Eagleton, who was running a full autopsy on Jasmine Green, the girl they'd found this morning, and would get back to him as soon as possible. Cass looked at the small pile of papers in front of him and wondered who was more intrigued by this case, the ME's assistant, or Cass himself. Eagleton's curiosity had been roused for sure, but as Cass sifted through the documents Armstrong had brought him, he felt a tingle in the pit of his stomach. He'd started to think he'd lost that feeling.

It appeared that a depressingly large number of young people felt the urge to end their lives before they'd grown up enough to realise they could live through a whole lot worse shit than the angst that comes from being somewhere between eighteen and twenty-two. As he scanned through their tragedies, he didn't let his eyes linger too long on the invariably smiling photographs. If you let too many of the dead grip you, they'd pull you down and drown you. He'd learned that fast.

Over the past three months there'd been nine suicides among London's student population. Cass put five of them in a separate pile, to be ignored ; there was nothing unusual about any of them – a teenager who had always been bullied; a young woman with a history of depression – and more importantly, all five dead had left notes explaining their actions.

The other four, however, he laid out carefully across his desk. Four suicides in just over two weeks, spread across the capital. The files were sparse on information, even Katie Dodds'. He looked at her photo. Dark hair, pretty. Green eyes. Then he looked at the second image, the words finger-painted in blood on the wall. *Chaos in the darkness.* No note, other than that one sentence. His eyes flicked over the attached sheet of paper. Popular student, talented artist. No hint of depression.

The second file was James Busby's, a twenty-year-old sports science second-year student at the Richmond campus of Brunel University. Cut his wrists in the bath in a student house in Hounslow four days before Katie Dodds slashed hers on her bed in Chelsea. He'd been the rugby team captain. He'd passed all his exams thus far, in the way that the popular kids always do: not top of the class, but doing enough work to get by and still have a social life. Cass's eyes caught on the final paragraph of the report.

No evidence of foul play. Deceased sent text to mother from bathroom. Chaos in the darkness. Mother didn't understand it, she tried to call and received no answer. There was no further communication from her son, who was found dead by another resident of his house thirty minutes later.

Cass's heart thumped more loudly. There it was again, in black and white. *Chaos in the darkness.* What did it mean – and more importantly, what the hell did it mean to these kids? He looked at the last two files. Angie Lane and Cory Denter. Angie had been an accountancy and business student at the South Bank University. She'd been quiet but friendly. Her flatmate had returned to find her dead on the kitchen floor a week ago. There was a pile of chopped carrots on the side. Angie had been cutting up vegetables and at some point decided that cutting her own wrists open was preferable to finishing whatever she'd decided to cook. She left no note.

Cass jotted down the address of her flat, the name of her flatmate and her parents' contact details. She might not have left an obvious message behind, but he needed to find out for himself. Cory Denter's story was similar: he was a second-year medical student at Bart's with no signs of depression. He'd slit his wrists with a scalpel the most efficient way, vertically, not horizontally, in his car on his parents' drive in Lewisham. He was a live-at-home student. Cass added his address to Angie Lane's.

Cory Denter had died only four days earlier, so he'd go there first. There had been no suicide note for Cory either, and Cass knew full well what he'd be facing when he turned up at the Denter house: all their grief, and wonder – and then, on top of that, he'd feel the awful weight of their expectation that maybe he'd be able to provide the answers for them, to give them some closure.

He stood up. The parents didn't concern him so much. Their grief would be painful, but it was their grief, not his own, and he could live with their expectations. He'd done that before. He looked down at the four faces on his desk once more before gathering up the files and putting them in his top drawer. It was the expectations of the dead that he had a hard time dealing with. The dead didn't let go.

Chapter Four

Abigail Porter had become good at being relatively invisible over the years, no mean feat for a woman who stood six foot tall in flat shoes, especially when most of that height was taken up by spectacular long, slim legs. Still, as she stood by the door in Alison McDonnell's private office it was clear that neither the Prime Minister, nor the Home Secretary, nor David Fletcher, the head of ATD, the Anti-Terror Division, the new hard core at the heart of the country's counter-terrorism agencies, considered her to be in the room. She was like a ghost imprinted on the wallpaper, there, but not there. As she idly listened to the serious voices, she was pleased about that. Next door, the PM's admin secretary would be just leaving for lunch. In ten minutes' time McDonnell would be leaving to meet the other members of the Cabinet for the emergency briefing. Abigail needed two or three minutes of unnoticed time between those two events.

'We're almost certain that all five of the 26/09 bombs were made of Semtex, rather than the usual home-made organic compounds used in 7/7 and 13/12,' Fletcher started.

'Semtex?'

'Military grade.'

'I take it this isn't a good thing.' McDonnell said.

'In itself, it shouldn't make much difference. Without

trying to be crude, it doesn't matter what it's made of; if it explodes and kills people, then a bomb is a bomb. What's of more concern is the lack of any polymer residue at any of the sites. All military-grade Semtex manufactured since 2002 has a post-detonation taggant which leaves behind traces of chemicals, allowing the batch to be identified and traced. And if it's not military grade, then it should be orange. None of these explosions left residue, and trace evidence suggests the plastique was white.'

'What does all that actually mean?'

'In essence, it suggests that your bombers are both well organised and well funded, and I would suggest that if they're taking time to purchase Semtex I'd be willing to bet they bought more than they used for 26/09. I very much doubt it's for sale in small quantities.'

'Small quantities?' The Prime Minister grimaced. 'They virtually *destroyed* Ealing Broadway and Hampstead High Street, and they brought the Underground system to its knees.'

'It's certainly efficient, but politically, the use of this kind of Semtex raises some questions. The Czechs are either selling old stock on the black market, or manufacturing new – untraceable – product.' Fletcher sipped his coffee.

He had strong hands, Abigail noted, with neat, clipped fingernails. He'd be a good lover, she was certain. The thoughts were idle. Two more minutes.

'Oh, that's great,' said Lucius Dawson, the Home Secretary.

'The whole world's in recession and keen to blow the hell out of everyone else,' said the PM, 'so what do you really expect? The Czechs aren't well known for their high-class exports, are they?' She sighed. 'Beer, Bohemian crystal and bombs are all they've got.'

'We also know the bombs were detonated with mobile phones, and given that at least three of the sites were underground, it's likely they used the alarm as the trigger – all you have to do is wire a detonator across the vibrate function and it's done.'

'That would make sense, especially given the precision of the explosions on Ealing Broadway. They were staggered perfectly to cause maximum casualties.'

Casualties, thought Abigail, was a horribly overused word, a soothing plaster over any number of rotten, cancerous wounds. At the last count, the *casualties* meant the four hundred and eighty-three people who had died on 26 September, and there were still at least thirty more who might join them any moment. And that was without counting the wounded, those blinded and limbless. *Casualties*. There was a true horror in the blandness of that euphemism.

'It also means there's no trace of a triggering call – although even if they had been call-detonated, they'll all be pay-as-you-go sims, so we'd be none the wiser. The best we could hope for would be to find a common link.'

'That has to stop,' the PM muttered. 'I don't want *anyone* in this country with a phone that can't be traced right back to them.'

'With your permission, ma'am' – for the first time Fletcher sounded hesitant – 'I'd like to share some of this information with my opposite number in Moscow.'

There was a slight hitch of breath from the Home Secretary.

'Why? For all we know Russian terrorists were behind these bombs, despite what happened today.'

Fletcher shook his head. 'We've had none of the normal claims of responsibility, nothing from the Chechens, Al

Qaeda or Red Terror. If the Russians were involved, Red Terror would have claimed it by now.'

'You may have a point,' she conceded. 'So does this mean we're dealing with a new terrorist threat?'

'We could be,' Fletcher admitted, 'and if we are, then I'm curious about the similarities between what happened here two weeks ago and what happened in Moscow today. Then we'll be able to gauge the level of threat, and perhaps get some idea of what they were hoping to achieve.'

'Terror.' The PM spoke softly. 'I should imagine they were hoping to achieve terror.'

'And we're no closer to IDing the bombers themselves?' the Home Secretary asked.

'No, although we're still piecing together CCTV images – a lot of cameras were damaged, as you can imagine.'

Abigail took a small step sideways and slipped out through the door and into Emily's office. The desk was abandoned, just as she'd expected. Emily was a mouse, and a creature of habit. She ate her lunch at exactly the same time every day, regular as clockwork. Death by routine.

Keeping one eye on the door in front of her, Abigail hit ctrl/alt/del and brought up the log-in screen. Emily had dutifully logged herself out, but it hadn't taken much to figure out her password. The morning she'd found the note pushed under her front door, Abigail had made it her business to have lunch with Emily. Abigail had asked her gently probing questions, and listening to the girl's mindless drivel had quickly produced what she needed – the minute Emily mentioned that she had a dog, Abigail had known what her password would be. It was predictably sentimental. She typed quickly and the home screen appeared. She went straight to the Internet browser and brought up Hotmail, her heart thumping, as it had been every time she'd tried this over the past two weeks. The beat was a strange reassurance that she was still alive, despite the cold grey cloud that had enveloped her soul. She hadn't brought the note with her. She didn't need to. The words on it were imprinted in her mind.

You'll need this. You'll know when.

Username: <u>Intervention1@hotmail.co.uk</u>
Password: Salvation

She'd found it the morning after the bombings: a small, sealed white envelope with the folded paper inside. She should have handed it over to Special Branch or MI5, or at least the PM – she should definitely have given it to *someone*. The note had been screaming at her to hand it over – but she hadn't, she'd brought it in with her. She'd intended to tell McDonnell, but instead she found herself eating lunch with Emily and thinking if she was going to compromise a computer, then Emily's was a better choice than her own.

So here she was again, her career in her hands as she stared at the home screen. The disappointment was almost overwhelming. The inbox was empty. The whole account was empty. She frowned. So what was the point of it – how was she supposed to know when she'd need it? She closed the screen down and deleted the browser history. Maybe if a message did ever appear, then she'd pass the whole thing on. *Maybe.* She replaced the chair exactly as she'd found it and headed back to the door. Or maybe she was just telling herself a big fat lie. There was a promise in that note, and it had been made to her.

'We're cross-referencing all the tapes,' Fletcher was still speaking as Abigail resumed her place by the door, 'checking for people entering the sites with bags and leaving without them. If they used alarm settings to detonate the bombs, then there's a chance the bombers weren't suicides. They could have left themselves time to get out.'

'Without raising suspicion?'

Fletcher shrugged. 'They wouldn't need long, just a few minutes. And even if someone spotted the bag between stops, whoever planted it could have got out at the previous station and left before it was detonated, if he moved fast enough.'

'You really don't think suicide bombings?'

'We can't be sure one way or the other at this point, but this silence is strange. Suicide bombers leave a message: it's the nature of suicide, to want to explain yourself, and all terror organisations use that to propagandise their message. They send us videos so we're sure who did it and why and in the name of which God they're blowing the shit out of themselves and everyone around them. And as yet, we've received no messages whatsoever from whomever is responsible for these attacks.'

'You think the Russians have had a message?'

'Nothing on intel about it.' Fletcher's stare was direct.

Abigail didn't think the man was capable of anything else. There was a straightforwardness about him that in the double-dealing world of politics might be mistaken for a lesser intelligence by the less intelligent politicians. But David Fletcher wasn't stupid; he was dangerously sharp in his clinical evaluations in just about any given situation.

'Speak to them,' the PM said, 'but don't give them everything. It will be tricky, because the media's been quick to put the blame on the Russians, and we haven't done much to dissipate that in case it disrupts the fragile peace we've got going with the Middle East. We can't be seen to be blaming *them* at the moment, can we? Not until next month's summit is done.'

'I'll tread carefully.'

The Prime Minister looked up at her counter-terrorism commander. 'Make sure you do.'

Abigail watched the woman she was paid to protect. Unlike David Fletcher, Alison McDonnell understood politics; more than that, she got how the world worked. She might not always like it, but she understood it, and that was what made her such a good player at the game. And that's all this life and death business ever really was – a game. *The* game. That was what Fletcher would never understand: that there was no point in taking it too seriously, because at the end of the day it was all just moves and counter-moves, winners and losers. Abigail thought of the empty Hotmail account. It might be a cold, dangerous game, but it was all there was. And now someone was trying to lure her back into it.

And that was interesting.

Chapter Five

Although the sun was shining brightly through the windows of the small house in Lewisham, it dulled in the sombre atmosphere of the sitting room, as if aware that the good spirits normally associated with it weren't welcome here. Cory Denter had died four days ago, and his grandparents and aunts had travelled from Trinidad to support the family in their grief. Large women dressed in black sipped tea and talked softly, their white eyes rimmed red from crying. The pain in the room was almost palpable. Cass had felt it too many times before.

'I'm sorry to disturb you,' he said, quietly. 'I won't take up much of your time.'

'Take whatever time you need, please.' Cory's mother looked up at him with almost desperate hope.

He knew why; all around the house were proudly framed pictures of this now-broken family unit, of Cory, smiling throughout the years of his short life. The whole family looked to be always smiling – but not any more. The future held only echoes now. And poor Cory's mother just wanted to know why.

'I'm not sure what you want.' Mr Denter watched him with suspicion, and Cass knew what that meant too: *Don't go bringing hope here if you can't deliver. Don't you do that to us, not now.* 'The car is gone. We didn't want it here.

There was too much ...' His voice cracked slightly as the sentence drifted away unsaid.

It didn't matter; Cass knew the end of it. *Too much blood.*

'There wasn't anything in it anyway, just the usual – maps, service book, chewing gum. Some CDs.' Mr Denter's eyes welled up, as if the memory of each item was stabbing him somewhere inside.

'Can I see his room?'

'He was always a good boy.' Mrs Denter looked up from the sofa. The hope had turned to a vague dread. The *why* wasn't always good to know. 'Always.'

'I'm sure he was, Mrs Denter.'

She shrugged, the weight heavy in her shoulders. 'I just don't understand. I don't understand.' The tears came, hot and fast from the endless well inside her, and big black arms engulfed and held her tight as an older Jamaican woman muttered soothing words in an accent like rum. Cass watched them with something close to envy. It would feel good to be held in an embrace like that. It had been a long time since he'd felt anything other than the grip of the dead.

He looked at Mr Denter and they shared a look that spoke more than words ever could, and for an instant Cass was back looking down the barrel of a gun at wide brown Jamaican eyes. He closed the memory down and followed the dead boy's father out of the room of crying women and up a narrow staircase.

At the top, Mr Denter spoke again, more softly this time.

'Was my boy in trouble? Had he got himself mixed up in something?' The man's Adam's apple bobbed nervously up and down, a mix of needing the *why* and the fear of it, that perhaps his child had secrets of his own already, and a life that was separate, darker.

'No,' Cass said, 'there's no evidence to suggest that. Really.'

Mr Denter didn't look convinced, and Cass didn't blame him. The police didn't investigate routine suicides, everyone knew that – these days the police didn't investigate half the crimes they were supposed to, let alone small personal tragedies like this one. Still, Mr Denter didn't look like someone who argued with the police. He was a good citizen.

'Well—' He shrugged helplessly from the doorway, as if his grief barred him from entry. 'It's exactly as he left it. We haven't ... moved anything.'

Cass nodded. He could see the Denters' whole lives in the neatness of this room. There were a couple of football posters on the wall, a set of clothes draped over the chair in the corner; a skeleton was standing against the back wall, next to a chart of the body's organs. The bed was made. Next to it was a desk, on which was stacked a pile of medical textbooks and folders of work, alongside the small lamp and a pen pot. Cory Denter had been the product of a hard-working family who had clearly scrimped and saved every penny so that their precious son could have a better life. It looked like Cory had appreciated it, too: there was a small photograph of him and his parents on a boat somewhere bright and sunny. They were smiling like that feeling would last for ever. It was the only photo in the room.

Cass carefully opened the cupboards and drawers, but he found nothing untoward – neatly folded clothes, a bank book that showed a young man careful with his money, football kit, jeans and a couple of suits, but no diary, no letters from a girlfriend, nothing personal. Cass would never meet Cory Denter now, but he felt like they were being introduced. A quiet boy. A private man. Someone confident in his life, but who kept his feelings inside.

He flicked through the various student files on the desk, aware of Mr Denter watching him from the doorway. The sheets of lined paper were filled with neatly written notes, which might as well have been in a foreign language as far as Cass was concerned. Some had diagrams drawn in, then crossed out and redrawn again: this was someone striving for perfection. Cory Denter worked hard. Had he not let his blood drain out all over his car, he might well have been a fine doctor one day.

Cass's hand froze as he turned the page. More lines of precisely printed words he didn't understand filled the sheet, but that wasn't what had caught his eye. In the margin, in tiny letters, he could see one sentence, written over and over, as if doodled absently in a lecture. There were no gaps between the letters, so it appeared as one long nonsensical word down the side of the page:

Chaosinthedarknesschaosinthedarknesschaosinthedarknesschaosinthedarkness.

Cass's heart thumped so loudly he was sure Mr Denter could hear it.

Chaos in the darkness. Another one. He closed the folder.

'It looks like Cory worked hard.' Cass kept the file in his hand and his tone light.

'He did. He was a good boy.'

'What about his social life? Did he have a big circle of friends?'

'He had some,' said Mr Denter, 'but he took his studies seriously. He stayed in most nights with us. Went to football and cricket at weekends. Maybe he'd go out another night or two in the week, but he was never home late.'

'Do you know where he'd go?'

'No. He was a good boy. He was a young man and we gave him his freedom. It wasn't like he came home drunk all the time, not like some of the other students you see.' A wistful smile crossed the man's careworn face. 'Not too often anyway.'

'Can I take this?' Cass held up the file.

The dread settled in Mr Denter's face. 'You would tell me if he'd been in trouble?'

Cass smiled. 'Mr Denter, I would tell you.'

They stared at each other for a long time, the unknown *why* hanging between them, binding them.

Eventually, Mr Denter said, 'Take it.'

Outside, Cass got back in his car before calling Armstrong. He had enough evidence that something was linking these deaths to push for a proper investigation, but he wanted to speak to Angie Lane's flatmate first. Amanda Kemble. He needed to find that sentence somewhere in the dead girl's belongings, and his gut was sure it would be there. What could possibly link these kids – some kind of suicide pact? But why? Cory Denter wouldn't see any romance in ending his own life; he'd have come across enough cadavers in his training to see how clinical death was.

He gave his sergeant the task of pulling the girl out of her lectures and taking her to meet Cass at the flat, then hung up on the other man's questions and lit a cigarette before dialling Eagleton. Armstrong could wait for his explanations. He hadn't earned them yet.

'Cass?' Eagleton spoke first. 'Spooky, I was just about to call you.'

'I've been looking at student suicides across London. You were right to be curious. So far we're up to four linked by this "Chaos in the darkness" shit, and I think I'm about to make that five. All slit their wrists in some way or another. They're all at different colleges.'

'I might have something else to add to the mix.'

'Yeah?'

'I'll need to see the other bodies to know whether it's a one-off or not, but I found a series of small lesions across the surface of Jasmine Green's brain. I'm running some tests to see what might have caused them, but they could go some way to explaining her sudden suicide.'

'Is this an injury thing?'

'Could be any number of causes. There was no external trauma to her skull so I would guess not. Could be disease, may be, or a reaction to a chemical. We'll see what the lab says before I hazard any guesses. If you can get the DCI to give me the rest of the bodies to play with, I'd be very grateful.'

'I'll do my best. I've got to persuade him that this is actually a case first.'

'Good luck with that.'

'Yeah, thanks.'

He started the car and pulled away from the kerb, aware that Cory Denter's father was still watching from the window of the house of mourning. He'd sewn a seed there, and it would grow, whether he watered it or not.

He stopped for a quick coffee and a cigarette before heading across the river to the address he'd jotted down for Angie Lane. His phone vibrated once in his pocket, Perry Jordan: *Sorry. Nothing new to report.*

Six months ago Cass had promised Charles Ramsey and DCI Morgan that he wouldn't start an investigation into what had become of his nephew Luke, or who the boy was who had been raised as part of Christian's family until the investigations into the corruption at Paddington Green station were done. There was going to be quite enough shit flying around without Cass hurling more at an incompetent

NHS, and if it had waited all these years, it could wait a little longer.

He took their point, and in a strange way, revealing that somehow his nephew had been traded at birth could weaken him as a witness. He'd look like a crazy, one who believed he was surrounded by conspiracy theories. Cass took a long last drag and then flicked the cigarette butt out of the window, breaking the law twice in as many minutes.

He wondered what Ramsey and Morgan would think of him if he'd told them everything he'd discovered while investigating the Man of Flies. The Bank, which owned practically every functioning government in the world now, was nothing but a front for a shady organisation called the Network. The man called Solomon had turned into a whirlwind of flies before Cass's very eyes before he'd died, and the ageless Mr Bright hadn't even batted an eyelash at it . . . they really would think he was a crazy then, that was for sure. Although given the way that the investigation had been told to stay away from Mr Bright, maybe Morgan or those above him already had an inkling of that man's power.

Despite their warnings, he'd put Perry Jordan on a small retainer a couple of weeks ago, just to start quietly digging around to see if he could begin tracing the boy.

So far the tenacious young private eye had found nothing of much use. Cass wasn't overly surprised. He'd pretty much tied Jordan's hands by telling him that for now he could only chase paper, not physically talk to anyone. He just wanted to be doing something. The boy was out there some-where, and now he was his only living relative. Cass had seen the Jones file on Christian's laptop, and it stood to reason that if Mr Bright and his network were so interested in the Jones family, then they'd be interested in the missing boy too.

'I don't want to go in there again. I really don't.' Amanda Kemble, Angie Lane's flatmate, stood in the hallway of the small flat with her arms folded across her narrow chest. She twitched, nervous and birdlike, as if she were desperate to flutter away back to the outside world.

'You don't have to.' Rachel Honey put her arm around Amanda's narrow shoulders before looking at Cass. 'She's been staying with me since it happened. She's handed in her notice and I don't blame her either.'

Cass was impressed with the girl. 'If you two want to wait in the sitting room, I won't be too long. Which was Angie's room?'

'Second on the left. Just past the bathroom.'

After a cursory glance into the freshly scrubbed kitchen – there was no hint of what had happened in there, either to the carrots Angie Lane had been chopping, or that she'd bled to death beneath them on the lino – Cass went into her bedroom. Several boxes filled with her belongings were lined against the wall. The first was full of clothes; the second was filled with paperbacks and textbooks.

'Are you looking for anything in particular?'

Cass looked up to see Rachel Honey standing in the doorway.

'I could probably help you if you are,' she continued. 'I packed her things up, so I know what's in each of those.' She nodded to the boxes. 'Angie's parents are coming to collect them in a couple of days. I don't think they could face it until after the funeral.'

'And when is that?'

'Tomorrow.'

'Will you be going?'

'I'll drive Amanda there, so yes. I wasn't as close to Angie as she was, but what I knew of her I liked.'

'Did she seem suicidal to you?'

The dark-haired girl looked thoughtful for a moment. 'I would say no, but then I would be wrong. She did kill herself. When Amanda found her she was still alive, and holding onto the knife.'

'Did she say anything before she died?'

'No. So, what *are* you looking for a week after she died? It seems a bit odd.'

She looked clever. Cass closed the lid of the first box. 'Just anything unusual. Something she might have said, or written down.'

'Something unusual?' Rachel's eyes narrowed and the widened slightly. 'There was something. We found it when we were clearing out her locker on campus. Amanda was with me. She found it.'

Amanda swayed backwards and forwards a little on the sofa, sniffing into a tissue. Beside her, Rachel Honey was a rock of calm; Cass was very glad Sergeant Armstrong had had the good sense to let the girl bring her friend. Amanda was too wrapped up in her own shock to have remembered by herself.

'She had a mirror on the inside of her locker door,' Amanda said, looking up nervously. 'She sometimes went out straight from Uni, so it was handy for her to just quickly put some make-up on if she was changing her clothes. The toilets there can be pretty grim, and they stink.'

Cass nodded encouragingly. 'Go on.'

'Well, there isn't that much to tell, really. When Rachel came to help me pack up her stuff we remembered her locker. I found her key and when we opened it up we saw it written on the mirror in her lipstick.'

'What was written there?'

'Chaos in the darkness,' Amanda whispered, as if somehow the phrase could hurt her.

'You didn't tell anyone?' Cass kept his face impassive.

'To be honest,' Rachel cut in, 'we thought it might be some kind of sick joke.'

'Why?'

'I work on the Uni news site. It's one of the best in the city – we think *the* best actually, we don't just run stories from South Bank but from across London. Everyone's heard the stories of the girl who died a couple of weeks ago, the one who wrote that phrase on the wall. And the kid who texted his mum. It's becoming a bit like one of those urban legends around all the campuses.'

'They say,' Amanda's eyes widened, 'that if you see those words somewhere then you'll kill yourself within the week.' She picked at her tissue. 'I should never have come to London,' she muttered. 'I should have stayed in Guildford. I don't want to kill myself. I don't want to die.'

'They' – Rachel rolled her eyes – 'are just a bunch of dumb boys wanting to scare girls into getting their knickers off. I've got no intention of topping myself in the next few days, and neither do you. That story's just a pile of shit.' Her grin froze and she looked back up at Cass. 'Is that why you're here? Have there been more suicides like these?'

For once Cass was lost for words. He hadn't for a second thought that the stories of the deaths would spread like Chinese whispers through the student community. Where the police hadn't bothered even looking for links, the kids had grabbed hold of them and run with it.

He ignored her question. 'Has anyone asked you about

48

her locker? Any students who might have been playing a prank like you thought?'

Rachel's smile fell and Amanda's shoulders curved further inwards as she sniffed into her tissue. 'No,' she said quietly, 'no one's said anything. I don't think it was a joke.'

'Is the writing still there?' Cass leaned forward.

'We cleaned it off,' Rachel said. 'Sorry. We didn't think it mattered.'

'It probably doesn't.' Cass smiled, but he could feel those sharp eyes digging in to him. Rachel Honey wasn't stupid. 'What was her social life like? You said she went out sometimes straight from college?'

'Sometimes. She was out two or three evenings a week. Sometimes at weekends we'd go to the Union together.' Amanda twisted the tissue between her thin fingers. She was talking, but Cass knew her mind was on the words she'd found in the locker and thinking about the newly born urban myth, and whether she would be next. What she was feeling wasn't grief. It was fear.

'She was quite a private person. We didn't really talk about boyfriends or stuff like that. I don't think she was seeing anyone, though.'

'I think she had a job,' Rachel cut in. 'She had one last year, waitressing somewhere. She was pretty good with money. I mean, I know you'd expect that from someone on her course, but that's not always the case.' She smiled. 'I'm doing accountancy too, but my overdraft is shocking.'

'You don't know where she worked, do you?'

Both girls shook their heads, before Amanda's red eyes focused slightly. 'I know she worked at Pizza Express last year. Maybe she got a job there again. The one right down on the river.'

'Thanks.' Cass stood up. 'Do you girls need a lift back to Uni?'

'No, we'll walk,' Rachel said. 'Bit of fresh air will do us good.'

Armstrong folded his notebook and tucked it back in his pocket. 'If we need you, we'll be in touch.'

Cass wondered how long it would take for the news of the police visit to spread across the student network. Their youth made him feel like a dinosaur; they were an alien race he really didn't understand. He was angry at himself for not having realised Katie Dodds' death would have been texted, tweeted, messaged and however else these teenagers communicated all across the city and beyond, probably within a few hours of her being found. He wasn't sure what bothered him most: the fact that he hadn't thought about it, or that he was so out of touch with the way young people behaved.

'You want to what?' The DCI didn't look happy, but then Hugo Heddings always looked like a man with a bad case of haemorrhoids who had sat down too heavily. Cass had never thought he'd miss Morgan, but since the old DCI had been shipped out he'd started to look like a dream boss.

'I think we need to look into this, sir.' Cass spread the files out on Heddings' desk. 'That's five students who have killed themselves, all linked by this one phrase.'

'"Chaos in the darkness"?' Heddings spat the words out as if he didn't want them in his mouth any longer than possible. 'It doesn't even mean anything.'

'To be fair, sir,' Armstrong cut in, 'we don't know what it means. It must mean *something*.'

Cass glanced up, surprised. He'd filled Armstrong in briefly before coming up to see the boss, but they hadn't discussed the deaths at all. He'd expected the younger man just to stay quiet at the back and pretend he wasn't there, but maybe his curiosity had been engaged too.

'Five young people dead in just over two weeks is a lot,' Cass said. 'Don't you think we should at least check it out? If Eagleton could examine the bodies, then perhaps we'll find some physical evidence to link them.'

'Examine the bodies?' The DCI's gaze hardened. 'That means exhuming at least two of them, surely?'

Cass didn't answer. His silence spoke for him.

'You want to dig up the bodies of two dead students?' Heddings was determined to drag the words out of Cass.

'Yes, sir.'

'Tell me, Jones' – the DCI rested his arms on the ignored files and laced his fingers – 'did these kids commit suicide or not?'

'It's not as simple as—'

'Yes, it is. Did they commit suicide?'

'Yes.' Cass's jaw tightened as he spoke. He'd thought the DCI would be a bastard about this, and it was turning out he'd been right.

'And have you got any evidence at all, from any of the crime scenes, that they might be anything other than suicide? Any suspicion of murder?'

'Not in the traditional sense, no. But there *is* something linking them.'

'Lots of people have crazy suicide pacts. We don't look into all of those. For all you know that phrase is a lyric from some current pop song that all the teenagers in Britain are singing.'

The suggestion gave Cass pause, and for the second time that morning he felt old and out of touch.

'It isn't,' Armstrong said. 'I did a search on the Internet.

There was nothing listed for that exact phrase.'

For the first time since they'd been partnered together, Cass felt glad to have Armstrong on his side. He kept his eyes on Heddings. 'There's something very odd going on with these deaths, sir. And yes, technically these kids all killed themselves, but none of them had any suicidal traits prior. They were all good students, and relatively popular. I think something or someone prompted them to take their own lives, and whatever it is, it's linked to this phrase. They deserve a little of our time to see if we can figure out why.' He paused. 'If these five have died in so short a time, then there might be more.'

'That's very noble.' Heddings glanced at each of the files and then piled them up again. 'But such sentiments don't pay the bills.' As he peered over the top of his glasses, the balding man looked like a headmaster, telling Cass and Armstrong off as if they were children. 'We don't have the money to start digging up bodies and investigating perfectly clear-cut cases of suicide, however tragic you might feel them to be. This station is virtually on its knees, Jones—' He jabbed a finger into the air between them. 'You know this better than most. We barely have the money to work on the criminal cases, without acting on a' – he gestured at the files – 'fanciful whim.'

'It's not a whim, sir.' Cass raised the whip to flog the dead horse once more.

'It is. There's too much shit going on around here at the moment—'

A knock on the door interrupted him, and a constable poked his head cautiously into the office, as if even from the outside he'd been aware that he might be walking into cross-fire.

'What is it?' Heddings snapped.

'Sorry, sir. There's a lawyer here to see DI Jones. He says it's urgent and can't wait. Desk Sergeant's rung up twice now, sir.'

Cass felt whatever slim chance he'd had of changing his boss's mind crumble into dust.

'And that' – Heddings leaned back in his chair – 'is the kind of shit I'm talking about. You've got enough to be contending with putting our own lot behind bars without chasing suicides.'

Cass refused to bite, but he felt the barb in the remark.

'Just for the record,' Armstrong spoke softly as he followed Cass over to the door, 'I think the DI is right. There's something odd about these cases. We should be looking into them.'

'Your point is noted.' The contempt in Heddings' voice was clear. 'But when I want your opinion, Sergeant, I'll ask for it. And I'm pretty sure that I didn't. Now shut the door on your way out.'

Cass had already gone, afraid he might growl something that he would technically regret if he stayed in his new boss's earshot for much longer. And he wasn't ready to thank Armstrong for his support just yet. The sergeant had said what anyone with half a brain would have said after seeing the files and hearing what Amanda Kemble and Rachel Honey had said earlier. But Cass had to admit Armstrong had risen dramatically in his estimation; if he carried on like this, then maybe one day they would be going for a beer after work. Not yet, but one day.

He found the lawyer sipping a polystyrene cup of coffee in a small office on the first floor usually allocated to duty solicitors when they needed to quickly catch up on some notes before being given a client.

'Be careful with that stuff,' Cass said, nodding at the cup. 'It'll kill you.'

He regretted his words the moment the man turned around. His skin was almost yellow, and had the waxy, leather appearance of a body that was already embalmed despite the beating heart inside.

'I'm DI Jones.' He nodded at the man to take a seat. 'I presume this is about one of the trials. Surely whatever you need is in one of the countless statements I've made over the months?'

'My name is Edgar Marlowe, from Marlowe and Beale. I've left a few messages on your answerphone at home.'

The message on his phone that morning. That was this man. Cass recognised his voice. 'Don't call me at home and then come here looking for ways to help your corrupt clients.' His voice was cold. He didn't have time for this shit. It had fucked up enough of his life already.

'I think you misunderstand.' Marlowe raised his hands. 'I'm not here about the police cases. I'm here about your brother.'

'What?' The sentence was completely unexpected, and Cass felt the world tilt sideways in a way he hadn't in months. 'What do you mean?'

'This is a slightly unusual situation.' Marlowe finally pulled a chair out and carefully sat down. Cass did the same on the opposite side of the table.

'I'm listening.'

'Marlowe and Beale mainly work exclusively for The Bank and some of its . . .' Marlowe hesitated, his sickly eyes shifting slightly away from Cass's. 'Shall we say, investors.'

Cass felt as if he were heading into an invisible game of chess. He'd been here before, but now at least he was aware of some of the pieces. The Bank. The Network. The *Glow*.

And of course, Mr Bright and his dead partner Mr Solomon, the Man of Flies.

'Go on.'

'Your brother was in contact with me on several occasions regarding some legal matters for various of The Bank's subsidiary companies. He was very highly regarded, it would seem. For a long time I'd dealt mainly with a man called Asher Red . . .'

'I've met him.'

'Well, then, you'll know he's not the easiest man to get to know, or to get along with.' Marlowe smiled and Cass could see where his gums were whitening. There was nothing healthy about the lawyer, despite the lack of grey in his thick brown hair. How old was he? Forty-five? Maybe fifty at most.

'That's the one.'

'Your brother was different. He used to come to my office to work through figures and details with me, and I suppose we developed – well, I'd call it a quiet friendship of sorts. He was an unusual man, wasn't he?

Cass nodded, once again feeling that twinge of shame which always came with any mention of Christian. The one thing he'd learned recently was that he really hadn't known his little brother at all.

'He had a brilliant head for figures,' Marlowe continued, 'but what I liked about him was that he saw past them. Most accountants, men like Asher Red, for instance, they can only understand the sums – they can only see the cash value of something. They assess risk or gain purely in numbers. Your brother wasn't like that. He also factored in the people. He was honest at his core, and I don't think he knew how to be anything other. He was a curious choice to work so high up in The Bank.'

Cass kept his face impassive. He hadn't told anyone about The Bank's shady background figures and their interest in the Jones family, and he wasn't going to start now, even with this man who professed himself Christian's friend. It wasn't his business, and anyway, as far as Cass was concerned the whole thing was over. His father and his brother had both got themselves involved with Mr Bright, and it had done neither of them any good. He intended to stay well away. *There is no glow.*

'He didn't value people in terms of money,' Marlowe mused. 'And that's very unusual, wouldn't you agree?'

His own thoughts of that morning came back to Cass: Christian's life insurance, the bonuses . . .

'Sometimes my brother could be a little naïve.'

'Yes.' Marlowe smiled. 'But there is a charm in that. I liked him. I liked him a lot. I was very sorry to hear what happened to him and his family.'

'Could you get to the point?'

Marlowe flinched a little, and Cass could read his expression clearly. *This brother has none of Christian's goodness. This one is cold.* Marlowe would be right.

'Your brother came out to meet me when I got my final diagnosis.' Marlowe didn't speed up; he was obviously determined to tell this in his own way. 'It's funny how, as you get older, you suddenly find you barely know anyone at all. When you're at school the lists of friends you have is endless, and it's the same at university.' He smiled. 'But then suddenly you're forty and the circle around you has shrunk so much sometimes it's barely there at all. You marry, you divorce, and then it's easier to leave the joint friends behind than work through all that awkwardness. Personally, I chose to drink through the awkwardness. To be honest, since I was about twenty, I found drink to be the best way to get through most things.' He looked down at his clipped fingernails. 'I suppose that's how I found myself calling Christian's office when I was told I was going to need a liver transplant. He'd been in the office the day before and we'd gone for dinner and when I needed a friendly voice, his was the only one I could hear in my head. Slightly pathetic, I suppose. But there was something about Christian that made you feel he cared.'

Cass listened to this new snapshot of his brother's life and found himself drawn in, despite his disinterested expression. Christian was the good brother; that he already knew. He'd always known it, even when Christian was still alive and their separate existences had seemed relatively normal. But he was always surprised to hear stories of his little brother's quiet 'care'. Cass had no patience for people. Most of them he didn't like, and even those he did, he didn't always trust. How had Christian managed to be so different?

'Anyway, the point I'm making is that we bonded. He'd been there for me, and I trusted him. He pushed his superiors at The Bank, to see if they could do anything to get me up the transplant list more quickly, but it appeared that they couldn't.'

For the first time Cass saw a hint of bitterness in Marlowe's smile.

'Or wouldn't,' he added. 'My liver disease is apparently my own fault, and that tends to make people less sympathetic.'

Cass said nothing. The man was sick, but that wasn't Cass's problem. He didn't know Edgar Marlowe, and he didn't care – he wasn't Christian. He didn't feel the suffering of strangers.

'Anyway, about seven months ago I got a call from your brother. It was perhaps three weeks or so before he died. It was from a payphone, which I found odd, and he sounded quite unsettled, which concerned me even more. He wanted to meet me, and I went, of course. At that point I was feeling quite good about things. I'd been told that the prospect for a transplant was good, and that I was moving quickly up the list. I'd stopped drinking. I was feeling positive about the future.'

'What did my brother want?'

'He gave me this.' Marlowe pulled a sealed envelope from his pocket. 'He told me that if anything should happen to him or his family, then I was to give it to you. He was a bit drunk, I think, and he said some things that I really didn't understand. He said that he didn't know what to do about it. He said he wasn't sure he could change anything, and that it wouldn't be fair on either of them if he tried. But what I did understand was this: Christian said that if any-thing ever happened to him, then you'd know what to do about it. He said you were good at things like that. And he said I was the only person he could trust to make sure you got it.' He paused. 'I never saw him again after that.'

Marlowe had been speaking slowly as he replayed the memory, as if determined to get it exactly right. Cass leaned forward and carefully took the envelope from him.

'Did you look inside?'

'No.' Marlowe shook his head. 'I might not have your brother's integrity, but I am a lawyer. I've handled many sealed envelopes in my time, and I've learned that often they are Pandora's boxes. Sometimes they shouldn't be opened at all.'

'Are you saying that after all the effort you've gone to find me that I shouldn't even open it?'

'No, not at all.' Marlowe smiled, his lips whitening as they stretched. 'That's entirely up to you.'

Cass looked down at the envelope. Expensive. It felt like

linen between his fingers. He'd felt paper like that before.

'Did you tell anyone about this?' He'd seen the way The Bank operated. They demanded one hundred per cent loyalty from their employees.

'I should have done. And I did think about it.' Marlowe's smile twisted bitterly. 'Why do you think it's taken me so long to bring it to you?'

'Why didn't you?'

'Things change – my diagnosis for one. It appears that things are worse than the doctors thought.' He paused, and then went on, 'I've got two weeks left, maybe three at a pinch. A transplant won't save me now.'

'So there's nothing they can offer you in return, is that what you're saying?'

'Perhaps. Life is a healthy bartering tool. But I think I'd made my choice already. Even back then when Christian gave it to me I think I knew I'd be here one day. Some things should be left to unfold uncontrolled.'

Marlowe pushed away from the desk, flinching slightly at the effort of getting up. He held out his hand. 'I doubt we'll meet again. Good luck.'

His palm felt cool and greasy, and Cass thought the lawyer would be lucky if he made it through the two weeks. They walked in silence to the front desk and Cass nodded a silent goodbye to the dying man. As he watched him move slowly down the front steps the envelope felt heavy in his hand. What could Christian have found out that he didn't want to tell Cass while he was alive? And why didn't he want to do anything about it himself? *It wouldn't be fair on either of them.* On whom?

Instead of going back up to his office he headed into the toilets and locked himself in a cubicle. The sudden silence buzzed in his ears as he stared at the envelope. He didn't have to open it; he could tear it up and flush it and let the past lie – the lawyer would be dead in a couple of weeks and no one would be any the wiser. Cass looked down at his shoes. For a brief second, he thought he saw red splashes on them.

'Fuck it,' he muttered. Not knowing something wouldn't change the truth of it. He tore the envelope open and tugged out the contents – a piece of notepaper, folded in half, the size paper used to be when people wrote letters with the lined sheet underneath to make sure the writing stayed straight and even. His heart thumped so hard he was sure his shirt was moving with the beat. He unfolded it. One sentence stood out in black ink against the white, printed in Christian's neat writing.

THEY took Luke.

And the world shifted again.

Chapter Six

Lucius Dawson was the last one in, ten minutes after the briefing had started. The Prime Minister hadn't waited for him, and Abigail wasn't surprised. The mood had changed since the bombs, and as Alison McDonnell's previously firm hold on the country was loosening, so the tension that surrounded her slowly tightened. People were grieving, angry and afraid, and the disruption caused by the damage to the Underground system was not helping the already fraught economic situation. And then there was the cost of repairs: Britain might have reached an agreement with the French about leaving the Chunnel closed, but London needed her tube lines working.

Now that the initial mourning period was over, the vultures on the Opposition benches were gathering, even after the explosions in Russia, and the PM was going to have to come up with some answers soon. Russia was too far away for anyone to care about. Since the world economy had begun to crumble, people had become more selfish. Charity began at home. The noose might not yet be around her neck, but McDonnell knew it was dangling above her somewhere, and she'd lost a little of her natural calm.

'I don't understand,' she said now, barely acknowledging the Home Secretary as he took his seat beside her. 'All of this CCTV footage is time-coded and date-correct. There couldn't be a mistake?'

'No,' Andrew Dunne answered. 'It's correct.'

'Run it again. More slowly.' She flashed a look sideways to Dawson. 'I don't think this is going to cheer you up.'

The head of Special Branch typed something into his laptop and the images on the screen started moving again.

'Okay, this is Ealing Broadway at 1.04 p.m. Security camera footage from the bank opposite and the Pri-Maxx clothes store where the first bomb went off both show this man exiting the store and heading left. Two minutes later the explosions started.'

'He's a big man,' Dawson commented. 'Moves well, though.'

At the back of the room, Abigail didn't look. This wasn't her business, and she was tired. Her phone vibrated in her pocket and she took it out. She stared at it for a second before the name registered. Hayley. What could Hayley want? Without answering, she put the phone away. It would have to wait.

'Yes, too well,' Fletcher added. 'That's the problem.'

'This is footage from Goodge Street at 1.09 p.m.' Dunne played a second clip. 'One minute before three carriages of the Northern Line train exploded just as it pulled into Tottenham Court Road Station.'

'But that's the same man,' Dawson said.

'That's what I just said,' McDonnell added. 'And this is where you came in.'

'I'm afraid it doesn't end there.' Fletcher leaned forward, resting his arms on the desk. 'CCTV evidence also places him outside Liverpool Street Station minutes before the explosions there. And he's seen leaving the 37 bus one stop before Ealing Broadway, one minute before cameras picked him up leaving the Pri-Maxx store.'

Abigail's phone buzzed again in the silence that filled the room. Hayley. She cancelled it quickly, but even as she waved an apology at the PM, her sister's name stayed in her head. There was no reason for Hayley to call her – it had been a long time since her little sister had called her for a chat, and if something had happened to one of their parents, Abigail would have heard first. There was a nine-year age gap between them, and although Abigail blamed Hayley's move to London and starting university for their distance as she started growing up and leading her own life, deep down she knew that wasn't the case. *She* was the one who had grown distant – she'd grown distant from all of them. Suddenly she felt sad, as if remembering a place that had once been special, and yet could never be returned to.

'It's impossible,' McDonnell said. 'He can't be every-where. There must be another explanation. There must be more than one of them.'

'That's the theory we're working on,' Dunne said.

'They look identical.' Dawson stared at the screen. 'Even down to the clothes – and the way they move. It's uncanny.'

'Where do they go?' The Prime Minister looked at Dunne. 'Have you traced a route, either to or from any of the sites?'

Fletcher and Dunne exchanged a glance. Abigail forgot the phone call; that look intrigued her. Dunne often showed his feelings, but never Fletcher. They looked like men who knew they were in trouble and there was nothing they could do about it.

'Unfortunately, we can't.'

'What do you mean? Not even for one of them?'

Silence hung in the air until Fletcher finally broke it.

'No. The one link we have is that they all go into the

nearest Underground station – and then we lose them as the cameras transfer. In one frame they're there, and then in the next they're not. And we've had teams trawling the footage of people leaving the stations that day. There's no evidence of even one of these men coming out of the Underground system at all.'

'That's impossible.'

'Yes,' Fletcher agreed, 'it is. And so there must be some explanation. We just haven't found it yet.'

'Have you got enhanced images?' Dawson asked. 'Can you bring them up through the overhead? I want to see two of these men side by side.'

Dunne started tapping and a few moments later the large LCD screen on the wall burst into life. Abigail stared, ignoring the phone that was now vibrating persistently against her leg.

'I know him,' she said, the words tumbling straight from her brain to hang in the silent room.

The four heads who had so far ignored her turned her way. She stared at the screen. The suit fitted neatly in both images. His skin looked sickly, mottled and shiny, on his face and neck. His eyes were dark, beyond brown, the pupils leaking out into the surrounding irises like black ink soaking into blotting paper. The images were undeniably identical. One man. Not two.

The PM spoke softly. 'You know him?'

'No,' Abigail said, 'I've seen him.'

'Where?' Fletcher was on his feet. 'When?'

'The night of the bombings. He was just standing in the street when I ran home. Near my flat.' Her words felt like water trickling down a drain. Her insides cooled. For a moment she was back there, out of breath and sweating, feeling again that blissful sense of emptiness she'd had when he looked at her. She remembered his finger rising to his lips. Her own pupils dilated and she bit the side of her tongue to shut it up.

'What do you mean, just standing in the street? What was he doing?'

Abigail moved closer to the screen and frowned. 'Maybe it wasn't him. It might have just been a fat man ...'

'Did he speak to you?' Fletcher asked.

'No.' Her phone buzzed again and this time she reached for it. 'Can I take this? It's my sister. She keeps ringing. Maybe something's wrong?'

'Be quick,' McDonnell said.

She felt all four sets of eyes watching her as she slipped out into the corridor. She'd lied, and she was going to keep on lying, and she didn't even know why. It *was* the same man; she knew it. She remembered the rise of his finger. There was a promise in that, just as there was in the empty Hotmail account. One day both would deliver something, she knew that deep down somewhere in a part of her she didn't understand. But not if she told. If she told, then whatever it was would never happen.

'Hayley?' Her voice sounded calm, normal. It surprised her. 'What's the matter?'

'I saw it all.' The breathing at the other end was wet and heavy.

'Hayley? Is that you?' Abigail stared at the closed door. They were waiting on the other side for her lies.

'I remembered.' It was Hayley, but the words were strained, as if she was having trouble forming them.

'What did you remember?' Abigail frowned. She really didn't have time for this. 'Are you stoned, Hayley?'

'Chaos in the darkness.' Hayley's voice was barely above a whisper. 'That was it. Chaos in the darkness.'

65

'Hayley?'

The phone clicked off at the other end.

The door opened. Fletcher looked at her. 'All okay?'

'I'm not sure. I'll call her later. Maybe she was drunk or something. She's a student.'

'This man you saw—'

'It wasn't him,' Abigail said, cutting him off. 'I'm sorry; I shouldn't have spoken like that without being sure. The suit's all wrong – and I think the man I saw had brown hair.'

'You sounded pretty sure in there.' His eyes were evaluating every move of her face, looking for some kind of *tell*.

Abigail didn't underestimate the man. 'I can take another look if you'd like, but I'm pretty sure it's a different man. It was the size of him that made me think I'd seen him before.'

'Maybe we should do that,' Fletcher said, 'see where the differences lie.'

'Sure.' Abigail smiled. 'Now?'

'Why not?'

She tucked her phone away. It didn't ring again.

Chapter Seven

They sat in their usual places, one at each compass point of the large round table. For a moment there was only the drumming of Mr Craven's fingers on the highly polished surface at the east.

Then Mr Dublin spoke. 'The others won't like us meeting without them. Not at this time. Everyone's a touch on edge, wouldn't you say?'

'We met as a whole two weeks ago,' Mr Bright answered, 'and anyway' – he sipped his espresso – 'the more of us who meet, the harder it is to come to any decisions. Everyone wants to have a say. And for now, I feel some things should stay between us four.'

'How's Monmir?' Mr Craven asked.

'Going downhill fast. From what I gather he's back in Damascus.' Mr Dublin smiled. It was wistful and kind. 'He always did like it there.'

'I've heard that Morelo is ill.' Mr Craven's fingers still twitched nervously. 'Collapsed overseeing the building of a new energy plant in Russia. Is that true?'

'He's having some tests.' Mr Bright's voice remained impassive. 'Our doctors, of course.'

'It's happening quicker then.' Mr Dublin's smile dropped. His high cheekbones were like flashes of silver under the pale lighting. 'The first ones didn't die so fast. And there were always so many years between them.'

'Some are saying it's a punishment.' Mr Bellew spoke softly. He leaned back in his chair and his tall, broad frame filled his seat. He looked at each of the others, his dark eyes finally resting on Mr Bright.

'Even for him—,' Mr Bright flashed perfect white teeth as he smiled at the dark-haired man, '—that would be an awfully long wait for vengeance. It's *ennui*, that's all. They started to believe they could die, and they started to fear it. And so they let it in. That's all.'

'Tell that to Monmir,' Mr Craven muttered. 'Tell him it's all in his head.'

'And what about the First? Is that what he thinks?' Mr Bellew returned Mr Bright's smile.

'Childish game to play, Mr Bellew.' Mr Bright carefully pushed his coffee cup aside. 'The First is sleeping. But it is what he *did* think. And look at us. We're perfectly healthy.'

'Some are saying that perhaps there's been a change of leadership, and that's why these punishments are falling on us now.'

'*Some are saying, some are saying*... There is always talk, and much of it is ridiculous, even if you won't tell them so. Who would have led this supposed coup?' Mr Bright asked. 'Even you, Mr Bellew, the perennial politician, know that all the serious challengers are here.'

'Since we allowed ourselves to become smaller,' Mr Dublin sighed, running one hand through his ash-blond hair, 'I find the notion of time has changed.' He paused. 'Sometimes I find it hard to be myself any more. It gets more difficult to remember.'

'We're still everything we once were, and this is still our kingdom.' Mr Bright leaned forward, his eyes sharp. 'If anything, we're *more* than we were then. We chose this place, and I – *we* – built it.'

'We were glorious.' Mr Dublin finally smiled. 'Weren't we?'

'We *are* glorious. And if we go back, then we go back to fight, not to beg forgiveness.'

'Always *if, if, if.*' Mr Craven sneered. He was the youngest of the four, perhaps in his early thirties, showing only the first hint of lines around the corners of his narrow, suspicious eyes. '*If* we find the walkways, *if* we can get back, *if* this crumbling *kingdom* doesn't collapse around us before then.'

'Speaking of getting back, how is the Experiment?' Mr Bellew asked.

'Complicated as expected,' Mr Bright said. 'We're using the Hubble. The Bank's scientific subsidiaries are also working on the development of a more powerful global deep-space remotely powered telescope. However, I'm hoping that won't be needed. We are making some progress.'

'We're trapped, aren't we?' Mr Dublin's voice had lost its wistful edge. 'How ironic that we've had to wait for them to develop their crude skills to even think about getting back.'

'If you remember,' Mr Craven said, 'until the First started sleeping and death found us, no one was interested in finding the way back.'

'We're lucky,' Mr Bellew added, 'that they turned their attentions *heavenwards* at all.'

'It's never luck,' Mr Bright said. 'We pushed them that way.'

'Sometimes I wonder if – after everything – they are still a mystery to us,' Mr Dublin said. 'Perhaps some part of them remembers.'

'Who knows?' Mr Bright leaned back. 'But the Experiment is not why we're here. We discussed that a fortnight ago with the full Cohort.'

'So why exactly have you dragged us here?' Mr Bellew lit a thin cigarette. 'We're all busy.'

'These bombings in London and Moscow are a concern.'

'I don't see why,' Mr Craven said. 'We know they're violent. They always have been. They were always more like us; that's how we all came to be here in the first place.'

'Don't you find it somewhat peculiar that no one knows who's responsible? That none of their terror groups have come forward? *We* don't even appear to know ...'

'We've been distracted,' Mr Dublin said. 'And London is your responsibility.'

'To be honest,' Mr Craven said, frowning, 'this was never about looking after them. We all have our own ventures to manage.'

'This is true,' Mr Bright conceded, 'but the leaders of these nations were suggested by the House to have the capacity to calm the current downward spiral. We all worked hard to ensure they found power. Now it looks like these attacks have been aimed at unsettling the balance we're creating. There are some far more hot-headed candidates eagerly waiting in the wings ...' His eyes lingered on both Mr Bellew and Mr Craven for a second before he continued, 'And that could cause us far larger problems. No one wants that.'

'You think too much,' Mr Bellew said dryly.

'I'm the Architect. I built it—'

'— and it would be ironic if after all this *they* destroyed it.' Mr Dublin smiled.

'Maybe we've given them too much freedom.'

'But freedom was always the point,' Mr Bellew said. 'For all of us. And we've always kept our eye on things.' He evaluated the silver-haired man in the impeccable suit sitting opposite him. 'You've always been confident you have everything under control. The First's right-hand man. You and Solomon ...' The sentence trailed away. 'Well, I'm sure we can all rely on you to get to the bottom of whatever you think is going on here.'

'What *do* you think is going on?' Mr Craven leaned forward. 'Are you suggesting that one of us is behind these attacks?'

'It's a consideration that perhaps one of our wider number is.' Mr Bright remained impassive. 'There's no denying we are less cohesive than once we were. Those who are sick are becoming desperate. We have been sitting back over all this time and watching the effect fear and sickness can have.'

'You want us to see if anyone is acting of their own accord?' Mr Dublin asked. 'You're suggesting we spy on our own?'

Mr Bright said nothing, but looked at each of them. 'Nothing that extreme,' he said at last. 'I just think it's time we tightened the reins a touch.'

'Good luck with that.' Mr Dublin smiled.

'I don't believe in luck. I never have.'

The meeting over, the four individuals made their way onto the quiet side street where gleaming black cars awaited them, always invisible in the dark until the headlights came on, set by set. Mr Bright left first, watched by the other three.

'Are you flying straight back?' Mr Dublin asked.

'No.' Mr Craven's thin lips almost disappeared as he grinned. 'I think I'll stay a couple of days and remind myself of what this First City has to offer.'

'Don't draw too much attention to yourself.'

'Don't worry,' he laughed, 'there are still those who willingly give me their children.'

Mr Dublin sighed. 'We all have our secrets. Perhaps even Mr Bright.'

'Perhaps even the sleeping First,' Mr Bellew added. 'Goodnight. Until next time.'

The car doors closed one by one and the limousines slipped out onto the brightly lit main road, losing each other as they headed their separate ways.

In the back of one, the occupant sighed and poured a whisky, sipping it thoughtfully before pulling a phone from his pocket and scrolling down to the required name. He typed one word, TOMORROW, into the text message screen and then pressed send. He leaned back against the soft leather and smiled.

Mr Bright's shoes clicked gently against the marble floor of the lobby of Senate House. Once part of the University of London, now it was owned by The Bank, and its functions were diverse. The university still used the north part for overseas studies, and some of the south side floors were used for various research projects. UCL had tried to stop the take-over of the building when The Bank had demanded these premises if it were to bail out the financially beleaguered university, but as it stood, they hadn't done too badly out of the deal. The building had certain advantages for The Bank – and therefore the Network – and one of those, as far as Mr Bright was concerned, was having the university occupying part of it. All the secrets of the world were hidden in plain sight, and young people were notoriously self-absorbed. They rarely saw the business of others.

His footsteps had an echo that continued when he stopped, and he turned to face its source.

'I've been waiting here for hours.'

The almost familiar figure walked towards Mr Bright. The once-dark olive Arabian hue of the skin had turned pale, almost sickly; the hair had thinned and lost its lustre.

'Monmir,' Mr Bright said. 'I thought you were in Damascus.'

'I wanted to come here first.'

'I thought you might.'

'He is here, isn't he?'

Mr Bright nodded.

'Can I see him?'

Mr Bright looked into the desperate yellowing eyes. 'Of course. Although he's still sleeping.'

The lift doors closed behind them. Mr Bright pushed the button on the small remote control in his pocket, the silver back panels slid open and they stepped through to the second lift beyond. It whirred silently upwards, and neither occupant broke its hum with speech.

The floor they emerged onto was brightly lit despite the late hour, but apart from the large men positioned outside the doors and the woman working quietly behind the glass desk who nodded a greeting at them as they passed, the corridor was empty. No one stopped Mr Bright and Monmir, nor spoke to them.

At the furthest door Mr Bright scanned his thumbprint and punched in a code. Inside, a nurse looked up from her station, recognised Mr Bright and went back to filling syringes. He smiled at her as he passed and led Monmir to the glass window beyond.

'You might be shocked by his appearance.' The air

shivered as he spoke. 'But he's still very much alive.' Mr Bright pulled up the blind.

'Jesus,' Monmir said, after a moment's pause.

Mr Bright's eyes widened slightly, and then he smiled at the memories. 'No, not Jesus. Not any more.'

Monmir didn't take his eyes from the view. The figure in the bed was barely visible. Thin arms lay still on the neatly tucked bedding, poking out pathetically from short-sleeved blue pyjamas. Tubes ran from the inner elbows to drips hanging from tall stands on either side of the hospital bed, and a pulse monitor was clipped to the tip of one finger. A mask covered the occupant's face, thick coils connecting it to a tank hanging on the wall behind, which in turn was almost obscured by the bank of machines displaying silently changing numbers and lines of activity.

'This isn't sleeping.' Monmir's sickly breath settled as condensation on the glass. 'This is life-support.'

'It's all perspective,' Mr Bright said. 'And most of this he doesn't need.'

'Then why is it there?'

'It's better to be safe than sorry, wouldn't you say?'

There was a long pause after that.

'We used to think he could do anything. How did it come to this?'

Mr Bright stared through his own healthy reflection at the figure in the bed. 'He *can* do anything. He'll wake again when he's ready.'

'We were so full of energy, weren't we? We were unstoppable. And now look at us. Everything's crumbling and so are we. Maybe it was never meant to last.'

Mr Bright looked at the sad acceptance in Monmir's face. There was pain etched in its once smooth surface.

'This doesn't have to happen to you, Monmir.' He spoke

softly. 'It's a trick of the mind. You can stop it.'

Monmir turned. 'Is that what you said to Mr Solomon?'

Mr Bright didn't answer.

'You can't control everything, Mr Bright.' There was something close to pity in Monmir's voice. 'Not you, not the First, not even with the bloodline traced, with the promise of the boy.'

Mr Bright's eyes widened slightly.

'We all hear the stories – you and Mr Solomon and the First, yes, you keep your secrets well, but there will always be rumours that even those outside the Inner Cohort hear. We trust you. We trusted you then, and in the main we trust you now. Most of us have been happy to simply fulfil our obligations to the Network and enjoy the power we have while you manage the bigger picture. But you mustn't forget free will. It's what brought us here, after all.' He paused to catch his breath.

'I have always respected you. From before you were Mr Bright, from the times and places that are getting so hard to remember. And I won't turn against you now. But be careful and tread softly. And keep your eyes open.'

'What are you trying to tell me, Monmir?' Mr Bright asked. His eyes twinkled. They always did.

Monmir watched him thoughtfully. 'Probably nothing you don't already know.' He smiled. His gums were pale. 'Perhaps I'm just being human. I think I've finally begun to understand what that means.' He winked, for a moment a shadow of his former self. 'Dying can do that to you.'

'You don't have to die, Monmir. You're just allowing it to happen.'

'No,' Monmir agreed, 'maybe I don't have to die. Maybe I'll use what strength I have left and try for the walkways. If I can become myself again.'

'Don't do that.'

'Why not?'

'Others have tried, you know that. It's not safe. You won't make it.'

'You think dying is better?'

Mr Bright said nothing.

Monmir smiled. 'You think you understand, but in reality, you know nothing. You built it, yes, but until *you're* dying, you will never understand all its magic and madness.'

'I never took you for a poet, Monmir.'

They stared at each other.

'I'll find my own way out.'

The sickly figure turned without looking back through the glass, and Mr Bright watched him go. He waited until the lift was headed back down to the ground floor before he carefully lowered the blind and turned away. Back in the corridor, he paused outside one of the guarded rooms. He slid back the small panel and peered in. Mr Rasnic sat propped up against the back wall. His face twitched slightly, and small tics at the corner of his mouth hinted at unformed words.

Mr Bright's own mouth pursed slightly. It was unsettling seeing him like this, in this endless state of nothingness, his body a dull shell. The Glow had gone. Mr Rasnic had volunteered to try and find the walkways in the early days of the Experiment. He'd been strong and powerful and full of wit. He'd shone, even when small.

Not any more. Five years on and there had been no change. Mr Bright didn't expect any. Mr Rasnic was empty. Just like the others who had tried afterwards.

He slid the hatch shut and glanced at the other doors. He didn't need to look inside. Had there been any changes he would have been informed. At least they'd stopped trying to claw at their dead eyes. That had been unsettling.

He sighed and turned away. He had never been tempted to try for the walkways himself. Neither had Solomon, back then, when his old friend was still sane. Sometimes he wondered if anyone actually remembered how it had really been, beyond the power and the glory. He smiled. He would always choose to take his chances here.

Chapter Eight

Dr Tim Hask swallowed the last of his third vodka and tonic, coughing in his enthusiastic need to speak, and then delivered the punchline of his rambling shaggy dog tale. It must have been funny, because Ramsey burst out in the kind of laughter that can only come from a joke well told. Cass forced a smile of his own and drained his pint. It was good to see both men – Hask's presence had been a surprise. After the Man of Flies case had come to its unusual end, the profiler had returned to Sweden, but following the bombings, he was back at the behest of the government for psyche evaluations for any potential suspects – not to mention the numerous corporations who were prepared to pay big bucks to have any of their employees who were caught up in the trauma that day checked over: heaven forbid post-traumatic stress should cause any financial errors to be made. Like the world wasn't fucked-up enough already?

It was good to see him again, but Cass just wished they'd met up another night. There was too much filling his head to concentrate on his friends, and the note the dying solicitor had given him was sitting like lead in his pocket. And then there were the suicides. Everything about them was all wrong.

'Does the phrase "Chaos in the darkness" mean anything

to either of you?' he asked at last, when the humour of the conversation had faded and they were left talking around the up-coming trials that they weren't supposed to discuss.

'No,' Ramsey said, 'should it?'

'A girl on your patch killed herself a couple of weeks ago. She wrote it on the wall.'

'Didn't land on my desk – but then, a suicide wouldn't. Although it's about the level of case I'm getting these days.'

'You and me both.'

'If it was in my part of town, how do you know about it?'

'A girl killed herself in mine last night and those were her last words. Eagleton called me. He'd photographed your girl. He made the connection and thought there might be something in it. He figured I'd be bored enough to dig around.'

'He's a good kid,' Ramsey said, 'and I guess he was right.'

Cass looked at Hask. 'Does it mean anything to you?'

'No, not without researching it.' The fat man leaned forward, threatening the stability of the wooden pub table. 'Is this what's got you so preoccupied tonight?'

'Partly, yeah,' Cass admitted. 'Not that it matters. The DCI won't allow it as a case.'

The beer had given him a sombre buzz and he could feel his mood sinking. For the first time in months he wanted some cocaine.

'I think I might head home.' He got to his feet. 'It's good to see you, Hask.' He meant it too. 'Let's do this again.'

'Of course we will.' Hask grinned cheerfully, the expression forcing its way onto his vast cheeks, but Cass could feel those clever eyes digging into him. Hask was curious – well, let him be. Cass had nothing to share at the moment. There was no point talking about a case that couldn't run, and the letter was private. He said farewell to Ramsey and headed out onto the pavement.

Despite being walking distance from the hubbub of Oxford Street, Marylebone High Street was quiet in the evenings, and Cass enjoyed the peace as he walked through the warm air towards the Marylebone Road, where traffic would be rumbling on all night; he'd be able to grab a taxi there. He stared into the dark city and wondered at its secrets.

THEY took Luke.

He knew who *THEY* were: the Network; the shadowy – he fought against the word *supernatural,* despite what he'd seen when Solomon died – group behind The Bank, who was in turn behind most governments, banks and big businesses, as far as he could see. And The Bank itself was also the owner of the X accounts, connected to a strange file called Redemption which he'd found on Christian's laptop six months ago, just after his brother was murdered. Cass hadn't wanted anything to do with them: the Network might have had files on the Jones family, but Cass had no wish to be drawn into whatever game they were playing, even if the mysterious Mr Bright had been claiming to be looking out for him. After all, that 'special care' hadn't done his parents or his brother any good. But now it appeared he wasn't being given any choice but to step back into that fray.

His soul was weary as he trudged past the shops and the last of the restaurants into the quieter far end of the High Street. A church loomed dark in the shadows, shrouded by trees and shrubs. Cass didn't look up. Faith hadn't done his family any good either.

THEY took Luke. It was a statement of fact, not a question. Christian had been a meticulous man, so to leave that note for Cass, he must have been certain that the boy he'd raised wasn't his biological son. Cass paused to light a cigarette and watched as he expelled the first lungful of pale smoke into the night. He also understood what Christian had meant when he'd had that last conversation with Marlowe: he loved Jessica and Luke – the boy he'd raised as his son – too much to destroy them with news like this, no matter how much it might have been tearing Christian apart.

Cass had always known he was different from Christian, but over the last six months he'd begun to realise how great those differences were. One was blond, the other brown; and they were light and dark in every way. Christian knew that Cass – the brother who had slept with his wife – would be able to do what he couldn't: find the baby stolen at birth, regardless of cost. Cass had believed they'd become strangers as adults, but that wasn't true: Christian really had understood Cass. It was only after his baby brother had been murdered that Cass had come anywhere close to understanding Christian.

THEY. Even Christian had been wary of using names or mentioning the Network, and he'd been so much more open to all of it than Cass had ever had. *The boys see the glow! Yay!* Their mother had scribbled that excitedly on the back of an old photograph, but in that picture the small dark boy had been frowning at it, while the blond boy looked excited. One had embraced the *glow* and lived with it, while the other had shut his mind to it, completely denied its existence. And now one was dead and one was alive. That was the comparison that held the most weight for Cass: the Network was dangerous for him on a personal level. He might not understand why, but he knew this to be the truth in every nerve and fibre of his body, and he did trust his instinct. That rarely failed him.

Music drifted down the path of the church grounds: the soft notes of a violin. Cass didn't know the tune, but it was something bluesy, born in the deep southern states, untrained music beaten out on the stoops of dusty shacks by rough hands.

Cass followed it along the flagstones and past the church door, round to the small graveyard at the side. A figure perched on the back of an old bench, his feet on the seat. With his mind still on his brother, Cass half-expected to see Christian's shiny black brogues there, but no, this wasn't Christian's ghost. The old man's face crinkled into a smile and he drew out one more long note before letting the violin fall silent. He leaned forward. Even in the dark Cass could see the man's hands were dirty, his fingernails almost black with the muck underneath them.

'Evening,' he said. The voice was gruff and London, and cultivated from years of living in cardboard boxes and door-ways. The man's trousers came halfway up his shins; when he stood up, they'd be a good two or three inches too short for his legs.

'I'm not sure you should be here,' Cass answered.

'As you don't know me, how do you know where I should be?' There was no aggression in the response, only a hint of humour.

Cass took a step forward. Was the tramp drunk? They were only a couple of feet apart now, and given the grime that coated the old man, he should stink. But Cass got nothing; no whiff of stale sweat, no alcohol, nothing at all.

'It's a little late at night for an outdoor concert,' he said.

The man laughed a little. 'I ain't disturbing the residents, son.'

It was a fair comment.

'Where did you learn to play?'

'Can't really remember.' There was a tooth missing from his upper set; the gap showed when he smiled. 'A long time ago. Prob'ly before you were born, and you don't look like a spring chicken from here.' He laughed again, and this time Cass couldn't help but smile with him.

'Well, take care of that.' Cass gestured at the polished wood of the violin. It looked old and well cared for, but he couldn't see a case anywhere. 'Looks like it's worth a few quid.'

'It's worth what it's worth. More to some than others. Like most things.' He leaned forward and looked hard at Cass. 'It's all perspective.'

'If you say so.' Cass ground out his cigarette and started to walk away. The old man was harmless; he could play his music in the graveyard if he wanted. 'You take care.' He didn't turn round. He had too much on his mind for an old tramp and his riddles.

'You take care too, Cassius Jones.' Cass was almost at the gate when the voice followed him. 'Watch your back.'

Cass's blood chilled and he turned. 'How do you know my—?'

—*name*. The question went unfinished. The bench was empty. The old man had gone.

He stared into the gloom for a long time before heading home. There was vodka there. He needed it.

The air should have been getting crisper, but at 8.15 the next morning it was warm and muggy, and nothing like early October at all. The heat drained any freshness from his earlier shower, and his hangover throbbed. He'd needed a cool morning with some bite in it after a night of thinking and drinking and then passing out on the sofa, but today the weather wasn't his friend. The Met Office had for once been right: London was heading for an Indian summer.

In the car he scrolled through the numbers in his phone until he found Artie Mullins. He quickly typed out one short sentence – 'Can I come by and get something off you later? C' – and hit the send button before he could change his mind. Mullins would be awake, no doubt – that old fucker never slept more than two or three hours – but if Cass's sometime friend was going to turn him down, then he could do without the awkward conversation. Things were strained between them, though Cass couldn't blame Artie, either for his irritation with Cass, or his wanting to keep some distance between them for now.

The old London gangster knew Cass hadn't damaged his operation on purpose; it was just a by-product of his investigations into Christian's death and the drive-by shooting of two schoolboys, but that didn't change the outcome: all the illegal 'bonuses' that had been passing between the London firms and the police had been sus-pended indefinitely as soon as the arrests started. Sure, it was DI Bowman's fault for having used them to set up a crime syndicate of his own, but it was Cass who had uncovered the plot. Now no one wanted to be seen taking any kind of bribe, at least until all this shit was cleared up, so if they weren't able to make money on the side, then every detective in London had to pay his mortgage the legal way, and that meant performance-related pay. All bets were off, and it was open season on the criminal fraternity once again.

No one was thanking Cass on either side of the fence.

On top of that, every copper in London was scrabbling to cover up just how far the hand-holding between the Met and London's criminal element had gone. It wouldn't have helped Artie that he was Cass's contact – shit sticks, and all that. Lucky for Artie Mullins that he ran so much of London, otherwise he'd probably have been in danger of landing in the Thames attached to a pair of sink-don't-swim concrete boots.

Still, troubles or not, Cass trusted Artie and his discretion more than any other dealers. Artie would either sell him the coke or he wouldn't, but he sure as fuck wouldn't grass Cass up, not to the media or his new DCI. And in the long term, Cass reckoned he'd probably done Artie Mullins a favour: his big rival Sam Macintyre was gone, and the Irish were struggling to find a solid replacement. Mullins was probably cleaning up.

The message sent, Cass turned on the engine and set the air-con running to cool himself down. Some things never changed. Here he was, still stuck on the fence, not belonging to one side or the other – not that either side would be happy to own him. He wondered if he should feel relieved about that. Sometimes the only side a man could be on was his own. He sent another quick text message, this time to Perry Jordan, asking him to call later. Fuck the court cases; it was time to put the private investigator to better use, tracking down his brother's child. He'd let the young man do the groundwork, then he'd take over himself. He wasn't going to risk anyone else getting hurt in whatever game the Network was playing.

'We need to go straight upstairs.' DS Armstrong was waiting outside Cass's office. 'Heddings wants to see us.'

'What, now?' Cass had hoped to spend the morning waiting for his hangover to give up and die, and then the afternoon trying to avoid thinking about the teenage sui-cides before talking to Perry Jordan about upping the search for his nephew Luke.

Armstrong shrugged.

'Well, I'm grabbing a coffee first. He can wait five minutes.'

The DCI was standing behind his desk when Cass knocked and let himself and his sergeant into his office. As soon as the door was shut Heddings threw down the newspaper he was holding. 'I take it you've seen this?'

Cass didn't answer, but bent and picked up the tabloid. The headline was printed large across the front page: **Sinister links between teenage suicides**. Katie Dodds' face smiled out in black and white, alongside Cory Denter's and James Busby's.

'No. I haven't.' He scanned the accompanying article. The hack, Oliver McMahon, who'd written it seemed to have a lot of information at his fingertips, especially about Cass himself and his role in 'uncovering the corruption at the heart of the London Met'. The piece claimed the deaths were linked by the single phrase, *Chaos in the darkness*, although it didn't go into detail about how each suicide had used the phrase.

Once he'd finished, he passed it sideways to Armstrong. Keeping his eyes focused on Heddings, he said, 'It doesn't surprise me, though. The two girls we met yesterday at Angie Lane's flat already knew about the others.'

'We really don't need any more bloody fiascos.' Heddings cheeks were flushed.

'With all due respect, sir, don't take it out on me. I haven't said a word.' It was only a small lie; mentioning the deaths to Hask and Ramsey didn't count, and it wasn't as if they'd even discussed the full potential of the case.

'They make you sound like the saviour of the Met.'

'Is that what's bothering you?'

'No.' Heddings flashed him a glare. 'Despite what you

think, I'm not that petty. I just don't like having my hand forced.'

'I'm not with you, sir.'

'Really? If it's in this rag today, then it'll be in all the others by tomorrow. We'll look like a right bunch of callous bastards if we do nothing about it.'

Cass bit back his smile. 'So have I got the case, sir?'

'You bloody know you have.'

Cass didn't let the grin stretch across his face until the door closed behind them and he was heading back to his office.

When Armstrong knocked on his door forty-five minutes later, Cass had a copy of the paper on his desk and was staring at the computer. He'd typed in the phrase 'Chaos in the darkness'. Even after hearing what the students had said the day before, he was surprised to see how many forums and message boards had picked up on it. He'd been going through them for nearly an hour and had yet to scratch the surface.

'We should be ready to dig up the bodies this afternoon. I've called Eagleton and he's getting prepped. I'm just waiting for the official go-ahead and then we can get a team in.'

Armstrong put the fresh coffee down. 'The Dodds and Busby families need informing, but her parents are in Guildford, and Busby's are somewhere in Buckinghamshire. Do you want me to get the locals on it?'

'No, you go with a WPC. I want to know about these kids' lives. I'll do their colleges.' He sighed. 'This shit is all over the Internet and it's spreading like wildfire. We're watching a new urban myth in the making.'

'I know, I did a search last night. What are you looking for?'

'Something referencing the phrase prior to these deaths.'

'Once you've briefed the team, get a couple of plods working on it.' Armstrong's face twitched into a smile. 'No offence, but they're probably more Internet-savvy than you.'

'I'm still in my bloody thirties, you know.' Cass couldn't help feeling slightly rankled. 'Maybe only just, but I'm not a dinosaur.' He sipped his coffee. 'You seem a little more enthusiastic about working with me today.'

'It's good to have a proper case.'

'I know that feeling.' Cass looked down at the newspaper. 'What was your degree in before you joined the force?'

'Politics and journalism. Why?'

Cass had half-expected the young man to lie, but he'd hoped he wouldn't. At least it showed he didn't take Cass for an idiot.

'This article has a lot of valid information. It surprised me to see Cory Denter's story in there. Even his parents weren't aware that he'd scribbled "Chaos in the darkness" in his work file. Didn't that stand out to you? I've just got off the phone to them. It probably would have been better for them to hear from us that there may be something dodgy about their son's death before reading it in the papers.'

'They knew. You were there yesterday. They might not have *known*, but the fact that you turned up? They'd have realised something wasn't quite right.'

Cass looked at the paper again. He wasn't letting his enthusiastic young sergeant get off that lightly. 'It's a clever piece. There's enough there to make it interesting, but not so much that it causes us any major problems in any investigation. It also says some overly kind things about me.' Cass watched his sergeant thoughtfully. 'You got friends at that paper?'

Armstrong met Cass's eyes. 'It was a case that needed

investigating, sir. And now we're investigating it.'

'So the ends justify the means?'

'I couldn't comment on the means.' Armstrong glanced at his watch. 'I'd better get the team ready for briefing if I'm going to see both sets of parents today. Anything else, sir?'

'No.' Cass leaned back in his chair. 'Just don't ever go to the papers without my say-so again. You'll end up getting fired for a stunt like that.'

'No, I won't.' Armstrong was on his way out the door. 'Trust me.'

The ambiguity of the answer wasn't lost on Cass; there was obviously more to his new sergeant than he'd at first thought. He could live with that, he reflected, looking back at the screen filled with short messages mainly written in some Internet version of teenage textspeak. A little ruthlessness could take you a long way in the force. But he'd be keeping an eye on Armstrong from now on. The young man might think he was clever, but the stupidity of youth stopped them all realising they were never as clever as they thought.

Chapter Nine

As the car pulled in through the barricades and onto Leicester Square, Abigail was glad that David Fletcher was back at the ATD and not with them on this public outing. He unsettled her. He was too straightforward. Where Andrew Dunne and the Prime Minister had believed her change of heart about the fat man and accepted that she had just been mistaken, Fletcher had not. He'd seen her initial reaction, and no matter what she'd said in the interview afterwards, he hadn't let go of that. She could read his face as well as he had read hers in that moment. They'd spent the afternoon locked in a wary battle, and however many times he had smiled at her politely, they both knew he *knew*.

Still, knowing and being able to do something about it were two different things. Fletcher had his hands full, and he could run as many searches on her as he liked, they'd always come back as clean. She *was* clean.

Through the tinted glass of the window she could see the memorial that was going up for all those who'd lost their lives, not only in 26/09, but in all the acts of terrorism that had taken place over the past decade. It was supposed to be modern art. Abigail wondered if anyone else thought the sculpted metal looked like the twisted wreck of a train carriage. She guessed not – or if they did, they weren't saying.

The surrounding roads had been temporarily closed off, but within the pedestrianised square a large group of grieving relatives were standing behind a smaller barrier about fifteen feet from the microphone. More onlookers gathered in crowds further away behind the Road Closed cordons. The Prime Minister had wanted this memorial up quickly, not just to draw a line under the events as much as she could, but also she wanted the public to be here to show the world that London was not afraid of terrorism, that Londoners were made of sterner stuff. Crowds had turned out, but nowhere near the numbers this part of the city should draw. Maybe Londoners weren't so brave after all.

The car slowed to a halt. Perhaps if the King had come, as he'd wanted to, the crowds would have been larger, but his health was failing, and McDonnell had persuaded him to allow the Prince of Wales to come in his stead at a separate time. The public would prefer that anyway; most people believed the old king should have passed his crown to his son, just like he'd wanted his own mother to do. The country needed a morale boost, and a young and dynamic king would raise spirits. Some leaders just didn't know when to step down. Even empty power could be addictive.

Cameras started flashing as soon as they got out of the limousine. The journalists had been kept behind the inner barrier. Special Branch officers would be moving among them, as well as the relatives and the main crowd of onlookers, further back, dressed in their civvies, monitoring the population for the slightest hint of any suspicious behaviour. Abigail didn't know their faces, but she could always pick them out by their posture and concentrated expressions as their eyes flicked across the crowd. Body language was the biggest tell of them all.

It was only ten a.m. but the day was already warm. For

once her expensive dark glasses – so stereotypical, thanks to Hollywood, and yet vital for masking the target of her gaze – did not look so out of place. Behind her, Barker pulled the large wreath of flowers from the car and followed the Prime Minister over to the steel and black structure. McDonnell took it from him and after placing it carefully on the ground, she turned to the crowd. Abigail moved so that she was slightly to one side of her boss, where she had a clear view of all the people in front of them, and the barriers beside. Her earpiece remained silent, but she scanned the buildings and windows, just in case the great Secret Service machine had missed anything. It hadn't, of course. Today, there would be no chance of any attack; highly trained individuals had flooded the area to be sure of that.

As the Prime Minister began to talk, Abigail remained focused. Her heartbeat stayed regular and even. She didn't think about the strangeness of her job, the ability to leap in front of a bullet without hesitation. They could dress it up with whatever title they wanted, but that was the essence of her position. Her sole responsibility was to ensure that should any attack on the Prime Minister happen, the other woman would have every chance of survival, which meant severely limiting the chance of her own. She'd been trained to move and calculate angles in order to take a bullet with the least likely outcome of death if she had to, but everyone knew that, really, it was just a matter of luck. The training was just something to help you sleep at night.

Abigail knew her colleagues viewed her strangely. They couldn't understand why a young, attractive woman would apply for that job, especially when so many world leaders were coming under attack. She didn't fit the image. She certainly hadn't throughout the interview process either, but she'd come top in all the tests, both physical and mental, and the psyche evaluation had proven her the most suitable for the position, and so here she was: death's body double.

More cameras flashed as McDonnell's speech continued. Abigail watched the crowd, her gaze moving from left to right through the group of relatives. There was nothing suspicious, as she'd expected. Her eyes moved again—

—and froze. Her heart thumped into life. A figure stood at the back, a step or two away from the last of the relatives. He hadn't been there seconds before. Her mouth dried as he smiled. *At her.* Even from the distance she could see the purple mottling on the skin that stretched across his fat face. He wore a dark suit. One hand undid the buttons of his jacket, his black eyes still fixed on hers. The earpiece was silent. Why the hell hadn't anyone spotted him? The finger to the lips, the note under her door, all her secrets were lost as her training kicked in.

Too much happened in too few seconds. The fat man held open his suit jacket. Something was strapped to his already oversized chest. Blocks of white. He smiled again, tilting his head to one side. He raised his left hand. He was holding something small in it. A triggering device? She looked at the white again. *Plastique.*

Action took over and she pulled her gun free with one hand while pushing the PM and her press officer to the ground. She shouted, not lowering her head towards the discreet mike attached to her suit jacket, but loud enough to be heard across the square. The sombre moment cracked, and the memory of the lost dead was replaced with the screaming fear of a crowd's sudden awareness of their own potential mortality. The barrier was shoved sideways as people fled. The officers who had hidden among them stood dumbfounded, looking this way and that for whatever the cause of the panic was. Why the hell hadn't they seen him?

On her feet, Abigail was running before she spotted the fat man again. He'd moved fast, already across the far barrier. Why had no one stopped him? What the hell was going on? Were they all half-asleep? Her feet pounded the tarmac and she pushed past the scattering people until she reached the metal, vaulting it in one smooth move. Someone was yelling in her earpiece but she couldn't work out what they were saying. She ripped it free. They could wait.

She spied the man at least one hundred yards away heading towards the empty Trocadero building. He'd paused and was looking backwards. What the fuck was he doing? Waiting for her? *Yes*, a still voice inside her whispered. *Of course he's waiting for you. He always has been.* She didn't listen. It was drowned out by the rush of her urgent breath. As she picked up her pace to a sprint, the suited man smiled. He ducked between a gaggle of pedestrians who'd frozen like rabbits in the headlights in the midst of the sudden commotion and she lost him again. Bastard. How did he move so fast? She hadn't even seen him running. Her shirt clung to her back with sweat as she chased him. Somewhere behind her, other feet would be coming fast. She wanted to reach this man before they did. Why the hell hadn't he detonated the bomb at the memorial? There was nothing she could have done about it if he had. No one else had seen him. Why was he taunting her?

He waited for her at the entrance to Piccadilly Circus tube station. She was almost at him when he disappeared inside. She swore under her breath and headed down into the stinking heat of the humid Underground. She spied him again as he stepped onto the escalator towards the Bakerloo Line. He was facing the wrong way, looking upwards, smiling at her as his face disappeared, carried down into the earth. Abigail's breathing was raw. Sweat itched her hairline. She pushed passed commuters and shoppers, their angry exclamations turning to sharp intakes of breath as they saw the weapon in her hand and fought with each other to get out of her way in the overcrowded station. Some were unsuccessful, finding themselves kicked and shoved aside as she tried in vain to keep her eyes on her target. She couldn't.

'Which way did the fat man go?' she shouted into the crowd at the bottom of the escalator. Wide eyes stared dumbly back at her. Two paths to choose from. He could have taken either. Fuck it, she thought, and turned to her left. If she picked the wrong platform he was likely to be gone by the time she fought her way to the other, even with the reduced services, but in a game of chance all that mattered was that you chose – the outcome was all about luck. She chose left. Someone tumbled on the stairs as she rushed down them, her voice ringing out loudly to *get out of the way* to people who had nowhere to go to. From the corner of her eye she saw a man bend to pick up the shaken woman. Abigail didn't give her another thought. The people around her were just hindrances: obstacles in the way of her target.

As it was, though she hadn't been able to get the commuter population to give her some space, the fat man had plenty. He stood just the other side of the 'stand clear' line with an arc of empty platform around him. The air was heavy with stale breath from the crowds jammed together in the surrounding area waiting for the next already over-loaded train, but despite the numbers present, the platform was eerily quiet. Perhaps they all sensed something odd about this man too.

'Don't move,' Abigail said, raising her gun. She walked slowly forward until they were only a few feet apart. His hand stayed clasped round whatever device he was holding, his pudgy thumb poised. From this close the mottled tone of his skin was more pronounced, the purple patches looking like bruised flesh. Although he wasn't sweating, he was shiny, as if somehow he was slick with damp, just on the other side of his pores. His eyes were black, she'd swear on it: not dark brown, but black, through and through.

'Put that on the floor and step backwards.' Her voice shook. She should be revolted by this strange man, but instead she was drawn to him. She wanted to run her hands over that obese body – but there was nothing sexual in the feeling. It came from somewhere deeper and more primal, somewhere in her cells, in her very being. She fought it, keeping her gun levelled at his head.

'I said put that down.'

The fat man smiled. His gums were bleeding badly, and thin rivulets of pink spilled onto his lips. What the hell was wrong with him – radiation sickness? How could he be so obese and move so quickly, and yet be so ill?

'How long have you been emptying, Abigail?' He kept his hand up, his thumb poised. His voice was a melody carried on the wind. It caught her breath.

'You can feel it, can't you? Everything draining?' His smile stretched wider and he tilted his head. 'Isn't it beautiful?'

'Who are you?' she asked. Her own voice was gritty and rough and ugly. *Earth to air.* Her words tasted like shit in her mouth. His felt like honey in her ears. Behind her came more shouts. Police. *Her* side. They'd be here in moments.

'I am family.' The grin widened. More thin blood oozed from his gums.

'Take it,' he said, and held out his hand. She leaned in and closed her palm around the cool flesh. Everything stopped. Her head filled with darkness and flashes of colour, hundreds of shades of gold and light. Images she didn't understand reached into the empty spaces that had been silently craving them.

She gasped as he let go. For a moment her body forgot how to breathe as the cells started realigning, part one thing, part another, into something new. A sharp pain ran from the base of her neck and up through her skull, as if a skewer had been driven hard into her head. Her gun clattered to the ground.

Feet pounded down the stairs. Male voices shouted, authoritative, threatening. *Empty.*

'Interventionist,' the fat man whispered, and the pain stopped. His beautiful word sounded wet, as if the blood that filled his mouth was now clogging his lungs. He winked at Abigail.

Her hair lifted in the hot roar from the tunnel. A train was coming. He stepped backwards. She couldn't speak. Hands grabbed at her arms, pulling her away to get closer to the target. Everything moved in a haze. *Dark eyes on hers.* The rush of the train. The smile, as the fat man elegantly stepped from the platform edge. She squeezed her eyes shut against the impact. Several women screamed. The train screeched in unison.

There was a moment of silence.

'Jesus fucking Christ!'

Abigail didn't look at the sweaty Special Branch officer beside her. Neither did she look over the edge at the mess that would no doubt be splattered along the tracks and up the sides of the platform for a hundred yards or so. She trembled. She tried to remember the feeling she'd had when he touched her. *Completeness.* It was gone – not far, she thought, but like something lost somewhere just out of sight, and no matter how quickly you spun round, you never quite found it.

'You okay?' the officer asked her.

She nodded. She unfolded her hand. She'd been gripping it so tightly the object had left an imprint of its familiar shape against her palm. A pen. An ordinary black ballpoint pen.

More voices.

'Get this place sealed off now!'

'You people there, don't move! You're perfectly safe—'

'—don't *move.* That includes you, sir. No, you can't leave—'

'Who saw this man? Who saw what happened?'

'You? You stand there, please.'

An ordinary pen. She clicked the end, no fear of what might happen. The nib slid out at the bottom. She clicked again. It withdrew.

'What the fuck are you doing?' Hands took it from her. 'What the fuck are you doing?'

'It's just a pen,' she said. She didn't look up. She didn't look anywhere. 'No detonator. Just an ordinary pen.'

Chapter Ten

Cass made the call to Cory Denter's father himself. The conversation was stilted, but this time there was no hint of aggression. The Denter family had perhaps decided overnight that any *why* would be better than living with the thought of their son killing himself for no reason they could fathom. The older man listened quietly. For Cass, they were words he'd used too many times to count: *We're going to have to run some tests on your son's body. We will have to do a full post-mortem. We'll be in touch when we can release him back to you. No, I can't give you any further information at this time, but as soon as I can, I will.* For some reason, the clinical nature of the phrases soothed. They took some responsibility for the grief out of the next-of-kin's hands. Unfortunately, that grief had to go somewhere, and that meant it usually landed squarely on Cass's shoulders.

A short text came through from Artie Mullins: a time and a place to meet, and Cass left Armstrong to speak to the other families and supervise the exhumation arrangements, while he headed into Soho to meet his sometime friend. As his car sat in the London traffic that had become even more interminable since the bombings, he rang Perry Jordan.

'I think it's time we step up a gear looking for Luke. Is that okay?'

'Not a problem this end. But how come? Thought you

wanted to wait until the trials were done and dusted?'

'You know me, I'm impatient.' He wasn't going to tell Jordan about the note Marlowe had delivered. 'It's still only you and me, though, not official. I just want to do some probing. All I need from you is the admin. I don't have time for that.' He really didn't want Jordan involved any more than necessary. This was his shit to deal with. Family stuff. The Jones family and *They*.

'Sure, I'll be your secretary – but don't expect me in heels.' Jordan laughed. 'So what do you need?'

'I want a list of all the people working in the maternity ward that night, and their contact details. Same for security – in fact, get me as many staff names as you can. Especially anyone with any kind of authority. Also, I want the details of anyone else who had a baby at approximately the same time. Boys only.' Christian had been at the bedside at Luke's birth, and Jessica had definitely delivered a boy. There was a possibility he'd simply been swapped with another child – why they would do that, he didn't know, but then, there was nothing about the Network he understood. And they'd have needed to get a new-born baby from somewhere; so either they brought one in, or swapped one from the ward.

'I've got some of that already. You around later?'

'No, I'm on a new case. It's going to wipe out most of today.'

'Let me guess – the weird teenage suicides in the paper?'

'Yeah, that's the one.'

'Whoever wrote that article loves you, don't they? I didn't recognise you from the description. Had to keep checking the name to be sure they weren't writing about someone else.'

'Oh, you're a funny fucker.' Cass kept his tone light. He

still felt unnerved by Armstrong's actions, although he wasn't really sure why. The newspaper stunt was something he might have done if he'd had the connections – and trusted them. Maybe it was seeing his own ruthlessness reflected in one so young that unsettled him. He knew where it could lead.

'Yeah, sadly that's what all the girls say. I'll get on the rest but I'll stick what I've already found through your letterbox when I'm out later. As soon as I've got more I'll let you know. And just call if you've got any questions.'

'Cheers, Perry. That sounds fine.'

There was the briefest moment of hesitation and Cass wondered if the other man had already hung up.

'Take care, Cass.' Perry Jordan didn't sound so funny. He sounded almost grown-up. Serious.

'I always do, Perry. I always do.'

Artie was at a tucked-away table at the far end of the pub when Cass arrived. He was already sipping from a pint of lager, despite it being not yet eleven.

'Fuck this weather,' he said, nodding Cass to the chair opposite and the pint that waited for him. 'Where the fuck is autumn? If I wanted year-round sunshine I'd go and live on the Costa del Crap.' He smiled at Cass, but his eyes were slightly wary. Cass figured his own expression was much the same. They hadn't seen each other in a while. Mullins looked exactly the same though; weather-beaten and indestructible.

'I took the liberty of ordering for you.'

'Thanks.' Cass took a sip. There was nothing like cool lager on a hot day.

'Stick your hand under the table, mate. Let's get the formalities out of the way.'

Cass did as he was told. Artie's thick fingers met his and the small bag of powder was exchanged.

'How much do you—?' Cass started awkwardly.

'Fuck off, Jones. You think I want your money?'

'With things being as they are ...' Cass sighed. 'I know I'm not your favourite person right now.' He felt like he had during his first days as Charlie Sutton, awkward ... stupid.

Artie watched him for a long few seconds, then sniffed. He took a swallow of his beer. 'This shit will pass. It always does. I was around long before the bonuses even existed, remember? Fuck, I've been around since before you had the dumb idea to sit the fucking police exam, or whatever it is you have to do to get in on your side of this fence.' He leaned forward and smiled. 'We always managed before. This ain't the end of the world. Right now there might be no money changing hands, but you can be sure as fuck no one wants to make any enemies. We're all just treading water, Jones, haven't you noticed? No one's really coming near us.'

'I haven't been getting much in the way of cases. Too much legal shit going on.'

'There's your fucking punishment, mate.' Artie laughed, and Cass could almost taste the cigarettes that fed that throaty rattle. 'When does that shit Bowman go to court? That fucker won't last five minutes inside.' He winked. 'I can guarantee you that.'

'No date's set yet,' Cass said, 'but rumour has it they want him in the dock in the next couple of months. PR and all that shit. I just want it done. Then I can lay the whole thing to rest.' He hoped so anyway. He still dreamed too much – of Kate, and Claire. And all of the rest. But mainly of those two women. He took a longer swallow of his beer. The light buzz felt good.

'So, we okay then?' he asked.

Artie sniffed again. 'We're okay. You're a fucking liability, Jones, but you didn't bring this shit down on purpose. But we still need to keep any meetings we might have low-key. You're not the only one getting hassle from lawyers, you know. We're all claiming innocence, pushing the blame onto Macintyre and those fucking Chechen cunts, but I can live without being seen with you. Same as, I guess?'

'Yeah, same as. They need me squeaky clean for this case.'

'Well, that'll take more than Daz and a hot wash.' Artie laughed at his own joke and Cass smiled along. The wariness was leaving him. He'd underestimated Artie Mullins and he shouldn't have. Artie was something else; always had been.

His phone vibrated and as he pulled it out of his pocket, he slipped the baggie in.

'We've got another dead student,' Armstrong said.

Cass stood and turned his back to the table. 'Where?'

'Soho. The flat above a shop called "Loving It" on Old Compton Street.'

'I'm five minutes away. I'll meet you there.'

The call ended and Cass found Artie watching him.

'They letting you work something proper again?' The gangster smiled.

'Not through any choice of their own, trust me. Sorry about the drink.'

'No problem,' Artie said. 'I'm a busy boy myself. You take care, Cass Jones. You know where I am.'

As he headed back out into the sticky heat, Cass wondered why everyone was feeling the need to express their concern for his wellbeing today. If there was one thing he'd always been more than moderately good at, it was looking after Number One. That wasn't going to change now.

*

The mystery of how a third-year student, most likely weighed down with debts, could afford a Soho address was answered within seconds of Cass passing the constable standing across the narrow doorway and heading up the tatty stairs to the flat. The sex shop 'Loving It' had looked sleazy enough, the grime on the unwashed windows visible even against the blackout on the other side of the glass, but the flat was basically a shit-hole. After twenty minutes inside, Cass felt ready for a shower, and he hadn't even touched anything. Dust lay thick at the edges of the carpet, and in the kitchen there were thick rings of grime in the sink. The rubbish bin was over-filled and a take-away carton of some description sat, half-full and rotting, on the side. On the lino, the foodstains were hard to distinguish from the original pattern, if there in fact was one. Cass thought someone would have to pay him fucking good money to open the fridge.

'I converted the main bedroom into a bedsit when things started getting tight.' Neil Newton, the live-in landlord and shop owner, was an over-cologned effete who was clinging to his younger days by wearing a styled shirt that was too tight across his growing pot belly. It wasn't working. He was clearly in his mid-forties – long past dead in gay years.

'We shared the bathroom.' His hands trembled, his cheap gold chain bracelets clinking, as he gestured around the dirty flat. 'He had his own cooking facilities in there, but I never minded if he wanted to use the bigger kitchen.' Newton swallowed. 'We'd become friends.'

Cass left him in the hallway and peered through the door to the other room. Joe Lidster, twenty-two, Media and Communications Studies student at South Bank University – the second of South Bank's kids to die – was lying on the double bed, on top of the neat spread that matched the two cushions behind his head. His pale arms were stretched out sideways, displaying the deep cuts in his wrists. Blood had darkened a circle of the bed under him, and had created two pools on the thin carpet either side, where his fingers hung over the edge. They were no longer dripping. There were also no shiny black shoes for the drips to land on. Cass was glad about that.

The rest of the room, although cheaply furnished, was meticulously clean and neat. There was a small fridge and a hob along one wall, and a wardrobe and chest of drawers with a TV on top. It was dust- and mess-free. Cass thought that if this boy had shared the bathroom with Newton, then that would probably be spotless too – and it would have been all the student's doing.

Beside the bed a piece of paper was tacked to the wall. The words written on it in thick black marker were clear even from the doorway. *Chaos in the darkness*. It hung slightly to one side. If Lidster had been alive, he would no doubt have wanted to straighten it.

Cass looked again at the room and couldn't help but remember standing in a similar bedsit not so many months ago. There were no dead flies here, and no rotting puppy, just poor dead Joe Lidster, bled out and cold in a shit-hole in Soho.

'With all due respect,' he started as he turned back to Newton, 'how did he come to be living here when he could have got something cheaper and better down by the South Bank?'

The applied grease in Newton's hair merged with small beads of sweat on his forehead. Cass wasn't sure if it was due to the heat or the situation, or if it was just Newton's normal appearance. The latter wouldn't have surprised him; the man wore enough cologne to hint at attempts to cover a sweat problem; he sure wouldn't want to be standing too close to him by the end of the day.

'He was at first. But you know what these students are like. He had a bad break-up, got himself into a financial pickle. Then he got a part-time job here, and I offered him the room.' His eyes darted past Cass to the body. 'He was a nice boy. It worked well.'

Cass was sure Newton had *loved* having the young man around.

'I think he liked being in the middle of Soho,' Newton continued. 'It's where all the media types are, after all. He'd just got a job as a runner for one company actually. Well, I say *job* – they didn't actually pay him anything. But still, he seemed happier.' He sniffed. 'I don't know what could have made him do this. I really don't. Perhaps if I'd been in last night instead of at my sister's, this wouldn't have happened. I feel awful.'

'Thanks for your help, Mr Newton.' Cass blocked the bedroom doorway. 'Now, if you wouldn't mind waiting down in the shop while we do what we have to do here?'

'Of course.' His mildly disgruntled facial expression disagreed with his words, but he did as he was told.

Armstrong emerged from the bedroom, holding a clear plastic evidence bag. 'We've got a mobile phone. It was by the bed. Do you want me to go through it?'

'Yes – and send someone to get any mobiles the families might have for the other suicides. Cross-reference the numbers and see if we can find a link that way.'

'No problem.' Armstrong was talking into his own phone within seconds, quietly instructing someone back in the Incident Room to get to work. Efficient as well as ruthless. And always so calm. Cass's jury was still out.

In the bedroom, Dr Marsden, the new ME, moved round

the room, silently photographing the dead man. He was a quiet man; precise. He lacked Farmer's ambition, but given what had just gone down at Paddington Green, that was probably no bad thing.

'I'm nearly done. Not much of a crime scene.'

'How are things?' Cass asked. He didn't need to elaborate. He meant the fall-out from the bombings.

'Finally slowing down, thankfully.' Dr Marsden sighed, and lowered his camera. 'Now we're onto all the report-writing next.' He looked back at Lidster. 'I'd say he bled to death. It's consistent with his wounds. But then, you probably don't need me to tell you that, not with all this mess.' His voice was devoid of emotion as he surveyed the clotted blood pools. Dr Marsden probably hadn't been an overly reactive man before the bombings, but after what he must have seen over the past couple of weeks, it would take more than a pair of slit wrists to raise an eyebrow.

'He's going to have to buy a new mattress before he gets any more pretty young men to rent a room from him,' Cass said.

'He doesn't look like the sort who buys a new anything,' Dr Marsden answered. 'Even his aftershave is twenty years out of fashion.'

Cass laughed. Maybe Dr Marsden wasn't without humour after all.

'I'll finish up here and get the body into the curious hands of my protégé,' the ME said.

'He's good, Eagleton, isn't he?'

'Oh yes, he's good. One day he'll be excellent. We're lucky we didn't lose him.'

Cass decided Dr Marsden was the master of the under-statement.

Armstrong, still on the phone to the Incident Room,

turned suddenly, his eyes seeking out Cass's.

'What is it?'

Armstrong flipped the phone shut. 'We've got another one, sir. Sloane Square.'

The two men stared at each other for a moment, until Cass spoke.

'Jesus fucking Christ.' It was all he could think of to say.

Chapter Eleven

Eagleton was in full flow by the time Cass got through the turgid mess that had constituted London's all-day-long rush-hour since the bombings. The morgue might be somewhat closer than Soho to Sloane Square, but Cass still wasn't sure how the young man did it. Maybe Josh Eagleton had taken to getting around on a moped. Cass wouldn't put it past him. He knew from experience that even the full blues and twos couldn't shift gridlock these days.

'At least you're keeping me busy until the exhumations arrive,' Josh said as he led Cass inside. 'And if it wasn't for the dead body, there would be worse places to spend the afternoon than this pad.'

Cass had to agree. It was a far cry from the dump where he'd left the earthly remains of Joe Lidster. With a smartly suited doorman and 24-hour concierge downstairs, this apartment lived up to its Sloane Square address. The high-ceilinged rooms were beautifully decorated, and there were three large double bedrooms, each with its own en-suite bathroom. One was unused, politely dressed as a spare, with the bed covered in cushions and a small basket of hotel-style toiletries by the wash basin. The kitchen had solid granite work surfaces covered in brushed-steel appliances, and in the lounge the Bang & Olufsen TV and sound system sat comfortably in pride of place. A thick cream rug lay in front of the inlaid gas fire – the arty kind with smooth, pale stones rather than faux logs. All this opulence didn't make the girl any less dead than Joe Lidster, though. In this they were very much united.

She was lying on the rug in just her underwear, in front of the fire which was, mercifully, turned off. Her slim, toned body was framed in blood. It looked like an expensive body, scrubbed and moisturised and exfoliated, and exercised on ski slopes. Her wrists were neatly slit, the small, sharp kitchen knife which had proved itself more than adequate for the job, lying untidily beside her.

The halo of blood that had soaked through the rug, travelling upwards as far as the fan of her hair, made it hard to see where her long tresses ended and the blood began. She looked like a fallen Rapunzel, thought Cass. She was – or had been – a real beauty. Even where her skin had turned blue and mottled, the olive warmth of its original hue clung on, and her brown eyes stared forever into the distance with a haunting quality Cass rarely found in the soulless eyes of the dead.

In the hallway, a similarly lithe and toned young woman sat on a chair by the lifts. Her knees were pulled up under her chin and her narrow shoulders shook as she cried. Under her blonde hair, her face was brown, not olive, like the dead girl's, but sun-kissed. There was something less special about this girl. Cass couldn't help the thought, as much as he didn't like it. *There was no glow.* He pushed that one away too.

The girl didn't wait for him to speak before she started, 'I stayed at Justin's last night.' Her voice hinted at expensive holidays, trust funds and a house in the south of France. The emotion was all human though. 'Hayley's been so weird lately – I thought maybe she'd been taking acid or something and I definitely didn't want any part of that.' Her perfect eyes filled with tears. 'I didn't realise she would do anything like this. God, I feel like such a bitch. She was my friend. She was *good* to me—'

'When you say she was acting strangely, how do you mean?'

'We've always lived our own lives. She does her thing and I do mine, but we normally find time to make dinner together or something and catch up. But the past few days she hasn't been herself. She wasn't sleeping or eating. She'd just sit on that rug and stare into the fire. That's why I thought it was acid, you know? She was acting all tripped out. Whenever I asked her what was wrong, she just said, "I saw. I saw it all. And I remembered." It didn't even sound like her.'

'Was that all she said?' Cass asked. 'Did she ever use the phrase "Chaos in the darkness"?'

'No.' The blonde girl shook her head. 'If she'd said that, I'd have stayed last night – and called someone. We've all heard what's happened to those students.' Fresh tears spilled over her cheeks. 'I didn't think. I just didn't think.'

'Can you stay at your boyfriend's again?'

She nodded. 'He's downstairs waiting for me.'

'Good.' He paused. 'This isn't your fault, you know.'

She nodded again, but there was no conviction in the gesture. Cass left a constable to take her details and went back inside. Armstrong met him in the doorway to the lounge.

'Her name's Hayley Porter. She's a second-year student of journalism at City University. Her parents are currently at their holiday home in Portugal. They own this flat, and the main family home in Highgate as well.' He smiled. 'Lucky for some.'

111

'Apart from the dead daughter,' Cass added.

Armstrong's grin dropped.

'I'll call the parents,' he said.

'But they do seem to be surviving the recession well,' Cass said. 'What does the father do? Do you know?'

'Yeah, he's on the boards of several conglomerates world-wide. Media stuff mainly. Guess that's why she was on this course.'

'A family of high-flyers then?'

'It gets better. You'll never guess who her big sister is.'

'If I'll never guess, then you'd better just tell me.' Cass didn't have time for games. There were enough of those being played out in his private life.

'Abigail Porter. The Prime Minister's personal protection officer.'

There was a moment's pause before Cass spoke. 'Then let's go and pay her a visit. See how close she and her sister were.' He looked around the plush apartment. 'I think this case just took a large step up the high-profile ladder.'

There was nothing in that thought that pleased him. He'd done enough high-profile for one career.

Abigail was tired and her head hurt. It had been thumping ever since her encounter with the fat man on the Underground platform; a dull, sick kind of petrol headache that just wouldn't shift. Fletcher wasn't helping. They might be calling it a 'debriefing' but it sure as hell felt to her like an interrogation. The head of the ATD had barely let her out of his sight as the tedious interviewing of bystanders had taken place and the remains of the fat man had been carefully scraped from the tracks. Now they were just going round and round in circles, because Fletcher was intent on making sense out of something that couldn't make sense.

'Okay, let's go through this again.' Fletcher sat on the edge of the desk and his shoulders slumped forward slightly. Maybe he was finally getting tired too. 'All the people on the platform say the man had been standing there for at least six or seven minutes before you came down the stairs – at least as long as they'd been waiting for the next train, anyway. We've got twelve separate interviewees who are adamant about that. It wasn't as if he was built to blend into the crowd well.'

'What can I say?' Abigail sighed. 'They must be wrong.' *How long have you been emptying, Abigail?* Her head throbbed louder and she fought a sudden bout of nausea. This was not a time to show weakness. 'Why would I have run down there if I hadn't seen anything?'

Fletcher couldn't deny her logic. 'I'm not saying you didn't see anything. We saw on the footage from the bombings that this man must have doppelgängers. I'm just wondering where they went.'

Abigail said nothing. There was something good about seeing Fletcher losing his cool. It made him almost more attractive. Not that seducing the head of the ATD was still on her list, if it ever consciously had been, but she couldn't help but wonder if she could break him. For the first time she thought that maybe she could.

'It's also strange that none of the Special Branch officers out on the streets saw him or his doubles either.' There was mild accusation in his tone, coupled with doubt. He was a man who knew something was very wrong, but couldn't put his finger on what it was, other than she was something to do with it.

Abigail kept her gaze level. 'I told you. He was standing at the back of the crowd in the inner cordon. He opened his jacket and I saw the explosives strapped to his chest.'

'Plasticine,' Fletcher said. 'It was fucking Plasticine.'

'Yeah, well, if you can tell that from a hundred yards away, then you have better than my twenty-twenty vision. And it was strapped to him to look like explosives. He lifted what I thought was a detonator, and that's when I raised the alarm. I chased after him, but I lost him in the crowd. Then I saw him at the barriers, and again at the tube entrance. It was just luck that I picked the right platform after following him underground.' She didn't mention his black eyes, or his bleeding gums. Those, somehow, felt private.

'How could you lose a man like that in a crowd?'

'How could no one else spot him?' Abigail stood up, her hands on her hips. 'You're talking to me as if I've done something wrong. I chased the guy down. I found him. What's your problem?'

'What did he say to you on the platform?'

'Nothing.'

'That's not what the men that followed you down to the platform say. They reported that he spoke to you before jumping under the train.'

'The same men who couldn't spot a fat man identical to the bombing suspect in the crowds?'

'Enough.'

Abigail had almost forgotten there was anyone else in the room with them until the Home Secretary spoke. He had faded as the game between her and Fletcher had grown more tense.

'We're all on the same side here, if you care to remember,' he continued. 'Our good lady leader would not want to see us bickering like this.'

Abigail thought that if McDonnell heard herself referred to like that, bickering would be the least of the Cabinet minister's worries.

'How long she's our leader *for*, however, is another matter.' Dawson rubbed his face. 'She's in another emergency meeting about how best to fight the growing call for an election or change of leader. And it says something about how that's probably going that I'd rather be here listening to this over and over again than in there. Let's stick to the point. When I get back to her she's going to be in a foul enough mood without me having nothing to deliver.'

Abigail stared at Fletcher. They might both have fallen silent, but the lack of trust was clear. Pain stabbed through the back of her neck and for a moment her vision was only black and white. What the fuck was the matter with her? Colour flooded back into the room.

'Is this dead man the suspect from the bombings – or at least one of them?' Dawson asked.

'Yes.' Fletcher turned away from Abigail. 'And he's probably the same man Abigail saw the night after the bombs on her way home.'

'I told you, I—'

'Leave that for now,' Dawson interrupted. 'What facts do we have?'

'Although he wasn't carrying any actual explosive, he'd rigged himself up to look like he was. The Plasticine that was taped to his chest is now all over the tube line. We've got the pen he was holding. It's an ordinary ballpoint, and the only fingerprints on it are Abigail's, even though he wasn't wearing gloves.' Fletcher held up his hand to stop Dawson's question. 'Don't ask me how because I don't fucking know. He also waited for one of us to arrive before jumping under the train. He clearly wanted to be seen.'

'It was perfectly timed too,' he added. 'He got Abigail to the platform just a minute or so before the train arrived. They're not exactly running frequently these days.'

'Although if our dead guy was on the platform the whole time, as the onlookers claim, then he could have been communicating with his mysterious doubles to act according to a schedule.'

'No, there was no sign of any radio device on him,' Fletcher said. 'Perhaps he thought that if the train didn't come, he could get himself shot somehow. If suicide was part of his original plan.'

'And it seems to me that for some reason he was targeting Abigail.' Dawson was thoughtful.

'In what way targeting me?' She let the fight go out of her voice. All she wanted to do was get out of here and check the Hotmail account. *Interventionist.* That's what he'd said. Now was the time. She knew it.

'Simple observation. He could have got the attention of one of Dunne's men much more easily than yours. He just needed to call out, and they'd have seen him. But he made sure you spotted him by standing directly in your line of sight, and a little back from the rest. He opened his jacket for *you.*'

'Maybe he wanted to get the PM's attention,' Abigail said.

'No, McDonnell was concentrating on her speech and would have been making eye contact with the relatives. She had specific faces to concentrate on, trust me. It was you he wanted to get to the platform. He even made sure the doubles or whatever waited for you. It's the *why* I can't figure out.'

'If he'd spoken to you, that would have made sense. Then there would have been a message,' Fletcher said.

'I told you, he didn't say anything.'

'Forget that.' Dawson pressed on. 'What about the Plasticine and the pen? He clearly wasn't intent on killing anyone but himself. Maybe the message is in that? Was this whole thing staged to be a dramatic admission of guilt for the 26/09 bombs? Or was it an act of repentance?'

'Or, of course, he could just be mocking us,' Fletcher cut in. 'There was no admission of anything in the act. It just made us panic. We still have no idea who these people are or why they've blown up half of London and Moscow.'

'*And* Moscow?'

Abigail looked up, as surprised as Dawson.

'Yes,' Fletcher said, 'Moscow. Came through from intel an hour or so ago. A man similar to ours – well, apparently *identical* to ours – was caught on camera in several locations throughout Moscow before their bombs went off. They're now officially as confused as we are.'

'They found him on their CCTV quicker than we did.'

'Not really. I gave them a full description. In fact, I emailed over a picture. We needed quick results from them.'

'Hang on.' Dawson got to his feet. 'But I was with you when you called your opposite number. We didn't even have this ID then. We just wanted to know if they'd had warning.'

'I called him back.' Fletcher's gaze was cool. 'You can screw your political bullshit.'

The door to the small office opened, and Andrew Dunne came in. He'd aged over the course of the day. Bags hung under his eyes and Abigail was sure the lines in his face were deeper than they had been. Whatever shit she'd been getting, he'd have been taking twice as much for his men not seeing the fat man in the crowd. No doubt it was getting passed down the line now.

'What now?' Dawson asked.

Dunne sighed and sat down. 'This gets stranger.'

'Go on.'

'It's the images of the suspects we had from 26/09.'

'What about them?' Fletcher asked.

'The tech boys have been working on them, comparing the dimensions of each man and creating 3D images and whatever else the fuck their computers can do. They're all identical.' He looked round the room. 'To the last millimetre. These aren't men who have made themselves look the same: according to the computer, *all those men* are *the same man*. One person.'

'But that's not possible,' Dawson breathed.

'That's what I said, but according to them, what's not possible is that there can be several people with exactly the same dimensions for their entire bodies. Not even with the best surgery. It's just not possible. They're now working on the images we've got from today's fiasco, but something tells me the result's going to be the same.'

Abigail let her mouth drop open in the following silence, but she didn't share the men's confusion and surprise. Somewhere beyond the blanket of the headache and the shifting in her cells, she'd known that this man was outside of the normal. The same laws didn't apply. This was just an example of that.

'What is this fucking shit?' Fletcher asked, but Abigail figured he wasn't expecting an answer. The phone on the desk rang and he grabbed at it.

'Yes?' he barked. 'What do you—?' He paused as someone spoke hurriedly at the other end. 'What, here? Who the hell let them in? . . . Oh, I see. Yeah. I told her to turn it off.' He looked up at Abigail, but the anger had gone out of him. His voice softened. 'If it's empty, put them in the White Drawing Room. No, don't disturb the boss. I'll come down with her now.' He put the phone down.

'There are some policemen here to see you.'

'What about?' Her heart thumped, the blood forcing her headache to the front of her skull. Was this some kind of ploy? Had they found out about the email account? The note? Even if they had, then why wasn't Fletcher talking to her about it?

'They said it was something to do with your family.' Fletcher ignored Dunne and Dawson's questioning glances and held the door open. 'Let's go.'

Family. *I am family.* All she could see were black eyes and bleeding gums. The headache faded.

'So, this is 10 Downing Street. Fuck me.' Armstrong's voice was barely more than a whisper.

It was good to see the normally over-confident sergeant less than cocky. Cass looked around the large room they'd been left in. It made Hayley Porter's flat in Sloane Square look like it had been furnished from IKEA. The large wing-back chairs were gilt-edged, as was the matching deep-seated sofa in front of the huge fireplace. Floor-length red curtains framed large windows, and highly polished mahogany tables did their best to fill the vast spaces in between.

'Don't be too overwhelmed,' Cass muttered. 'It's a house of puppets.' He'd seen more impressive rooms in the elusive lost floor at The Bank. How much influence did Mr Bright and the Network have here? He tried not to think about it – that road led to paranoia. Wheels within wheels. He shut it out ... for now.

'I can't believe they let us come here – I thought the Commissioner would have wanted the kudos.'

'There's no kudos to be gained from telling someone their sister is dead,' Cass said. But still, Armstrong had a point. Even though no one had been able to get hold of Abigail Porter, it was strange that he and Armstrong had been the ones sent to Downing Street – not just by Heddings; the Commissioner had apparently agreed. Cass had assumed someone far higher up the ranks would deal with it first, but maybe they didn't want to be associated with it.

'I think they're distancing themselves, in case we fuck the whole thing up.' Cass smiled at his sergeant. 'Welcome to the world of the expendable.'

The door opened and a young woman stepped in, followed by a man in his late thirties. His eyes were hard and sharp. Although he was not skinny, there wasn't a trace of fat on his body. Just looking at him made Cass want to smoke. He also wondered what the man was doing here. There was nothing in the body language of either man or woman that suggested they were close – if anything, there was some tension there. He wondered what they had been in the middle of when he arrived.

The woman didn't even glance at the man as she stepped forward and held out her hand. 'Abigail Porter.'

Cass didn't need the introduction. He could see the resemblance with the dead girl straight away: the same olive skin, and shining long dark hair. Abigail was taller than her sister, a match for Cass's own six foot, maybe even slightly taller, and there was a cool confidence about her. This Porter sister had grown into herself. She was all woman. Cass found himself looking into the corner of her eyes, half-expecting to see the *glow* that he fought so hard to deny. It wasn't – but there was something. Something *other*. Something he was sure he'd be able to see, if he'd just allow himself to.

'They said this was something to do with my family.' Her voice was soft. Cass had expected an edge to it – nerves, or fear – but he couldn't sense either.

'We've been trying to reach your mobile. So have your parents.'

'We've got a lot on right now.'

Cass suddenly recognised the man. David Fletcher, head of the ATD. No wonder he looked so fucking pissed off.

'Don't you watch the news?' Fletcher continued.

'When I have the time,' Cass answered. 'Mainly I'm too busy trying to deal with ordinary day-to-day crimes.' He turned his attention back to the woman in front of him.

'I'm really sorry to have to tell you this, Miss Porter, but your sister's been found dead in her flat in Sloane Square.'

The moment settled between them: the one that existed between belief and disbelief. It filled the silence.

'Hayley?' Abigail said eventually, her eyes wide. 'I don't understand. *Hayley's* dead?'

Cass wondered if she had any idea how beautiful she was. There was something truly unusual about her. Something beyond the skin. He watched her reactions. She didn't sit, but stood still, only her hands trembling slightly by her sides. She clenched her fists and then released them. The trembling stopped. Cass had never seen someone so utterly self-contained at the loss of a loved one.

'What happened?'

'Would you like to sit down?' Cass asked.

'No, just tell me.'

'It would appear she took her own life. She slit her wrists.'

'She killed herself?'

'Yes.'

'But Hayley wouldn't ... She just wasn't that kind of person. We're not like that.'

'Were you close to your sister?'

'We used to be.' She crossed her arms across the chest of her fitted trouser suit and hugged herself.

David Fletcher didn't move closer to her. Whatever the deal was with them, they definitely weren't friends.

'But my job isn't exactly ordinary, and she's at Uni.' Her breath hitched slightly. 'She *was* at Uni. I don't understand why she would do it. I really don't.'

'Have you spoken to her recently?'

'Yes.' Abigail looked up. 'She called me— We were in a meeting. I didn't talk to her for long.' Dawning realisation crept across her face, swiftly followed by the shadow of guilt. Cass knew exactly how she was feeling. He'd been there himself six months earlier.

'She was strange. She didn't sound like herself.'

'What did she say?'

'It was odd. I thought she was drunk or high or something.' A tear almost broke and fell from her left eye, but she blinked it away. 'If I'm honest, I didn't think too much about it at all.'

The dark eyes flashed at Fletcher with something close to anger, or resentment at the very least. Why was the other man even here if he wasn't a friend?

'It's important you tell me what she said. It could be useful.'

'She said, "I saw it all. I remembered," and then she said something about "chaos in the dark". No, "chaos in the darkness", that was it.'

Cass looked over at Armstrong. *Bingo.* Two more in one day. What the fuck did that phrase mean?

Abigail frowned. 'I think I should call my parents now.' She looked up at Cass. 'They'll need me.'

The cool had returned. *They'll need me.* What about her? Didn't she need them too? She hadn't even asked if the words meant anything.

'Keep your mobile on though, please,' Cass said. 'Just in case we have any information for you.'

She was almost at the door when she looked back. 'Do you think there is chaos in the darkness?'

Cass watched her, surprised. 'I don't know what the darkness is. What do you think it is?'

'I think it should be empty.'

'I don't understand what you're saying, Miss Porter.'

'Neither do I.' She smiled sadly. 'Just random thoughts.'

She closed the door quietly behind her.

Silver. That's what was in her eyes. No golden glow, but silver. Mr Bright shed silver tears for Mr Solomon, and this woman had a silver glow.

'That was odd,' Armstrong said, breaking the moment.

'She's an odd woman.' Fletcher didn't sound impressed by her oddness. He looked over at Cass. 'I *do* listen to the news,' he said. 'I've read about these student suicides. Is there any way they could be linked to something political?'

'No.' Cass stared at him. 'Until this girl died they were all just ordinary students. Probably not so interesting to you. To me, however, they're all equal.'

'I had to ask.' The slight dig didn't even touch Fletcher's calm. 'I'm the—'

'I know who you are,' Cass cut in. 'Fletcher. Head of the ATD. We sometimes see your lot at Paddington Green.'

'And they rarely even say hello,' Armstrong added. 'I can see where they get their manners from.'

Cass bit back a grin. Maybe he was warming to his sergeant after all.

'Not that your visits are quite so frequent now you've moved on to bigger and better things.'

'Only because the world got nastier.' Fletcher's smile sat somewhere between cynicism and weariness. 'Trust me, I could live with a smaller office.'

Cass figured the man had a point. He wouldn't want to

trade places with him, that was for sure, even with all the shit that had come his own way.

An hour later and the sleek dark-windowed limousine had redelivered them to the mundane surroundings of Paddington Green Police Station, where they'd satisfied DCI Heddings that they hadn't brought any disrepute to the force on their visit to Number Ten, and had delivered the news to Ms Porter as gently as possible. Although Cass wished the DCI had taken as much care with the relatives of all the other dead kids, he was bloody glad he hadn't. There was only so much not being trusted to do his job properly that he could handle at one time.

They took the stairs back down, and Armstrong paused at the doors to the second-floor Incident Room.

'You forget something, Toby?'

'I thought I might just go and take another look at the board. Make sure the notes on Lidster and Porter have been added, and then see if there's anything staring us in the face to link these kids.'

'There's no point in hanging around here. Eagleton won't have anything of any use for us until tomorrow and you're tired. Go home. Mull it over there if you want, I can't stop you, but your day in the office is over.'

'With all due respect—'

'If this job gets to be twenty-four seven,' Cass said, 'then you'll get bitter and die lonely.'

With one hand pushing the door open, Armstrong paused.

'Trust me,' Cass continued, 'my missus went way beyond thinking about divorce.'

For the first time in their short relationship Armstrong looked awkward.

'It's okay. I've dealt with it.' Cass found that the lie came easy – but then, he had to admit, it always had. It was part of who he was: he'd had a lot of practice at hiding the truth.

Chapter Twelve

It felt strange walking with David Fletcher. But then, everything had felt strange to Abigail all day; why should this be any different? He had a game plan though, and she knew it. Fletcher didn't care that Hayley was dead – the thought sat awkwardly in her head, as if it was information that belonged to someone else – all he cared about was her link to the fat man. The thought of his touch made her shiver with pleasure. It would take someone more than Fletcher to make her give that up. Nothing could. Not even her sister's suicide. Maybe Hayley had been emptying too. Perhaps that had confused her. Abigail wondered when she'd start grieving, if at all. The world had changed for her today. Fletcher's obvious plans barely registered.

After the police had left, he'd said he see her home in his car. She'd rather have gone with the detective. She'd liked him – no, *liked* wasn't the right word; she'd recognised him a little, as if she'd met him somewhere before and come away with a good memory. When she'd told Fletcher she'd rather walk, he insisted on coming along, saying he needed some fresh air. He'd wasted his time because she'd barely said a word. If he thought grief would loosen her tongue then he really didn't know her at all. She glanced over at him, and he was looking back, just as he had been the whole silent journey. She didn't let her eyes drop. He looked handsome. Warm.

'Are you sure you're okay?' he asked. 'I mean as okay as possible.' He was as uncomfortable as she was discussing emotions.

She nodded. 'We don't cry, Fletcher. You know that.' Her words sounded like lines from some cheesy secret service show.

'That's bullshit. Everyone cries. Everyone should cry. It keeps us human. And sane.'

Abigail didn't believe that Fletcher had shed a single tear in his entire adult life.

'When are your parents coming back from Portugal?'

She opened her mouth to speak and then had to leave her jaw hanging as she struggled for an answer. They had told her, but the words were forgotten. Bits of her head felt fuzzy where the headache had faded.

'Tomorrow,' she lied. Was it tomorrow or tonight? It was one of the 'T' words, anyway. They seemed unimportant, and that felt wrong. God, it *was* wrong. But right. Something was happening to her. The emptiness was taking hold at an alarming rate of knots. The last of the headache nestled in a quiet space in her head and watched.

They reached her front door. The street around them was subdued. Not so long ago it would have been filled with the hustle and bustle of life and the rage against death that was calmed by constantly moving forward. Now the rage had slipped into fear, and kept people at home as the evenings drew in. Abigail wondered what they could possibly fear in the darkness that couldn't happen – or in fact be more likely to happen – in the brightness of the day. For her the darkness was soothing.

She slid her key into the lock while Fletcher stood

awkwardly on the doorstep. She liked seeing him slightly uncomfortable. It made him more attractive.

'If there's anything you want to talk about, then you know how to get hold of me.' His voice was sympathetic, but his eyes didn't lie. He wanted to know what the fat man had said before he jumped. He didn't trust her. He'd probably already organised a car, or maybe a surveillance team to watch her flat. She needed them to relax. She also wanted some warmth. Her own blood was cooling and she had a feeling this might be the last time for a while; maybe for ever.

'I don't want to talk.' She held his gaze as she pushed the door open. 'I want you to fuck me. Make me feel alive.'

They looked at each other with mistrust for a long time before he stepped inside and slowly closed the door behind them.

'We only need you here from eight until ten on Tuesday evenings. It's a six-week trial.' Dr Shearman smiled at the girl who peered wide-eyed through the small window of one of the cubicles. 'You have nothing to worry about. The hypnosis is perfectly safe.'

'I can't believe you want to pay me so much money to cure me of my sleepwalking.' Jenna Smart grinned back under her blonde bob that turned shocking pink at the bottom inch. 'What's in it for you?'

'I can't guarantee we'll cure you, but we'll do our best.' Most of Dr Shearman's face was covered by a curly, greying beard. He was just past forty – by the time he reached sixty he'd be doing a fair impersonation of Father Christmas unless he took up shaving. 'Our interest is in the changes in brain patterns during the hypnotic state and why they vary between people. Very dull, I'm afraid.' His smile widened. He had a friendly face and she smiled back.

'So just a couple of hours once a week?'

Dr Shearman nodded.

'I'm *so* up for that.'

The doctor let out a laugh at her gleeful enthusiasm. 'Then if you'll step this way, one of my colleagues can take all your details and I'll see you on Tuesday.'

After depositing the student at the reception desk, Dr Shearman headed back to his office where the results of the previous session were waiting for him to analyse. He grabbed a coffee from the machine and then wandered back to the end of the corridor. He was tired. He hadn't been sleeping so well himself, but unlike Jenna Smart, his body no longer had the bounce-back capabilities of youth. He opened his door, looking forward to a break from the harsh fluorescent lighting, and froze.

'Close the door, Dr Shearman. Please.'

'What are you doing here?' The doctor did as he was told, leaving them with only the glow from the desk lamp in the windowless room. He kept his distance. Even after all these years the other man still made him nervous.

'Just taking a look at these results. There are some very interesting patterns here, wouldn't you say?' Under his silver hair, the older man's eyes twinkled.

'They might not seem like much for all of this space but I—'

'Stop panicking. We're not about to cease your funding.' He looked down at the various scans in front of him. A well-manicured hand pulled three from the stack. 'These in particular have caught my attention. Who are they?'

'I can get their details for you. I'm not overly sure from the top of my head. I think one is a boy called Elroy Peterson.'

'Thank you. How far through the course are they?'

'They finished two weeks ago. I was just sorting through my files.'

'Perfect.' The man smiled cheerfully before turning his sharp eyes to the doctor. 'You look tired, Dr Shearman. Is something the matter?'

'No,' Dr Shearman started, 'no, obviously, I'm very grateful for your continued and generous support ...'

'Just get to the point, if you will.'

'I was just wondering,' Dr Shearman's voice dropped, 'why do your people have to hypnotise them to not talk about this experiment? I don't understand that stipulation.'

'We're just very private about where we choose to invest our money, Dr Shearman. You can understand that.' He picked up his wool overcoat from where it was folded neatly over the back of Dr Shearman's desk chair. 'If these students started telling their friends and parents about a well-equipped research centre that can pay them two hundred pounds per session, it wouldn't be long before someone came sneaking around to see who was backing it.' He paused. 'The Bank has always looked out for you, Dr Shearman. Things could have gone badly for you. But they didn't.'

'I know and I'm grateful, of course I am, and I suppose that makes perfect sense.' His shoulders slumped slightly. 'I'm sorry. I'll go and get those details you wanted.'

The other man's eyes twinkled as he smiled.

Dr Shearman was happy to get back out into the corridor, despite the ache behind his eyes. Mr Bright was a man who looked as if he'd never lost a night's sleep in his life – and although Dr Shearman refused to admit it to himself, that scared him.

Cass took a long swallow from the bottle of beer down by his feet. It was cool against the cocaine burn at the back of his throat. The ashtray was filling unnoticed, each cigarette smoked out of habit rather than choice, and he frowned as he looked down once again at the spread of papers that Perry Jordan had posted through his door at some point during the day. There was a report on Luke's birth weight and measurements, and Jessica's admission and release forms. Translating the medical jargon wasn't too hard; from what he could understand, there was nothing at all out of the ordinary about the birth, for either the baby or the mother.

He looked again at the baby's information. Had it been gathered before or after his nephew was taken? *THEY* took Luke. *There is no glow.* He pushed the phrase away. As the thought of the Network pushed the coke faster round his system, his foot tapped. Maybe it was just the frustration: the constant presence of *They* in his life, however much he fought to keep them out, and despite his own hungry curiosity to know more. Maybe he should just go to The Bank and demand that smarmy Asher Red get hold of Mr Bright because Cass Jones wanted a word. Perhaps he should pin that ageless man up against a wall and get his answers the old-fashioned way. He took a deep breath. There was no point in that – all it would do would be to alert them that he was looking.

A series of names and job titles filled most of the sheets. None stood out. Which one of these mundane people had played a part? He was tired, and his head was too full to concentrate. The baggie was still on the table and he chopped another line of the white powder and snorted it quickly. One thing he didn't want to think about was how much he enjoyed the tingle and steady buzz – six months had been too long. He leaned back in his chair, allowing the powder to trickle down the back of his throat, bringing a familiar numbness with it. His jaw tightened over his tongue, clenching the edges of it between his teeth.

Chaos in the darkness. The names on the sheets might have just been words, but that phrase brought with it a host of ghosts. There was only a side-lamp on, and in the gloomy corners of the room's ceilings and floors, he was sure he could almost make out the faces of the dead students, pale and drained of blood, glaring at him with their dulled eyes. *What about us?* they asked jealously. *Don't you care about us?*

'Day job,' he muttered under his breath, as if that would somehow make them disappear. They never went away. Every night as he slept, his dreams were still overshadowed by wide accusing eyes in a brown face, and a single gunshot. The dead never left you alone. Not if you owed them.

Shivers ran through his limbs with renewed confidence as he forced his attention back to the paperwork. The dead could go and fuck themselves. For now, he wanted to concentrate on the living: the stranger of his blood that he sought while still grieving for the loss of a nephew that was someone else's blood. Wheels within wheels.

She sits with her knees drawn up under her chin. Her eyes are shut, but she's not sleeping. Her hair shines Titian red under the single bulb hanging naked above her in the centre of the ceiling. The room is empty of furniture apart from this one wooden chair and the state-of-the-art stereo on the floor against the wall.

Paris is warm, despite the lateness of the hour and the dying of the year. The window is open. She's tired. She's been tired ever since she got here, and that has come as a surprise. She thought she was stronger than that. Still, she has a job to do, and she has enough energy to do it. Sounds drift up from the streets outside. She likes the voices best. The speed of the words and the smoothness of the language intrigue her. London can wait. She has to go there eventually, but for now she's happy to be in 'gay Paree'. She can still do what she has to from here, and it isn't as if she came alone. Without opening her eyes, one slim arm drops to her side and touches the tiny remote control balanced beside her. 'Rhapsody in Blue' bursts perfectly from the stereo. She smiles. She likes this one.

Cass was definitely high. His upwards progress might have been satisfactory but he wasn't getting very far with the papers spread out in front of him. He jotted down the midwife's name alongside the obstetrician and paediatrician who had been on the ward that night. They'd be a good place to start. He also needed to know how the whole birth process went in a hospital. He and Kate had never gone down the children route in their ill-fated marriage. So how hard was it to swap a baby ten years ago? What he really needed was CCTV footage. The Portman had been a relatively new hospital then; they must have installed cameras. The likelihood of any of the tapes from so long ago still being stored anywhere was, however, more than remote.

It was a moment before he noticed the music coming from the street outside. He lit a cigarette and frowned. Was that a violin? He knew who he was going to see before he'd even got the window open. As he leaned out, he wasn't disappointed. The tramp stood under the street lamp as if serenading him, his bow making smooth movements across the tight strings of his instrument. He was playing in a different style to last time; Cass knew this tune. 'Rhapsody in Blue'.

The old man looked up and smiled, the gap in his front

teeth matching the night. He was wearing the same too short trousers and dirty clothes that he had been in the graveyard. He nodded. 'Evenin', officer,' he said, without a break in the music.

'What are you doing here?' There were no coincidences. How the fuck did the tramp know where he lived? Had he followed him at some point? It was unlikely. Cass would have noticed – in the past six months he'd learned to keep looking over his shoulder. He was bringing a lot of shit down on the force, and he was wary of revenge.

'Just keeping an eye out for you, mate – nothing more, nothing less.' He grinned, and his eyes twinkled. Cass didn't like that something in that expression reminded him of Mr Bright. The same eyes sunk into a much older face.

'Who are you?'

'Just a friend, my friend.'

Cass was sure he winked. He bit down on his tongue, the coke and his own irritation joining forces. This weird shit was something he didn't need. And how the fuck had he not noticed this man following him?

'I don't trust that word,' Cass growled. 'But you can trust me that I don't need you keeping an eye out for me.'

'But I will anyway. You can trust *me* on that.' Still smiling, he turned his back and started to stroll up the street as he played.

'If I see you around here again, I'll fucking arrest you.' Something about the old man made his blood boil and he wasn't sure why.

'Get some sleep, Cassius Jones.' The man's voice was full of light-hearted humour. He didn't look back as he spoke, just called the words up into the air. 'You've got some long days ahead.'

Cass watched until the old man and his music turned the

corner at the bottom of the street. There was no surprise disappearance this time, and Cass flicked his cigarette butt down to the pavement and shut the window hard. He was just a crazy old man who'd fixated on him. There didn't have to be anything sinister about it at all – his name had been in the papers plenty of times in recent months – it was unlikely he'd get away with no weirdos coming after him. It didn't stop one word filling his head as he sat back down in front of his work. *They*. It always came back to *They*.

Chapter Thirteen

Abigail wrapped the sheet round her like a towel to let Fletcher out. They kissed upstairs at her door, rather than at street level, and she watched him all the way down. At the bottom he opened the front door and then turned and half-smiled back up at her. She didn't expect anything less. It had been good sex. She'd done everything he hadn't expected from her and it had an effect. He'd been expecting animalistic, but she'd given him gentle.

There was still an awkwardness between them when they'd finished, but she'd seen that 'thing' in his eyes. Even a man as tough as he was couldn't quite shift all the conditioning that made men think women were helpless and vulnerable underneath the surface. Men could never believe that women could be soft and warm in bed and yet still have a hard soul. It didn't compute. They never learned. Ever since Eve, women have always been tougher. *There* was a woman who took what she wanted, and then dragged her man down with her to share the blame.

She smiled back, leaning in against the door frame in the knowledge that she made a sensuous picture. Fletcher probably thought she was keeping some secrets and that she knew something about the fat man that she was refusing to share, but from his hesitant look she could tell that he was perhaps already making excuses for her in his head. It was what straightforward men did. She didn't really care. She'd enjoyed the warmth of him, but it was done now. She waited until he'd closed the door behind him, before letting the smile slip and locking herself into her flat.

It could wait ten minutes. It would have to. She needed to be careful, and she needed to be sure that Fletcher really had gone back to work. She showered and wrapped herself in a robe and then filled the coffee machine, counting each minute off as it bubbled and steamed and filled the jug. There could be no room for error or haste. If she did this wrong, then she was quite sure that she would die. Her soul at least would crumble like a tin can in a vacuum. There wouldn't be any second chances, she was certain of that.

Second chance at what, Abigail? At first she didn't recognise the inner voice, and then she realised it was her own, from a long time ago. *You don't even know. Something's changing in you and you're not even afraid. What's happened to you?*

She shut herself up and poured the coffee. Her fingers drummed on the work surface until the black liquid was cool enough to drink, and then she finally went over to the computer in the corner of the clinical lounge. If Fletcher was coming back to catch her out at something, he'd have done it by now. She brought up the Hotmail screen that flashed for her login details. Maybe she should be in an Internet café doing this, but if ATD was watching her, then that would draw too much attention. Her younger sister had died; she should be at home crying. *Her younger sister had died.* It felt alien, as if that information belonged elsewhere. She wouldn't dwell on it. She wouldn't give that inner voice anything to shout about. She stared at the flashing screen and took a deep breath. The note had told her she'd know when, and whoever had written it was right. She logged in.

Username: <u>Intervention1@hotmail.co.uk</u>
Password: Salvation

For a moment there was nothing but overwhelming disappointment as she stared at the *No new messages* displayed on the home screen. What was left of her heart almost broke and then something different on the screen caught her eye. The small (1) next to the Drafts folder. Her breath held. With a trembling hand she sipped from her mug. As she swallowed the bitter liquid she clicked on the highlighted icon.

This was the point of no return. Every cell in her body knew that. Or perhaps there had never been any choice in it. Maybe this was just her destiny, and had been ever since she'd felt herself separating from the world. The message opened up.

Call this number tonight from a payphone.

She jotted the mobile number down on the inside of her arm before continuing with the short message:

When you leave your flat, you will not be returning. Take only what is essential.
  You will learn all you need to know when we meet.
  Delete this message now.

She stared at the screen for a few more seconds before hitting the delete key. The message disappeared as if it had never existed. She turned the computer off without bothering to wipe her Internet history. That would only slow Special Branch and Fletcher's lot down by an hour or two, and there wasn't anything on her hard drive that could link her with anyone.

Over by the window she peered out between the wooden slats. A car was parked on the opposite side of the road, on a double yellow line. The two men inside weren't even trying not to be noticed. Perhaps Fletcher did understand her better than she thought. Maybe he had a hard soul himself.

Ten minutes later and she was dressed in black leggings and a black sweater, her hair pulled back into a ponytail. She took some change from her wallet and tucked it into her bra before looking around the apartment that had been her home for some years now. There was nothing in its bland interior that she wanted to take; no personal items or photographs. Those were stored in her parents' attic in the Highgate house. The flat was simply somewhere she slept and bathed and ate, and now that she knew she was leaving it behind, it felt alien already. Had she been subconsciously preparing for this day since she moved here? Or before then, even?

She left the lights on and walked towards the front door. Thinking about it was irrelevant. She was here now, and ultimately *how* you got to a place rarely mattered once you'd arrived. Instead of heading down to the main entrance, she went up a floor and stopped in the landing by the small sash window. She pushed it up and peered out. The air had lost the deceptive heat of the day, and now an October chill owned the night. She shivered involuntarily as it wrapped itself round her.

There gap between the wall of her building and the one next to it was barely three feet wide, giving her a limited view of the street either side. How closely were they watching her? It was more likely that Fletcher had placed the car so obviously in order to warn her off going out, and was instead monitoring her mobile and landline phones. Her sister had just died, after all, and despite his suspicions about what she had or hadn't seen on the platform of the tube station, she was the one who had chased the fat man down while Special Branch had been bumbling around like something out of a silent black and white film.

Black and white. That meant something. Hadn't she seen only in black and white for a moment earlier in the day? It had felt good; she knew that. There had been something soothing in that fleeting absence of colour. Along the wall, perhaps a metre to her left, a drainpipe ran the length of the building. Although paint-chipped and tatty, the brackets holding it at regular intervals to the bricks looked firmly screwed in, the metal tight against the wall. She hoped she was right.

The window only opened halfway, but it was enough. Bending backwards, she managed to slide her slim torso out and then pulled upward against the glass, one hand hooked round the frame and her stomach muscles holding her in place. When she felt secure, she eased one long leg out and shuffled herself to the edge of the window. She stretched along the outside wall and reached for the pipe. It was greasy under her touch. She sighed and then took a deep breath, swung herself out and grabbed for the pipe. She didn't look down – not because she was afraid of heights, but because there was no point. She knew what was down there: uneven, hard concrete. Evaluating a landing didn't take much thought – if she fell, there would be broken bones, at the very least.

With the precision of a cat she pressed her free foot into a gap between the bricks, curling her toes up to get some form of hold on the filler and then, with every muscle in her body taut, she pulled her other leg out of the window and instantly swung them both sideways. Just at the point her hand had to let go of the window, her feet found purchase on the pipe and she used the momentum to carry the rest of her torso over.

She shimmied quickly to the ground, and stood panting against the wall for a moment. Her top had ridden up and her stomach had grazed against the bricks. Her ribs ached. It had been a long time since she'd done something like that, and no amount of jogging and yoga could prepare your body for the completely unusual. She trotted to the back of the building, her muscles recovering as she went. She scanned the road. It was quiet, and there was no sign of any suspicious vehicle. With her head down, she stayed close to the shadows of the wall and walked in the other direction, away from her flat. When she reached the end of the street she peered backwards. As far as she could tell, no one was following her. The night was still.

Once clear of her own immediate vicinity, she broke into a steady jog, nothing fast enough to draw suspicion from any passing police car, but setting a good enough pace to draw out anyone who might have been tailing behind. Her footsteps were not matched, but echoed lonely in the darkness and soon she eased into her stride, running as much for pleasure as purpose.

After three miles she stopped at a phone booth. Her breathing was even and her muscles were loose. She felt good as she inserted some coins and then tapped the number from her arm into the pad. It rang twice before a voice, sounding smooth and exotic, answered.

'Asher Red.'

'Abigail Porter,' she replied.

'Good. I've been expecting your call. Now listen carefully ...'

Abigail could hear the pleasure in the man's voice as he spoke, and it warmed her.

The boy on the bed had finally stopped crying, although, to be fair, it hadn't taken much to make him start. Mr Craven didn't really mind. It could be more fun that way, if he was in the right mood. The bed was vast and the boy looked tiny in it. Mr Craven wasn't sure how old he was; somewhere above six and below nine would be his experienced guess, and unlike the children he'd become used to, this one was pale and blond with a layer of puppy fat covering his small bones. It was a welcome change.

Mr Craven leaned back in the low regency chair in the corner of the large bedroom as he finished his thin Cartier cigarette, letting his silk dressing gown fall open. Although the boy's tear-stained face was looking in his direction, he showed no sign of fear at Mr Craven's naked body, even after all the damage it had inflicted on his own damaged flesh. This was nothing surprising. They all retreated into themselves at some point, as if what was happening to their body was elsewhere. Children, Mr Craven had discovered over the long years, had an interesting capacity for that. Perhaps it was because they had yet to doubt their own immortality and realise just how important this fresh new body was to them. They soon learned under Mr Craven's, tutelage, though. He made very sure of that.

The boy's skin was bright pink in patches, and as he looked at the small stain of blood on the Egyptian cotton sheet from where the child's anus had torn, Mr Craven became aroused again. Recovery time was not something he'd ever needed. Perhaps he'd use a knife on this one. That would bring the life back into his piggy eyes. It was feasible. He was a nothing, this boy, a runaway in a care home, ironically having run away from a situation like this. It could always be reported that he'd run away again. The manager of the care home wouldn't mind. Any doubts she'd had were dispelled when he showed her everything he truly was – and on top of that, she'd been paid well. As he looked at the silent boy again, his thoughts fixated on the knife. Mutilation wasn't something he indulged in too often – he wasn't cruel – but he was feeling over-stressed, and in need of some release. Too much was changing, and it was starting to look like they had come here under a false promise. He smiled. He wanted to score the boy's buttocks and hear him scream as he tried to wriggle away. He wanted to—

The doorbell echoed through the huge apartment and Mr Craven sighed, his delicious train of thought broken. He didn't have to wonder who it was; no one came up here apart from the Network or their lackeys. It was two a.m. What could be so important now?

He tied his dressing gown around his waist and left the room, locking the door behind him. The boy looked broken, but you couldn't be too careful. There were no staff working that night, at his own request. Of course they would turn a blind eye and do what they were told, but in recent times he'd preferred to keep his hobbies private.

A man in an expensively tailored suit stood on the other side of the heavy wooden door. Mr Craven glared at him.

'Don't tell me – another meeting? If it's to tell me Monmir's dead, then that's hardly news.'

The besuited man didn't speak and Mr Craven gritted his teeth and pressed his thin lips together so that they almost disappeared completely and fought the urge to beat him or tear him limb from limb. He still had the strength – he wasn't weakening – but he also knew that Mr Bright wouldn't take that kindly. This man in front of him might not know exactly who he was working for, but he was still Mr Bright's man. Not that Mr Craven really cared what Mr Bright thought, but for now he needed to play the game.

'Let's go then.'

There was the slightest flicker of surprise in the man's eyes. 'Aren't you going to dress?'

Mr Craven looked down. 'Am I naked?' His eyes were hard.

The man didn't say any more.

Mr Craven looked back into the apartment. There was never any telling how long a meeting could go on for, and if he was still in the mood, he could always arrange for another.

'There's something in the bedroom that needs taking back to where it belongs.' He paused. 'Perhaps clean it up first.'

The man registered no surprise, and as Mr Craven followed him out, his irritation rose. It appeared that everyone was aware that he continued the practices of his youth, even the bloody lackeys. Were there no secrets? Was nothing sacred?

Mr Bellew and Mr Dublin were already there when Mr Craven arrived. His bare feet slapped against the marble floor and the sound echoed slightly against the curved walls and ceiling of the old tunnel.

'Just the four of us again?' he asked. 'How sweet.'

'Glad you made an effort.' Mr Dublin was, as ever, impeccably but casually dressed, the tan of his trousers and the off-cream of his soft shirt making him almost a ghost under his ash-blond hair.

'Someone else is in there with him,' Mr Bellew said. He

144

looked Mr Craven up and down and didn't disguise his distaste.

'So we've been left outside to wait?' Mr Craven's lips tightened as he sneered, 'Is Mr Bright the First or have I missed something?'

'Just because your fun has clearly been interrupted, there's no need to throw your toys out of your pram.' Mr Bellew leaned against one of the pillars in front of the carved double doors, but he kept his eyes on Mr Craven. None of the three sat down on any of the variety of sofas and wing-back chairs in the atrium.

'It's not like you to take Mr Bright's side,' Mr Craven said.

'Oh, both of you, please just be quiet. This bickering is sounding like the old days.' Mr Dublin looked at Mr Craven. 'We've only just arrived ourselves; he doesn't even know we're here. We thought we might as well wait for you. So now that we're all here, gentlemen, shall we go in?'

As they took their respective places at the compass points of the table, a small man made the back of the room untidy as he paced up and down, worrying at his hands.

'What's he doing here?' Mr Craven directed the question at Mr Bright. 'He's not one of the Inner Cohort.'

'We appear to have a problem.' Mr Bright poured four brandies as he spoke. He didn't offer a drink to the worried man at the back. He clicked a silver remote control and a canvas hanging behind him slid up the wall to reveal a large flat-screen monitor.

'These are some of the images that Special Branch and the ATD discovered while looking through CCTV footage of the London bombs.' Pictures flashed across the screen. Mr Bright clicked again. 'And these are from the Moscow bombs.'

The men around the table stared at the screen. After a few moments, Mr Bright turned it off.

'I would say our problem is obvious.' He sat down, resting his hands on the table.

'But that's—' Mr Craven looked over at the chubby, pacing man who had moved further towards the corner of the large room. 'How did this happen, Mr DeVore?' There was a sharp accusation in the question. 'How did it get out?'

'I don't know.' The man called Mr DeVore visibly shivered. 'I don't understand it.'

'How it got out is almost irrelevant,' Mr Bellew cut in. 'What is it doing?'

'And stop trembling like that.' Mr Dublin looked at DeVore. 'We're better than that kind of fear. You're shaming yourself. Pull yourself together and sit down.'

DeVore did as he was told, taking his own regular seat between the south and west points of the table, with Mr Bellew at the south and Mr Dublin at the east. He sank into the chair.

'How could you not have known it was gone?' Mr Craven asked.

DeVore's forehead shone with sweat despite the coolness of the room.

'To be fair,' Mr Bright answered in his place, 'being in several places at once is what they do. We know this. We use it all the time. DeVore didn't realise he didn't have the real one until the Reflection disappeared this lunchtime. The Interventionist itself died under a tube train at the same time.'

'And that's when it disappeared from the thought chamber,' DeVore repeated Mr Bright's point.

'Don't you check them?' Mr Craven wasn't letting go.

'Yes,' DeVore answered helplessly, 'of course we do.'

'I'm sorry.' Mr Dublin sighed. 'I'm missing something. If you *check* them, how could you not have known it was a Reflection?'

'They've developed a new skill,' Mr Bright said.

'What?'

'We all know they've been evolving since they came through the walkways with us.'

'Evolving isn't perhaps a word I'd choose,' Mr Craven muttered.

'Mainly those changes have worked in our favour.' Mr Bright ignored the other man and continued, 'As their other skills have grown, they've lost their individual personalities—'

'— and their looks.'

'And they've become empty vessels for their abilities. Their reclusive natures make them harmless. The House of Intervention has served us well.'

'But the Reflections they use to see the world have always been insubstantial,' Mr Dublin's voice was eternally soft. 'Like holograms.'

'That would appear to have changed.'

'The Reflections are now *solid*?'

'That's why DeVore's team didn't realise the one in the Chamber wasn't real.'

There was a thoughtful pause before DeVore started babbling, as if to fill it. 'And I have other responsibilities to take care of. There is the constant stream of data coming from them to check. I have to oversee the analysis and make sure we're reading them properly. I can't do everything!'

'So, if all the Reflections are now solid,' Mr Craven asked, 'how did you know which was the real one in this case? Surely the Reflection could have been what we saw on that footage?'

'Because of this.' Mr Bright started the film again. The silent film lasted only a few moments. 'As this one went under the train, so the one in the House simply disappeared.'

'Where did you get all this footage?' Mr Bellew asked.

'Luckily, DeVore acted fast.' Mr Bright's eyes hardened on Mr Bellew, ignoring the question as if it were a slight on his power. 'When the Reflection disappeared, he contacted me straight away.'

'Of course he did,' Mr Craven sneered. 'Everyone runs to the First's right-hand man.'

'We now have the body – at least what they could scrape up of it from the tracks. We'll feed them back some regular results – something anonymous. We need to keep this away from *Them* as much as possible. Even those who know need to think we have complete control.'

'Why did it go under the track? I don't see a gunshot.' Mr Dublin frowned, delicate lines furrowing his perfect skin.

'It was wearing a dummy bomb – I presume to create the impression that it was going to commit an act of terror, like the others. There was no apparent reason for it to take such an extreme measure. The only conclusion I can draw is that this was suicide.' Mr Bright paused. 'And a very public one, although for whose benefit I'm not yet sure.'

There was a long silence.

'It doesn't make any sense,' Mr Bellew said at last. 'Why would one of them kill itself? If it could create a hard Reflection, why not send that instead? And on top of that, they don't *think* – not like us, or even *Them*, for that matter. They don't even like being out in the world, otherwise they wouldn't just sit like vegetables in the House of Intervention.'

'Look at the gums.' Mr Bright magnified the image. 'They're bleeding quite badly. I think it was dying anyway.'

148

'So death has come to them too?' Mr Craven's voice was low.

'Is this your *ennui* too, Mr Bright?' Mr Dublin leaned back in his chair.

'I doubt it. Perhaps the centuries spent inside have made the world intolerable to them. Who knows?' Mr Bright smiled, calmly. 'What's happening to them and what's happening with us is unlikely to be related.'

'We all travelled,' Mr Dublin said softly.

'But they were never *us*. They were lower.'

'They were fucking servants, and now they're fucking freaks,' Mr Craven exploded. 'We should have left them behind.'

'I'm surprised by your vehemence,' Mr Dublin said. 'I didn't think you would care one way or another, women having never been to your particular taste.'

Mr Craven downed his brandy. 'Well done, Mr Dublin. You've discovered your sense of humour.'

'This is all relatively irrelevant.' Mr Bright took a careful sip of his own drink. 'The Interventionist itself isn't the problem. Perhaps they're dying. It would be unfortunate, but we could manage without them and their abilities.'

DeVore opened his mouth to comment, but one look from Mr Bright closed it.

'But this footage confirms the suspicions I aired the last time we met. The Interventionists don't care about the machinations of this world. I don't think they even care about us. They have become something of their own – we just tap into that. Someone in the Network – maybe one of us, even – is using them. To create an imbalance, perhaps. Whatever the reason, I can assure you it's not for the greater good. Wouldn't you agree, causing devastation in two major cities is hardly to our current benefit?'

'London is your city. Your base,' Mr Craven said.

'It's the *first* city, as well as mine. Perhaps this is an attack on me.'

'You never were short of ego, Mr Bright.' Mr Dublin's laughter was shards of diamonds on a mirror. 'Maybe someone's tired of following the lead of the puppet rather than the sleeping puppet-master.'

'Then they should bring it to the full Cohort. I have no problem with that. *This*,' he said as he pointed back at the screen, 'I have a problem with.'

'I never thought I'd be the one to say this,' Mr Bellew started, 'but this is no time for us four to fight. We led them here, and they've let us lead since.' His dark eyes moved around the table. 'We have to keep our hold now, or we're in danger of losing everything.'

'But what about the others?' Mr Craven turned to DeVore. 'Is there any way we can tell if they're Reflections or not? How many others are out?'

'I can't tell,' DeVore answered, a little of his composure returning. 'They all seem to be exactly as they normally are. We're trying various tests.'

'Things are unravelling,' Mr Dublin mused in the silence that followed.

Mr Bright ignored him. 'Go back to your cities and meet with your sections. If anyone doesn't turn up, or is acting suspiciously, then I want to know. We have to spy on our own, now, unpleasant though that may be. I fear this *ennui* is causing cracks in our unity.'

'You'll have a long list,' Mr Craven said. 'Everyone's acting strangely. This fear of death is definitely spreading – and on top of that I don't meet with my section often. As long as the accounts are maintained, everyone puts their share in, business is going well and the rules are being followed, then

I don't really see why I should nursemaid them. They don't need it.'

'Mr Craven—,' Mr Bright lowered his voice, and the first hint of menace crept out, '—you were included in this council only when the First started to sleep. You can easily be replaced if you're not up to it.'

Mr Craven said nothing.

'From now on you I will expect you to do as I say.'

'It's dying,' Mr Dublin continued, as if the others weren't there. 'The world is dying and so are the Interventionists, and so are we. Interesting, isn't it?'

'You sound like Mr Solomon,' Mr Bright said, 'and he, brother that he was, was quite, quite mad.'

'We'll see, Mr Bright. Until then, let's play this farce out.' Mr Dublin smiled. 'And there's no need to look at me like that. I for one have no intention of dying or giving up yet.'

After they had left, Mr Bright replayed the final film several times. Eventually, he froze it on the tall, dark-haired woman pointing her gun so ineffectually at the fat creature as it reached forward and touched her.

'Why you?' he muttered, drumming his perfect fingernails on the table. 'What did it want with you?'

Chapter Fourteen

Cass had to give Dr Marsden and Eagleton their due: they'd pulled an all-nighter, or as near as damn it, to get their work finished for first thing in the morning. Perhaps it was just his imagination, but beneath the clinical, chemical smell of the morgue lingered the earthy scent of a fresh grave. The bodies were lying on several stainless steel slabs behind the two pathologists, covered by regulation green sheets. Cass had no desire to see the mutilated bodies; he didn't need to – he could feel their hold on him inside. They weren't people any more, merely physical evidence.

'Jasmine Green wasn't alone with her brain injuries.' Eagleton rummaged on his desk and then held up some slides. 'You want to see?'

'Will I understand them?' Cass asked.

'Probably not.'

'Then let's not bother. The others have the same lesions?'

'Yes. There's no sign of any disease that I can find, but they all share similar damage. Angie Lane was harder to match because she banged her head on the corner of the work surface on the way down, so she'd already sustained some head trauma.'

'Did you find anything else that links them? Drugs maybe?' Armstrong asked.

'Not that I can tell. We've run all the tests we can, but

nothing's leaping out. Even the chemicals we'd expect them to share vary in quantity, because they all died on different days, at different times. Even after death our bodies still strive to retain their individuality.'

The young doctor leaned back against the desk and stretched one leg out, wincing. Cass didn't comment. Eagleton had recovered well, and being left with the odd ache or pain wasn't necessarily a bad thing: everyone should have a reminder that the world couldn't be trusted. Cass had his memories, but Eagleton was younger – emotionally he'd bounce back and the memories would fade. It was good that his body would serve to remind him that a little caution is sometimes a good thing.

The assistant ME got back to his feet. 'So now you've got a physical link as well.'

'These six students have all been through *something* together,' Dr Marsden said, browsing through the slides Cass hadn't declined to see. 'Something caused these lesions – but to be honest, I've never seen anything like them.' He looked up. 'Which I know isn't something you lot like to hear. My gut instinct would be to tell you to look for something chemical. Apart from Angie, they have no physical trauma other than the fatal wounds at their wrists. And yet—' He frowned. 'It's almost like small lines have been seared into their brain tissue.'

'Like a computer that's burnt out?' Armstrong asked.

'Could the damage have caused suicidal tendencies in them?' Cass cut across his sergeant.

'Any form of brain injury can have any number of effects, so it's hard to tell. There are some side-effects we would expect to see from various areas of damage. Armstrong's a little out of date with his medical knowledge.' Dr Marsden smiled. 'The myth of the brain being one large computer is pretty much defunct now; we prefer to think of it as more like an orchestra – every part has a function and has to work in co-ordination with the other parts for us to behave properly. The spinal column is the information highway. When you touch, taste or feel something, the spinal column decides which part of the brain is required to process it and then sends it there – for example, these kids have all got some damage at the rear right side of their brains. The right side deals with organising information, but the rear part deals specifically with vision. Might have led them to have a "denial syndrome" side-effect. Impaired vision but unaware of it.'

'Can that happen?' Cass asked.

'You'd be surprised at the weirdness the brain is capable of. I knew of a patient with a brain injury who was blind in his right eye and didn't realise because his brain refused to acknowledge it.' Dr Marsden looked at the sheets in front of him again. 'Most of these also have some slight damage to the left side. Did any of these kids show signs of confusion, strange speech patterns, something like that?'

'Yes,' Cass said, 'Hayley Porter's flatmate said she'd been behaving oddly for days, and Jasmine Green's boyfriend said she'd been strange for most of the day.'

'This could be a contributing cause. The left side of our brain deals with language and analysis. Damage there can also cause depression.' He put the sheets down. 'They all have damage to the frontal lobe too – I'll presume it in Angie Lane's case, as the haematoma makes it hard to tell without further investigation. That area controls our emotions. It houses the stop switch when we get angry.'

Cass thought back to six months ago, in his dead brother's house. It had taken a lot of willpower on top of the 'stop switch' to stop him blowing Bowman's head off.

'However,' Eagleton cut in, 'despite how interesting everything the boss is saying is, there is no way a side-effect of any of these lesions would be to commit suicide in exactly the same way as several other people, let alone make them leave the same message behind.' He looked over to Dr Marsden for confirmation. 'Right?'

'This is true,' he agreed, 'although it might have made them far more susceptible to the suggestion of it.'

'So these kids have all been to the same place, and been exposed to something that has caused this damage?' Cass wanted to hear someone say it out loud.

'Yes,' Dr Marsden said, 'without a doubt they've had a shared experience – but not necessarily at the same time.'

'*Great.*' Cass frowned, thinking of the dead and their puzzle. 'Hold on, you said *six* students. We've got seven.'

'Gotcha.' Eagleton grinned. 'We have an anomaly.'

'What?'

'Allow me my dramatic pause!' Eagleton's face had lit up with childish enthusiasm.

'What's the anomaly?' Cass growled.

'Not what, but who,' Eagleton said. 'Joe Lidster. He has no lesions on his brain at all.'

'What?' This time it was Armstrong interrupting.

'His brain looks fine.' The Assistant ME sounded almost cheerful. 'Apart from being dead, of course.'

Back at the office, Cass had taken a few minutes to pull in a favour and get a current address for Adele Stratham, the midwife who'd been working at the Portman on the night Luke was born. At least it was a London address, so if the day got too busy he'd still be able to visit her that evening and get home by a reasonable hour. He'd been awake most of the night – the drugs had kept his heart pumping fast long after any trace of the buzz had faded, and he'd been unable to turn his brain off. Now all traces of the coke had faded and he was just dog-tired and irritated. He'd left the remainder of the baggie at home, and although a big part of him wished he'd not, so he could just perk himself up with a quick snifter, his wiser self – what was left of it – was glad he couldn't. Getting caught with white powder around his nose in the current climate at Paddington Green wouldn't be good. He was drinking strong coffee instead, though it wasn't really cutting it. It was going to be a long day, he concluded. He might as well get on with it.

He found Armstrong working on the case board, rearranging photos and notes.

'Have we got the kids' mobiles back from their families yet?'

'Just, I think.'

'Good. I want all their numbers cross-referenced and call records checked straight away.'

'How far back do you want to go? A couple of months?'

'No,' Cass said, 'as far back as we can. I don't want to miss anything. There must be a computer here somewhere that can do it.'

'Anything else?'

Yeah, I want their bank statements, for the past six months at least.' He frowned. 'What are you doing?'

'Moving Lidster over away from the rest until we figure out why he had no lesions.'

Cass stared at the dark-haired young man's picture – a ghost smiling from the wall – and suddenly it was clear. He railed at his own tiredness for making him so fucking slow. *Lidster didn't have the lesions.* Of course he didn't.

'Armstrong.'

'Sir?'

'If you wanted to murder a student in London and get away with it, what would you do?'

Armstrong looked at him.

Cass jabbed a finger at the board.

'You'd give us a scenario we wouldn't look beyond.'

'You think?' Armstrong's eyes widened slightly as he caught up.

'It's got to be worth a second look.' Cass smiled. 'Grab your coat. There's a sex shop in Soho demanding our immediate attention.'

'That's not a line I thought I'd ever hear when I joined the force.'

Cass laughed. It was beginning to look like Armstrong might just turn out to be all right.

Despite the door being wedged open, there was a distinct tang of sweat filling 'Loving It' that probably went some way to explain the lack of custom. As Cass drew closer to the chubby man behind the counter, the smell grew stronger. It didn't come as any surprise; Neil Newton was wearing the same shirt as the previous day, and even if it had been fresh on, it was too tight and too nylon for a man with an odour problem. Cass tried to keep the grimace from his face as the warm sweat and overpowering cheap cologne fought for supremacy.

'Mr Newton?'

Newton, who had been staring at a catalogue page of over-large dildos, looked up, surprised. Dark circles had formed around his eyes and fresh spots were breaking out on his chin. He looked very much like a man who hadn't slept in some time. It was a look Cass recognised; it had been staring out at him from his bathroom mirror that morning.

'I didn't expect to see you back here,' Newton said. 'What can I do for you?' The nasal quality of his voice grated, and as much as Cass tried to sympathise with Newton, he found it hard. He was just too damned oily.

'We'd like to take another look at Joe's room,' Armstrong said.

'Not a problem; just let me lock up down here.' Newton fluttered his cheap-jewellery-laden hands as he hunted down his keys.

'It's fine; we can go up by ourselves.'

'No, no – I can't concentrate anyway,' Newton sighed. 'I don't know why I bothered opening up really. Just didn't want to sit in the flat.' He moved in small, precise steps as he ushered them out. 'You know how it is.'

Cass said nothing, but waited for Newton to lock up and then followed him up the side stairs to the flat. Luckily the smell was less invasive there; maybe it had settled into the fabric and furniture rather than hovering in the air as it did below.

'I haven't been in his room,' Newton said, the rings on his fingers glinting as he worried at his hands. 'I can't bring myself to. And your lot said they'd send someone to deal with all the—' He struggled for a word, settling finally on, '—mess.'

Inside Lidster's room, the two policemen started searching the young man's drawers and cupboards for anything that might give them an insight into his life.

'You were at your sister's when he died, is that right?' Cass glanced back at the shop owner. His pudgy hands paused in their constant finger-picking.

'Yes, yes I was. Why do you ask?'

'Just routine.' Lidster's drawers were as neat as the rest of his room; even his socks were paired up and folded on the opposite side to his boxer shorts. 'When did you get home?'

'Late. I had to get a taxi because of all this awful business with the tubes. I probably wasn't home until after 2 a.m.'

'And can your sister verify that?'

'Of course – of course, she can. It was her husband's birthday. We had a lovely dinner.'

'I don't need all the details.' Cass closed the drawer. There was nothing in there. 'Just your sister's phone numbers and address. Did you use a minicab?'

'No, a black cab.'

'You'll need to buy yourself a new mattress.' Armstrong lifted a pillow and looked underneath. 'Maybe your insurance will cover it. Our lot will clean the carpet, but this mattress is wrecked.'

Newton flinched. 'Well, perhaps they will dispose of it for me.'

'I'm sure they will.' Armstrong smiled.

Cass watched the interplay between the two. His sergeant clearly disliked Neil Newton as much as he did. He crouched down and peered under the bed. He grinned to himself before pulling out the laptop bag.

'I knew there'd be one around here somewhere. A media student with no computer or Internet wouldn't get very far.'

'I didn't know he had that.' Newton frowned. 'I don't have the Internet up here – only in the shop. I find that serves my uses.'

The sleek model was exactly the kind Cass would have expected a student to have, stylish but inexpensive. A thin silver dongle sat in one of the many holders on the inside of the case.

He pulled it out.

'Pay as you go Internet,' he announced, satisfied.

Back on the street, and thankfully away from any lingering scents Neil Newton might have wanted to share with them, Cass handed Armstrong the laptop.

'Get that back to the tech boys and let them dig around in it. Shouldn't take long to get an idea of Mr Lidster's life. And while they're doing that, I want you to check out that smarmy twat's alibi. I'll see you back at the office in a couple of hours.' He flagged down a taxi.

'Why? Where are you going?' Armstrong frowned.

'That's the advantage of being the boss.' Cass winked. 'I don't have to answer all your questions.'

There were calls for the ever-increasing congestion charge to be scrapped in the wake of the bombings, since it had become a fee for simply sitting in a continuous traffic jam in the heart of London, but the government was stoically avoiding the issue. Cass figured they couldn't afford to stop the charges; the government was as broke as everyone else in Britain.

The cabbie weaved his way as best he could through the slow-moving roads, but by the time they'd reached Wimbledon, the meter had clocked up a healthy fare. Though Cass might have been able to get there quicker and more cheaply on the tube, he liked being above ground, where he could see the city, and look up whenever he felt the urge. He'd rather be sitting in traffic than crammed like a sardine in one of the overloaded trains rumbling beneath their feet. Given a choice between breathing in a hundred strangers' stale air and damp sweat and the noxious output of a thousand belching vehicles, he'd take the car fumes any day.

Adele Streatham lived in a large semi-detached house not too far from the famous tennis courts. The front garden was no-nonsense smart: a neat lawn edged with enough shrubs to stop it looking boring, but not so much as to need too much upkeep. The red brick doorstep looked scrubbed clean. Adele Streatham was an efficient woman; Cass knew that much about her before she'd even opened the door.

She took a long look at his police ID before letting him in.

'You're lucky to catch me,' she said, ushering him into the sitting room. 'I'm between home visits.'

She was a stout woman in her mid-fifties. Her silver-blonde hair was pulled back into a neat bun. It was a severe look, and Cass wasn't sure if she wore it that way out of preference or practicality. She didn't offer him a cup of tea, but took the seat opposite and looked at him expectantly.

'Nice house,' Cass said.

'The recession and a divorce have both been good for me. Unusual, I know, but all the fiasco of the NHS becoming so limited has been great for us midwives. We can charge a good rate privately. No one skimps with their babies. Especially the first one.' She gave him a tight, satisfied smile. 'I specialise in those now.'

Cass couldn't help but feel there was something mercenary about that: she sounded more child-catcher than midwife. Perhaps this recession was making everyone bare their teeth a little and show their harder side, even those in the traditionally caring professions.

'You say this is about a missing child?' she asked.

'Sort-of missing, yes. I'm looking for a baby born in the Portman Hospital when you worked there. Nine years ago.'

'That's a long time ago. I'm not sure I'll be able to help. I'm not even sure what "sort-of missing" means.'

Cass ignored the hint for further information; that could

wait. He passed her over a sheet of paper with a list of names on it.

'These are the people who were working on or around the maternity ward with you that night. Anyone on there ring any bells?'

She scanned it, and laughed. 'Of course they do – I worked with them. It's not the staff I forget, love, it's the patients.'

'Was there anything unusual about any of them?'

'In what way?' Her eyes hardened.

'Is there anyone there who might have been having particular debt issues? Or any sort of problem that might make them do something stupid?'

'What, like steal a baby?' She snorted with contempt. 'Not likely. We take our jobs seriously. And everyone had money problems back then, especially if you worked for the NHS – but I can assure you that none of those people would stoop to selling a baby, or whatever it is you're very badly implying.'

'I'm sorry.' Cass raised his hands slightly. 'I didn't mean to offend you, Ms Streatham. I just have to ask these questions. A baby did end up going home with the wrong parents that night, and I'm trying to understand how it could have happened.'

'It's ridiculous,' she snorted, adding, 'Nigh on impossible, in fact.'

'There's a big difference between "nigh on impossible" and "impossible", Ms Streatham. And it happened.' He paused for a moment to let the woman calm down.

'The couple in question were Jessica and Christian Jones. She gave birth to a baby boy.'

'Jones?'

'No relation,' Cass lied. 'It's a common name.'

'Too common. It's not ringing any bells for me. I've been

midwife to a lot of babies, and back then I had maybe three or four visits maximum with each mother before the birth. They were nearly all quick and routine, and unless there was a problem, I was too busy and too tired to make idle conversation or to become friendly. Unless something went wrong at the birth, I wouldn't remember their faces six months later, let alone nearly ten years later.' She shrugged slightly. 'The world might be facing financial ruin, but it's not stopping people having children. If anything, they're having more.'

'I'm sorry if I've touched a nerve, but you can understand why I need to ask.'

'And I apologise for snapping.' Her tone smoothed out. 'But you have to understand that we all worked bloody hard, and we did our best to stay on top of the game. You should be chasing the people who worked on the private ward – they made far more mistakes than we ever did, and they worked half the hours.'

'There was a private ward?' Cass frowned. 'A maternity ward?'

'Of course there was. Didn't you know? Flush5 ran it. It was one of their first wards, actually. I think they own the whole hospital now. Them or The Bank, anyway – one or the other owns pretty much all of London's hospitals these day, if my pay slips are anything to go by.'

'Thank you, Ms Streatham.' Cass smiled. 'Thank you very much.'

He called Perry Jordan as soon as the door had closed behind him. Jessica and Christian hadn't used a private service – their records showed up clearly in the NHS records – but that didn't mean the baby hadn't been swapped with a child from the private ward.

'A private ward?' Jordan sounded put out. 'But that's weird – I didn't get anything come up about that when I started. Sorry, mate; I'll get back to it right now.'

Cass knew Jordan would be fast – the young investigator was annoyed at himself for having missed something, and he didn't like to lose any more than Cass did.

He checked his watch. If the traffic was in his favour, he'd be back at the office before anyone too high-ranking had noticed he wasn't there.

'So what do we know?' Cass leaned back against one of the desks in the Incident Room. Armstrong hadn't asked where he'd been, but it was clear the sergeant wasn't overly happy at being left out of whatever was going on. Claire had never questioned him when Cass disappeared during office hours; she had just covered for him if required. Armstrong might never be that loyal, but he was going to have to get used to it. For all he knew, Cass could have been in another interminable legal meeting – that was the lie he'd been planning to use if pushed.

Cass stared at the board where the six smiling photographs stared back. Somewhere beyond the shine of the paper lurked dark shadows and accusing eyes. He ignored them.

'According to the phone records, none of them have ever phoned any of the others,' Armstrong said. 'Nor have they called any of the same landline or mobile numbers. A couple used their phones to call the same utilities companies, but there's nothing in that – they all lived in London, and they all had to pay bills.'

'They were students,' Cass added. 'They were probably calling the gas board because they *couldn't* pay their bills.'

164

'Whichever, what we do know is that they didn't know each other.'

'Or at least not well enough to swap phone numbers,' Cass clarified.

'True,' Armstrong said. 'And the computer print-outs of their bank records are all on your desk. I had a quick look. I hate to say it, but I doubt you'll find much there.'

'Great. Haven't you got anything good for me?'

'Actually, yes – well, a good and a bad. Which do you want first?'

'Hit me.'

'Neil Newton's alibi checks out. I rang his sister, and she confirms that they had a birthday dinner for her husband that he attended. And he left late, saying he'd grab a black cab.'

'What's the good news?'

'Joe Lidster was Internet dating. There were two sites bookmarked that he used quite heavily. He emailed a couple of men with his number. They didn't email their numbers back, though – I guess they would have texted. Tech are tracing them through their emails, and I've got a constable calling the numbers from his phone book and call log. We should get something to go on soon.'

'Good. Let's see if we can end the day with something positive.'

At his desk, Cass picked up the first of the bank statements. Katie Dodds. He scanned the list of details and numbers. There was something about bank records that was like reading someone's diary – it was the bones without the flesh of emotion and detail, but it nonetheless gave a clear view of their life. He put Joe Lidster's statement to one side – something bad had come his way, that was for sure, but

Cass was quite certain it wasn't the same as the others – and flicked through the rest. Aside from Hayley Porter and Cory Denter, the other three had at least one utility bill going out each month. Perhaps the rest were in the names of other housemates or sharers, splitting the responsibility, like taking the first step into adulthood – a journey that was over too quickly for these youngsters.

Their transactions were depressingly mundane. Student loans came in; rents and bills went out. Various cash withdrawals were made and pay-as-you-go phones were topped up. And then there were the debit card purchases for the kind of stores that implied fashion, music, movies and downloads, all vital necessities for students who were struggling to stay out of the red. It was all what he had expected to see.

He laid the long print-outs side by side and looked again. An itch tickled at the back of his mind and he ran his eyes up and down each one. There was something odd about them. Something that he couldn't quite—

And then he saw it.

He rummaged in his desk drawer until he found a pair of scissors, and then cut each long sheet into sections, divided at the first of the next month. After he was done he laid out the past four months, one above the other for each student.

'Armstrong!' he shouted. 'Get in here!'

He had to give the young man his due, Armstrong could move fast.

'What is it?'

'You were right when you said I wouldn't see much. But that's the point!'

'I'm not getting you, sir.'

'Look again. I've cut each student's statements into

months. The last two months are much shorter than the rest. The transactions are mainly basic – rent and bills and stuff – but there are hardly any withdrawals or purchases.'

'I'm still not—'

'Wake up, Sergeant! They weren't taking any cash out of their accounts, but don't tell me they weren't spending any.'

'What are you . . . ?'

'Cash! They were getting *cash* from somewhere – maybe someone was paying them cash-in-hand for something.'

'Something dodgy?'

'Maybe, maybe not. But *that* is what we need to find out.'

Chapter Fifteen

M r Craven was half-listening to the debate raging on the large screen on the wall in front of him. Politics were the same worldwide, he concluded: men screaming at each other from different sides of an opulent room, decrying each other's values when really it was all just about the power. He liked to watch them playing it out sometimes; it reminded him of the old days.

He swallowed a mouthful of his lunch and smiled as the Leader of the Opposition received a standing ovation, and not only from those on his own side of the bench. The McDonnell woman looked around her, trying to remain calm, but clearly flustered, as the other – Merchant, Mr Craven believed his name was – enjoyed his moment. Mr Craven couldn't help himself; he always favoured the Opposition, even though the man who was ranting and pacing and shaking his fists in the air on the screen appeared to be promising a dictatorship in the name of protection if he ever got into power.

Hedonist that he was, Mr Craven still kept abreast of the potential for change that hung in the air of every major city of this world. The McDonnell woman, the House's choice, if the Interventionists had been interpreted correctly, favoured peace and tolerance. This man Merchant was a different breed. Even listening to him was exhausting: more death sentences for lesser crimes, merciless vengeance on any nation or group who attacks the British Isles, a return to a one-religion state. There was no *glow* about him, but Mr Craven couldn't help but wonder if this was what had been planned all that time ago – a man made in his God's image. Still, if people were stupid enough to support him, then so be it. He'd never been interested enough to get involved; the others could handle that. He just found it entertaining.

His knife cleaved the steak like butter and he lifted another slice to his mouth and chewed. It was perfectly cooked, as was only to be expected. A small pool of pinkish blood oozed out of the meat and ran into the dauphinoise potato and vegetable medley on the side. He swallowed, and then took a long sip of red wine. The man hovering in the doorway could wait.

At last he put down his cutlery and beckoned Draper forward. 'Yes?' he said. 'Is it organised?'

'She won't give you any more children, sir.' Draper didn't move any further forward into the vast lounge.

Mr Craven picked up his knife again.

'What do you mean?'

'The boy who was here last is sick.'

'Sick?' Mr Craven frowned.

'Strain II. The bug.'

'Her concern is noted, but it's not as if I can catch it,' he said impatiently. 'Tell her to send a different one. And there are a few letters on my desk that need taking back to some lawyers or other.'

The man didn't move, and Mr Craven's irritation shifted into annoyance.

'What's the matter with you?'

Draper's hesitation hung in the air between them before he finally spoke.

'It's the boy. She says he didn't have the bug. Not before.'

'Not before what?'

Draper swallowed. 'Not before you, sir.'

Mr Craven froze as the world stilled. A sneeze tickled in his nose and he let it out. He'd been sneezing a lot recently. Draper flinched, and suddenly it was all very clear; he understood why the man had stayed hovering in the doorway. Mr Craven looked at him properly. Draper's pupils were wide. A bead of sweat on his forehead reflected the world. A world that had suddenly changed. A chill gripped Mr Craven's stomach.

Draper took a tiny step backwards, perhaps hoping that if he moved slowly enough, then his exit wouldn't be noticed. Mr Craven smiled.

'Scared of something, Draper? Suddenly not so keen to serve me?' He carefully lifted his napkin from his lap and placed it next to his unfinished dinner. He stood up.

'No sir, I just have ...' The sentence hung unfinished. Draper didn't have to speak. Mr Craven could see his fear on every inch of his skin. It pulsed through his pores. Death.

He smiled.

'If you can get to the front door before me, I'll let you leave.'

Draper turned to run.

There was light, energy and movement. The flap of wings tore shreds in the curtains. For those few seconds, Mr Craven thought it was good to feel like himself again.

Draper hadn't got very far at all. Mr Craven leaned against the heavy wooden door and smiled at him.

'I just want to hug you.'

The fight had gone out of Draper. His shoulders slumped. 'Please, sir—'

That was all he managed to say before Mr Craven pulled him close.

Draper's body was hot.

'Sometimes in life we don't get the rewards we were hoping for,' Mr Craven whispered gently into his ear. 'Today is a day where I think we're both learning that lesson.'

He bit down on the soft lobe. Draper mewled.

When he returned to his meal his dessert was cooling, but still delicious. Draper was on his knees, sobbing in the hallway. Mr Craven hoped he'd get up soon – those letters still needed delivering, and he was pretty sure Draper would be healthy long enough to manage that, at least.

The man on the other side of the interview table was the epitome of ordinary. Though Richard Elwood worked for an advertising company, he was in charge of inputting numbers rather than anything creative. Forty-four years old, and married for seventeen of those, with whatever limited good looks he might have once had now faded into blandness ... Cass couldn't help but wonder what could possibly have attracted the handsome young Joe Lidster to him.

He slid a cup of bad instant coffee across the table, and Elwood picked it up and started to sip from it gratefully. He was upset, there was no doubting that, but the emotion didn't make Cass warm to him. You could be upset for any number of reasons, including fear of being caught.

'You must have seen the papers reporting his death,' Cass said, ignoring his own coffee.

'Yes. It came as a terrible shock.' Elwood's hands twitched as he played with the polystyrene cup. 'I was trying not to let it show at home. I just can't understand why he'd have done something like that. What's going on with these students? How many have died now?' The last few words came out in a sob.

Cass stared at him and gritted his teeth. He had never been able to stomach men who cried too easily. 'We don't believe Joe Lidster died in the same way as the others.'

'What?' Elwood's tears magically stopped.

'Why are you on a gay dating website when you're married with two children?' Cass asked.

'What do you mean, he didn't die in the same way as the others?'

'You answer my question first.' Cass didn't really care about Elwood's personal life – everyone lied to one extent or another. He just wanted to see his reactions.

Elwood looked down at the table. 'Life is messy,' he said. 'Complicated.'

Cass had been expecting him to come out with the usual crap about loving his wife and not wanting to hurt anyone. The honesty of his answer pushed Elwood up a little in his estimation, but he didn't let it show.

'Not for Joe Lidster. Life is decidedly un-fucking-complicated for him now.'

'I don't understand how I can help you.'

'We believe Lidster was murdered,' Cass said.

Elwood's eyes widened. His mouth dropped open, as if he was about to speak, but Cass didn't give him time. 'We need to know about your relationship with him and when you last saw him. Did you fight?'

Elwood shook his head, his hands spreading slightly helplessly, as if he wished they could do the talking for him, but they couldn't oblige.

After a moment he said, 'He answered an ad on the site. We started messaging, and then he gave me his number and we arranged to meet. The first time was three weeks or so ago. We had coffee. I was honest with him about my situation and he was fine with it. He said he wasn't long out of a bad break-up and wasn't looking for something overly serious. It suited us both.' He paused. 'I liked him. He was very funny, but very gentle. He was a kind young man.'

'When did you last see him?'

'The night he died. We'd met a few times before in hotels, but this time he said to come to his. We went for something to eat and then went back to his flat.'

'Did you have sex with him?'

'I suppose so. We did stuff, anyway.' The question clearly made the man uncomfortable, and Cass wondered how much time he spent wrestling with his desires. One day he'd figure out it was rarely worth the struggle. At some point or other the desire would eventually win out.

'We mainly chatted. He told me about the awful man he lived with – well, whose flat he rented. We laughed a bit about that, and the state of the place. I think Joe felt sorry for him. He said he thought the old boy had a bit of a crush on him, but all his attempts at seduction were like something out of an awful seventies sitcom – just like the landlord himself. I had to get home by eleven, so at about half-ten I left Joe upstairs and went down, unchained the door and let myself out. That was it. I thought it was odd that he hadn't texted me, even though he never did much when I was at home, and then the next time I saw his name it was in the paper.' He looked down at his watch.

The day was creeping away, and he'd be expected home soon. Cass thought he'd let him go in time. Elwood might be many things, but Cass was pretty sure he wasn't a killer, not in this case, at least.

He was about to stop the recording and let the man go

back to his family when something occurred to him. 'You said you unchained the door?'

'Yes, on the way out.'

'Are you sure of that?'

'Yes – you've been in that flat, right? You saw how old and filthy everything is? Well, the chain was stuck and I had to yank at it a bit to open it. I remember it clearly.'

Cass didn't say any more until they'd seen the man out and were back in his office. Then he started, 'Don't you think it's odd that Lidster put the chain on?'

'Maybe,' Armstrong said, 'but maybe he just wanted to make sure they had privacy.'

'His bedroom had a lock. He could have had privacy without putting the chain on the front door.' Cass leaned against his desk. 'Most people only put the chain on at the end of the evening, when they're not expecting to go out again.'

He thought for a moment, then looked at Armstrong. 'Get on the phone to Marsden's office and tell Eagleton I want Lidster's blood testing again, for anything unusual or out of the ordinary.'

'What are you thinking?'

'I'll tell you when I'm sure.' He reached for his jacket. 'When you've done that, you can get off home. I've got a couple of visits to make and then I'll be doing the same.'

'More secrets?' Armstrong asked.

'Thought I'd go and see Jasmine Green's boyfriend, and then call in on the Denters. See if either of them had a cash-in-hand job.' He smiled. 'No secrets.'

'I'll call the next of kin and the roommates of the others before I go home.'

Cass was at his office door when he paused. 'And get

someone watching Neil Newton's place. Nothing obvious. I just don't want him doing a runner.'

'But his alibi checks out.'

'Maybe, but we've got the budget for some overtime and that door chain is really bugging me.'

Cory Denter's father answered on the third ring. His greeting was in a monotone, the voice a reflection of the man's broken heart. Cory had had jobs, yes, but as far as his father was concerned, nothing cash in hand, nothing regular – he'd done some silver service waiting during the Christmas holidays, that kind of thing. He took his studies too seriously to have had a regular job. He was a good boy; he worked hard. He paused the call for a moment to check with his wife, but she knew no more than he did.

The conversation was stilted. Cass didn't have the answers to their pain; worse, he knew that even if he did get them answers to the questions surrounding their son's death, they'd find that it couldn't really take the pain away. It would just change, that was all. They didn't know that yet, though. Their ignorance might not be bliss, but there was some mercy in it. At least for now they had a semblance of hope.

'Cash in hand?' The dread was back in Mr Denter's voice. 'Does that mean my son was involved in some bad business after all?'

'Not necessarily,' Cass said. 'A lot of companies are trying to fiddle the taxman these days. Everyone's struggling. It could be that he didn't even know that whoever was paying him wasn't putting it through the books.'

It wasn't likely – Cass had looked through Cory's stuff and he hadn't seen any payslips, dodgy or otherwise. If he'd been working quite recently, there'd have surely been something somewhere. There was a word hanging in the air.

At last he said, 'I don't think your son was mixed up in selling drugs.' There they were: the word was out there. Drugs. Done. 'Kids who sell drugs normally do so to pay for their own habit. Your son's body showed no evidence of any usage – nor did any of the other students.' He spoke slowly, letting each sentence sink in before starting the next. 'I can't give you any guarantees on that, obviously, but my gut instinct tells me it is very far from likely. You had a good son, Mr Denter. He was a boy to be proud of. Whatever I find out or don't, you should enjoy that memory of him.'

When the other man started crying softly into the phone, Cass hung up, for both their sakes.

There was no answer at Jasmine Green's house. He'd call in there later. First he had a personal visit to make.

Perry Jordan's flat was less flash than Cass had expected, given that the private investigator was an East End boy through and through. But then, he thought as he sat on the brown leather sofa, they were all getting older, Perry Jordan included. The man who opened the door was no longer the laddish boy-about-town who'd been thrown off the force for a stupid moment of misplaced loyalty a few years ago. The lanky body was thickening in the chest and shoulders, and his smooth face was starting to roughen, ready for the creases that would settle there as the years went by. Time waited for no man, that much was for sure.

'I've got some info for you, but it was like getting blood out of a stone.' Jordan dumped a few sheets of paper on the coffee table between them and leaned forward. 'The more I do this job, the more I realise the world is full of secrets.'

'How do you mean?' It wasn't news to Cass.

'The government bangs on about Flush5 being virtually independent. That's a load of bullshit. They are owned by The Bank, or at least by several of The Bank's holding companies. The paper trail is ridiculously complex.' He looked up. 'Over-complex, if you know what I mean – dig as I might, I reckon I'll never get to the bottom of who truly owns it, but trust me, Flush5 is not the new fucking BUPA, no matter what anyone says in public. It's not just hospitals and doctors' surgeries they're into, there's pharmaceuticals, research – you name it, they own a part of it. I can't even find out who founded the fucking thing, you have to go through so many paper hoops.'

'Forget about The Bank,' Cass cut in. The last thing he needed was for Jordan to get a bee in his bonnet about the nefarious practices of that particular institution. The Bank was Cass's problem, not Jordan's. 'That's the Big Boys' league and I doubt they'll like you digging around too much. Play safe. Stay invisible. You know that.'

'Yeah, but they're *too* big – doesn't that make you curious?'

'Remember the cat, Perry! It's a cliché because it's true.'

The younger man smiled. 'Okay, Dad, I'll leave the big boys alone. Spoil all my fun, why don't you?'

'You'll thank me when you live to be old and grey.'

'Yeah, you look like you're enjoying that phase of life. I've never known a man who smiles less.'

'Cheeky fucker. Now, what have you got for me?'

'Okay, so, this private ward? I've got someone on the case at Flush5 who's trying to get the staff records for that night; I'm hoping to get those to you tomorrow. I'll email you the list when it comes in. I doubt it'll be long – from what I can gather, from the limited access to records, Flush5 had only been around a couple of months by then – unless of course there are layers of companies with different names disguising whatever they did before, none of which would surprise me, but it does appear that they were new.'

'Stick to the point, Jordan.'

'Sorry.' His hands went up, giving in, but he was grinning. 'It's fascinating though, don't you think?'

Cass said nothing. Maybe Perry Jordan hadn't grown up that much after all. From outside came the strains of a violin playing the blues, fighting against the traffic to be heard. Cass concentrated on the sounds of the engines and drowned it out.

'There were five children born on the private ward that night, two girls and three boys. One of the boys died of cardiac arrest six minutes after birth.' The humour had bled out of Jordan's face. 'Which was almost the exact time that Jessica Jones, down in the NHS ward, gave birth to a healthy boy, Luke.'

'What was the dead boy's name?'

'Ashley Gray. His parents were Elizabeth and Owen Gray. I did a bit of digging around on them too. They were killed in a car accident in France four months after the baby died. They drove off a cliff, apparently.'

'Jesus,' Cass muttered.

'It wasn't suicide. It's been recorded as accidental death. The hired car they were in had a faked Contrôle Technique – that's the French MOT – and several faulty parts. Add a duff vehicle and bad weather conditions, and make of it what you will.'

'Thanks,' Cass said. The tiredness in his bones was disappearing. Could this boy, supposedly dead, be the one he'd known as his nephew all his life? 'Any relatives that I can speak to?'

'Of course.' Jordan slid a piece of paper over to him. 'The grandparents on the mother's side – they live in Putney Bridge. Sure you could squeeze in a visit without it eating up too much of your working day?'

'Let's hope so. My new sergeant seems to want to nanny me.'

'Is he working out?'

'We'll see. He's starting to show some promise, at least.'

Neither of them mentioned Claire, and Cass was glad. He had enough difficulty prising off the fingers of the dead as it was, without anyone speaking their names aloud.

'There's a phone number on there too, if you want to call ahead. You going to see them tonight?'

'No, it's rush hour – it'd take me for ever to get there. I've got a work visit to make. I'll see them tomorrow.' He smiled. 'Thanks for this.'

'The bill's en route, don't you worry.' Jordan frowned and moved over to the window. 'What is that? Is someone playing a fucking violin down there?'

'Sounds like it.'

'London's full of nutters these days.' Jordan smiled. 'Guess that's why I love it so much.' He peered out. 'It is – it's a bloody tramp, just standing in the street and playing the violin. How about that?'

Cass found himself laughing along. At least whoever this musician was, he wasn't a ghost like Christian – other people could hear him too. The wave of relief came as something of a surprise. *There is no glow.* There was only so much crazy he could take.

'When you get them, email those staff details to my Black-Berry. I don't want a chance of anyone at work seeing them and questioning what I'm doing.'

'No worries. Take care, Jones.'

'I always do,' Cass said. 'You take care yourself.'

Perry Jordan just laughed.

Thirty minutes later Cass was at Jasmine Green's house, standing in the narrow kitchen and trying to avoid leaning against the worktops which were sticky with coffee and other substances Cass wouldn't want to guess at. Neil Newton would be right at home here, although he guessed that at some point these students would most likely grow out of their laziness and invest in some cleaning products. For Newton that time was highly unlikely to ever come.

'Do you need to go into Jasmine's room?' Craig Mallory asked. He had dark rings around his eyes and his pupils were wide and dark. The heavy scent of cannabis resin that hung in the air was no doubt the explanation. Cass didn't care. The poor kid had watched his girlfriend plunge her arms into the TV screen and then tried to pull her out as she died in his arms. Cass didn't really give a shit if he wanted to get a little stoned to help him sleep.

'Because if you do, that's fine, but most of her stuff was picked up by her parents, so you might be better off going to see them? We threw the TV out before they came. Figured they wouldn't want to be faced with that ...'

Mallory had been half-heartedly looking into the cups scattered across the kitchen worktop to see if there was one clean enough to provide coffee in. He gave up and turned to face Cass. The DI was relieved; E.coli was something he could live without right now.

'It was you I wanted to see, actually,' he said, offering the student a cigarette and lighting one for himself. 'You must have heard by now that Jasmine's suicide seems to be linked with others in the city.'

Mallory nodded. 'Yeah, I heard. I didn't know any of the others, though.'

'That's fine; it's Jasmine I want to ask you about. Did she have a job at all? Something that paid cash, rather than directly into her account?'

'Not that she told me about.' The youth frowned. 'But it's funny you should ask that, because I did notice she had more cash on her, like when we were buying food and shit, she wasn't paying on her card. She said she was trying to get her overdraft down.'

'Did you ask her where the money was coming from?'

'Yeah. But she told me she was taking it out of her account every week so she could see what she was spending better. Like she was budgeting.' He looked at Cass as if the word was from an alien language. 'She said she got the idea off one of them "get your life organised" shows that are on all the time.' He paused and frowned as the significance of the question started sinking in through the smoke clogging up his head. 'I guess she wasn't, then.'

Cass didn't comment, but changed the subject. 'Can you think of any times she was out regularly during the week?'

'It's hard to say – I had a job in the summer at an Ed's Pizza's so I was out quite a lot on odd shifts. And we try – tried – not to live in each other's pockets, you know? That's why we didn't share a room. We both liked our own space.'

'Sensible move,' Cass said.

'Yeah, but now I wish we hadn't.' Mallory's shoulders sank. 'This whole thing is too weird. I don't know how I'm supposed to feel or act or nothing. It's like everyone's looking at me the whole time.'

'Trust me, I know how that feels.'

Mallory didn't look convinced.

'Are you going to stay in this house?' Cass asked.

'I haven't decided yet. We've got a couple of months left on the contract, so I'd have to find someone to take my room. We still need someone for Jasmine's. I guess I could get something cheaper further out, so I'll probably move when the lease is up. We only lived here because of Jasmine's claustrophobia – she wouldn't get on a tube, and there's good bus routes here, especially for Uni.'

An awkward silence settled between them.

Cass wasn't going to get any more here.

'If you think of anything that might help, give me a call, right?'

'I will,' Mallory said.

As he showed Cass out, the DI was relieved to find the only music in the air was the badly tuned orchestra of the traffic.

Adam Bradley's almost-black hair was still shoulder length, but these days instead of hanging lank and greasy it was well styled and shone with health. He still picked at his nails and smoked four cigarettes a day, but as the boss man said, a few vices didn't hurt, just as long as you kept them under control. Bradley's life *was* under control now; that much was for sure – it had been ever since the man had come back five months before and had two heavies haul him out of the squat and into the back of a waiting car. To be fair, there probably hadn't been much hauling involved; he hadn't exactly weighed much then. In his vague memory he'd been hauled; in reality, he'd probably been tossed into the back seat with no sign of exertion on the part of either of the large men.

He remembered the smell of those leather seats clearly, and the way the boss had looked right into his eyes and said, 'I thought so.' He didn't remember so much of the month that followed, apart from the sense of having lived through an eternity of hell. There had been no anodyne easing off the junk for Adam, no morphine to see him through. It had been a not-so-short, sharp drag through cold turkey for him, a dip into the freezing waters of the insanity of the true addict, and he had screamed and cried and scratched and shat himself as he climbed and clawed at the walls in that locked-away room. The boss had told him – with a smile – that he'd either die, or come through the fire purified, and if he survived with his mind and body intact then there was a job waiting for him.

He'd made it. He'd come out the other side whole and healthy and suddenly in possession of a upmarket, fully furnished flat in Canary Wharf, and with a car and driver at his disposal, and an exceptionally generous wage slip. In return, all he had to do was whatever task the boss required of him. It was a good job – an *interesting* one. Adam Bradley no longer had any need for junk, and when he found himself looking at the scars and pockmarks left on his body by the stranger who had inhabited it before, he couldn't remember why he'd ever wanted that shit in the first place.

He'd asked the boss why he'd saved him once, but all he'd said was that Adam had the *glow*; he'd seen a hint of it that first time they'd met, lurking under all that sickly addiction. Adam had asked what the *glow* meant, and the boss had smiled, and said it was something in his blood, his *history*. He said that they were almost family. Adam hadn't understood, not back then; he'd wanted more explanation, but none had been forthcoming. Now that he was healthy and clear-headed, he didn't think he'd ask again. He could feel the *glow* inside him, he was sure of it: there was a kind of strength that he was certain he could focus into something, if he tried hard enough.

Even though it was warm – the Indian summer that had gripped London was refusing to let it go – he wore the long, dark overcoat that he'd bought with his first pay cheque. Bradley's homage to the man who'd pretty much raised him from the dead had made the boss smile. Now, clothed in its unnecessary warmth, he stood on the corner of a tatty street of terraced houses two minutes from Queen's Park station. He'd been waiting there ten minutes, and he'd be happy when he could leave. It was the kind of place he'd once dreamed of living, but now he just looked at with a vague sense of disgust, as if the filth and grime and tattered paint-work would somehow recognise a kindred spirit in him and drag him, kicking and screaming, back to the person he used to be. He just wanted to get this job done and get back to civilisation.

He had three people to get to, and specific words he needed to say to each. He wasn't nervous; he'd fulfilled this particular task several times before. If anything, he was somewhat bored of it, although the power amused him. He'd never realised people could be so easily influenced.

Eventually the boy emerged from the tube station and headed towards the street. He was alone, and wearing a headset to drown out the sounds of the city; no doubt he'd be listening to something heavy and unpleasant. In his baggy jeans and hoodie he looked so much younger than Adam felt, despite there being only a year's age difference between them. According to the small printout Adam was holding, Elroy Peterson was twenty-one, and Adam Bradley himself was coming up for twenty-three – but there were worlds between them.

He stepped out from the corner, timing it perfectly so he would bump into the student. He dropped the unzipped leather wallet that had been under his arm and various papers scattered across the pavement. Elroy Peterson's eyes widened and he yanked his head free of the earbuds.

'I'm *so* sorry, man,' he said.

'No problem,' Adam answered, 'I should have been looking where I was going.'

They both crouched and started to collect up the irrelevant letters.

Adam Bradley smiled.

'Is there peace in the dark silence of your mind?' he said.

Peterson's hand froze, then started trembling slightly. He looked up. He said nothing.

Bradley held out a small piece of notepaper; the only one that counted. He said quietly, 'There will be a taxi waiting for you here tonight at nine. It will take you where you need to go. I'll meet you outside. You won't tell anyone. Do you understand?'

His head moving as if through thick glue, the student nodded. 'I understand,' he said.

Bradley leaned forward and pinched the thin skin between the boy's thumb and forefinger. 'The dark silence is fine. Ignore it.'

His hand free, he scrabbled at the papers again, letting mindless drivel about his own clumsiness and ineptitude spill from his mouth.

'Really, no worries, mate,' Peterson said, 'I was listening to my iPod; I should've been paying attention.' He handed over the last of the stray sheets and they both stood up. 'I hope they weren't in any particular order.'

'No.' Bradley smiled. 'So no harm done.'

'Good.' Peterson nodded an awkward goodbye and reinserted his earbuds before carrying on towards his house.

'No real harm done,' Bradley muttered again, a satisfied smile twitching at his lips. He waited until Peterson was out of sight before crossing the road and heading down the opposite street where his car was waiting. He had two more visits to make before he could go home and relax for a couple of hours. No rest for the wicked.

Cass had all the lights blazing in the sitting room and kitchen of his flat. He might not believe in ghosts, but neither was he in the mood for the company of the jealous dead. If there were no shadows, then they couldn't lurk in them. His right nostril was numb and the back of his throat burned. He swallowed a mouthful of beer to try and wash it away. He wasn't doing the lines frequently enough for a big high, but he felt more awake than he had all day. Cocaine had a place in the world; there was no doubt about that. He'd missed it.

Staring at the computer screen in front of him, he sifted through the old newspaper and online reports of the crash that had killed the parents of the apparently dead baby. There was a picture of Elizabeth and Owen Gray, smiling and carefree, when she was clearly several months pregnant. Another showed them on their fatal holiday; still they smiled, but now the expressions didn't quite reach all the way to their eyes, and both looked thinner, with lines creasing in places they hadn't been such a short time earlier.

Cass couldn't help but feel a link with them. They were strangers' faces, but they tugged at his own damaged heart. He chopped out another long line. Fuck it. Maybe getting high was exactly what he needed. There was too much loss in the world. His own family were all gone; had this couple's 'dead' child been the much-loved cuckoo at the heart of the Jones family nest? Like Christian and Jessica, they had fair hair; were their blood types a match too?

What choices had they made that led them to their fate?

Or had the choices been made for them? He looked down at the patient notes that Jordan had managed to unearth: Jessica Jones and Elizabeth Gray had given birth within minutes of each other, but where Jessica's birth was natural, Jordan hadn't mentioned that Elizabeth's had been a C-section. Had that been planned? Had Elizabeth's pregnancy been monitored for the whole term, the happy parents blissfully unaware that *they* had a plan for their first child that didn't involve the natural parents?

He scribbled down questions he needed the grandparents to answer: who did Owen Jones work for? Why had they gone private? Had there been any unusual events leading up to Luke's – he crossed the name out; it was *Ashley*, not Luke – Ashley's birth that they could remember? Were they present at the birth? When had they last seen the baby? He leaned back in his chair. There were so many questions, and they would open up the scars of the old couple's grief – and it wasn't as if Cass could ever give them anything positive at the end of it. Even if he was honest with them, what could he say? Yes, there was a mistake in the hospital and your real grandchild lived until he was blown apart by a shotgun while he slept in his bed? That would be a neat parcel of fresh grief to haunt them for their remaining years. There were some truths that people really didn't need to know. He could show them photos, and tell them anecdotes, but they would never know the boy. No, best to leave it alone; they'd no doubt made their peace with their grief before losing their daughter.

His body was buzzing, but although the drug was doing its physical job, mentally it was dragging him down into his black mood, instead of lifting him out of it. He thought of Claire and Kate and Christian's family and his parents, all gone, and none of them naturally. Was there a cloud of death around him? How did he remain so untouched?

He lit a cigarette and went over to the window to smoke it. Maybe he should just leave the search for the boy alone. Maybe the dying lawyer had been right; perhaps some envelopes were best left sealed. He breathed out into the London air. But he *had* opened it, and he couldn't ignore his dead brother's request. He owed it to Christian, the good brother. He owed it to all his family.

Violin music drifted up at him, and he found he wasn't surprised. This time the tramp was playing 'Summertime', holding each long note perfectly between the bow and the strings. Cass didn't look down. He didn't give a shit who the musician was, or what he wanted. He could fuck off and play somewhere else.

Both phones started ringing at once, his mobile vibrating on the desk and the landline pealing out, cutting through the sound of the traffic and the strains of music from the old man outside. He picked up the mobile. There was no user name, simply the word International. Without answering, he checked the landline handset, which said the same. He stared at both for a moment, letting them continue with their demand to be answered. Coincidence? There were no coincidences, that's what Mr Bright had said not so long ago. *There is no glow.*

He answered the mobile, and as soon as he pressed the Connect button, the landline stopped ringing. In his ear he heard 'Summertime', the notes a perfect match for those outside, but this music was clearly a recording, with more than one instrument playing, and someone singing the haunting lyrics across the surface. Cass stared at both phones, and then back at the window. What the fuck was going on?

'Hello?' he said. He'd meant to hang up, but the word

had just slipped out. He knew what the fuck was going on. *They* were fucking with him. This was another part of whatever the game was that they had drawn his family into.

The laugh at the other end was soft and kind and sweet, like honey. It made Cass catch his breath. The music was lost behind it. His insides warmed as his blood pumped through his veins. He was suddenly hard.

'The boy is the key,' she said.

His cock throbbed. What was that accent? French? Russian? Neither and both.

'Don't let them keep the boy.'

The phone clicked off, and he was left with the dial tone. The violinist outside had stopped when he hung up. Cass wondered if the old man would even still be there if he looked out the window. His hands trembled, and he put the mobile down and sat at his desk. His balls ached even as his hard-on subsided. What had she done to him? No single voice had ever had such an effect on him. His insides burned. *He was glowing.* He could feel it. His vision sharpened on the edges of the shapes around him. Fuck this, he thought, taking a deep, shaky breath. She could fuck off too. He needed more drugs. He needed the arrogance cocaine could give him.

He wouldn't let them keep the lost boy. He'd find him, but he wouldn't do it for her or for anyone else. He'd find him for Christian, and woe betide anyone who got in his way.

Chapter Sixteen

Mr Bright said nothing as Mr Dublin peered through the hatch window into Mr Rasnic's room. He hadn't visited for more than a year. Mr Bright had thought maybe he wouldn't come again, but he'd been wrong. Perhaps this trip to the First city in dark times had brought out the melancholy in Mr Dublin. The other man's face remained still, but paled to the colour of his hair. The sight of one of their number like this could do that.

'I still can't believe it's him. He was always so—' He tilted his head sideways. 'He was special, even among us.' Mr Dublin's voice was like running water, crisply melodic.

Mr Bright said nothing.

'And now he's just empty. Not my brother at all.' Mr Dublin lit a slim turquoise Sobranie cigarette. On this quiet midnight hospital corridor there were no rules about smoking. Here, no outside rules applied.

'Is there any change?'

'No. Like the rest he's less agitated, but that's it. They're almost catatonic these days.'

Mr Dublin took one last long look, and then closed the hatch. His mouth twisted a fraction, the only hint at his disgust. 'He's become like them. Has he any *glow* left at all?'

'We can't tell,' Mr Bright said. 'I don't think so.'

'Then where the hell is it?'

'Lost out in the chaos before the walkways, wherever they are.' He turned and walked further into the heart of the building, past the guards standing outside various doors, and beyond where the First lay sleeping. Eventually he reached the atrium, and the indoor balcony that looked down on the activity on the floor below.

'They came back without it,' he said. 'They were scream-ing.' He looked over at the pale, slim man who had followed him. 'I had never heard a sound like it. Not even before, during all the fighting.'

'Why didn't you tell us? The Cohort? Perhaps then some of the others would be less keen to try for the walkways themselves.'

They spoke softly as the men in white coats below them checked readings and adjusted heavy white equipment. No one looked up.

'Solomon thought it was best no one knew the horrors they had suffered. I think perhaps he was right.'

'This dying would be a mercy for them. Why doesn't it take them?' Mr Dublin's question was merely thoughtful. Mr Bright had never heard him shout, or lose his temper or speak in a raised tone. In many ways, Mr Dublin was quite remarkable.

'Are they half here and half out there?'

'It would seem so. The Glow can't be destroyed, so it must be somewhere.'

'Then he is lost – this smaller body left behind isn't him; it was never him, merely a coat.' He let out a long breath of smoke. 'Perhaps we should kill them.'

'Then they would have no chance. As it stands there might come a time when we can restore them. Or they find their way back and restore themselves.'

Mr Dublin said nothing. He clearly wasn't convinced,

and Mr Bright didn't blame him. It wasn't an entirely honest answer. They needed to watch and see what happened. Maybe one day they would recover enough to speak, or at least to be one of *them* . . . if they could only let go of the madness. It would be interesting to see if it came about.

A scream ripped out through the atrium, and Mr Dublin visibly flinched, even as the men and women below continued in their work unfazed.

'What is that?'

'The experiment isn't without pain, even for them. We're making them see further than they ever have, and though we started using them so as not to lose any more of our own, when we enhance them they can travel further than we can. They don't remember the pain when they leave, that we ensure.' Mr Bright paused. He was surprised by how good it was to talk about these things to another. 'It damages them, though. I think they leave something behind, too.'

'What do they have to leave?'

'Those with some Glow leave that. I think there is something more, however.' He smiled. 'I think perhaps they have this "soul" after all. Perhaps it is the Glow for them, some kind of downgrade of our own.'

Mr Dublin stared down towards the terrible sound, as if he could somehow see the colour of it. 'Their capacity for pain astounds me.' He looked over at Mr Bright. 'He wasn't very kind to them, was he?'

'No. He was never very kind at all.'

As more screams followed the first one, they found the elevator and rode it up to the roof, where they walked out onto the terrace. The city still raged beneath them, despite the late hour and the fear of explosions. Streetlights shone down on the cars and taxis ferrying the masses through the streets. Neither Mr Bright nor Mr Dublin looked down.

The sky was clear above them, the air holding the first real chill of winter. Mr Bright smoked a thick cigar as Mr Dublin lit another of his elegant cigarettes. For a while they said nothing but stared up at the stars. Mr Bright decided that he liked Mr Dublin; there was a gentle kindness there that reminded him of Solomon. He was perhaps a touch maudlin at times, and he lacked the sort of fire Rasnic had had before the Experiment destroyed him, but beneath his fragile exterior was a quiet intellectual strength that Mr Bright respected. Also, though Rasnic was technically still alive, Mr Dublin understood the loss of a brother.

'Do you think the others have forgotten?' Mr Dublin asked. 'How it really was, I mean?'

'Some of them.'

'Or perhaps it's us,' he added. 'Have you considered that in all your machinations?'

Mr Bright said nothing to that. It had been such a very long time, and perhaps they had all changed – maybe even at the other end of the walkways. But he could clearly remember how he had felt then, the fights between the First and the despot, the need to take a side and fight on that side, the side of right. And then they'd collected the Unwanted and made their own Kingdom. Looking back, he wondered where they found the energy for it all.

'I hope you're right about your *ennui*, Mr Bright.' Mr Dublin sounded sad. 'It would be terrible for it to end like this, in a slow decay.'

Mr Bright drew on his cigar, which tasted hot and sweet. In a rare moment of self-pity he wished Solomon were here and the First would wake and they would be filled with the hope and the glory and the sheer joy of days gone by, when it was all new. He was the Architect; that was all. That he had become more to the Cohort was by chance – and as much as he enjoyed leading, and though he was well equipped for the task, he missed his brothers-in-arms. Their absence made him feel old.

'I used to find it peaceful to look up at the sky.' Mr Dublin's perfect features looked like alabaster in the moonlight. 'But now I know that somewhere out there, my brother is screaming. Him and the others.' He ground out his cigarette beneath his Italian leather sole. 'And those poor creatures in all their mortal pain as you tear at their minds, using them to serve our ends?'

He looked up again.

'There's no peace in it any more. We are merely standing in the shadow of their tormented souls.'

He smiled at Mr Bright; it was a beautifully pained expression. 'In all of this, this *ennui*, this decay, I wake every day and give thanks that I am not you, Mr Bright.' He turned away. 'Take that as you will.'

Mr Bright stood in the half-light and finished his cigar. He smiled. They had a long way to go before decay took hold. He would make sure of that.

'Tell me you've got something.' It was nearly eleven, and Cass had spent the past hour twiddling his thumbs at his desk, waiting for the secondary blood tests to come in. Eagleton had promised them by ten; if he'd known it was going to take this long he'd have gone and spoken to Elizabeth Gray's parents on the way in.

He bit back his irritation; he knew how the labs operated, and he also knew that on top of the stress of the cases, and his urgent need to find Luke, he was also on a massive coke comedown. After the strange phone call of the night before, he'd stayed up and finished off the bag. The high had been good, but this was the payoff: now he felt like shit.

'Certainly have.' Eagleton was chirpy on the other end of the phone. 'Nothing new, but something that could be relevant.'

Case put the call onto loudspeaker. 'Spit it out.'

'Gamma-Hydroxybutyric acid. GHB. Liquid X. Call it what you will.'

'You didn't pick it up in the first tests? What is going on over there?'

'Of course we picked it up.' There was a hint of professional irritation in Eagleton's voice. Here was another boy who was fast becoming a man. 'There are two problems with finding GHB in the body. First, if it's taken from an external source it only stays in the system a short while – four to six hours for the average dose. Second, and most pertinent, is that the body makes its own, post-mortem. I expected to find it, and I did – in all of the dead students. Lidster had slightly more than the others in his results, but every corpse breaks down differently. Now that we're definitely looking at him as separate from the rest of the students, then the result might mean more. GHD is recreational, but would definitely work as a sedative if someone wanted to keep him alive until his wrists had been slit.'

'Would it be easy to give it to someone without them knowing?'

'Yep—,' Eagleton was chirpy again, '—it's normally sold as a clear liquid. Pretty tasteless, maybe slightly salty, but if mixed with something with a strong taste, and if you weren't expecting it, I doubt you'd notice.'

'And I guess you can get this stuff from any street dealer?' Cass knew full well how easy drugs were to get hold of: drugs, guns, murder; anything was available to anybody in the city of London these days, especially if you had ready cash.

'Pretty much. The club scene, definitely. It's class C, so no real comeback. My money would be on GBL2 being used, rather than GHB itself. GBL2 is legal and you can get it online, and some sex shops stock it under the counter. It's from the same family of chemicals and coverts to GHB in the body, so has the same effects. The second generation is cheaper, cleaner and more dangerous – in the real world they use these chemical to strip paint and clean floors, and kids want to take them to get high? It's a crazy world we live in.'

'You were never tempted when you were at med school?' Cass asked.

'I was always high on life, Detective Inspector. Irritatingly high on it, I'm guessing now.'

'You still are. But you're getting to be fucking good at your job.'

'I love you, too.' Eagleton laughed into the phone before hanging up.

'Some sex shops keep it under the counter?' Armstrong had been listening on loudspeaker. 'Do you want to go and speak to Neil Newton's sister?'

'No,' Cass smiled, 'not the sister.'

'We can stay here all day.' Cass pulled up the blind exposing the window that separated Aaron Long's office from the throng of the work space outside and eyes peered in as they passed on their way to the photocopier or the water cooler or wherever it was people in offices went with that determined, busy stride.

'Is that your boss's office over there? Looks like he's curious too.' Cass wasn't lying. A large, middle-aged man stood watching from the doorway of an office far larger than Cass's and Long's put together.

'For God's sake, you can't do this.' Aaron Long almost kept the whine out of his voice, but the hint of it over-shadowed the strength of his conviction. 'Emma told you how it happened – you've spoken to her already.'

'Yes, we did.' Armstrong had taken a seat. 'But you know how women can be: confused, muddled. Forgetful.'

'And sometimes they just downright lie.' Cass turned back from the glass.

Aaron Long looked from one policeman to the other. 'It's like Emma said. We stayed up late after dinner, and then Neil got a cab.' His eyes darted out the window and across to where the silent figure stood appraising the tableau they'd created. Cass recognised the insecurity and fear in that glance.

'If all this is a lie out of some sense of misplaced loyalty, then you need to know that we *will* find out. I'm known for my solve rate, and this murder isn't even complicated. You'll get the sack – that's if they don't throw you in prison – and you won't get another job, because, let's face it, there aren't any.' Cass spoke calmly, his eyes never once leaving Long's. 'All of this I could understand – and to be fair, I'd probably admire you for it – if you were taking that risk for your wife. But for Neil Newton? That odious little twat? I doubt you even like him. Shit, I doubt your *wife* even likes him.'

Aaron Long swallowed, and Cass watched the bump of his Adam's apple rise as if willing him to spit out the words. He didn't look at Cass, but out through the glass.

'I can't stand him. He gives me the creeps.'

'That makes you sane. Don't let him make a cunt out of you. There's a dead boy in this story.'

Long looked towards Cass. 'Dinner was over quickly. I got snappy with him and he took it personally. He left just before nine, I think; around then, anyway. He did take a cab though.'

'Thank you.' Cass smiled. The pressure inside that was pulling him to the ground eased a little in his shoulders. Perhaps Joe Lidster's fingers were starting to let go.

It didn't take long for Newton to break. His sweat levels had reached critical mass before they'd even got him into the interview room. Cass has been tempted to line the chair with a plastic bag before the man sat down.

Newton snivelled into the back of his jewelled hand, 'I didn't mean it! I didn't really want to do it.'

Cass didn't offer any platitudes, but he lit a cigarette and slid a box of tissues across the table. It was a lie, of course. What Newton really meant was that he wished he hadn't done it now. Then he'd meant it. This was no crime of passion with a handy tyre-iron. This was, in its own way, premeditated. To Cass, anything outside of a moment of instinct was premeditated. Newton had thought this through before he'd started it, and the sneaky fucker had almost got away with it.

'We know you left your sister's house before nine. What happened next?'

Newton ran his hand over his greased-back hair, adding more odorous liquid to the dampness of his palm.

'It had been a God-awful evening,' he sniffed. 'They look down on me, you know. Always have. He makes out it's because I occasionally borrow money from my mother and he thinks that's wrong in a son, but then I don't have the luxury of a high-paying job. I had the initiative to go into business for myself, and they're stupid if they think I don't see how they look down on me for what I do ... And then of course there's my lifestyle.' His words were turning into one long whine.

'If you could keep to the point, Mr Newton?'

'I am.' The angry eyes that darted up to Cass's were feral and mean and full of self-pity. 'It's what started it. Emma asked me if I'd started seeing anyone – its been a while since I last had any meaningful relationship – and although part of me knows she doesn't really care and just thinks if I met someone then she wouldn't have to bloody invite me to Christmas, I was almost about to tell her about Joe and then that awful husband of hers made some joke about how I was dead in gay years, surely. I sniped back with something about him not being able to give Emma any children, and after that I left. You can imagine the evening had gone a little sour.'

Newton's sneer made clear that he felt his brother-in-law's barb had been worse than his own. Cass liked him even less for that pettiness. Murder was one thing, and everyone was capable of it in some circumstance or other, but this self-pitying prissiness was something else.

'You were seeing Joe Lidster?' Armstrong asked.

'No.' Newton shook his greasy head and blew his snotty nose before taking a deep breath and sitting up slightly taller in his seat. 'But I had hopes. I loved him, you see.'

He met Cass's gaze with a look that defied the DI to challenge the purity of that emotion.

Cass didn't give a fuck. He knew enough about love to know that there was nothing pure about it. It was a greedy, selfish emotion that rolled like a pig in the muck of life, and Newton was testament to that.

'And you killed him,' Cass said.

'I got home and heard Joe talking, so I locked up. First of

all I thought he must be on the phone, and it actually cheered me up a bit. I thought I'd persuade him to have a sherry or beer with me, and then I could unwind and laugh about Emma and her awful husband and all their middle-class ways. As I got up the stairs and heard a second voice – a male voice – I realised he'd brought someone back to the flat.' His mouth tightened. 'It came as a bit of a shock. He'd never done that before. Anyway, I thought perhaps I'd offer them both a drink, you know, be sociable. I could hear them talking, so I presumed they weren't actually doing anything and I was curious to see who this man was. It may sound odd, but it encouraged me, that he had a man there, I mean. I hadn't realised that he'd been looking for someone, so I hadn't been overly forward.'

Cass could only imagine what kind of clumsy flirtation Neil Newton had been attempting up until then. Their ideas of subtle were undoubtedly miles apart.

'It was stupid of me. I found that out.' Newton blew his nose again.

'What happened?'

'I went to knock on his door and I heard them. They were laughing. The other man said something about how my home was a "shit-hole", and he didn't understand how Joe could live there and not go mad. Then Joe said ... He that if the other man met me then he'd understand the flat.'

His brow furrowed and his eyes dried. Cass, Armstrong and the interview room were gone and Newton was back in that moment. 'They were *laughing* at me. Joe said things about me – hurtful things, worse than anything Emma's Aaron ever said. He said things about how I looked, and what I wore. He called me a preened chicken who thought it was a peacock – they both laughed a lot at that one.' He stopped, and blew his nose again.

He looked down at his hands, then whispered, 'I just stood there and listened. I couldn't bring myself to move even though I felt sick. They were laughing at me as if I was *nothing*. Joe was laughing. He called me pathetic and pitiful – and then he said that I meant well, in my own simpering way.' He looked up at Cass. 'Can you imagine? After *everything* I'd done for him? After I'd let him share my home?'

'He paid rent,' Cass said. 'He was your *lodger*.'

'You don't understand,' Newton said. 'It was all unsaid, but it was there.'

'So what did you do?'

'I went back to my room and sat there for a few minutes, just feeling numb and angry. The newspaper was still on the floor, from where I'd been reading in bed the night before, and the whole front page was going on about these student suicides.' Newton's mouth twitched nervously. 'I waited until I heard the other man leave. Then I went down to the shop and got a bottle of GBL from the stock-room and two sets of fluffy cuffs.' He looked at Armstrong nervously, as if having a bottle of a controlled substance in his possession was somehow going to make the murder charge worse. 'Then I made two Irish coffees and poured a couple of capfuls into one of them.'

He took a deep breath before continuing and Cass noticed his hands were trembling. Was Newton only just realising the enormity of what he'd done?

'I took the drinks into his room and pretended to be interested in his new boyfriend. We chatted as if everything was perfectly normal and I told him about what Aaron had said and Joe told me to take no notice and that I was a very attractive man. But this time I could see him laughing – he was just a boy, and he was *laughing* at me. He'd *always* been laughing at me and I just hadn't seen it.' He gritted his teeth at the memory.

'He started to get woozy pretty quickly. I told him I must have made the drink too strong and said I'd get a glass of water. I came back with the cuffs and the knife. He panicked a bit then, I could see it in his eyes, but he couldn't get himself off the bed. I wrote the "Chaos in the darkness" sign and then I cut his wrists.' Newton's lip trembled and tears spilled over his cheeks. It was the moment. Every killer like this had it: the instant when they saw what they'd done, and what they'd become, when they really couldn't believe the awfulness of it.

He was speaking almost by rote now, as if all the emotion had been leached from him. 'It was harder than I expected, and my hands were shaking so much, and I couldn't look at him. Right then I hated him. I didn't want to look at those beautiful dark eyes. I left him there and I went back to my room. I changed my clothes and drank my coffee. After half an hour I went to check on him and he was dead. I just had to look at the amount of blood all over the bed to know that. I hadn't realised—' His breath caught in his throat. 'I hadn't realised there'd be so much blood. He looked so pale.'

Finally, he burst into tears. 'I loved him.'

Cass watched the man snivel and sob and mutter empty words into his damp sleeves and crumpled tissues. Joe Lidster had been right. Neil Newton *was* a pathetic little man. What Lidster had not yet learned about the world – what he now never would – was that the weak and pathetic could often be the most dangerous.

'No, you didn't,' Cass broke in to Newton's self-obsessed litany, 'you killed him. In cold blood.'

The words hit Newton like a slap in the face, and he

blinked several times. Reality was settling in, and it didn't look like it was a good feeling.

Cass threw a follow-up punch. 'We will be charging you with first degree murder. You had better get your affairs in order.'

He stood up and headed for the door. Despite the cigarettes he'd smoked throughout the interview, the room was still filled with Newton's cloying stench. Now, beneath the cologne and the sweat and the hair gel, the pungent smell of fear fought its way to the surface.

'Wait – first degree murder?' Newton's pudgy face had paled. 'But that— That's the death penalty, isn't it?'

Cass said nothing.

'But they can't— I mean, I didn't mean to— Oh dear God! Oh dear God . . .'

Newton was still muttering pleas to a God that couldn't help him when Cass closed the door and left him to the booking sergeant. His belt and shoes would be gone soon, and then reality would really grip Newton. There was nowhere to hide in a prison cell. Cass had spent his own time in one a long time ago. But unlike Newton, Cass had got out.

Cass carefully took Joe Lidster's smiling face down from the board and slid it into the buff folder. It was good to have one less to look at.

'His parents will sleep better tonight,' Armstrong said.

'Let's hope so.' Cass wasn't convinced. Answers didn't always bring peace. They just brought knowledge, which was a different thing entirely. The trick was to make your peace with the knowledge, and not everyone could do that.

He looked at the board, and the young faces that stared

back at his own. There were no answers for them yet. He frowned as he paused at Jasmine Green, so different in the laughing photo from the dead body half in and half out of the television. The earlier conversation with her boyfriend echoed in his head.

'I want to see their medical records. Jasmine's boyfriend didn't know anything useful about a cash-in-hand job, but he did say she had claustrophobia. Let's see if the rest of them had any personal issues like that. There has to be something.'

'I'm on it.'

'Put in the request and we'll take a look at them in the morning with fresh eyes. We've worked hard enough for today.'

This time Armstrong didn't argue with him. Back in his office, Cass pulled out the piece of paper with Elizabeth Gray's parents' address on it. If he left now he could be there by half-seven, even in the rush-hour traffic.

'You seen this, Cass?' the desk sergeant asked as he headed out the door.

'What?'

'More bombs.' The man nodded at the TV screen under the high desk wall. 'New York, this time. These people are fucking crazy.'

Cass watched the images for a second. More burning, more smoke, more death. People pouring out of Metro stations, and the wreck of a bus filling a street. It was London and Moscow all over again – it was the wood, though, and not the trees.

'Yeah, it's terrible,' Cass said, turning his back on the miniaturised devastation. 'But I've got smaller things to worry about.'

*

He was at his car when David Fletcher rang from an unknown number. When Cass answered, he half-expected to hear that beautiful voice from the previous night on the other end. It took a moment before he registered it was the head of the ATD, even after he'd introduced himself.

'What are you calling me for?'

'It's about Abigail Porter,' Fletcher said, 'the woman whose sister killed herself.'

'What about her?' Tall, willowy limbs, and a flash of silver in her eyes. Cass didn't need reminding who Abigail Porter was.

'She's gone missing.'

'She's not with her parents?'

'No. That wouldn't qualify as missing.'

For a moment Cass said nothing. Porter was the PM's bodyguard. The suicide of a sibling was terrible news to hear – Cass knew that himself – but he doubted it would make her do anything crazy. She'd have been psyche-evaluated a thousand times over in her job, and whatever grief she felt would be normal and manageable ... Unless she'd just snapped, of course. You could never tell what was going on under the surface.

'I can only repeat my question,' he said, eventually. 'What are you calling me for?' It's not my fucking problem, was what he really wanted to say, but David Fletcher was a person who could make his life difficult, and though it might be late in the game to learn diplomacy, Cass had quite enough shit to deal with without adding to it by being unnecessarily rude.

'Trust me, I didn't want to. Personally, I don't see what some fucked-up DI from Paddington Green can do that I can't.'

'You've read my file, then.' Cass almost laughed. At least Fletcher was honest.

'Several times.'

'And you're still calling me?'

'Apparently you have friends in high places. This is a national security issue and I didn't want to share it with you at all, but it appears I have no choice.'

'So who told you to call me?' The first stirrings of a chill knowledge settled in Cass's stomach. *Wheels within wheels.*

'My boss, but I don't know who the fuck told him. And I don't care. The outcome's the same. I'm supposed to get you transferred to Special Branch. You need to come in and be debriefed.'

Fletcher sounded like he was talking through gritted teeth, and Cass didn't blame him. They were both getting their strings pulled, and Cass knew who was doing it: the elusive Mr Bright. What the fuck did he want with Cass now? What did Abigail Porter's disappearance have to do with him – and why would he give a shit anyway?

'They're telling me it's because the CNS have their hands full dealing with this spate of global attacks, but I'm not buying it. I don't know who you are, Jones, but someone obviously thinks you're better at your job than I am.'

'I wouldn't bank on that,' Cass said, 'but tell your boss this: there's no transfer to Special Branch – I've got cases I'm working that I'm not leaving. But I am curious, and I'll listen to what you've got to say, because, trust me, I want to know as much as you do why someone would want me in particular on this case. But there're no promises.'

'He's not going to like it.'

'Well then, we'll see how much he really wants me on the case then. Those are my terms.'

'Okay. I'll see you at the CNS in an hour.'

'No, I've got some stuff to do. It can wait until tomorrow.' He paused. Fuck it, he might as well push as far as he could. 'And you can come to Paddington Green.' He hung up before Fletcher could protest. He fought the urge to look around him. Even if Mr Bright was watching him, he wouldn't see it. The Network were too damned good. He hadn't noticed their presence in his life for the first thirty-six years; he was unlikely to spot them around now.

He pushed Abigail Porter out of his head. She was tomorrow's problem. For now, he had other issues to deal with.

Chapter Seventeen

'Turn that TV down, Roger.' Cathleen Watson placed the tray on the table between her and Cass as her husband begrudgingly did as he was told. The devastation in New York faded to a gentle hum as the images screamed more quietly from the screen.

'I don't see why anyone would be asking questions about it now, that's all,' Roger Watson muttered. 'No offence, but I'd have thought there would be more pressing matters for the police these days. What exactly are you here for?'

'Don't be so rude!' Cathleen apologised for her husband as she poured.

Cass hadn't known anyone still used a tea service any more outside of period drama, but this one even had a sugar bowl that matched. His hand felt clumsy around the thin china handle. 'It's all right; he has a point,' he said with a smile. 'I'm really investigating Flush5 – there have been some complaints about the way they operate. Nothing I can go into detail about; I'm just trying to get a sense of their background. I hope this won't bring back too many painful memories for you.'

'It's nice to talk about them. We don't do that much now.' Mrs Watson sipped her own tea. 'You know how time is. It doesn't heal, but it does put things in boxes for you. It's how we all go on, I suppose.'

Cass's smile was genuine. He liked this woman. He understood boxes.

'Why did Elizabeth have a C-section? Can you remember?'

'She hadn't thought she'd needed one. As far as she was concerned, everything was fine, but then she got a call that morning saying the doctor had been double-checking some scans and they thought her placenta might be obstructing the birth canal. She went back for a secondary scan that evening when Owen got home, and they decided to get the baby out straight away.' A ghost of pain flashed across her eyes. 'Not that it helped the baby, poor little mite. She barely saw him. I don't remember if she even held him, not when he was alive.' She stirred her tea, even though she hadn't added sugar to it. 'They didn't let her see him for hours; he was cold by then. She didn't want to see him again after that.'

Cass looked down at his own cup. Of course the baby was cold. They'd probably had to source one. Where had they brought it up from, the hospital mortuary? A nearby morgue? A time-share dead baby. He fought the image of the two women, both now dead: one crying and one smiling, both over the same child, while another was stolen away.

'And then of course the accident happened such a short while later.' Mrs Watson's smile was wistful. 'They'd gone away to recover. Life is full of cruel ironies, don't you think?'

Cass wondered how the woman would feel if she realised just how ironic her words really were. Part of him wanted to tell them that the baby they thought they'd lost had grown to be well loved, even by a father who had doubts about whether they were the same flesh and blood. He wanted to tell them about the things Luke had liked and disliked, the things that made him laugh and made him smile. Maybe they'd recognise their own daughter in some of it – but he couldn't share any, because the story would end with a shotgun and a cold, dead child, and then their grief would be fresh all over again. He wasn't sure these two could live with that knowledge. Their pain had settled into a quiet ache over the years, he could see that. He wouldn't tear open those scars.

'Why did she go private for the birth? Was that a personal choice?'

'It was Owen's job. He didn't even realise it was part of his package. I mean, he had some medical benefits, but he hadn't realised they covered his spouse as well, especially not for maternity. She was six months gone before he found out. His boss told him.'

'Who did he work for?'

'I can't remember now – some financial company with a foreign name. Something Swiss, I think.'

'Cathleen,' Roger Watson cut in, 'you're not supposed to talk about any of this. For God's sake, woman, can't you ever keep your mouth shut?'

'It's all such a long time ago now – surely it's all right? I mean, we're not talking about the case, are we?'

'What case?' Cass asked. His fingers tightened around the fragile handle of the cup so hard he feared it might snap. 'Why aren't you supposed to talk about this?'

'They were going to sue.' Roger Watson leaned forward in his chair. Perhaps he'd had enough of staying silent. 'Owen was unhappy with the way the hospital had handled the birth. It was nothing we understood because we didn't get there until it was all over, but he had a bee in his bonnet about something. To be honest, I just wanted him to calm down and let my girl grieve, to let all of us get over this terrible thing. But he wouldn't let it go.'

'That's why we paid for the holiday. Owen was getting into trouble at work for kicking up a fuss, and he was starting some kind of malpractice suit, but none of it was going to bring little Ashley back. So we thought the holiday would be good for them.'

Her face twitched with feelings she couldn't express – or couldn't allow herself to express.

Cass wondered at the weight of her guilt. He wondered if he should tell her that by paying for the holiday they hadn't influenced Fate or Luck, or any of that bullshit. He had a feeling that all the Watsons had done was just make things slightly easier for the people who were finding Owen Gray's refusal to let go of his son's death an inconvenience.

'And then they died,' Roger Watson said, 'and we thought about carrying on with it, like Owen would have wanted, and Elizabeth would have wanted because she would have stood by him, but then there were all these complications with their life insurance payouts, because of the faulty car. We were having problems getting their bodies back from France.' He looked back at the television, as if the devastation showing there was a comfort compared to what he'd lost.

'And then a man came to see us and he offered us a settlement.' Cathleen Watson's eyes darted across to her husband and back again. 'We were tired. We'd lost everything.'

'We took their money.' Roger Watson glared defiantly at Cass. 'And I don't regret it. We got our daughter's body back and we laid them all to rest. Together.'

'Was the life insurance issue resolved then too?' Cass asked.

'Yes.'

'And didn't you find that a little odd?'

'What I found odd,' Roger Watson stood up, 'is none of your business. I didn't care about odd. I just wanted it over.'

Cass took the other man's action as his own prompt and got to his feet. 'I'm sorry if I've caused you any offence or upset, Mr Watson. I'm just trying to do my job.'

'That's fine.' Cathleen Watson favoured her husband with a glare. 'You haven't caused any trouble at all.' She smiled. 'Let me walk you to the door.'

In the hallway, Cass stopped. 'I don't suppose you remember the name of the doctor working on the ward that night, do you?'

Mrs Watson opened her mouth to speak, but it was her husband, in the sitting room doorway, who got some words out first. 'No. We don't.'

Cathleen Watson shut her mouth and smiled apologetically.

'I don't suppose you do,' Cass said, and smiled at the man whose grandchild he'd bounced on his knee and kicked a football around with.

The door closed behind him.

Cass got in the car, but sat watching the house for a few minutes longer. The curtains didn't twitch. They were glad he was gone, and were probably turning the TV up and talking loudly to each other about the news to shoo away any ghost of his presence. Maybe money truly was the root of all evil. It was the root of their guilt, that much was for sure. They'd taken the settlement rather than find out the truth, and they'd learned to live with that, but living with something and thinking you'd done the right thing were poles apart. He'd seen that in the defiance in Roger Watson's eyes. His phone buzzed. An email from Perry Jordan. He smiled.

At home, he opened a beer, plugged the BlackBerry into the printer and waited for it to spit the sheet of staff names out. It was a short list, and that was fine with Cass. Next to the names were phone numbers and current addresses. He sighed and leaned backwards in his chair, stretching his arms out so far that his shoulders cracked. Outside, the violin played something light, nineteen thirties, maybe, with a flavour of France between the notes. Cass ignored it. The old tramp wasn't causing him any bother, and if he was Mr Bright's spy in the camp then he wasn't seeing very much from out there. Somehow it didn't feel likely. The violinist was too obvious for Mr Bright's methods. Mr Bright was a man who lived in the shadows; a puppet-master in the darkness high above the gods of this theatre – it wouldn't be like him to let the strings show.

He looked down at the list of names. The doctor listed as working the maternity ward of Flush5's wing of the hospital was Andrew Gibbs. His current address was Muswell Hill, London. Cass's stomach turned slightly. It was a small world. He punched the attached number into his phone and stored it. He could find out where Gibbs was working now easily enough, after he'd heard what David Fletcher had to say. His eyes ached from too many sleepless nights; it was time for an early one.

His turned the sitting room light off and headed for his cool, empty bed. As darkness ate the room up, Cass turned his back on the hungry eyes of the dead that screamed out at him from the corners. He hadn't forgotten them. Tomorrow he'd go through their medical records and see if he could find some similarity between the students that way. For now, they could get off his case. He needed to sleep.

He dreamed of Owen Gray and Christian. They were standing side by side and smiling.

'How much more do we have to do?' Mr Yakama said.

The man being addressed turned back from refilling his tea cup and looked around at his audience. Mr Yakama was somewhere near the back. There was no formal meeting table here; Monmir had dispensed with that some time ago. Now the vast space was filled with huge cushions and ornate chaises longues, each with its own hookah alongside. There was an elegance to the place that recalled Monmir's own understated elegance.

'Plenty,' he said, sipping the sweet mint tea. 'This is only the beginning.'

The hookahs remained untouched. It didn't surprise the man. He remembered the lepers of old as they clutched with rotten hands and begged to be healed, back when all this was just part of some glorious game. These of his number had that same desperate look.

Morelo coughed, a loud, hacking sound that set off a wave of flinching around the gathering. It had taken all that one's energy to get out of the hospital in Russia and make his way here, and now it was obvious to all that he didn't have long left. That suited the man who stood healthy among the sick. When they lost all hope they became a liability.

'You have to keep your dyings hidden for as long as you can.' He wondered if they hated him for his health. Probably. He would despise them if the roles were reversed. 'If Mr Bright comes to realise that this *ennui*, as he calls the cruel fate that is upon you, has spread so far, he'll start to look for a conspiracy and come for you all.'

Eyes widened. Morelo was the only one of the Inner

Cohort present; the rest of the number came from the First Cohort, with a few from the second.

'He's not a fool.' Morelo's voice was barely audible; bark crumbling on an old tree. 'He knows.'

'Yes, he does, but he doesn't know *who*, and that's what counts.'

'We need to get home soon,' Morelo said. 'How much more do we have to destroy for his forgiveness? All of it? Ourselves?'

'How much sacrifice does he want?'

'Is the emissary here?'

'Yes, I saw the signs. There is one.'

'Can we see them?'

'I can't die here.'

The voices came all at once on breath that stank of dead earth. He lifted one hand. 'I understand your concerns. I feel your pain. But we are on the right path and all the pieces are nearly in place. The Interventionists you helped release have caused chaos in three of the major cities. More cities will follow. Their leaders will fall. The world will sink into the collapse that has been its destiny for years, and then we shall be allowed home.' He paused for full effect. 'But you must be patient. And in order for me to undertake this during your sicknesses, I will need access to command some of your businesses and resources. Documents have been prepared and are waiting in your cars to be signed. I have planes ready to take you back to your sectors as soon as we are concluded here. From then, you must be strong and await further instruction.'

'It seems so very little to do after all this time.' Morelo sank back into the chaise longue. 'I would have thought he would demand more.'

It would be better if Morelo went to his dying sooner

rather than later, the man mused. But then, dying, from what he had observed, could be a sudden occurrence. Especially in the very sick.

'It's been a long time,' a voice from the back argued for him.

'Yes, things might have changed.'

'I can't die here.'

He said nothing. The sickly were tiresome and an embarrassment, but for now a necessity. He'd learned that during the millennia that had passed; there was no greater motivator than fear of death, and the dying always allowed themselves to be fooled quite easily in the name of hope. He sipped his tea.

When they had gone, he dismissed his man and walked through the long stone corridors of the mosque. It was not yet time for prayer, and his feet barely made a sound on the red patterned carpet. Above his head, pale lights hung in bronze baskets from the pinched archways. The mosque had been built more than a thousand years before, when Monmir had had a sense of humour. In those days the area, part of the medina quarter, had been surrounded by sellers of manuscripts, so its name had been derived from the word *al-Koutoubiyyin*, the Arabic for librarian. Beneath the surface of this iconic place of worship were now housed one of the original scrolls of the Story, kept safe and revered, and only ever seen by the Inner Cohort. It truly was a place of history.

The air was cooling, but was still too warm for a jacket. As he stepped outside, the noise from Djemaa el Fna tumbled towards him. He watched the mêlée, hundreds of people filling the dusty square, and as a light breeze from the desert teased his hair, he understood why Monmir liked this part of the world so much. It reminded him, too, of places long forgotten. Unlike Monmir, he wasn't sentimental enough to make it his home, though. What was done was done.

He wandered towards the square, enjoying the freedom and wildness of the sandy city. Lights from the dozens of food stalls shone upwards, forming a halo in the clear sky, and mopeds screeched and buzzed their weaving way through the acrobats and storytellers who entertained the crowds. Others cried their wares, selling henna tattoos, rare spices, bottles of water ... Of course, here as everywhere, the world had become smaller, and the flash of pale skin would prompt the hawkers to use the only English phrases they knew: *Asda price! Tesco price! Lovely jubberly*, and the tourists would smile in amusement, and perhaps it would make them stop and sample the fish, or taste a vegetable tagine, before heading into the narrow alleys of the souk. There they'd be pestered into buying leather goods or fili-gree silver, and though they'd be proud of their haggling skills, cutting the price down to what they considered reasonable, still they would invariably walk away feeling done out of their precious dinars, regardless of the sum finally agreed.

He recognised Mr Craven in the distance as the man emerged from the hustle and bustle of the medina's main square and wandered in his direction. It was always easy to spot one of their own; he would have picked him out of a crowd anywhere, even now, after they had all been small for so long. He didn't change his pace, and neither did Mr Craven. Both men strolled casually through the night, and eventually they came face to face.

'It appears we both wanted a change of scene,' Mr Craven said. He pulled a paper bag of sugared almonds from his jacket pocket and gave it to the children around him with a command in French to go and entertain themselves for a few moments. They scuttered off in the sand, squealing at each other in guttural Arabic as they fought over the sweets. Mr Craven watched them and smiled for a moment, before turning back.

'Coincidence?'

'I don't believe in coincidences, Mr Craven.'

'Who does? I heard a whisper of a secret meeting. I was curious.' Mr Craven's thin lips were barely visible in the gloom of the evening as he spoke. 'Not curious enough to attend, though. Not yet.'

'There are always rumours of secret meetings, you know that. There's rarely any truth in them.'

Mr Craven laughed a little, and the two men walked for the sake of it, their slow pace matched.

'I hear the missing Interventionists might be down to you,' Mr Craven said.

'Be careful of making accusations you can't prove.' He kept his tone light. Menace was often best delivered that way.

'Ah, but this is merely an observation,' Mr Craven countered. 'You have nothing to fear from me. I've just been considering whether I too should hedge my bets. And if indeed there is something to hedge them with, or whether this might just be a ruse disguising some other motivation.'

'Sometimes I think you think too much, Mr Craven.'

'How ironic. I've recently been thinking that I haven't spent enough time thinking at all.' Mr Craven kept his gaze forward. 'Don't you trust the Experiment?'

'It's hardly producing results. One can't help but wonder if perhaps there is another way to get home, before this dying comes for us all. Hypothetically speaking, of course.'

'Of course.' Mr Craven's thin lips split into a tight smile.

'And we all know forgiveness never did come without a price. It's just that you had never struck me as being overly concerned with the common good.'

'We're all concerned with the common good when its interests merge with our own.'

'Too true.' Mr Craven's laugh was dry as the parched sand that danced in the breeze. 'Well, consider me, in this case, a trustworthy ally.' His feet stopped. 'Of course, I'll still support the Experiment, and I am, as ever, loyal to the Inner Cohort.'

'As am I.'

'But I presume this meeting is best kept between ourselves?'

'That would be preferable.'

'As I thought, then.' Mr Craven turned and headed back in the direction of the playing children.

'Might I ask why you're so interested?' He couldn't fight his own curiosity. Despite his clever brain and his promotion to the Inner Cohort, Mr Craven had shown little interest in their politics in a long time.

'Let's just say,' Mr Craven looked up at the night sky before letting his lips form a wistful smile, 'that my circumstances have changed.' And he walked away, strolling through the sand as if he didn't have a care in the world.

For the first time, looking at the receding figure, he felt a twinge of fear. He pulled out a slim mobile phone and dialled.

'Asher Red,' said a voice before the second ring had quite finished.

'How are things?'

'We have the three. One seems to be having difficulties, however.'

'What sort of difficulties?'

'Slowed responses. I think perhaps it's affecting her more quickly than the other two. She might be of no value to you in this endeavour.'

'Make sure the other two are ready.'

'They will be. The British one in particular … well, I do believe she must have had some of your blood in her. She's quite remarkable.'

He hung up the phone. As each day passed he was placing himself in a more dangerous position. The sooner he acted, the better. Mr Bright was no fool and he still had the First; despite his *sleeping*, as Mr Bright and Mr Solomon insisted on calling it, that one was still revered. But still, he thought, analysing the small moment of emotion he had just experienced, fear was a great motivator.

Thunder roared over London's dawn, trying in vain to catch the lightning that darted across the city. Mr Bright watched the endless dance from his apartment in The Bank's headquarters by the river. He hadn't used the place much since Solomon's demise, but he had always liked it, and being back gave him a sense of stability in these uncertain times. Not that he was overly worried. He understood the chessboard, and all the pieces on it. There was very little that could surprise him these days. He might not have names or numbers, but he was aware that a conspiracy was brewing – it had ever been thus with them. They had maintained their peace and camaraderie with each other for a long, long time, and he'd always known that couldn't last.

This, however, this was causing him some mild concern. He looked down at the phone on his desk.

'So another has gone?'

'Yes. Just vanished, an hour ago. I was at home. I was …'

'So that's three.' One dead on the Underground station

in London, the second vanished from the House two afternoons before, and now this third. He might not have any photographic evidence of it yet, but he knew these two must have died in Moscow and New York. Three lots of bombings; three Interventionists dead . . . but to what end? And who was pulling the strings?

'I find it so hard to believe that they could do these things – that they would go out there. They've never wanted to. And now this? This I just don't understand.'

Sudden light flashed in a sheet across the uneven skyline outside, highlighting every tiny drop in the mass of rain that tumbled from the sky. For a brief second each one stood alone, and then it was gone, caught up in the driving force of those behind it.

'Calm down and speak slowly, DeVore. What is it you don't understand?'

'They're not projecting. They stopped twenty-eight minutes ago.'

'All of them?' Mr Bright turned away from the mesmerising weather.

'Yes. The data flow just stopped – from each – in the same second. I don't understand it.'

'Are you sure they're not reflecting?' His question was stupid and he knew it; his irritation with himself grew. It annoyed him more that DeVore thought he actually needed the question answered.

'If they were reflecting the stream would still be coming in. We'd see what they were seeing. They haven't reflected in a long time, and I still can't tell if any in the House are hard Reflections and now this . . .'

'The point, DeVore? If they're not projecting, then what do you think they're doing?' *Are they dying?* The thought came to him from nowhere and he carefully swallowed it down. There was no *dying*. There was only *ennui*. He would not be fooled by the panic. He still had control, and the First and the boy were still breathing.

'They're singing,' DeVore said, 'listen. It's astounding.' Somewhere in a warmer climate the man on the end of the phone released the noise from within the Chamber and an orchestra of sweet voices poured down the phone.

For a moment, the sound almost touched Mr Bright's heart. He hadn't heard singing like that in such a long time.

'Isn't it beautiful?' DeVore could barely be heard over the flood of voices.

Mr Bright listened for a few seconds longer. Yes, it was beautiful, but he didn't much care for it. What did it mean? Why were they singing now?

'Keep this to yourself, DeVore,' he said after a moment, 'and let me know when they stop.'

He put the phone down and turned back to the window, staring out at the rain to steady his thinking. Something was being added to the game. He made himself fresh coffee and sipped it thoughtfully. Eventually he smiled. It was nice to feel surprised occasionally, and there were very few outcomes that he hadn't prepared for.

An hour later, though, as he sat by the First's bed, he wished he could get the strains of 'Rhapsody in Blue' out of his head. It was starting to annoy him.

Chapter Eighteen

As he closed the main door to the flats behind him, Cass noted two things: first, that the thundering rains of the early morning might have passed, but they'd taken the warmth of the Indian summer with them, and second, that the violinist had gone back to his old favourite, 'Rhapsody in Blue'. It took him a moment to spot the tramp – he'd expected him to be closer, but this morning he'd chosen a place further up the street. It was a surprise. The music had been clearly audible from upstairs, and even now it appeared to weave through the pedestrians towards Cass as if it knew its mark.

The tramp flicked his wrist between notes, the bow coming up in a gesture of hello, and his dirty face cracked into a smile. Cass didn't return it. He should ignore the crazy old bastard; he should go straight to his car and drive to work where the head of the Anti-Terror Division would be waiting and to where the grip of the dead was impatiently dragging him. There was no time for this. His feet, however, didn't move.

Fuck it. Leaving his car behind him, he walked towards the violinist, who made no movement to meet him halfway but carried on smiling and playing as if jazz on the streets of St John's Wood at eight o'clock in the morning was the most natural thing in the world. As he drew closer, Cass saw the small pile of coins scattered at the old man's feet and felt a moment of surprise. There was no hat or tin or sign begging for change – this money had been given without any prompt. A woman in a suit barely paused as she passed, but two gold one-pound coins slipped from her fingers to the pavement. She smiled sweetly to no one and everyone and kept going. It had been a long time since Cass had seen anyone give away money on the streets. Hard times made people mean and selfish.

He looked up at the tramp. He was dirtier than before, and he thought perhaps there was another tooth missing from the man's upper jaw. In the bright morning light, blue varicose veins were visible in the gap where his too-short trousers ended and his shoes began. As far as Cass could see, none of this degradation was dampening his spirit; the filthy fingers moved deftly across the strings as his smiling eyes stayed firmly on Cass.

'Who's the woman?' Cass asked. He didn't have time for pleasantries.

'Woman?' The gruff voice was at odds with the notes that poured from his hands.

'The one on the phone.'

The smile widened, and Cass noted the dirt wedged around the yellow teeth. It was black and earthy. How the hell did someone get mud in their mouth? Surely that would take some concerted effort?

'She's something else, isn't she?'

'It looks like everything turns out to be something else these days.' Cass didn't smile back. He didn't want to be friends with the tramp. He wanted the tramp to fuck off and play his music to someone else, and save Cass more questions he couldn't find answers to.

'Never a truer word spoken in jest, son.' The old man

laughed a little, the sound a rattle in his chest. It reminded Cass of Artie Mullins. It was the sound of too many nights spent in the company of cigarette smoke and hard liquor. 'Although some would say that also ain't exactly possible,' the tramp continued, his fingers never missing a note. 'What is, is. It's just your perspective on it that changes.'

'Who is she?' Cass asked. He didn't need this head-fuckery bullshit.

'I told you – she's something else.' He grinned and winked.

'You need a fucking toothbrush,' Cass muttered before turning and heading to his car. *Something else.* What kind of a fucking answer was that? Exactly the kind he'd expected, he thought as he lit a cigarette and slid behind the wheel. Questions as answers. It was the story of his fucking life.

Cass had barely stepped inside his office when Armstrong appeared in the doorway.

'The students' medical records have just come off the printer and the ATD are downstairs to see you. With David Fletcher.'

Cass hadn't needed telling. There had been three sleek, dark cars and a Mercedes van parked up outside, and anyone working out of Paddington Green nick who'd had anything like a half-decent car had flogged it after the 'bonuses for cocaine' scandal – even those bought entirely legitimately, to avoid drawing attention to their owners: guilt by association. As it was, they were all guilty to some degree, even if they hadn't been part of Bowman's personal drug gang. Cass had kept his Audi, though. They could get screwed if he was going to be a pariah *and* drive an old banger.

'They can wait ten minutes while I grab a coffee.'

Armstrong stepped inside. 'According to the desk sergeant, they got here at half-seven. They must get up early over at the CNS. He said they even brought their own equipment.' He finally got round to the question Cass had been waiting for. 'What do they want with you? Is this to do with the case? If so, maybe I should come down with you ...'

Cass turned on his computer before he looked up. In the corridor outside, people were wandering up and down, and he felt their eyes stray into his office as they passed. It wasn't only Armstrong who was watching him strangely; he could almost hear the worries of the people around him: *What's he up to now? How is he fucking up our lives this time? What's he doing that we don't know about?*

'Apparently it's a matter of national security. That miserable bastard Fletcher will probably shoot me if I open my mouth. And with your track record with newspapers, telling you might not be the best idea I'd ever have had.'

'You're full of secrets.'

'You wouldn't believe it. But you can tell that lot out there that this ATD shit has nothing to do with them – and trust me, I could well do without it myself.' He picked up the small pile of printed records. 'Go through these; see if any of the rest had anything similar to Jasmine Green's claustrophobia. Or if they were taking the same medication. If there's nothing in the files, speak to the doctors. You know how these people are, they don't always log everything.'

Armstrong left the office, his eyes still questioning Cass, but Cass had no intention of giving him any answers. As soon as he was alone he clicked into the mainframe and brought up the information he needed for Dr Andrew Gibbs: his current employer, home address and telephone number. He scribbled the details down before logging off, and wondered if having a quick cigarette before heading down would be taking the piss. He did it anyway.

Fletcher had three men standing by the door of the basement conference room and the whole corridor was sealed off to ensure no access by any unauthorised person. They could bring in Jack the Ripper upstairs and no one would be getting to the secure interview rooms that had once been the home of the ATD. Cass wondered whether he should point out that perhaps a more subtle approach would have elicited less curiosity from the rest of the nick, but decided that Fletcher probably didn't much care. He'd wanted their conversation secure and private, and he'd made sure of it. Cass wasn't sure subtlety was part of Fletcher's repertoire.

'So this guy is definitely the London bomber?' Cass asked. 'But this time he's wearing *fake* explosives?'

'Yes.'

'Why would he kill all those people, and then kill himself while wearing a dummy bomb? Isn't that odd?'

'There's a lot about this situation that's odd.' Fletcher shuttled the image along on his laptop. 'This is where Abigail Porter gets down onto the platform.'

Cass looked up at the hi-res screen: the picture had been enhanced as much as it ever could be, but there was still a grainy quality to it, and the angle wasn't great. The ATD might have state-of-the-art equipment, but the source material was still London Underground CCTV.

Abigail Porter came down the steps and onto the platform. She raised her gun at the fat man standing near the edge opposite her.

'She's on her own?'

'No one else saw him in the crowd. She'd shouted the alert, taken the PM down and then was off and running before our people in the square could figure out what was going on. She took her radio off too.'

'Strange that no one else saw him.'

'Trust me, we have a list of strange about this bomber that keeps growing. Most of it is classified and doesn't concern you – be grateful for that. Abigail had seen this man before. On the night of the London bombings. She said he was standing on her street, and then she changed her story and said it wasn't him at all – but I didn't buy it. She was too well trained to make a mistake like that. And this is hardly an ordinary-looking man.'

At the sight of a gun, some commuters on screen had turned and tried to push their way back up the stairs they'd just come down. The crowds still on the platform pressed back into each other, creating a small amphitheatre for the drama unfolding in front of them.

'But this doesn't make sense.' Cass frowned. 'He's on the platform for several minutes before she arrives. He doesn't even come down the stairs, just appears from somewhere in the crowd. Whoever she was chasing, it couldn't be him.'

'It seems our man has an ability to be in two places at once.' Fletcher smiled ruefully. 'Another thing you don't have to concern yourself with. What I want you to see is the interchange between them. Whatever the reason for her disappearance, it started here.'

'No, it didn't,' Cass said, 'it started with the lie: when she told you she hadn't seen him in her street. That's when she made her choice. What happened next?'

The story continued on screen. Two still figures, one with gun raised.

'Are they speaking?'

'Yes.'

The screen split in two and on one side the fat man's face filled it. The movement of his lips was quite clear.

'Another thing she denied. Porter tells him to put what she presumes is the detonator down. He doesn't. So far, so good. Everything normal. It's what he then says that doesn't make any sense.'

'Which is?'

'He asks her how long she's been emptying.'

'What?'

'I know. It means nothing to me. And then he says, "You can feel it, can't you? Everything draining. Isn't it beautiful?" I thought maybe it was some kind of code, but no one we've got working on it can crack it.'

Cass said nothing, but he looked at the man on the screen. Mottled skin on fat cheeks. Black eyes. He wondered if the man would glow if he saw him in the flesh. He thought of the brief flash of silver he'd seen in Abigail Porter's eyes. This wasn't any kind of code. This was Network business, he could feel it in his gut. But if this stank of Mr Bright, then why was Cass being pulled into the game? Why wasn't Mr Bright sorting this out himself?

'She asks him who he is,' Fletcher continued, 'and he answers, "I am family."'

This was a puzzle, right in front of him, and although he'd had no intention of helping Fletcher in his search – there was no way he wanted to be drawn into the Network's business – he still liked the buzz in getting a feel for all the pieces.

'So she might have seen him before, but she didn't know him.' Cass looked over to Fletcher. 'I take it he isn't actually related to her?' The fat man on the screen didn't look like he was related to anyone, certainly not the leggy brunette holding a gun on him.

'Not that we can ascertain – but then, we've got no fucking idea who he is. We scraped him up, but even with DNA there's nothing on the system.'

'What's that?' Cass watched the fat man's mouth twitch. 'Just after she takes the pen or whatever from him – does he say something then?'

'One word. "Interventionist". Mean anything to you?'

'Should it?'

'No, but it would be good if it meant something to some-one.'

Cass was still watching the silent man and woman on screen. 'He holds her hand for a long time – longer than needed to hand her the pen, anyway. Can you close up on her face?'

'Sure.'

Abigail Porter's much more pleasing visage replaced that of the fat man. Her eyes were wide and her pupils were dilated. Her mouth had dropped open slightly, as if maybe she was gasping.

'She's reacting to something. Look at her. She looks surprised.'

Fletcher tilted his head and studied her. 'You're right. What is it? Maybe he gave her something else along with the pen?'

'Would she feel it in her hand? No, this looks like some-thing else. Play the rest.'

There were only a few seconds of footage left. The fat man let go of Abigail's hand and then lightly jumped from the platform and in front of the train that was screeching to a halt. Other plain-clothes officers came down the stairs and grabbed at Abigail. She still looked vague, half-asleep, as if whatever had shocked her a moment earlier was lingering. For a moment, Abigail Porter was lost behind the carriages, and then the tube backed up to reveal the panic on the platform.

'Look,' he said, pointing as on screen Abigail Porter unfolded her hand to reveal the pen. 'There's nothing else in her hand – unless she moved it while the train was there, but your team had joined her by then, so she'd have been taking a risk. To be honest, she looks too spaced-out to have tried a good sleight of hand.' Something had happened when the fat man touched Abigail Porter – something that stunned her momentarily.

'Could he have injected her with something?' Fletcher asked.

'I don't see how. His hands are visible right up until he jumps. You didn't find a syringe on the track?'

'No, and we probably would have. He was spread all over that line.'

'Nice.'

'Glad scraping him up wasn't my job. I should imagine there were a lot of bags used.' Fletcher froze the screen. 'During the debriefing you turned up and told us about her sister's suicide. After that, of course, the PM insisted she go home on compassionate leave. I walked her home – to be honest, it was half because I still wasn't happy with her behaviour and wanted to dig a bit deeper – then she invited me in for coffee. I stayed a couple of hours and then went back to work.'

'Coffee?' Cass asked. 'Your relationship didn't look overly friendly when I came to Number Ten.' He nodded at the screen. 'I can see why now, but my point is, she must have felt your hostility too. So why did she invite you in? If she was grieving, I would have thought you'd be the last person she'd want around.'

'She didn't seem overly grief-stricken. I presumed she was keeping it inside.'

He watched Fletcher's eyes shift slightly as he spoke.

'Plus, in our line of work we don't tend to have hundreds of friends to call on when we need one.'

He was trying hard, but Fletcher was not a great liar. If Abigail Porter had invited him in, it wasn't for coffee. They might have not liked each other overly much, but Cass knew from experience that didn't necessarily stop people wanting to fuck each other. The last few years of his marriage had been about two people who'd only liked each other in bed.

'I had a car outside her place after I went. She's something to do with all of this, and I didn't trust her.'

Cass almost laughed. Maybe he and Fletcher weren't so different after all. It would take more than a good fuck for either of them to let their guard down. Sex was easy. Trust was something else completely.

'She must have spotted it and gone out through a window at the back, because in the morning she was gone.'

'Any ideas where? Did she leave anything at her flat that might help?'

'We found her on CCTV footage at a payphone a few miles from her flat. The number she dialled doesn't give us anything – it's just a cheap pay-as-you-go, bought in a shop in Oxford Street for cash one year ago and never used until now. The shop doesn't keep their tapes that long, so we can't get an ID on the purchaser from them. Cameras later picked her up going past Oxford Circus Underground Station.'

'You were lucky to spot her.'

'We have good trace facilities and image recognition software.'

'Remind me to come to you next time I need to find some murdering fucker.'

Fletcher smiled, albeit briefly. 'Then we got this.' Fresh footage rolled on the screen. 'The lobby of the Latham Hotel in Portland Place.'

Dressed all in black, with her hair pulled back, Abigail Porter strolled into the hotel. She didn't hesitate, but walked smoothly past the reception desk and through the large marble foyer until she disappeared down a side corridor and into the lifts.

'Where did she go?'

'The lift camera shows her getting out on the eighth floor. After that we don't have anything. She simply disappears.'

'No footage of her leaving?'

'No, but the hotel has plenty of black spots without cameras. If she didn't take the lifts or come out the front entrance then it's likely she wouldn't have been picked up. We've been through the footage for that day and we've got no match with anyone in our system, no likely figures from any terrorist organisations in our database.'

'And you're sure she's involved? Admittedly it all looks pretty cloak and dagger, but could she have gone to meet someone else – a secret lover, perhaps? Maybe someone the job might not have approved of? Perhaps she knew you were watching her and didn't want to call them from her own phone?'

'Does she look like she's dressed for a lover?'

'To be fair, a girl like that could turn up dressed anyway she likes. And hotels have showers,' Cass mused. 'It just seems odd. She chased him down to the Underground; she stands there with her gun on him. Why all this show if she's already involved?'

'We went through her home computer. Her most recent

Internet activity was to a Hotmail account. The username was Intervention1 and the password was Salvation. Coincidence?'

'I don't believe in them.' Cass didn't like his own words echoing those spoken to him by Mr Bright not so many months ago, but he found it was true. 'Were there any messages?'

'No, and I'm not surprised. We're used to this; it's one of the simplest and most effective ways that terrorist cells can communicate with no trace. One person sets up the account and then gives the username and password to the other members of their cell or group. When they want to communicate with them, they write a message but don't send it. Instead they save it in the Drafts folder. The other logs in, reads it and deletes. If they need to reply they do it the same way. No data is ever sent, so the message is irretrievable.'

'Clever bastards.' Cass smiled; he couldn't help himself.

'So that's what we've got.'

'Can I see her file?'

Fletcher opened his briefcase and pulled out a thin buff file. 'I'd rather you read it here and I'll take it back with me.'

'Ah,' Cass said, 'I love that we're starting from a position of trust. But as I still haven't decided whether I'm going to help you or not, that's fine with me.'

He flicked through the pages. There was all the usual: a good school, better university. McDonnell wanted female personal security; Porter had served in the military locations and excelled at the training; she'd been a dead cert when she'd applied for the position. His eyes snagged on something.

'Have you looked at this file?'

'Yes. Why?'

'What happened with this psyche evaluation? There's a

fail in the application form box that's had a void stamp over it and then next to it a pass.'

Fletcher peered over his shoulder. 'I don't know. Admin error, maybe?'

'Who did the psyche evaluation on her?'

'It should be attached.'

Cass flicked through to the back of the long form, where extra pages had been stapled in. There was Abigail Porter's personal statement – several pages of it – all written in small, neat handwriting that was perfectly presentable but lacking any sort of personal flair. He didn't bother reading it. No one ever told the truth in those things, and he doubted Porter was any different. Finally he reached the top sheet of the evaluation. The writer had scrawled impatiently across the relevant boxes. He recognised the handwriting at once, and double-checked against the signature.

'Tim Hask did the evaluation?'

'If it says so. Do you know him?'

'He worked on a case with me.' He turned the page to find it went straight to copies of her driving licence and the results of her physical. 'The actual evaluation isn't here.' He flicked the papers over and examined the area around the staple. There was a tiny ragged edge visible between Hask's sheet and the next photocopy. 'Someone's torn it out.' He looked up. 'That's interesting.'

'You think there was something in that no one wanted us to see?'

'That's normally why people rip things out of files in my experience.'

Cass smiled as Fletcher flashed him a glare. 'I'll talk to Dr Hask for you if you like. See what he made of her, and if he's still got a copy of his original notes.'

'So you're going to come in on the search?' Fletcher

looked like asking the question was sticking in his throat, and Cass didn't blame him. He sure as hell wouldn't want the ATD coming and trampling all over a murder scene where they didn't belong.

'I doubt it,' he said. 'There's someone I want to talk to first.'

Fletcher's face was a mixture of relief and the knowledge that he was going to get a right royal bollocking for not getting Cass on board.

'A couple of things before I go,' Cass continued. 'The hotel footage – I'd go through two or three days before, and in the time after she goes in.'

'We've already done that. No known terrorists or affiliates inside.'

'Did you just scan for them? What about politicians? Overseas aides? I don't know what all the job titles are those fuckers dream up for themselves, but there are a lot of dangerous people out there that you and I spend our lives protecting.' He stood up. 'Plus, who you know and who I know might be completely different. If I do come on board I'm going to want to see the faces of everyone who came in that day.'

'What was the second thing?' Fletcher was speaking through gritted teeth, and although Cass found himself warming to the head of the ATD, he still liked seeing it. There was nothing better than seeing one of the bosses brought to their knees, and them seeing that you knew it.

'You said the body brought back no DNA you could use?'

'That's right.'

'Was there any explanation for his bleeding gums and the way he looked?'

'Some evidence of various cancers was all they said. I'm

236

no medical man; I just wanted to know if he was wanted anywhere. I presumed that his illnesses made him a better subject for a terrorist organisation. He was clearly already facing a death sentence – perhaps he was after a glorious exit.'

'Well, he sure as fuck didn't choose one, strapped up with fucking Plasticine and jumping under a tube. Where was all the analysis done? In-house?'

'Sure – well, I presume so.'

Cass thought about how he'd been pulled into this meeting from people on high who were having their strings tugged by someone else, someone he assumed was Mr Bright. He thought about the unnatural look of the fat man. If this was Network business, and if this fat man was somehow involved with the elusive Mr Bright and The Bank, then surely Mr Bright would want the body parts under his control?

'I'd double-check that,' he said. 'Oh, and make sure you take everything when you go. Wouldn't want any of this glamorous equipment ending up in police hands.'

Cass left Fletcher to find his own way out and headed back upstairs. His nerves were twitchy at the thought of seeing Mr Bright again. He had vowed to do his best to keep himself out of the web the ageless man had trapped the rest of his family in, but the invisible gossamer was stickier than he thought, and whichever way he turned, he got pulled further in. There was no point in telling Fletcher he wasn't interested in helping find Abigail Porter – in this case the head of the ATD was simply the monkey; likewise his superiors. Cass needed to tell it to the organ grinder himself. There was only one Porter sister he wanted to help, and that was the cold, dead one. Hayley. She was the one who had the claim on him, and the government and the Network could carry on playing their games without him.

Armstrong was standing behind Cass's desk. 'Making yourself at home?'

'Just bringing these back.' The sergeant held up the print-outs. 'I didn't know how long you'd be.'

'Did you find anything?'

'Yep.' Armstrong grinned. 'All of them except Angie Lane had spoken to their doctors about phobias.'

'Really?' Cass's heart picked up its pace to chase speed. 'Fuck me, is something actually starting to go our way?'

'It would seem so. James Busby was afraid of deep water – a problem for a Sports Science student. Katie Dodds had extreme arachnophobia, Hayley Porter was afraid of flying and Cory Denter was afraid of heights.'

'Were they on any of the same prescribed medication?'

'No, unfortunately. Hayley had a prescription for Valium, but only for days she had to fly. The other two both had therapy recommendations, but there's no record of if they undertook any.'

'So we have a link.' Cass leaned against his desk. 'Thank fuck for that.'

'But not for Angie Lane.'

'Just because there's nothing on her medical records doesn't mean she didn't have one. We need to talk to her housemate again. She'd know.'

'I'm way ahead of you,' Armstrong said, holding up his car keys. 'I was just about to head off there. She's in a lecture, due to finish in twenty minutes. If we leave now we should be there for when she gets out.'

Chapter Nineteen

'We might as well let the others go first,' Amanda said. 'No point in getting crushed.'

Rachel figured she had a point: there was only one door to get out of the lecture theatre, and every student in the class was currently trying to get through it.

'There's never a crush on the way in,' Dr Cage said. 'Funny that.'

Rachel smiled at him. Of all the classes on the Accountancy and Business Studies course, Dr Cage's were always well attended. For an old man – he had to be at least fifty – he was quite funny, and he managed the difficult feat of making the study of numbers and business models pretty interesting.

'I don't want to get caught up with Emma,' Amanda continued, 'she's such a cow. Last time I saw her, she was going on and on about how Angie was a slag and had dreadful taste in men, and all this stuff that just isn't true. I had to get really shitty with her to get her to believe Angie didn't even have a boyfriend.' They took a couple of steps forward towards the door. 'People are so quick to believe rumours, aren't they? I always thought you were supposed to speak well of the dead.'

'Soon they'll all forget about it and poor Angie will be left in peace,' Rachel said. 'Either the police will get to the bottom of it, or some other kid will kill themselves here and they'll move on to ripping him or her apart.'

'Oh God.' Amanda frowned. 'Is that the police?'

Rachel peered out over the huddle of students fighting their way out into the corridor; the man studying the students as they exited was definitely the dark, moody-looking detective.

'What can they want now?' Amanda asked.

'Let's find out.' Rachel started to weave her way through the remaining stragglers, Amanda following in her wake. She needed to get to her locker and put these books down anyway. Accountancy was a heavyweight subject.

'Are you here to see us?' she asked as they finally pulled themselves free. 'Have you found anything out about Angie?'

'Nothing specific, I'm afraid,' the DI answered. He kept his voice as low as Rachel had, but unlike hers, his had the edge of a growl in it. Rachel thought it probably always did. She kept walking down towards their bank of lockers and as the policeman stepped in between her and Angie, his fair-haired sergeant fell slightly behind. Around them, students nudged each other and glanced in their direction.

'We need to know if Angie had any phobias.'

'Phobias?' She glanced over at Amanda. 'You'd probably know better than me.'

The thin girl was struggling to balance her books on her knee as she fiddled with her locker key.

'None that I can think of,' she said. 'Not that she mentioned, anyway. She always seemed so together.'

'Sorry.' Rachel looked back at the policeman. 'Are phobias relevant?'

The creased face cracked into a smile. 'I take it you're working on a story for that news site of yours?'

'Could be.' She smiled back.

'Well, if you keep that piece of info out of it for now, I promise that if we get to the bottom of what happened to these kids you'll be the first to know. How's that?'

'Sounds like a deal.'

'She was sometimes scared of the dark.' Amanda leaned against the lockers, her books tight against her chest. 'She slept with a night light on. She never actually told me, but I noticed the light under her door.' She looked over at Rachel. 'I don't know if you'd call that a phobia though, or just a fear.'

'Sounds like it fits the bill,' the sergeant said. 'Thank you.'

A phone vibrated, and the DI tugged it free from his pocket. 'If you think of anything else, anyone she might have seen to try and deal with it, then please let us know.' He gave them a smile. 'And thanks again.'

He turned away from them to take the call. 'Jones. Yes. Yes, I want in on that. What's the address? I'll see you there.'

Rachel looked at Amanda and shrugged slightly, awkward alone with the young sergeant. 'Is it okay if we go now?'

'Yes, of course. Thanks for your help.'

'No problem.' They walked away, Rachel waving one hand in a quick wave to the DI as he spoke into the phone.

'I wonder what phobias can have to do with it?' she said to Amanda once they were out of earshot.

'Who knows?' Amanda tucked her books under one arm. They looked like they'd unbalance her tiny frame, but she kept her back straight. 'Let's get out of here anyway. Everyone's staring at us.'

'So, if you're still not agreeing to help find Abigail, what the hell are you doing here?'

David Fletcher was waiting for him outside the Porters'

house in Causton Road, Highgate. Cass looked up at the clean brown stone and the large driveway. A Merc and a BMW, both top of the range, were parked side by side. Porter really was a high-flyer.

'You might be after the live sister, but the dead one is still very much my priority.' He looked back at the black cab; the engine was purring impatiently. 'And he needs his fare paying.' Fletcher glared at him, but pulled out his wallet. The head of the ATD had more chance of claiming the fare back than Cass ever would from the Met's increasingly tight purse strings. He thought of the little girl who grew up here in order to end up dead beside a fireplace, her blood spilled all over the expensive carpet. Had her older sister over-shadowed her all her life? Even now, the world was far more concerned with finding the very-much-alive Abigail rather than figuring out what happened to poor dead Hayley.

'Tell me about the family,' he said as Fletcher tucked the receipt into his wallet and the cab drove away.

'Melanie Porter – née McCorkindale – is a society type. Upper middle class, I suppose you'd call her. A beauty in her day; she'll be where the girls got their looks from. She's bright, though, she's got a Law degree from Oxford, but has never practised. Instead she got married and stayed at home to bring up the girls.'

'And the dad?'

'Alexander Porter. He heads up the ASKDAL Con-glomerate.'

'Which is?'

'Big and successful – one of the biggest of its kind in the world. It owns several media organisations, building companies in the Middle East, and I think some Korean electric goods manufacturers.'

'Spreads his interests wide, then.'

'Not really. He's a newspaper man himself – used to be the editor-in-chief of *The Times*, and according to his file got promoted to the Chair of the Board. Fuck knows how. I've never really understood all that boardroom politics. He must have done well, though, because it wasn't long before he was racing up the ranks of the parent holding company. And now he's responsible for running the whole show.'

'Remind me to wipe my feet,' Cass muttered as he pressed the doorbell.

A middle-aged woman in a sharp suit let them in and led them into a downstairs room. Mrs Porter had her back to them; she was staring out at the garden through one of the high windows. Her husband stood by the large mantelpiece, nursing a drink – whisky, maybe – in a crystal glass. He looked up, though his wife didn't turn round.

'Are you the police?' He wore jeans and a sweater with a shirt under it, the top button undone with casual elegance, and his face was tanned rather than ruddy. His body had just started to run into the typical corporate fat cat shape.

'I'm DI Cass Jones, Mr Porter. I'm investigating Hayley's death, among others.'

'He isn't.' Porter's eyes swept over Cass and focused on Fletcher. 'I know who he is.' He raised one thick finger and jabbed it. 'My girl had nothing to do with those bombings; I don't care what you think. You try and accuse her of it and I'll come after you with all I've got – and I have quite some artillery.'

Cass watched Fletcher hold the other man's gaze. If this was going to turn into a cockfight, he wanted to get his business here done first.

'It's currently being treated as a missing person's case, Mr Porter,' he said.

'As far as anyone she works with is concerned, she's on

243

compassionate leave.' Fletcher's voice was calm but firm.

'Good, because if any of the news agencies gets wind of this, then that's my career over.'

'Please forgive my husband.' Mrs Porter finally turned around. Her voice was cold and clipped as if she had no intention of doing what her words requested of others. She was still a beauty, Cass could see that, but it was her eyes he was drawn to. A silver glow poured from the edges, just like he'd glimpsed with Abigail. His guts curdled. *There is no glow.* He was having a hard time believing his own mantra these days.

'I sometimes think he's spent so much time working he forgets that real life exists outside of it.'

'For God's sake, Melanie,' her husband hissed.

She didn't look at him, but smiled softly at Cass. 'One of our daughters is dead and the other is missing. How could that have happened to us?' A small tear shed silver down her cheek. To Cass it looked like mercury, and part of him wished she'd just turn back round and keep on looking out of that window. He didn't want to see her strange silver glow – *the glow* was *gold*, not *silver*. It always had been. He gritted his teeth. But then, Mr Bright had shed a silver tear in the church all those months ago – so silver and gold, maybe it was all *the glow*.

Whichever colour it was, he wanted no part of it.

'I used to dream of Hayley dying, you know,' Melanie Porter continued. 'When she was little. I dreamed it for a month every night. So did Abigail. It was the oddest thing. I would wake up crying, and I'd have to go to her room to check she was all right. Twice I found her big sister already in her room, driven there by her own dreams.' Another tear broke free, but her breathing didn't hitch; it was as if her crying belonged to a different person. 'The dreams stopped eventually, but after that I think I always knew that we wouldn't have her for very long.'

'Please excuse my wife,' Alexander Porter cut in. 'Too much sun, I think. She spends all her bloody time laying out in it in Portugal. I'm surprised she's not riddled with skin cancer with the complexion of a dried prune.'

Cass studied the dark-haired woman with the olive complexion. She was far from wrinkled; her forehead and the area around her eyes were smooth and only a single crease ran down one side of her mouth.

'We grieve in different ways,' Porter continued. 'I have never been able to do tears. I don't see the point in them.'

Everyone did grief in different ways. Cass wondered if he should point that out to the magnate. These two with their distance, the Denters with their fear, his own contained emotions – he would never judge people on how they dealt with death.

'Have you heard from Abigail?' Fletcher asked.

'No, not since a brief call after the news about Hayley.' Alex Porter sipped his whisky, and Cass wondered if it was only so he could stare into it rather than look at Fletcher. 'But that didn't surprise me. That job of hers gives her so many excuses not to call us or come home. I think that's why she likes it.'

'She was a grown woman,' Melanie snapped. 'Why would she want to come home all the time? To talk stocks and shares with you over dinner? To have you probe her for inside news?'

'Can you think of anywhere she might have gone if she wanted to get away from everything?' Fletcher's voice was calm and steady, cutting through the tension between the couple. 'Any old school friends, or favourite places?'

245

'I can't think of any.' Melanie shook her head. 'There was no one she was overly close to.'

'Including us,' her husband added.

'We have people watching your house in Portugal and the flat in Sloane Square. We'll know if she turns up there.'

'Of course you do, and of course you will.' Porter stared at Fletcher with an open dislike that washed over him. Cass thought Fletcher must be used to it, but with Porter he couldn't help but think that the dislike was purely a power issue – Porter was used to having it, but with a man like Fletcher, all his money and influence counted for nothing. And Fletcher had power of his own.

'Can I ask you a few questions about Hayley?' Cass asked.

'Of course.' Melanie smiled gently, and Cass focused on her mouth rather than the silver in her eyes.

'She had a fear of flying?'

'Yes, it was dreadful – she'd be in a panic for days before she had to go anywhere. That was why she tends – *tended* – to stay in London for the holidays, rather than come out to Portugal with us. She'd had it ever since she was a little girl.'

'She did fly though,' Alexander Porter cut in, and for the first time Cass heard a little pride in his voice. 'She'd make herself do it. She'd take a Valium to calm herself down and force herself on the plane. She wasn't the kind of girl to let fear get in the way of her life.'

'Had she seen anyone about it recently? A new doctor?'

The line at Melanie Porter's mouth creased slightly deeper as she thought. 'She did mention that she was thinking of trying some experimental therapy, but that was a few months ago. She hadn't mentioned it again and I didn't like to ask. I thought she'd think I was pressuring her.'

'Would you mind taking a look through her things and

letting me know if you find anything that might indicate if she went?'

'Of course I will.' Melanie Porter didn't ask why Cass might want to know, but the flash of silver in her eyes did. Cass ignored it.

'Find my girl.' Alexander put his glass down on the mantelpiece and stared at Fletcher. 'We need her back.'

Fletcher nodded curtly, but said nothing.

Cass wondered what the honest man would say if he spoke: *I intend to get her back, but it won't be to come home and play happy families with you, to repair all the fractures in your lives* – something like that, he was sure. Wherever Abigail Porter was, if Fletcher found her, she'd be spending a lot of time in an interrogation cell, and none of Porter's much-vaunted power or influence would have any sway.

Armstrong put a bottle of beer for Cass and a vodka and Coke for himself down on the table. Cass wondered when coppers had stopped drinking good, honest pints – probably about the same time they'd stopped beating the crap out of people to get the confessions they needed. The world changed; that was guaranteed, and change was relentless.

'Cheers.' Cass tapped his bottle against the younger man's glass. Here they were, finally having a drink in the pub together. Cass wasn't entirely sure how he felt about it. Armstrong was no Claire May, but Claire was gone and Armstrong was here and as much as he might not like it, he had no choice but to get used to it.

'I've spoken to the families, and as far as they are all concerned, their kids weren't being treated by anyone for their phobias.' Armstrong pulled his stool closer into the table and sat down. 'It's really surprising how much parents don't know about their children – neither Denter's nor

Lane's parents were even aware that their kids had phobias.'

'Children grow up,' Cass said. 'They learn to keep secrets. No adult likes to publicise their weaknesses.' He took a mouthful, swallowed, and asked, 'Where's your car?' There was no way this was going to be a one-beer-only night.

'I've left it at the station. It's parked right beside yours. My tube line's running okay.'

'Good.' Cass settled back in the chair. 'There must be something else. These kids didn't know each other, but they were all getting cash payments, and they all died the same way. This phobia link must go somewhere – that, or we're barking up completely the wrong fucking tree and wasting police time ...'

'And what does "Chaos in the darkness" even mean? I've had two PCs searching libraries and the Internet for the phrase, or some kind of variation, and they've come up with sweet FA.'

'Fuck knows. Maybe if we find what links them, we'll find that.'

'I've done some digging into their childhoods – schools, clubs, secret societies, that kind of thing. As they were all in the same age range, give or take a year or two, I wondered if they might have been on the same school excursion or something. You know those places where loads of schools go on some stupid river-wading Geography field trip, or visit war memorials?'

'Even at my advanced age I can dimly recall those.'

'I couldn't find any common ground, though. I really don't think these students had ever met.'

'That must have taken some time.' Cass sipped his beer again. 'You've been busy. Good use of initiative.' He knew he sounded patronising, but right now he didn't much care. He'd earned the right to patronise.

'You've been off doing whatever it is you've been doing. I had the hours.'

The two men watched each other across the table for a few moments, and Cass internally groaned. He was going to have to give Armstrong something. The problem with men who worked on their own initiative was that they couldn't just switch their curiosity off when it suited him. It had taken years for Cass to train himself to remember what happened to the fucking cat.

'There's a lot of people wanting pieces of me at the moment.' He didn't break the stare.

'All work?' Armstrong asked.

'Some personal.' That was as much as he was willing to give the sergeant. If he wasn't careful, this would be the last beer they'd share after work, and that was no good for a team.

'Maybe whatever it is would be best done officially. Through work?'

'Maybe, Toby, you don't know shit about that of which you speak.' Cass leaned on the table. 'Are you going to be a problem for me here?'

'You're the boss.' Armstrong finally looked away.

'Your curiosity is what makes you a detective. What'll make you a good detective is knowing when to keep your nose out.'

Silence hung awkwardly between them. Even the general clink of glasses and the chatter from the rest of the pub refused to come near it.

'Listen,' Cass said eventually, 'it really is personal – nothing to stress about. It's just some family business.'

The image of the strange fat man on the tube platform with Abigail Porter rose up in his mind. *I am family.* That's what he'd said, and it made Cass shiver. *Family business.*

Who were these people who'd made his family their business and so royally fucked them up? He still dreamed of Solomon's death sometimes: the explosion of light, the explosion of *flies*. There was nothing *natural* about it: it was *glow* business.

Abigail Porter. The fat man. The Underground platform. All thoughts of *the glow* left him as the dead students gathered closer. His heart raced.

'How are you getting home?'

'I told you.' Armstrong frowned. 'The tube.'

'How are you paying?'

'I'm not – well, I'll be using my Oyster card.'

'Exactly.' Cass grinned, the pieces forming a whole in his mind. 'And if you were a student living here who had to get around London every day, how would you do it?'

A light went on in Armstrong's eyes as his brain caught up with Cass's. '*A student-discounted Oyster card!*'

'Is that your first drink tonight?'

'Yeah—'

'Go back to the office, get your car and then go and find those Oyster cards. If we can see their journey histories, maybe we can find a link that way.'

'Now?' Armstrong looked at his unfinished drink. 'But it's half-past seven. I thought you said I had to get the work/life balance shit sorted?'

'I lied. I want those cards by morning. And ring whoever the fuck runs Oyster and tell them we want a man with a scanning machine at the station by ten tomorrow.'

'What if they didn't register their cards?'

'They'll be registered – they'd have to be to get their student discounts, and you know what students are like: they'll save money wherever they can to pay for their beer.'

He drained his bottle and got to his feet. 'I'll see you in the morning.'

'Where are you going?'

'Since you're now too busy to be a drinking partner I think I'll go and fry some other fish. You don't need me holding your hand.'

He felt Armstrong's eyes on his back as he left the pub, but he didn't look back. He walked for several blocks before calling Directory Enquiries.

'The Bank, head office, London, please. Just put me straight through.'

The woman at the other end did as she was told and the line rang out in his ear.

'The Bank, good evening, how can I assist you?' The voice was soft and professional and entirely feminine.

'Put me through to Mr Castor Bright, please.'

'I'm afraid we have no one of that name here, sir. Could anyone else help you? Unless your business is with our overseas division, most of our staff have already left for the evening.'

'Just tell Mr Bright that Cass Jones called and I'm on my way in to see him. I'm sure he's expecting me.'

He ended the call before she could speak again. Despite the chill in the air, his palms were sweating as he slipped the phone back into his pocket. He stared out at the life on the London streets, cars and buses fighting each other to get to where they were going. He suddenly felt very apart from it all. The Bank and Mr Bright were waiting for him. It was time to play the game.

'They're saying what?' Alison McDonnell stared across the table at the man standing there so casually, his hands jammed in his pockets as if he were telling her the time, or

251

what he had for breakfast. Spin doctors had no soul, she was sure of it. If only politicians didn't need them so badly.

He repeated, 'That perhaps you staged an attack on yourself to raise your ratings.'

'But how could that possibly be?' She pushed her coffee cup away. She was exhausted and running on adrenalin, and more caffeine really wasn't going to help her think straight. 'What kind of person would do that – is that really what they think of me? I didn't even raise the alarm!'

'The problem you have,' Desmond Simpson continued, 'is that no one saw this apparent assailant, not a single person in the crowd, nor in fact any of our Secret fucking Service men. All they saw was Abigail bloody Porter pushing you to the ground and then chasing a phantom.' He sipped his own coffee. 'Add to that all the journalists and news crews who were filming at the location, who also have no record of our fat man being there, and . . .' He stared at her, then looked down at his cup. 'Well, you can see how we need a fucking miracle to make sense of any of it, can't you.'

'So who's actually saying this?' The Prime Minister leaned back in her chair.

Lucius Dawson looked more tired than she felt, if that was possible; he didn't see her glance at him because he was too busy looking at Simpson for an answer. Sometimes she wondered if any of them ran the country at all, or if it was all done by these shadowy figures in the background who spent their lives making new truths out of old ones.

'It started somewhere on the back benches – nicely anonymous. But it's spreading now, and Merchant will grab it and run with it as soon as he thinks there's enough support.'

'He's the leader of the Opposition,' McDonnell said. 'He'd never be allowed to make such an outrageous claim.'

'He would if he thought there were people within your own party who agreed with him.'

'And are there?'

Simpson looked over at the Home Secretary. McDonnell did the same.

'I've heard people talking,' Dawson said, eventually. 'They're worried about what a story like this could do to us.'

'We're not dead in the water yet.' Simpson sat on the edge of the desk. 'I know she's on compassionate leave, but we need to bring Abigail Porter in. You need a scapegoat, and it needs to be her. She can say she overreacted and thought she'd seen something when she hadn't; that she panicked, forcing a poor civilian who happened to have some mental illness – I'm sure we can make up some shit about him – to jump in front of a train because he thought he was about to get fucking shot. I don't care if we say she was on LSD and cracked, we just need to make it her fault and not yours.' Despite his language, his voice was calm. This destruction of careers – of *lives* – for the greater good was what he was paid for, and he was damn good at it. It exhausted McDonnell to even *try* to think like him, and she heartily disliked the fact that she needed him.

'In some ways, she's the best choice,' Simpson continued. 'Her sister's just died, so the press – and any inquiry – will go easy on her, and her father can get her another security job, and one that pays a damn sight more than she's on at the moment. If we get her in tomorrow ...' He paused and looked at the Home Secretary. 'What? What am I missing?'

Dawson looked at McDonnell. If she'd been less tired, she might have laughed. It was all becoming something of a farce. How quickly empires crumble.

'It's Abigail,' she said.

'What about her?' Simpson's eyes narrowed.

'She's not on compassionate leave. She was, but she disappeared. She went out the back window of her flat and hasn't been seen since. Fletcher's got people looking for her, but so far the trail's dead.'

'Holy mother of shit.'

'But surely,' McDonnell continued, 'if we tell people that she's gone, they'll think that if anyone planned this, it was her. Which is exactly what we're thinking – so what's wrong with telling the truth?'

'Two things.' Simpson stood up and looked down on her. 'First, if they want to get rid of you – of all of us – they can do it by blaming you for hiring her in the first place: they'll say you were incompetent and naïve.'

'Technically, Alison didn't hire her,' Dawson cut in.

'Save that bullshit. She's in charge, she takes the buck on this. No one gives a shit who actually does the hiring and firing; they'll say if you can't see a security threat in the middle of your personal security team, then how the hell are you going to spot an external one? They'll crucify you. Before you know it the London bombs will be your fault. *Personally.*' He barely paused for breath. 'Second, those who aren't busy calling you a stupid fool will think you've got her hidden away somewhere because you *did* organise the whole thing to boost your ratings and don't want anyone getting to her for the truth. It's a lose–lose situation for you.'

'The truth?' McDonnell looked up at him. 'God forbid we should ever speak the truth, or care about people's lives and integrity.'

'Don't get sanctimonious with me.' The spin doctor's eyes hardened. 'If you care so much about the fucking truth and people, go join a bloody nunnery, or work with fucking disabled children. This is *politics.*'

'You're right.' She raised her hands in submission. He wasn't right, and never would be in her book, but she didn't have the energy to argue with him, and it was pointless anyway. She wouldn't win. She was just a piece on the chessboard, and right now she had the feeling she was the most expendable of pawns.

'Are we fucked then?' Dawson asked quietly.

'Well that all depends,' Simpson said. 'Do you want to save your leader, or this government?'

'The government.' McDonnell didn't hesitate. 'We can't let Merchant get in. The man's a lunatic. If he has power, then this country will really be wrecked.'

'Then we need to create a viable take-over in-house. Something we can control.'

'What do you mean?'

Simpson smiled. 'Of all your Cabinet do you trust Dawson the most?'

'Absolutely.'

'Then he's who we'll use to destroy you.'

Chapter Twenty

Despite what the telephone receptionist had said, The Bank was the business that never slept. The sleek building on the Thames was the hub of all The Bank's worldwide activities, the nominated head office, although The Bank no doubt owned equally impressive buildings in other cities. Once it had been the MI6 building; now, in Cass' eyes at least, it was a front for something far more threatening: the Network, with their X accounts and the Redemption file. This was where his brother had worked, lured there by a good job and benefits in a world where both were increasingly hard to come by; before long he'd become inextricably entangled in his own section of the Network's web. And now he and his wife and the child he'd believed to be their son were dead.

Cass passed the external security guards and through the newly installed metal detectors just inside the sliding doors without incident. He wasn't carrying a gun – even if he'd been licensed, he wouldn't have brought one; that kind of weapon was unlikely to do him any good here. His heels clicked on the marble.

'Can I help you, sir?' The woman sat behind a long glass desk of black and silver, the colours of the company. She smiled over at him. This wasn't the same woman he'd spoken to half an hour before. Although undeniably a beauty, she was in her mid-fifties, older and doubtless infinitely wiser than the young woman who'd answered his call. Her voice has been smooth and professional, but lacked the harder edge of this woman.

Cass didn't answer her, but stopped in the middle of the vast foyer, ten feet or more from where she sat, tilted up his head and spread his arms wide. Slowly he turned in a circle. From within the large black glass boxroom behind the reception desk – it doubled as a security centre and modern art – two men in dark suits emerged. They stood either side of the woman, watching him cautiously. Cass ignored them as the lights of the embedded security cameras above his head flickered quietly.

A phone buzzed and the woman with the wise eyes answered it. After a moment, she carefully replaced it.

'Mr Jones?'

Cass stopped his circling and looked at her.

'You can go up now. I believe you know the way.' She didn't smile, but Cass favoured her with a grin.

'Thank you.'

The clear security gates clicked and opened for him and he headed towards the lift. There were obviously people in the building still working, but the communal areas were eerily quiet. The doors of the lift slid shut behind him. Cass didn't press any buttons; he'd not be operating this lift. After a moment the central panel between the two banks of numbers lit up green at the edges and the machine purred into life, just as Cass had expected. This ride was taking him to a floor which didn't exist, and to a man who didn't feature in any of The Bank's employment records – the man who had introduced his mother to his father with a smile, and who hadn't left his family alone since, even now, when they were nearly all gone. He was here to meet Mr Castor Bright.

The lift slowed and pinged its arrival. Cass's heart thumped and his mouth dried. Nothing had changed. The cherry-red floor still shone in the wash of light from the standing lamps positioned at various points of the room. The opulent Eastern rug still stretched lazily out towards the chesterfields and armchairs in the living area of the vast open-plan space. As he stepped out, Cass's eyes automatically followed the wide spiral staircase that rose alongside the wall of antique books to his right to the second floor beyond. It was from there that the mysterious Mr Bright had emerged last time Cass visited this place. Tonight, it was empty.

'Would you like a drink?'

This time the silver-haired man was sitting in a wingback chair, one leg casually crossed over the other, the pressed seams of his tailored suit trousers still perfect.

'No, thanks. I won't be here long.'

'You never are.' Mr Bright's sharp eyes twinkled. He hadn't changed – but then, he hadn't changed over several decades; why would six months make a difference?

'You've been keeping busy, Cassius.' Mr Bright put down his own drink, and with a well-manicured hand gestured at the *Telegraph* on the table beside him. Cass looked at the headline. MURDER DISGUISED AS TEEN SUICIDE.

'I thought you'd be more of a tabloid man,' Cass said, keeping his tone cool and nonchalant. Mr Bright chilled him to the bone, but there was no way he intended showing it.

'I always did like your sense of humour.' Mr Bright smiled. 'It's important to keep it. I've always tried to keep mine.' He looked back down at the paper. 'Suicides. Such a terrible business. Sometimes I think the dead should just be allowed to rest, don't you?'

'Most of the time I find the dead can't.' Cass glanced across to the far side of the room, where two office doors sat on either side of an unlit modern fire. Both still had bronze name plaques attached, and although he was too far away to read them, he could clearly make out the shapes of the names: Mr Bright on one and Mr Solomon on the other.

'And if you're so keen, perhaps you should lay him to rest then. We both saw the crazy fucker die, after all.'

For a brief second, the twinkle in Mr Bright's eyes hardened to diamond and then he smiled again: all perfect white teeth.

'I haven't been here for a while. Trust me, finding someone to fill that office is on my "To Do" list.' He spread his hands in an elaborate shrug. 'But I've been busy. There's always so much to do.'

The words were just games, and Cass was getting tired of them. The less time spent around Mr Bright the better, as far as he was concerned.

'I presume you're responsible for the ADT wanting me to help find this Porter woman?'

'It would be pointless of me to deny it.'

'What does Interventionist mean?'

There was the slightest widening of pupils and a surge of bright gold that obliterated the colour in the sparkling eyes.

It was over in a flash, and while Cass was glad he'd got a reaction, he tried to hide that he'd seen it. Whatever *the glow* was, Castor Bright could control his – maybe that was because he had so fucking much of it. He'd half-answered Cass's question in that instant, though; whatever the word meant, it was something to do with the Network, just as he'd thought.

'I want you to find the girl David Fletcher's looking for.' Mr Bright got to his feet in one elegant movement. 'I need to know who's behind this business. It really shouldn't be too taxing; I just need you to inform me of anything you find that you think' – he smiled again, one eyelid dropping in a quick wink – 'might interest me.'

'Why do you need me? Are you losing your touch?'

'It would be very foolish of anyone to think that.' He strolled over to the window, then turned to face Cass. 'I trust you, Cassius Jones, despite yourself, and for reasons you don't yet understand. The others have never thought of you as important. I, on the other hand, have always liked to hedge my bets and play the numbers.'

'What the fuck are you talking about?' Cass growled. Being around Mr Bright always ended up making his skin burn with anger and frustration and disbelief. He wanted to get back into the grimy real world, where people lived and died, and no one else gave much of a shit about it.

'I need someone on the outside who knows a little bit about the inside. Someone who's not a fool – someone who is part of everything – and that, of course, would be you, Cassius Jones. It always has been.'

'Then you're the fucking fool. I'm not going to help you – I'd rather cut my own right hand off.'

Mr Bright laughed, ice tinkling in a glass of warm spirit. 'Let's hope I don't hold you to that.' He sighed. 'Of course you'll help me. I wouldn't have involved you if I wasn't sure of that.'

'What makes you so sure?'

'Because—,' and Mr Bright smiled cheerfully, '—you won't find Luke without me.'

Cass's blood chilled and the world shattered a little at the edges. 'What?'

'This hunt you've started: it's pointless.' The smile

stretched and Mr Bright's white teeth glinted. It was a shark's smile.

Cass had heard the expression before; fuck, he'd used it himself, but he'd never *felt* it like he did in that moment.

'If you do this for me,' Mr Bright continued, 'then I'll tell you who gave Luke up.'

'You have him, don't you?' The words were grit in his mouth.

'Does this place look child-friendly?' Mr Bright gestured around him. 'But help find the girl and I'll tell you what happened that night.'

'Maybe I'll find out myself.'

'No, you won't.' Mr Bright's voice dropped. 'You don't even know if he's alive or dead. Only I can tell you that.'

'You bastard.' Cass's lungs tightened. He didn't want to breathe the same air as Mr Bright.

'I've been called many, many things over many, many years.' Mr Bright kept smiling. 'One day you'll understand that all of this has been in your best interest, despite some of the unfortunate incidents along the way.'

'*Unfortunate incidents?*' Cass's blood was so far past boiling it felt like ice. 'My brother is fucking dead.'

'To be fair,' Mr Bright said, then paused to sip his drink before continuing, 'I didn't kill him.'

'You're a cunt.' The world shimmered as Cass spat the word out, and his vision sharpened. Heat fled from his eyes.

'It's good to see the real you is still in there, Cassius. Look at that Glow.'

There is no glow. His eyes burned.

'I won't help you.'

'Yes, you will.' The sentence was sharp and hard. 'Because I know where Luke is.'

For a moment, gold filled the room, bathing everything

it touched in its light. Cass wasn't sure where his ended and Mr Bright's began. He didn't know where *he* ended and Mr Bright began. With a gasp, he swallowed the colour back down again. His skin cooled. The lamps faded, as if aware they could never compete with that unnatural light and so no longer saw the point in making any attempt to dispel the gloom.

When the world had settled back to normality, Mr Bright pulled a card from his pocket and handed it over. It was thick and textured and expensive, and on it was embossed a mobile number. There was no other information.

'Let me know about anything that comes up that I might wish to hear of. And trace that number if you want, but your time would probably be better spent on other things. It won't give you any information on me.'

'I'm not interested in you.'

'Of course you are.'

Cass turned and headed towards the lift. 'I wouldn't *bank* on it.'

Tinkling laughter followed him. 'Very droll.'

'I don't trust you,' Cass said as the lift doors opened. 'What if you're lying?'

'I never make offers I haven't thought through, Cass Jones. And I haven't lied to you. And to be fair, you really don't have any choice, do you?'

'There's always a choice, Castor Bright,' Cass said. 'We just don't always like the options.'

Mr Bright was still smiling when the doors closed, separating them. With trembling hands Cass quickly stored the number on the card into his phone and saved it as 'A' for anonymous – he didn't want to key Mr Bright's name into his phone; that would be almost as if they were friends, and he felt Judas enough for what he knew he was going to do without adding that to it.

He screwed up the card and let it drop to the floor, not wanting to touch what Mr Bright had given him for any longer than necessary. There was no point in tracing the number; Cass had believed him when he'd said it wouldn't lead anywhere. But if Mr Bright thought Cass was going to give up his own chase for Luke, then he was very, very wrong. He had the leads; he was damned well going to follow them. Until he had something of his own to go on, he'd play Mr Bright's game. He didn't give a shit about Network business anyway.

The bright foyer was still empty as he strode through. He didn't acknowledge the woman behind the desk, just kept walking until he was safely back out in the night. He didn't look back, and he certainly didn't look up. Brian Freeman's advice from so long ago had no place here.

He waited until he was around the corner and out of sight of the building's security cameras before pulling out his phone. Of course Mr Bright knew he would be calling Fletcher, but the idea of the man watching him from a window as he did it grated on him. He felt dirty enough as it was.

Fletcher answered on the second ring.

'I'm in,' Cass said.

'What made you change your mind?'

'My sense of social responsibility.' He hung up. And then sighed. Ahead of him, the old tramp perched on the low street sign, his legs crossed in a poor imitation of Mr Bright's elegance. The lower foot tapped on the pavement, a gentle drum beat, and he grinned as he played. The tune was light and cheerful as if this were early May, and the tramp would be spending a night in a five-star hotel after dinner at the Savoy. It was old-school music from a bygone era of top hats and tails. Cass wondered if life had been simpler then. He doubted it. Most people probably just had to walk more and work harder.

'Evening, officer.' The tramp's voice was still gravel and earth. 'You taking your place in the game?'

Cass stared at him for a moment while lighting a cigarette.

'Oh, just fuck off,' he said eventually before turning away to find a taxi. The old man didn't stop playing, but at least he didn't follow him, and that, Cass thought, was something.

'What's that music?' The question drifted out as Abigail sank into the cushioned foam that moulded itself to her body. The white sides of the shiny oval rose up a little all around her, preventing her from seeing anything but the plain ceiling high above. At least she thought the sides were white. It was hard to tell any more.

'Can they hear the music?'

There were two other women here now; one, like her, was quiet; the other was screaming and shouting in Russian, something like *Pazhalsta! Pazhalsta!* Please! Please! She recognised the language, but it was hard to focus. Something was happening to her – it had been for what seemed like for ever. She'd got to the hotel and met the man from the telephone, and he'd taken her out through the fire escape and down to the alley at the back of the kitchen, where a black car had been waiting. She clung to the timeline, pulling herself along it: it was important that she remembered something that was *hers*, rather than all this other stuff that was filling her head.

The man had been waiting for her in one of the closed tube stations, and he'd led her down here, so far under the streets of the city. She hadn't been afraid of him then, and she wasn't now, even though some part of her – the old her – was sure that she should be. But he glowed golden when everything else had turned to black and white, and there was goodness in that glow, she was sure of it. He'd left her here, locked in a small room for hours, maybe days, but now he was back and there were two more girls, and there was this strange, bright room, with its strange white seats. And the music. Though the music was new.

Hands strapped her arms down. She didn't resist, though she wondered if perhaps she should – but she didn't have the energy, and anyway, where would she go? Something was happening to her; she was changing. Her head was filling again, and if it didn't stop, she was sure her skull would burst from the pressure.

The golden man leaned over her and his brow furrowed. Somewhere apart, the Russian girl screamed again. Abigail didn't think her cries would help. It sounded like she was getting strapped in anyway.

'Can you hear it?' she asked the glowing eyes. 'It's so *loud.*'

He smiled, and the beautiful light shone brighter.

'What have you done to me?'

'This will calm down,' he said. 'You'll settle. You'll learn to control it, and this place will help you. When you're ready, there is something I want you to do.'

'You've changed me,' she whispered, but the words were loud in her head.

'I haven't,' he said softly, '*They* did. *They* wanted something, and I allowed them to have it. You're just the added benefit. You will make me proud. Lie back and relax. This fear will pass.'

Abigail did as she was told and someone leaned over her and strapped her head down, and then the glow was gone.

Voices muttered, one of them deep and rich and golden, and a door clicked shut.

Soon after, the lights above went out and she was left with just the hum of the machines. The Russian had finally stopped wailing, but occasionally her breathing hitched in a low moan. Abigail wondered if perhaps she should cry too, but the concept felt alien. There were many things she *should* be crying about, but she was damned if she could remember them. Instead, she began to sort the images crowding her head: unfamiliar faces and places, city streets, politicians and paupers. She found that if she stopped being afraid, she liked the pictures; they came in colour in a world that had become black and white. They calmed her. She just wished the music would stop. It didn't *belong* here.

'These belong to the dead kids, don't they? I recognise this name from the paper.'

'If you could just scan them, Mr Conroy.' Armstrong smiled politely at the chubby man as he spoke.

Cass scowled. To give his sergeant his due, he'd managed to get hold of all five Oyster cards, and organised Mr Conroy from London Transport, complete with a scanning machine which could be attached to their computer to upload the information – and all by half-ten – but Cass wished he'd just let Armstrong finish the job by himself. He didn't have the energy for the niceties of dealing with someone else's curiosity right now.

'I'm sure you're as busy as we are,' he muttered.

'Ha! Yes, but we don't get the newspaper inches for what we do. I know your face too.' Conroy nodded at Cass. 'We're just the little people.'

'My heart bleeds.' Perhaps that was a bit harsh, but Cass was tired, and there was nothing 'little' about Conroy.

'It should, mate – I lost friends, you know? In those bombs? And others spent hours helping the police and ambulance men digging people out. They saw some things, I can tell you.'

'Where were you?' Cass asked.

'Day off.' Conroy sniffed as he fiddled with the cables and finished attaching it to the slim laptop. 'There but for the grace of God and all that.'

'Does God do the shift rota then? Fuck me, you lot are special.' Cass couldn't help the sarcasm. He was full of bitterness, left over from his meeting with Mr Bright, and nothing had been able to shift the sour taste in his mouth. He hadn't slept properly, just tossed and turned under the glare of the dead eyes that watched him from every corner. When he did finally manage to drift off, it had been into dreams of shiny black brogues with spots of crimson on them. He'd half-expected to find Christian's ghost sitting neatly on the end of his bed when he finally forced himself awake, but he was alone in his room. His brother had left him to it for now.

'You look tired,' Armstrong said. 'Busy night?'

'How far back can you go with these?' Cass asked Conroy, ignoring his sergeant's question.

'As long as they've had them. How far back do you want to go?'

'Do a year. If we find nothing, we'll get you back in. In fact, you can just leave the machine with us and that'll save you the journey and the time out of your day. We'll get it back to you when we're done.'

'This is London Transport property,' Conroy said as he started the upload. 'I'm responsible for it.'

'I'm sure London Transport is as much in hock to The Bank as everyone else, and trust me' – Cass looked over to the laptop screen that started filling with the mundanities of Cory Denter's daily journeys – 'The Bank doesn't really give a shit about one ticket machine.'

His phone buzzed and the screen flashed up Fletcher's name.

'When these are done, get someone to drive this bloke back to work,' he said to Armstrong. 'Without his bloody machine. Then figure out how to get the computer to cross-reference all the cards.' He answered the call. 'One minute, I'm heading to my office.'

'"This bloke"?' Cass heard the railway man say as he left them behind. 'I don't much care for your boss's tone.'

'No,' Armstrong answered, quietly, 'he takes a bit of getting used to. I'm not sure I'm entirely there myself.'

Cass closed the door to his office and shut them up.

'What can I do for you?'

'How did you know the bodywork on our bomber was outsourced?'

'Call it a hunch. Who took it?'

'God knows. The order went out to our ME almost immediately he got the mess back to the lab. He was told he had to release it to some anonymous outfit. Experts, apparently. The order came from somewhere in the Home Office. And I thought I was in charge of the fucking ATD. Should I be chasing to get the body back?'

Cass almost laughed. Fletcher had to be as tired as he was; he wasn't thinking straight. Even if he did request the body back, he wouldn't get it – maybe something that looked similar, but it wouldn't be the strange fat man's body. Nor would he be able to trace where it had actually gone. The ATD might have the nation's resources at their fingertips, but the Network owned the nation. Whoever had placed that order from within the inner echelons of government wouldn't have even known where it had gone, or why, let alone truly understood the nature of the powerful shadowy men requesting it. It was all wheels within wheels.

'Not worth it. It won't help you find Abigail.'

'You sound very sure.'

'Let's just call it a hunch.'

'If you say so.' Fletcher sounded pissed off, and Cass didn't blame him. It must really grate on him that a fucked-up DI looked like he knew more about what the ATD were investigating than he did.

'We've been through the hotel footage right up to last night and rechecked those coming in and out. Two other women went in after Abigail who had no right being there. One is Mary Keyes, personal assistant to the Governor of New York, and the other is Irena Melanov, a known face in the Russian security services who is normally to be found in the presidential entourage. Neither US nor Russian intel will confirm or deny whether these two are missing, but they were both *very* keen to be kept informed on any developments, which is as much confirmation as we need. Those girls aren't on holiday.'

'Both from places that got bombed.'

'Yes – and with bombing suspects who look identical to ours,' Fletcher said. 'So whatever is going on here isn't just our problem, but it looks like I'm carrying it.'

'That's your business, Fletcher. My only concern in this is getting some idea of what's happened to Abigail Porter.'

'Aren't you the lucky one? I'm going to send these images from the hotel over on disk. See if you recognise anyone we don't.'

'Print them out and send them. I might need to look at them on the move,' Cass said. 'Also send me whatever family history you've got on the other two. I'm curious.'

'On the way.'

With the call ended, Cass scrolled through his phone until he found the numbers for Dr Tim Hask. He dialled the office line.

'Mr Jones, what a pleasant surprise.' Hask was cheerful as ever at the other end of the line. 'Is this a social call, or business?'

'As much as I'd love to say I've called for a chat, I'd be lying. I need to pick your brains about a job you did a couple of years ago. Where are you working? Can I call in?'

'Sounds intriguing. I'm at the ISISOR building in the city, stuck here all day, so come by any time. What was the job?'

'A psyche evaluation on a woman called Abigail Porter – she's part of the Prime Minister's personal security team. Your assessment feedback is missing from her file.'

'I remember her. Very tall, very striking.'

'That's the one.'

'I'll have her notes somewhere on my laptop. Give me twenty minutes to dig them out, then I'm all yours. I need a break from all this banality anyway.'

'And I need an excuse to get out of the office.'

He hung up, then dug out the piece of paper with Dr Gibbs' home number scribbled on it and punched the digits into the phone. It rang out; no one answered. He'd already stored Gibbs' mobile number in his own phone; when he rang that it went straight to answerphone. The doctor must be working; Cass decided he'd try the hospital after speaking to Hask.

Armstrong knocked once on the door and then opened it, grinning as he came inside.

'We've got something.'

Cass looked up. 'Go on then.'

'For a period of six weeks all our dead kids, except Angie Lane, went to Temple Underground Station on Tuesday evenings, arriving there at roughly seven-thirty and leaving to head home at approximately ten-thirty. Jasmine Green took the number 42a bus, which stops on the Embankment, just by the tube.'

'When was this?' For a second, all thoughts of Abigail Porter, Mr Bright and even Luke were gone. 'They *all* went there during the same six weeks?'

'No,' Armstrong qualified, shaking his head, 'not exactly, but they do all overlap. Wherever they were going, for a few weeks they were all there together.'

'When was this? Just before they died?'

'No, but the time between the end of their six week-periods and their deaths are approximately the same: four weeks, roughly.'

Cass frowned. 'Explain it to me.'

'James Busby made his first trip to Temple on 14 July. He went for six weeks, then nothing. Four weeks after his last trip he sent that "Chaos in the darkness" text to his mother, then slit his wrists in the bath. Katie Dodds started her visits to Temple the week after Busby, on 21 July. She did her six weeks, and then she died slightly less than four weeks after her trips ended, killing herself four days after Busby. Cory Denter started on 28 July, and Jasmine Green and Hayley Porter the week after that. Given that Angie Lane died within days of Cory Denter, then I guess we can presume that she started her six weeks at Temple at the same time as he did.'

Cass looked up at the tatty wall calendar. 'So there were three weeks where all their journeys overlapped. Wherever they were going is the link. They must have met there. But why no travel record for Angie Lane?'

'It was summer and she lived just across the river, a mile

271

away at most. Maybe she walked? Or got a cab?'

'And they killed themselves four weeks after finishing whatever they were doing there,' Cass mused. 'So what caused the delay?' He roused himself from his thoughts and turned back to Armstrong.

'Take two or three PCs and get up to Fleet Street with blown-up pictures of our kids. Go in all the local shops, the usual routine. Someone might recognise them. While the plods are doing that, I want you in every business in that area that's open in the evenings. *Someone* was paying these kids cash: what kind of job only lasts six weeks? Look for something unusual. Whatever it was, I doubt it was stuffing envelopes. These kids weren't using their own bank accounts much right up until they died, so whatever money they were getting, it was enough to see them through four weeks or more.'

'I'm on it. You coming?'

'I've got to follow up something for this ATD shit, but I'll have my phone on. I'm expecting a package to come from Fletcher. Tell someone on the desk to have it biked over to the ISISOR building in the City when it gets here.'

Armstrong nodded. He looked pissed off, but Cass let it wash over him. He was letting the young sergeant do most of the gruntwork on this case, but it wouldn't do him any harm. He'd get over it.

The ISISOR building was one of the last high-rise structures to go up before the recession really hit, and its sleek glass walls were home to twenty or thirty companies. ISISOR itself had gone bust within weeks of moving in as stocks and shares collapsed around the world, but the name lived on as a highly prestigious address for the most successful of those companies which had somehow survived the recession.

Cass found Hask on the eighteenth floor, in a boardroom that was bigger than the whole of Paddington Green nick's Incident Room, and with a side-table full of cakes and sandwiches sitting next to a bubbling coffee machine. The pastries looked fresh, and Hask looked, as ever, larger than life.

'So this is how the private sector live,' he said.

'You'd hate it, Cass. All this wealth and privilege.' Hask got to his feet and picked up a miniature Danish from the plate. 'Let them eat cake.' He popped it whole into his mouth and wiped his fingers on a napkin.

'They still got you assessing people after the bombings?'

'God, it's interminable.' Hask rolled his eyes. 'Most of these people are cold as sharks anyway. Whatever psychological problems they have don't stem from whether or not they were stuck in London on 26 September.'

'I presume you've told their employers that?'

Hask laughed cheerfully and poured two cups of coffee. 'I will do. Eventually.' He handed Cass a mug. 'Drink that and weep.'

The coffee was strong and rich and a million miles away from the vaguely brown liquid dispensed from the nick's vending machines, or the over-brewed gravy that came out of the coffeepot, if anyone even remembered to fill it in the mornings. 'Yeah,' Cass said over the fragrant steam, 'life here must be hell.'

'So, what is this about Abigail Porter? I thought you were working this teen suicide thing?'

'I am. Porter's sister is one of the dead students.'

'And that got you access to her personal file?' Hask's eyebrow rose. 'Call me old-fashioned, but since when did an ordinary DI get access to such highly confidential information?'

'Don't ask,' Cass said, 'because I can't tell you.'

'Fair enough.' The fat man grinned. 'I do like a bit of cloak and dagger.'

'I wish I could say the same.' Cass took a sip of his coffee. 'So how come your report's missing?'

'Probably because I didn't pass her. If they gave her the job anyway it's likely the panel chose to remove it and therefore hide any personal liability, should anything go wrong with her. I'm surprised they didn't replace it with a different doctor's evaluation. I should imagine that there are plenty of respected professionals out there who would have passed her.'

'If they would, then how come you didn't? Was it because she was young?'

'God, no. Young people will die for any Tom, Dick or Harry. In her line of work, youth's an advantage.' Hask leaned against the large highly polished wooden table, and the solid frame creaked under his weight.

He looked up at Cass. 'There was just something about her that didn't ring true. She had all the right answers, and on paper she was the perfect candidate for the job, but I just couldn't pass her.'

'She was lying?'

'No.' Hask shook his head, and his chins wobbled. 'No, I don't think she was aware of what was missing. It was something else.' He reached forward and picked up another small cake, this time breaking a small chunk off and chewing it thoughtfully.

'She was too detached. I felt that she was faking her fear.' He looked over at Cass. 'Part of the evaluation consists of reaction and image tests. Her face and heart-rate showed exactly the right result for every image or situation we gave her to look at.'

'And this was a problem?' Cass asked.

'It was too exact – no one reacts perfectly to the model, especially not every time. That's part of the test. We all have our quirks and secrets – things that excite us that shouldn't; things that we're afraid of. It was as if she had no personal responses of her own; as if she had learned the required reaction and duplicated it.'

'Can you do that?'

'Technically, yes. These tests are supposed to be confidential, and they get varied from year to year, but of course people get hold of them. The thing is' – he swallowed the rest of the cake – 'whether someone's seen the test or not, they shouldn't be able to fake their reactions, and certainly not to such a great extent that they'll fool the testers. It's a bit like a lie detector in that it picks out your involuntary responses: dilation of pupils, increase in heart-rate, that kind of thing. The verbal reactions are almost irrelevant. Cheating is pretty much impossible.'

'But you think Abigail Porter did?'

'She scored perfectly, and that's not possible. It was enough for me to know that I couldn't pass her. I've never done an evaluation like it.'

'And yet they still gave her the job,' Cass said.

'There's no accounting for people. Maybe she had friends in high places.' Hask smiled, but Cass felt a chill ripple down his spine. Someone had wanted Abigail Porter to get that job and if it wasn't Mr Bright, then it must have been someone else in the Network. Maybe the Jones family wasn't the only one being toyed with by the hidden organisation and their endless funds in the X accounts.

A knock on the door interrupted his thoughts, and Cass

turned to see a young woman hovering nervously.

'DI Jones?'

Cass nodded.

'A package had come for you. Apparently, he' – she stepped aside to allow a tall, dark-suited man through – 'has to give it to you personally.'

The man didn't smile, but stared hard at Hask and then Cass before approaching.

'Can I see some ID?' His voice was devoid of accent, and even when walking he moved with athletic ease.

Everything about him made Cass want a cigarette. 'Keep your knickers on.' Cass grinned as he showed his police ID. 'I'm sure you know exactly who I am.'

The man scanned Cass's badge, and then handed the package over. 'It's from Fletcher.' Without another word, he turned and left, leaving the poor woman to scurry after him.

'I'd have passed him,' Hask said, 'without a moment's hesitation.' He looked down at the thick envelope Cass held in his hands. 'Fletcher, eh? You're always involved in the serious stuff, Cass.'

'You don't know the half of it.'

'Are you sure it's not too soon?'

The question came out of the blue, and for a brief moment Cass didn't know what he meant, and then the weight of it came flooding back. Kate, Claire, Bowman. The Man of Flies. That's what Hask was talking about.

'I'm fine.' It was all he could think of to say.

'You look tired, that's all.'

'I am, but I'm fine.' Cass smiled.

The doctor smiled back. 'Good. Well, when you've cleared your plate a bit, let's go for a beer again, shall we?'

'Sounds like a plan.'

Cass lit a cigarette before opening the envelope. It was the middle of the day and the brightly lit basement car park was empty. He tugged out the contents, on top of which was a handwritten note from Fletcher. *I presume you're smart enough to get rid of all this when you're done.* Cass stared at it. If he was presumed smart enough, then why the fuck had he felt the need to mention it? He threw the note onto the passenger seat and then flicked through the brief dossier the ATD man had included on the US and Russian women. Cass figured he was getting the watered-down version, but that was fine; he wasn't sure what he was looking for himself.

Both women were young and attractive, and both had been promoted quickly in their adult lives – just like Abigail Porter – and both came from successful, wealthy families. He scanned through their family backgrounds. The Russian girl's was scant, mostly a list of unpronounceable companies that her parents had worked for, but from the job titles Cass could see her father, like Abigail's, had been promoted fast over the past fifteen years. The American woman's father hadn't started rising up the corporate ladder until he was fifty, normally the time that workers were getting thrown out with the waste in this new buyer's market. How was it that he suddenly, like Abigail's father, started making waves in the boardroom? Even if they were late starters, no one would be listening to them by then, however much business sense they were making. Fuck it. Those questions weren't his to answer and they could wait.

He put the personal notes aside and turned his attention to the stack of glossy ten-by-eights. Each had a date at the top, and under each picture was the time the person had entered the Latham Hotel. Cass went for the day Abigail Porter disappeared first and flicked through. There were at least thirty on that day alone. No wonder Fletcher had wanted to send them all over on a disk – and so much for the recession. He peered at the strangers' faces, forcing his eyes to dwell on each one, rather than dismissing them quickly. He settled back in his seat and threw the cigarette butt out of the window. He was going to be there for a while.

The man who came into the hotel that day at 16.54 p.m. according to the time code didn't need focused attention to jog Cass's memory; he recognised him straight away. Despite his determination to stay on the periphery of the hunt for Abigail Porter, he couldn't fight the buzz of excitement that fizzed in his gut. Mr Bright was going to love this. Or not. Cass did, though.

Without taking his eyes from the image, he dialled the number stored under 'A' in his phone. It rang three times before it was answered. Cass wondered if Mr Bright was really busy, or just creating the impression that he was in no overwhelming hurry for whatever information Cass might have discovered.

'Yes?'

'I've got something for you.' The words almost stuck in Cass's throat. He didn't like this bargain he'd made, and could only hope the end justified the means, and that Christian would forgive him – no, not Christian. Christian was *dead*. What mattered was whether he could forgive himself for one more betrayal of his little brother.

'Which is?'

'Firstly, I don't know whether this will interest you but it appears two other women in similar positions to Abigail Porter have gone missing from their home towns, and each turned up on the Latham Hotel's somewhat limited CCTV footage on the same day. One is Mary Keyes – she works for the Governor of New York – and the other is Irena Melanov, apparently a member of the Moscow Security Service. Both families are successful and influential. You might want to check them out. I'm not doing any more of your dirty work than I have to, and we both know you can dig deeper than I ever could.'

'Is that all?'

'Oh no,' Cass said, 'none of the women have been seen since they went into the Latham over a period of two days. But guess who else I saw going into that same place, just a few hours earlier than Abigail Porter?'

He particularly enjoyed the long pause at the other end.

'Go on.'

'Someone who clearly thought no one who might recognise him would ever see the photographs. Someone just a little too smug for his own good.'

'You might have to narrow it down,' Mr Bright said, dryly.

'Asher Red.'

Cass was quite sure that for a nano-second at least Mr Castor Bright had held his breath. Cass didn't blame him. Asher Red, the smooth-talking face of The Bank during the Man of Flies investigation, and Cass's brother's boss, now looked as if he was perhaps not quite so loyal after all.

'Now that is interesting,' Mr Bright said eventually.

Cass hung up without saying another word. He checked his watch. Armstrong would be busy for a while yet, so there was no point heading back to the office. He probably had time for another visit first.

He had to show his badge at the desk of St Bede's Hospital before the woman would even page Dr Gibbs for him, and even then she watched him warily from behind the toughened glass that separated her desk from the general public. He didn't blame her. St Bede's was one of the few hospitals left in London that treated NHS patients, as well as those who couldn't afford to go anywhere else, and he was sure many of those would be infected with the bug. It wasn't worth the risk of getting spat in the face any more. The bug would find whatever way in it could.

A nurse finally came and collected him and took him down to a small lounge deep in the heart of the hospital, where he found a middle-aged man pulling on a jumper. A pile of green scrubs sat at his feet.

'Dr Gibbs?' Cass asked.

'You were lucky to catch me. I was just on my way home,' the doctor said as he tugged his sweater down over his stomach. 'Eight hours on A&E is quite enough for anyone.' He smiled, but there were heavy bags under his eyes, and Cass was sure that the man's scruffy hair had nothing to do with styling and everything to do with lack of time to get to a barber's. He'd finally found someone who looked as tired as he felt.

'So, what's this about? The RTA brought in earlier?'

'No,' said Cass, 'I wanted to ask you about an incident during your time at the Portman Hospital. On the Flush5 maternity wing.'

'Really?' Dr Gibbs frowned. 'That was a long time ago. Ten years?' He smiled. 'I'd like to say I've come a long way since then but that probably wouldn't seem entirely true. What is it you want to know? If I can remember that far back.' He dumped the scrubs in a large green bin in the corner of the room and then pulled a pair of trainers out of his locker.

'A baby died on your shift a couple of months after the ward opened. Ashley Gray. His parents were Owen and Elizabeth Gray. I want to know more about what happened that night.'

'I'm afraid you've made a wasted trip,' Dr Gibbs said, changing his shoes. 'I wasn't working that night.'

'Yes, you were. Your name is on the shift records.'

'I wasn't working. There was only one baby lost in my time there, so I'm not mistaken. I was swapped off-shift at the last minute.'

'What do you mean?'

'Exactly what I said. I was literally about to leave the house to come to work when I got a call saying they wanted to give a new doctor a trial shift.' He put his work shoes in his locker.

'Didn't you find that odd?'

'Not overly. I was old enough to be grateful for the time off, and even in those days you didn't argue with Flush5. Plus, they said they'd pay me anyway, so I wasn't complaining. I guess that's how my name is still down on the staff list. Must have been a glitch with the payroll. Of course, the next day I heard what had happened – it came as a bit of a surprise, because Elizabeth Gray's pregnancy had been pretty textbook. But you never can tell.'

Something was off here. The doctor might not know what had happened that night, but something was very wrong about this.

'Who called you about the change of shift?'

'I think it was the ward sister, if my memory serves me correctly – which, to be fair, it often doesn't. Most days I can't remember what I had for lunch by teatime.'

'Do you know the name of the doctor they gave this trial to?'

'Sorry, no.' Dr Gibbs shook his head. 'I don't remember if anyone actually told me. He never came in again. The baby's death probably didn't look great on his CV.'

'What about the ward sister? Would she know?'

'Susan? Yes, I'm sure she would have, but she died of a heart attack a couple of years later.' He frowned as he got to his feet. 'How come you're so interested?'

'I'm afraid I can't tell you that. But it's nothing too major. Just routine.' Cass's stomach sank. Maybe Mr Bright had been right. Perhaps he wouldn't get anywhere looking for Luke on his own.

'I know who might know, actually,' Dr Gibbs said suddenly. 'Nigel Powell – he was the Portman Hospital administrator. I didn't know him then, but we've since been on a couple of committees together and we're pretty good friends, in a kind of "game of golf every couple of weeks" way. I'm sure Flush5 would have had to keep him informed of some things for the hospital's admin. Even if it didn't go down on record anywhere, he'd have known who was working that night.'

Cass had to fight back a grin. Fuck you, Mr Bright. You're not the only one able to get information.

'Did he ever talk with you about what happened to the Gray baby?' Cass asked.

'No,' the doctor said, 'it was just a dead baby – oh God, I know how harsh that sounds, but I haven't thought about it since it happened. You must know what I mean. You must have cases like that. Someone else's tragedy is just routine for us.'

Cass knew exactly what he meant. 'Have you got a number for Mr Powell?'

Dr Gibbs opened his mouth to speak, and then hesitated. 'I think he's just changed it. Last time I rang I got a dead tone. I do know his address though, if that will help?'

'That'll do.' Cass grinned.

*

Andrew Gibbs watched the policeman head out of the hospital before heading into one of the small offices off the reception area. He could have walked out with the DI: he was on his way home himself. He probably should have . . . Whatever this DI Jones was digging around in the past for, it was probably nothing. He was tired and he had his coat on; he should have just gone home. He looked at the phone on the desk. Why would anyone be interested in a baby that had died so many years ago? Maybe that was what was troubling him. That, and that he might have inadvertently dropped his friend in it.

Powell was only just coming out of divorce fugue; he really didn't need any more aggravation. Perhaps that's why he'd lied to the policeman about not having Powell's number. At least this way he could forewarn his friend to expect a visit.

He sighed and picked up the phone.

'Hey, it's Andrew Gibbs. Glad I caught you. Look, it's probably nothing, but I've had a policeman here, a DI Jones. He was asking questions about a baby that died on the Flush5 ward. Ashley Gray? You probably don't even remember it.' He paused. 'Nothing strange happened that night, did it?' He smiled. 'I didn't think so. Just letting you know, really. He might call round and see you.'

'Gibbs?' A face appeared in the doorway and broke into a grin. 'Glad you're still here – get your scrubs on, you've pulled a double. Markham's called in sick.'

'Great,' he said into the phone while waving an acknowledgement at the disappearing figure. 'Looks like I've got to go. So much for an early finish. I'll call you for a game when I eventually get a day off. We should make the most of this mild weather.'

He hung up and stared at his locker in disgust. Time to change his shoes again.

'So, are you going to come to the Union tonight? Johnny's band's playing – Cream Face Pie. It should be good.'

'Yeah, probably.' Rachel followed James outside the main building. A night out did sound like fun, but if James thought it meant that he'd be getting a drunken fumble at the end of the evening, he'd got another think coming.

'Great!' James grinned.

Inwardly, Rachel sighed. The grin was too large and the excitement in his voice just a little too much for a few halves of lager in the Uni bar with a friend. It was her fault, of course; after a couple of pints James always seemed funnier than he actually was, and the acne that covered the lower part of his face miraculously disappeared ... until the next morning, of course. Thankfully, she'd never been so drunk that she'd got herself in the terrible position of seeing him first thing, but if she kept up with the random snogging, then that day would eventually come, and at this rate it was going to be sooner rather than later. Then she'd have to face the idea that on some level she did find geeky James attractive, and that maybe he was the kind of man who was waiting for her in her future. That really wasn't a place she was ready to go yet.

'They're putting a demo together and going to take it out round to all the major labels. Someone's bound to pick them up. I'm doing their website. It'll be the first in my portfolio. I mean, they can't pay me or anything, but who cares at the moment? I mean, really, it's just so cool they asked me.'

Rachel smiled at him and wondered if he talked with this much over-abundant enthusiasm to everyone, or just to her.

She had to admit it was nice to see someone looking at her with that much shine in their eyes. She was attractive, she knew that, but she wasn't a great beauty – and Uni seemed to be filled with the slim and long-limbed. James didn't seem to notice them, though. He only ever noticed her – it was one of the things that made her wonder if there was something wrong with him.

'Shall we go and get some chips?' he asked. 'We've got an hour till the next lecture, and it's always pretty empty about now.'

Would chips be giving him the wrong impression she wondered. Probably not – it was only food, and she was pretty hungry. She looked over towards the refectory, and then her eyes snagged on something in the car park beyond. She frowned. That was odd. It was quite a distance but she was sure that that was . . .

'What do you think?'

'What?' She looked up at James and then back at the car park. They'd gone. She was sure they'd been arguing. What could they have to argue about?

'I was just saying we could maybe go to the cinema this weekend if you wanted. Nothing in it or anything, just a film.'

'One thing at a time, James,' she said. 'First let's get some chips.' She glanced back at the car park. It was probably nothing, she decided.

Chapter Twenty-One

'Who called you?' Mr Bright sat behind his office desk, enjoying the smell of rich leather that always filled this space. It had been a while since he'd been in this room for any prolonged period. The phone call was somewhat dampening his pleasure, though.

'Is he panicking?' He tapped out a beat on the blotting pad with his perfect nails and then stopped himself when he recognised the tune. 'Rhapsody in Blue'. Everything was coming to a head at once, but then, it had always been thus. He listened to the man at the other end. They were always so predictable.

'Call him back and tell him he has nothing to worry about. It's all under control. In fact, tell him to stay where he is, say you'll call round and reassure him this afternoon.' He paused. 'No, of course you won't be going to see him. I'll take care of it.'

He hung up the phone. It was irritating, having to be fighting someone who should be on his side, as if there wasn't enough of that already in his world. Still, it wasn't entirely unexpected. He smiled. Perhaps it was time to move things along a bit. He pressed a button on his desk and then went out into the main lounge area.

From upstairs, a tall, dark-haired figure emerged and made his way down the spiral stairs. Sometimes even Mr

Bright found it hard to recognise this confident, dedicated young man as the junkie he'd dragged out of a gutter only a few months previously. It was quite amazing what they could achieve when they had a touch of the *Glow* in their blood.

'Ah, Mr Bradley. I have a task for you.'

The young man smiled, and Mr Bright could see the adoration in his hard, cold eyes. For a moment he almost felt sad, but the pity was a self-indulgence. So many were ultimately expendable, and in every game there were pieces the master strategist needed to sacrifice in order to win.

'I need you to tie up some loose ends for me, and help me teach your old friend Detective Inspector Jones a lesson while you're at it. At some point he's really going to have to learn to do as he's told.' Mr Bright smiled. 'But only when it suits me.'

'I don't understand why you take such an interest in him,' Bradley said. There was something close to jealousy in the sneering downturn of his mouth. So predictable – but at the same time there was something amusing in that much loyalty.

'You don't have to understand. Understanding my motives is certainly not in your job description.'

'What do you need me to do?'

'You're going to enjoy this, I think. But you're going to have to work fast.'

Cass was about to ring Perry Jordan to get him a number for Nigel Powell when Eagleton called.

'What can I do for you, Doc?'

'I'm not really sure,' the young man said. 'It's Angie Lane's brain. It's bugging me. The thing is—'

'Don't tell me on the phone, I'm driving and I can't concentrate with all this fucking traffic. I'll come by the morgue.'

'You sure?'

'Yeah, I'm out and about anyway. I'll be there in about twenty minutes.'

He hung up and smiled. He wouldn't bother to call Jordan; Nigel Powell had a Chelsea address and Eagleton's lab wasn't too far from there. He could go straight to the former hospital administrator's house without drawing too much attention to the fact that he wasn't either in the office, or out and about with Armstrong. He wanted to see Powell today; the closer he got to finding out what had happened to his brother's child on the night of his birth, the more Cass felt as if the trail might get tugged away from him. He turned the car around and headed to the west of the city.

A little over half an hour later he was staring up at several images of brains taken from various angles and pretending very hard to have some kind of idea of what he was looking at.

'Don't go into acting, whatever you do, Jones.' Eagleton grinned. 'You're shit at it.'

'Cheeky fucker. Have you got any idea what caused the brain damage yet?'

'No. That's why I recognised your blank expression. Neither me or the boss can figure it out. It's not been caused by any disease that we can identify; it's almost as if the brain has torn itself slightly in several places at once. Like some kind of intense pressure burst. But each of the areas has been damaged really neatly – there's not even much inner bleed. Dr Marsden says he's never seen anything like it, and

I've hunted through all the textbooks and they're not giving us anything either. The boss' – Eagleton looked down from the scans and over to Cass – 'who is a really interesting bloke under that serious exterior, did some research and found some Swiss research article that says severe psychological trauma can cause some physical damage to brain matter in the moment of experience, often so tiny that it's not picked up by doctors, but the article claims it could be what causes personality changes in sufferers of extreme post-traumatic stress.'

'Do you believe it?'

'Hell, no, and nor does Dr Marsden – it's a crackpot theory with no clinical evidence. But if it were true, then these kids would have had to have been through some completely fucked-up shit to get this kind of damage.'

'So what's bothering you about Angie Lane?' Cass dragged him back on topic. He needed some hard facts, not more theories to tease his brain with.

'It's just that I'm not sure any more.'

'What do you mean?'

'I'm not sure she's like the others. It's been bugging me, ever since you arrested that guy over Lidster's death.' He pointed to a scan right in front of him. 'She's got a lot of damage, and a brain bleed from where she hit her head so it's really difficult to see whether she has the same lesions as the others underneath it. At first I just presumed that was the case, but I can't be sure.'

Cass looked along the line of backlit images, the scans identified by a printed surname underneath: LANE, BUSBY, DODDS, DENTER, GREEN. All those young lives so clinically reduced to a body part and a surname.

'She also must have gone down hard to hurt herself this much. I mean, it is possible, but she really dented her skull.'

289

He chewed the inside of one corner of his mouth. 'I'm just saying that whatever happened to her isn't as clear-cut as the others.'

'Are you saying she might not have been a suicide?' Cass frowned. His heart thumped. Angie Lane hadn't been to Temple tube on any Tuesday evening, as far as he could work out, and her fear of the dark wasn't on any doctor's records. It was just hearsay, and teenagers always exaggerated things. Shit, he'd even asked them outright if she was scared of anything. He'd fucking auto-suggested an answer.

'No,' Eagleton said, 'I'm not saying that. I'm just saying that I was wrong to presume and I wanted you to know that I had doubts.'

'As it happens, I think you might be on to something. There are other inconsistencies between her and the others.'

'Really?' Eagleton smiled. 'Does that mean I get a share of the bonus when you catch her killer?'

'Ha fucking ha.' Cass raised an eyebrow. 'If it leads to something you can have the whole fucking bonus. I'm all bonused out.'

In the corridor outside the lab he called Armstrong. The last thing he needed his nosy sergeant to hear was background traffic; that would only prompt his '*Where the fuck are you?*' question, either outright, or in the subtext.

'We haven't got anything yet,' Armstrong started. 'A couple of people think they might recognise one or other of them, but there's nothing concrete yet.'

'Forget about that for now. Leave the others on it and get back to the office.'

'How come?'

'I'm at the morgue with Eagleton. He thinks that Angie

Lane might be different to the others. Don't ask me for details, because I'm fucked if I understand any of that medical shit, but I want you to check on a couple of things. First, look at her Oyster card records. We presumed she must have just walked to Temple, but what if she wasn't there at all? See if she went anywhere else during the six weeks that she should have been going there if she was following the pattern of the others. That would rule her out of doing whatever they were. Also, get back onto the phone records people. If she wasn't part of this suicide pact shit, then someone killed her and made it look that way. I want the names of the people she called the most. And not just calls, check who she texted, too. You got that?'

'Yeah. You think she's a murder like Joe Lidster?'

'I don't know, but I don't want us to end up looking like arseholes because we didn't check thoroughly enough that all of these kids really were linked.'

'True.'

'Students had that *Chaos in the darkness* stuff all over the Internet before we even knew about it, even that the kids involved had slit their wrists. If Neil Newton thought he could use it to get away with murder, then why not someone else?' The more he thought about it, the more it made sense. So what the hell had happened to Angie Lane?

'I'll head back now. Will I see you there?'

'No,' Cass said. Armstrong was starting to sound like a nagging wife. 'I want to go over a few more things with Eagleton first. Put the request in for the phone records and then head home. I'll check the Oyster card stuff when I get back. You've worked hard enough for one day.' Although it meant he'd just added to his own workload, it was better than thinking of Armstrong back at the office clock-watching and waiting for Cass. As it was, the trip to Powell's house shouldn't add more than half an hour or so to his journey. How long could it take for the man to give him one name?

'If you're sure.'

'There's nothing we can do until we get her phone records, and those bastards finish dot on five. Fucking admin.'

'Although there's something to be said for not working for bonuses,' Armstrong added.

'You're telling me.' Cass kept his tone light. He'd thought Armstrong would have known better than to raise such a sensitive subject with him. Was the sergeant trying to get a reaction? If so, he was shit out of luck. 'We could all go home at the end of our shifts and still get paid,' Cass said. 'Wouldn't that be nice?'

Nigel Powell lived in the lower half of a large Georgian terrace in a side street not far from the Fulham Road. The residential nature gave the area the feel of a leafy suburb. Cass parked in a residents' parking bay a few doors up and let himself in through the low front gate. A short path led through what passed for a front garden to the main door. Beautiful as the house and street were, you didn't get much bang for your buck in this part of town, that much was for sure.

He rang the doorbell and waited. When no one answered, he tried again, and this time he heard a short cry. Cass froze for a second before slapping the palm of his hand hard against the wood.

'Mr Powell?' he shouted.

He crouched and peered through the letterbox. He could just make out two pairs of legs, woven so closely together that if one had been female, Cass might have wondered if they were dancing. Something crashed to the ground out of sight and someone grunted as the pair twisted out of view in their struggle.

Shit.

Cass yanked off his jacket and wrapped it round his arm before turning his face away and punching his elbow through one of the square glass panes of the closest window, thanking God it was an old-fashioned sash – no UPVC replacements round here. He reached through and grabbed at the catch, unlocking it with one hand and giving the wood a hard shove upwards with the other.

Somewhere further back in the house furniture crashed to the ground, followed by a heavy, softer thud. With his heart racing, Cass clambered inside. Why the fuck wasn't he licensed? Why the fuck didn't he have a gun? He followed the noise through the elegant dining room and into the hallway.

'Mr Powell?' he called.

Someone groaned and a sudden gust of cool air accompanied the blood that oozed from the doorway on Cass's left onto the black-and-white chequered tiles beneath his feet.

A middle-aged man was lying on the kitchen floor beside an upturned wooden chair that he must have grabbed at as he fell. Beyond him, the back door was open. *Shit.* Cass leapt over the injured man and out into the garden, screaming, 'Hey! Hey you! *Stop!*'

A thin man with shoulder-length dark hair swung one leg over the high wall with athletic ease. In the brief second before he disappeared over the other side he flashed Cass a smile, his face half-hidden by a veil of black hair. Something in Cass's memory jarred. That face was familiar. Where the fuck did he know it from?

He grabbed at the rough brick and hauled himself up in time to see the young man already sprinting off into the distance. This wasn't the movies, and Cass didn't have a hope in hell of catching him. Instead, he dropped back to the grass and headed inside. He'd come here for a name, and he intended to get it.

Nigel Powell wasn't looking good. The large stab wound in his stomach had turned his white shirt crimson, and his face had turned a sickly grey as his life bled away into a warm pool around him. Cass crouched beside him.

'Ambulance,' Powell muttered, his mouth working hard to force the one word out.

'What was the name of the doctor who worked that night? And don't pretend you don't know. Someone's just given you a very nasty stab wound over it.' He looked around at the top-of-the-range fittings lining the vast kitchen. 'Did what happened that night pay for all this?' He leaned in. 'Was it worth it?'

'Ambulance.' A hand clutched at his arm. The fingers were cold and clammy.

'Name.' Cass tried to keep the urgency out of his voice. The wound in the man's stomach did not look good at all, either the location, or the amount of his blood that was pumping out of it. He didn't have a hope in hell of surviving.

'Dr Shearman,' Powell whispered. 'Richard Shearman. It wasn't anything to do with me. I didn't organise it. I just ... I just facilitated it.' His breathing was a wet rattle. 'Now call an ambulance, *please.*'

Cass stood up and shifted backwards slightly, keeping his feet out of the sticky red mess. Powell's eyes followed him. They were full of panic. Cass stared at him. *I just facilitated it.* What the hell kind of word was facilitated? He'd been part of a conspiracy to steal a baby, a conspiracy that had killed the Grays, who'd just happened to be unfortunate enough to be due to give birth to a baby boy at the same time as Christian and Jessica Jones. A couple who thought they'd been lucky enough to get private care. A couple whose 'luck' had always been someone else's choices. Thanks in part to this man, that couple were now dead and two little boys had exchanged fates, one to be blown away by a shotgun while he slept. The other was out there somewhere. *Faciliated.* Cass felt bile rise within his chest.

'You don't understand.' The man on the ground tried to raise a limp arm, but it flopped back down. 'I know who you are. You don't understand.' Powell flinched slightly, his mouth tugging downwards at the sides. His face had moved beyond grey to a deathly white. 'Ambulance. *Please.*'

'There's no time for that, don't you think?' Cass's anger burned cold. 'You've spent enough time in hospitals to know that, surely?'

Powell's mouth moved again, but this time he couldn't get the words out. He stared at Cass with whatever small glimmer of life he had left pleading silently to the policeman to *do something.* Cass matched his gaze until the light finally went out of the dying man's eyes. It didn't fade. It just clicked off. Death came like that to everyone.

It took a moment before Cass realised his hands were shaking. A chill rippled from deep within his gut. Why did he feel as if he'd plunged the knife into Powell himself? Because part of him was glad the man had died? Because, just for a moment, the dying man had represented everyone who'd ever fucked with his family? Who had killed him anyway, Mr Bright and the Network – because Cass was looking for Luke? If they'd paid him off all those years ago and he'd never said anything, why were they suddenly afraid he might talk now? It didn't make sense.

He went to the sink and splashed water on his face before turning and leaning against the counter. Whatever the reasons behind it, this was a murder, and he needed to call it in, if one of the neighbours hadn't already. How he was going to explain his own presence without killing his already half-dead career he didn't know, but he'd hopefully have something figured out by the time the squad car turned up.

He let his head drop and took a deep breath to slow his heart down. He needed to get his shit together. At least he had the name of the doctor who must have swapped the babies that night. He'd find that fucker, and then there would be hell to pay.

Halfway through the exhale, he frowned. There was a knife under the kitchen table. He stared at it for a long second before crouching to take a closer look. The silver blade was slick with blood, but the handle was relatively clean. Instead of a straight handle, on this one the wood curved slightly at the end where the little finger would be if you gripped it. Small steel pieces in the shape of diamonds ran up the centre. It was exactly like the ones he had at home. He looked round to the far work surface and the full knife block there. Silver handles shone brightly. They didn't curve.

Back on his feet, he grabbed a tea towel and used it as a glove to yank open kitchen drawers and cupboards, searching in vain for a second knife block. There wasn't one. He slammed the last cupboard shut with a grunt of frustration before picking the knife up and washing it.

It was *his* fucking knife. From his own fucking kitchen. Jesus Fuck. Someone had been to his house and taken it and then come here and killed Powell. What the fuck for? And *who*? His mind raced. He couldn't call it in, not now. He'd been set up before, when his brother had died, and he'd managed to prove himself innocent; this time he had a feeling he was up against someone cleverer and better connected than Sam Macintyre and DI Gary bloody Bowman. He needed to get rid of all trace of himself and get out of there.

He wrapped the knife in the tea towel and slipped it into his inside jacket pocket before hunting under the sink. With a J-cloth he carefully wiped the handles of the cupboards before retracing his steps back out into the hallway and cleaning every surface he could remember touching. He cleaned the sill and the catch on the dining room window and then checked the hallway for footprints. There were none. He glanced in each of the downstairs rooms, his eyes scanning for anything else that might belong to him that might have been planted to incriminate him further, but there was nothing.

He was checking the upstairs rooms when his phone rang. Armstrong. Shit. He raced down and through the kitchen to the small garden outside and took a deep breath before answering. He couldn't afford to miss this call; he needed someone to hear him sounding normal. Then he really needed to get the fuck out of here.

'Yep.' He was pleased to find his tone was steady.

'I've checked her Oyster card.'

'What?' Cass scanned the houses on either side. There was no one at any of the windows; at least that was something in his favour. He needed the sounds of outside, but he didn't like the chance of anyone seeing him there. He moved under the partial shade of a half-lowered table parasol. If anyone did spot him, then at least they might not see his face clearly.

'Angie Lane's Oyster card,' Armstrong was saying. 'Well, I didn't do it, technically the computer did. I just figured out the dates she should have been going to Temple and punched them in. The laptop told me the rest.'

'Which is?' Cass felt like his brain was going to explode. The killer had run from here at least ten minutes before. If he'd called the police himself, intending to get Cass found there, the cars wouldn't be far away now.

'Two of the evenings she should have been in Temple, she wasn't anywhere near the place. Once she was around Piccadilly Circus – she got the tube home from there at 9.30 p.m. anyway – and the following week she was out at Turnham Green. She stayed an hour and then got on the tube back. That was at eight in the evening. She's looking increasingly separate from the rest.'

'Isn't she just?' Cass said. *Another murder.* He was surrounded by the dead. The first drops of rain began to patter onto the canvas of the parasol. Perhaps the dead wanted to drown him.

'Where are you?'

'Stuck in fucking traffic. Any news on her phone?'

'They've promised us the numbers first thing. I wish I'd requested all that in the first place rather than just a cross-reference with the others' calls.'

'Well, it didn't seem important at the time. And anyway, it can wait until the morning. Whoever's at the bottom of it thinks they've got away with it. They're not running.' He looked at the wall. Running was exactly what he should be doing.

'As you've done my job for me,' he continued, 'I might as well head straight home rather than fight my way to Paddington. You do the same. Good work today, Armstrong.'

'Thanks, sir.'

Andrew Gibbs waved goodbye to the woman at the Accident & Emergency reception desk and headed out towards the car park. She was pulling a full double; at least he'd only had to do an extra couple of hours before a relief had turned up. She was a pretty thing too, even with her face hardened from dealing with all the abuse from the drunks and the foolish and the just plain rude all day long. A few years ago, he might have tried to play there, but these days he was just too tired, and there was something grubby about the hospital and the sicknesses of the poor that rubbed off on everyone who worked there. She probably felt it too. Unlike most hospitals in the country, there were very few doctor-nurse relationships in this one. If you were going to sleep with someone, you wanted it to be someone *cleaner*, someone untouched by the grime of the A&E ward.

Still, it wasn't as if his social life was a whirl at the moment. For the first time, he'd started to feel middle age creeping up on him, and it wasn't just a number any more. He was tired, not so much physically – although he was certainly feeling the aches and pains of being on his feet all day – but mentally and emotionally. A&E wards had always been the stage for what ailed society; these days there was so much more wrong with the country. The bug was on the increase, stretching its deadly fingers to grip even the middle classes and the happily married: those who'd believed themselves safe from the original strain of HIV. They'd forgotten the big message of the eighties – to wear a condom – believing love and fidelity went hand in hand. TB and hepatitis strolled casually behind in their more aggressive colleague's wake. These days executive women worked as call girls to pay the mortgage on the houses they couldn't sell, while their corporate menfolk turned to drink, and always there were the junkies and the pushers and the petty criminals. The A&E ward was full of those who should have gone to a doctor, but couldn't afford the charges. Perhaps they'd hoped whatever was wrong would get better with time. It wouldn't, though, Dr Gibbs thought sadly. It was life that was ailing them: this grim life and its inevitable end.

It was raining, the drops falling in a steady, gentle rhythm, but he didn't pick up his pace – it was refreshing, and he needed something to clean out the dark shadows in his mind. It wasn't like him to be so bleak; his optimism was one of the reasons he'd chosen to work in this field. The policeman's visit had bothered him: it had made him remember how calm things had been in the Flush5 ward during the few months he'd worked there. Maybe he should have stayed in the private sector – the past ten years would certainly have been different.

His car was parked on the far side of the large lot, in the hospital employees' section, away from the pay and display machines patients and visitors alike had to fill with pound coins if they wanted to get to the hospital without using public transport. It was all so self-defeating for a hospital that the government held up constantly as an example to prove that it still cared about society's impoverished and weak and forgotten.

The problem was that when everyone was struggling, those in extremis no longer counted. If ordinary bus driver Joe Bloggs had to pay for his medical treatment, then why the hell shouldn't everyone else? That was the world's view. Charity certainly did begin at home. It wouldn't be long before the emergency services lost their NHS access too, although most of them had already bought into private plans for anything more than a trip to the GP. Dr Gibbs couldn't blame them – he wouldn't want NHS treatment himself; even with an accident he'd opt for a private A&E ward: have credit card, can travel.

He rummaged in his pocket for his car keys. He got to

help people who needed it though. He had to hang on to that. Most of the time it didn't seem like so very much, but there were always those magic moments in medicine where you held someone's life in your hands and then felt the scales tip in the right direction. Life could be worse, he concluded. Working on the NHS A&E ward certainly showed you that too.

The tatty old Ford Focus blipped as he hit the unlock button and he finally picked up the pace a bit as the rain found its rhythm and tumbled heavier to the ground. He'd just reached for the door handle when a young man in a long dark overcoat got out of a car a row back.

'Dr Gibbs! I don't believe it!' he said, grinning as he walked forward. 'I haven't seen you in ages!'

Gibbs frowned. He didn't recognise the young man with the thick black hair at all – not that that meant much; he saw so many people. Had he been a patient? No, he was greeting him like a friend, so perhaps a medical student? That must be it. Even so, his eyes wandered up to the CCTV cameras that whirred on tall posts above their heads, quietly monitoring the activity in the car park.

'I'm sorry, I can't quite place you.' His own smile was awkward, but it didn't stop the confident stride of the other man, and before he knew it, he was wrapped in a tight embrace, his face pressed into the wool of the man's shoulder. It smelled expensive. Savile Row. Not a medical student after all then.

'Goodnight, Doctor,' the young man whispered in his ear, and before he could pull back, the wind was knocked out by the sharp blow to his guts. He felt his eyes widen and his mouth drop. This wasn't right – in fact, this was very wrong. The arm around him tightened and a searing pain ran through his insides as the out-of-sight arm jerked suddenly upwards. He felt the young man tense before stepping back. Blood splattered across the tarmac between them and dripped down the side of his car. Crimson stained the young man's highly polished black shoes.

'Why?' The word wouldn't come out. He slid down the side of the car and watched the man turn and walk, head down, out of the car park. Wasn't his car. Just been waiting. Why? He stared at the ground as rain and blood mixed. *His blood.* His life. His *death.* The first wave of panic ran through his veins, veins that were so desperately trying to pump the blood that was so keen to leave him.

He felt dizzy, and the black spots that appeared at the corners of his eyes were spreading. Someone would come ... there were cameras ... someone would see ... This was too surreal. He couldn't be dying. Not here. Not now. Not *him.*

A few moments later his body proved him wrong.

The weather isn't as warm as it was in Paris, and it's raining. The heavy drops patter on the small metal slide and climbing frame to her left as she swings open the damp gate and strolls into the gardens of Woburn Square. The path is made of yellow grit, and she thinks it's pretty against the green of the central lawn. It makes her think of the walkways, and for a moment she is filled with a feeling she doesn't recognise – an ache, something new amidst so many new things. A longing for home. She shakes it away and breathes in the air that smells of wetness and petrol and the sweat of millions.

Water spills from the leaves of the trees that are spread out at regular intervals between the cast-iron fence and the path to afford some sense of peace and privacy in the midst of the bustling city, and she feels a splash of cool trickle down the back of her neck and slip under the collar of her baggy jumper.

Perhaps she should have worn more, but she likes the feel of the soft jeans on her legs and the wool brushing her body. Still, goosebumps prickle the fine hairs on her arms. She's not sure if she likes them or not.

A bus horn blares and a bunch of schoolkids pass on the other side of the fence, cussing each other in the vilest terms. The language sounds rough. London, she is realising, lacks the romance of Paris, and yet, she thinks with a smile, it has something of its own. It is old and gritty and filled with harsh truths hidden in plain sight. It is clever and fast and full of life. Its gestures are cynical, but made with a cheeky grin. London is a city that winks at you as it steals your wallet. There is no mistaking that this is the Architect's home. It stinks of him.

She smiles at the figure waiting for her in the wooden hut at the far end of the square. It is a quaint structure, with its white, waist-high fence that is almost picket-like, and the pale blue benches that line it within. There's a miniature pavilion, which on a sunny day is probably filled with students, or workers eating their lunches and chatting, or maybe lovers, curled up together watching the world go by. She likes it. It's a simple thing that has been built purely for the quiet pleasure of others. A good person designed it, she is sure of this.

'I like the look,' she says.

The tramp grins back, running a tongue over what are left of his teeth and highlighting the gaps as he plucks at the strings on his violin. 'I thought you would.' He puts the instrument carefully down on the bench beside him.

'Don't stop on my account,' she says. For a moment everything in the world falls silent, and then her head fills once more with the sounds of the city.

'There's always music. You don't need me to play it to hear it.'

And this is the truth. She hears the tunes in everything. 'It's good to see you.'

'I thought you'd come soon.' His eyes shine with his good mood. She's glad he's enjoying himself. 'It's all happening here,' he continues.

'Isn't it just?' She looks around her. 'Everything is happening all the time.' For a moment she is overwhelmed. 'This place is . . .' She isn't sure of the words she's looking for. 'This place is . . .'

'. . . wonderful?' He finishes her statement with a question, but she leaves it unanswered. Perhaps it is wonderful, but its wonders aren't why either of them are here, and it would be best not to forget that.

'How is he?' she asks instead.

The tramp lets out a throaty laugh. 'Oh my, he is something else. Do you think we should help him?'

The rain is coming down heavier now and she steps inside and sits beside him. 'Not just yet. I think we'll just watch a while longer.'

She smiles up at him. It really is good to see him.

'Play something lovely for me.'

And so he does.

Adam Bradley didn't run but walked fast from the hospital car park and rejoined the main streets and the flow of pedestrians moving quickly, all eager to get out of the rain. No one followed him. He hadn't expected anyone to. Someone was probably only just getting round to calling the police once they'd stopped trying to perform a miracle on Dr Gibbs' body. They would be wasting their time. Not even God could resurrect that man.

He slowed and turned down a side alley before pulling the mobile phone out of his pocket. He had one more job to do before he could head back. He smiled. So far the day had gone well. Mr Bright would be pleased with him.

The phone, a disposable pay-as-you-go – and one of hundreds he had access to – had only one phone number stored in it and that was on speed-dial, the direct line number for Chelsea Police Station. Under the limited protection of a fire-escape doorway, he pressed call.

'I'd like to speak to someone in the Murder Squad, please,' he said. 'I think I just saw someone kill a man.'

The desk sergeant tried to take his name and details, and Bradley speeded his breathing up slightly, making his words panicked. 'Look, if you don't put me through, I'll hang up. I probably shouldn't have rung anyway. What if he saw me? What if—?' He smiled as the voice at the other end did its best to soothe him before putting him on hold. After a moment a second voice came on.

'This is Detective Inspector Charles Ramsey. You have a crime to report?'

'Yes, I think there's been a murder. 36A Dayton Gardens.'

'What makes you think a crime has been committed, sir?' The man was American, every word spoken in a strong Yankee drawl.

'One of the front windows is smashed. I looked through the letterbox and saw blood on the hallway tiles. I think someone's dead in there. There was a man in there too. Tall and dark. I saw him come out of one room and cross into another. That's when I ran.'

'What did he look like, this man?'

'I don't know, maybe six foot? Dark short hair. He was wearing a suit. Maybe late thirties. Craggy face.'

'Sounds like you got a good look at him.'

'I was scared, man. There was so much blood—'

'I'm going to need to take your name—'

Bradley hung up and then turned the phone off. The Detective Inspector could call that number back as much as he liked and he wouldn't get an answer. Once he'd found the body, of course, the anonymous caller will be like so many others: an ordinary citizen not wanting to put himself in the firing line of a court and the justice system, because they couldn't afford the time off work, or had too many skeletons in their own closet to want to have their name on any police file. England was full of such people these days, all ordinary, all grubby. No one would spend much time looking for him. He took the phone apart and crunched the sim card under his well-polished shoe. On the main street he dropped the front of the phone in one rubbish bin and the back in a second.

There was a spring in his step that came from the satisfaction of a job well done, and knowing that his boss would be pleased. He looked around at the bland faces of the populace as they passed him by, their pasty bodies covered in cheap anoraks and tracksuits and off-the-peg suits. Once they would have considered him worse than the dirt on their shoes, and looked at him with fearful disgust, if they'd looked at him at all. These days, those same people still gave him a slight berth as they passed, and still looked at him as if he was different, but now the looks were filled with fearful awe. They recognised, if only subconsciously, the presence of superiority. It was in the fine wool of his coat, and the sleek cut of his hair. It was in his eyes. He was better than them all: he knew it, and so did they.

The black Mercedes pulled up along side him as he strolled down the pavement, and for a moment his smile fell.

He hadn't organised his driver. He'd planned to make his own way home from here. He stopped and frowned. The tinted window slid down and from inside he saw a flash of silver hair and a sharp smile.

'Get in, Bradley. I've got one more thing I need you to do.'

Bradley's frown disappeared and he grinned. There were still some hours of daylight left, plenty of time in which to make whatever mischief his boss required.

'Anything, sir.'

The door clicked shut.

Hours later, when night had fallen, Mr Bright stood on the roof of Senate House and stared out over the city. It glittered in the falling rain and he wished for a moment it would bring him more pleasure. He thought of Adam Bradley. It wasn't remorse that he felt, perhaps something close to passing regret, but the boy's death couldn't be helped. He'd had a few months longer than he'd probably have managed if he'd been left on that estate with a needle deep in his arm. As it was, right from the start he'd had a part to play in something much bigger than his own short, pathetic life.

Somewhere in the tangled network of streets below, Bradley's body lay waiting to be discovered next to an over-flowing skip. He had no identification on him and his neck had been cleanly broken. At least there had been no need to make him suffer. From the flat in Canary Wharf, various items of his possessions were being moved to a smaller council flat in his name that he'd never known about. His bank account details had been amended and a sum of cash placed in a drawer of the flat he'd never seen. New truths were so easy to create.

Castor Bright wondered if he should be feeling a small

sense of satisfaction that things were going according to his plans, but now, when there were divisions and mistrust everywhere he turned, it was hard to find the excitement he'd had in the early days. New truths were so easy to create – they always had been.

He turned his back on the city and headed inside. He needed to find out who was using the Interventionists against them. He wouldn't be hearing from Cass Jones again, not just yet, and certainly not about Abigail Porter. But then, whether Cassius Jones could find Abigail Porter or not had never been the point of the meeting. It was just a convenient excuse.

He allowed himself a small, self-satisfied smile. If Mr Solomon were here, then he would be laughing and slapping Mr Bright on the back for his masterful control of the pieces of the game. The Solomon of old, at any rate, before the testing got out of hand and the Dying took hold of his sanity. Back when they had been brothers, Solomon, with all his gentle charm and charisma, would have appreciated with Mr Bright was doing. He would have 'got it'. Sometimes people had to be immersed in the fire before they could rise out of the flames, better and stronger than they ever had been. That was Mr Bright's plan for Cassius Jones.

Of course, sometimes – it was Mr Solomon's voice that rose unbidden in his head, the Solomon of aeons before, whose voice was filled with light and humour – *if you put something in fire, it just screams and burns.*

Mr Bright ignored the thought and pressed the button to take him down. Later, he would check in on the Experiment, but for now he thought he'd go and sit with the First. It was peaceful in there with his old friend. They understood each other. And he listened well.

*

At Cass's flat, there was no evidence of a break-in. Whoever the fucker was who had stolen his kitchen knife – glaringly absent from the block – he had used a key. Cass had chucked the knife into a bin several miles away from Powell's house. Now home, he regretted the action. He should have brought it back and bleached it clean, but he'd just wanted rid of it. Left with no choice but to destroy the rest of any potential evidence, he grabbed the block and remaining knives and shoved them into a carrier bag before going back outside into the rain and dumping the bag in the wheelie bin belonging to one of the flats in a block much further down the street. Back upstairs, he locked the door and put the chain on. He stared at it. It was like closing the fucking gate after the horse had bolted. Someone had been inside his flat. His blood simmered. He wanted to rip the fucker's head off. Who was trying to play him now?

In the kitchen he washed the soles of his shoes and then stripped off his clothes. He'd been careful in Powell's house, but he knew better than most how easy trace evidence could be picked up, as well as left behind. After scouring every room for any sign that more of his possessions might be missing – or, conversely, that something else might have been planted, he finally had a shower, forcing himself to try to relax under the hot stream. Maybe he should have called Powell's death in and trusted in his colleagues to find the truth, but there were too many secrets wrapped up in this, and he had too many enemies on the force who'd be more than happy to see him go down for a murder he didn't commit.

He still wasn't in the clear. He chopped out the last of the cocaine into one long line and snorted it, hoping to quell the greasy fear in the pit of his stomach. He needed to speak to Dr Gibbs again. When he found out about his friend's death, the first thing he'd think about would be the policeman who had been asking questions about the Flush5 ward. He'd tell him some bollocks, like he'd forgotten the address, and could he have it again. Hopefully, Gibbs would be too tired and busy to be suspicious of a policeman's motives. It wasn't good, but it was all he had unless a brainwave hit him by the morning.

In the meantime he had one thing he could do. He sent Perry Jordan a text telling him to find out the whereabouts of a London doctor called Richard Shearman, and to email him the details. He was probably working privately somewhere, maybe within a Flush5 hospital.

The numbness that crept over his teeth and up his nose was pleasant, as was the confidence that came with it. He'd find out what the fuck was going on and he'd deal with it.

He grabbed a bottle of beer from the fridge and turned the TV on, needing the background noise to help him refocus. There was nothing more he could do tonight. He thought about trying Mr Bright again, but decided against it. There were no answers to be had there, and whatever deal they'd done, Cass didn't trust him. Did he have something to do with this set-up, or was it whoever was behind Abigail Porter's disappearance? Either way, for now his communication with Mr Bright was done.

'I believe that Alison McDonnell has served her country well in the past, but it is with some regret that I say that I no longer trust that she is competent for the great office she holds.' On screen the Home Secretary was trying to make himself heard over the jostling journalists pressing cameras into his face and shouting questions. 'Yes, I do intend to challenge her for the leadership of our party. I believe that I have the support of those on our benches, both the front and the back, who want the best for our government and, more importantly, for the people of Great Britain.'

'Do you have any comment on the alleged assassination attempt?' a faceless voice asked from somewhere behind the thrusting microphone.

'I can't comment on that at the moment, but have called for an official inquiry into those events. I find it hard to believe that any politician would consider creating false terror in these already strained times in order to bolster their public opinion; however, there are several security issues that I will be raising with the inquiry.'

Cass swallowed his beer. Fuck, with friends like that, the PM really didn't need enemies. By denying that McDonnell had been involved in whatever had led Abigail Porter down to Covent Garden Underground Station, he'd raised the question in the minds of those who maybe hadn't thought it before.

The camera cut to the woman herself. She looked tired and beyond strained. 'I have nothing to say at this time except that I'm confident that I will continue to have the support of my Cabinet colleagues and the rest of the party at this time.'

She didn't look convinced, and neither did the tight bundle of people around her as they all disappeared back inside 10 Downing Street. One man turned, his eyes calmly scanning the small crowd of journalists who had been allowed up the famous road. He must have been Abigail Porter's replacement, Cass figured. As the door closed, he could only imagine the collective slumping of shoulders on the other side. He sympathised with McDonnell – he knew only too well how it felt to have someone coming after you, and whatever had happened on that Underground platform, none of it had been the Prime Minister's fault. It wasn't she who had arranged it. It wasn't about *her* at all.

By the open window he lit a cigarette and peered out. Where was the musical tramp when he needed him? He might have seen whoever had broken in and taken his knife. But it looked like the old man had taken a couple of nights off, just when he might have been useful. The night air was cool; Cass liked its freshness against his skin. It made him feel alive when he was surrounded by the impatience of the dead.

Despite finding a link between the kids, they were still technically no further in finding out what had caused them to kill themselves, and his stomach tightened as he remembered the hope in the eyes of Cory Denter's mother. It reminded him of another pair of pleading dark eyes, much younger, and long dead. Cass had blown that kid's face away. *He had no glow. Chaos in the darkness.* The thoughts drifted in the dark spaces of his mind, adrift from the normal.

He was heading towards letting Mrs Denter down, unless it began to look like Cory Denter might have been murdered too, but that was unlikely. Whatever had happened to Cory had been something less ordinary than murder. A breath of smoke drifted free for a brief moment before being ripped apart by the London breeze. Murder. Within a couple of days it was possible that someone might be coming after him for that if he wasn't careful, and then the dead kids would be someone else's problem. They could take hold of someone else's soul. He wasn't sure they'd leave quietly, though; the dead seemed to like his company.

Powell's dying face refused to stray far from his mind, and as it rose up once again, Cass remembered the power he'd felt knowing the man was dying: that overwhelming sense of anger and vengeance. Even now, so many years and so much guilt later, he was still Charlie Sutton. He'd shot that kid, and he'd felt almost nothing watching Powell die.

That wasn't natural. How much black was there in his soul?

His thoughts froze and he frowned as an image filled the screen. It was a photograph, a head-shot of a man laughing: Dr Andrew Gibbs. He sat down and turned the volume up.

... stabbed to death by an unknown stranger in the hospital car park after finishing his shift in Accident and Emergency. His death is prompting calls for better security ... Two images came up, obviously taken from the cheap car park cameras that should have been replaced ten years ago. The first was of two men standing beside a car. The other showed a tall man with shoulder-length dark hair in a long overcoat as he walked away. His face wasn't visible, but he looked nothing like Cass.

Mixed emotions thudded through his veins as the news moved swiftly on. The doctor's death had had its allocated fifteen seconds. The relief that there would now be a suspect in the Powell case other than him was good, but it didn't pierce the web of grey worry that clung to him: Gibbs was dead, as was Powell, so what was the purpose of their murders? Was it simply to implicate Cass, or was that just an added bonus while stopping the trail to Luke? Was someone else looking for the boy, too? *Why* were they so interested in his brother's child anyway – what the fuck was it the Network found so special about the Jones family? And who was the woman who'd called him? *The boy is the key. Don't let them keep the boy.* Her words echoed those his dead brother had spoken six months and a lifetime ago. *Redemption is the key.* There were too many keys to unlock too many secrets.

The answerable questions hung around him in the flat that felt much less like home since a stranger had been inside. The chair beneath him was an unfamiliar shape. The colours in the room were a shade off-kilter. The world was shifting again, leaving the ground unsteady beneath his feet as something unseen nudged him into his place in the game. He felt entirely alone. It wasn't the first time.

Chapter Twenty-Two

Elroy Peterson finally stopped screaming as the machines around him powered down and one of the technicians slowly removed the various pieces of equipment from over his eyes and head, as well the monitors from his chest. There were no goosebumps on his bare torso, but Mr Bright wasn't surprised – the Experiment rooms were kept hot. The students were able to travel further that way. Perhaps it was the contrast with the cold *out there*. He wasn't sure, but he didn't need to understand why; it was enough for him to know that it helped. His remit had always been the bigger picture.

The boy's eyes were wide and dark and there were flecks of blood lining the edges of his pupils. His whole body trembled and sweat dripped from his hairline. The doctors had been unanimous in agreeing that the procedure was causing the subjects brain damage, and Mr Bright wasn't surprised. They never came back whole, and with each attempt it looked like they left a little more behind. In this, they were all united: this boy, the ones who had killed themselves, and those like Rasnic, whose *Glow* had been ripped from them, leaving them empty and mad and very, very human.

The young man sobbed quietly, and Mr Bright felt pity for his pain. Still, within an hour all memory of his time here would be forgotten and he'd be free of the Experiment until his feet led him back to take part again. He'd been a good find, this one. He'd gone further than any of the rest as the equipment sent his consciousness up and out through the Hubble to the darkness beyond.

'What did you see?' he asked. He didn't normally take much interest in the subjects themselves, but as he was here and this one was unusual, his curiosity got the better of him. Perhaps the events of the day had made him nostalgic.

'It was beautiful,' the boy breathed. 'It was terrible.' His forehead knotted as he searched for a word in his damaged mind. 'Chaos,' he said eventually.

'Yes, that's it.' Mr Bright smiled.

'So much darkness, and then chaos. Chaos in the darkness.' He tilted his head. The technician continued to put the equipment away, paying no attention to the boy's words.

Mr Bright leaned forward.

'What else?'

'They're still screaming.' Elroy Peterson gave no indication that he'd heard the silver-haired man's words. '*I'm* still screaming. I can still hear it.' He blinked rapidly. 'It's behind my eyes.'

'Could you see the colours? Could you see beyond?'

'Colours.' The pupils widened again. 'So many colours. New colours.' His hands clutched at the sides of his head. 'I remembered.' Tears ran down his sweating cheeks. 'I remembered.'

Mr Bright watched him impassively. In many ways they were dull and predictable, but somewhere in their circuitry these first flawed failures had the memory of all that had been. He felt a sudden wave of fondness for them, one that he hadn't felt in very many years. Perhaps it was good for him to take time to remember.

'You have to look for the lines.' His voice was soft and filled with kindness. 'Next time, you find the lines.'

'I can't,' Peterson whispered, his voice thick with snot. 'I can't.'

Mr Bright stood, and stroked the boy's hot head with his cool, dry palm. 'Of course you can.' If he couldn't, then eventually one would surely come along who could. Despite his small wave of nostalgia, he himself had no desire to take the walkways, or even to see them again, but if anyone were to have the knowledge of where they were, then he wanted it to be him. He would protect that for the First in the ways he thought fit. He turned and left the disturbed young man to dress in peace, happy to get out of the stifling heat.

The walkways hadn't crossed his mind in aeons, not until the Dying came and those among his own number had started clamouring for the Experiment to find their way home. Now he found that the very concept plagued him. The Network might not be able to find them, but that didn't mean that there hadn't been traffic from the other end. Who would know if there had been visitors among them, looking perhaps to see what they had achieved? He wouldn't necessarily send an emissary, that wasn't how he worked.

There were rumours, of course, but these days there were always rumours of something. But perhaps he should take a little more care – if suspicion of the boy's existence got back, then who knew what the outcome would be? Perhaps he would care, perhaps not: it was always so difficult to tell with *him*. His moods had never been predictable. Mr Bright stopped a passing technician.

'Tell the doctors to raise the intensity on this one when we start up again. Undo his hypnosis for now, just like the others; I don't want them coming here for a couple of weeks. But keep track of him. We'll need him again.'

His mobile phone rang and he smiled as he listened to the voice on the other end. 'Excellent,' he said. 'I'll be back shortly. Deal with the arrangements; I don't want any mess. You can access his passport information and bank accounts if you follow the instructions I left.' He paused. 'Good. I don't need the details. I'm sure you can make it believable.'

On his way back down to the earthy grit of London at street level he considered calling the other three and confronting them, but whoever was attempting to betray him and their age-old alliance would never be drawn into admitting it. They were all too strong, and in these times of slow decay and *ennui*, teeth were being bared within all the Cohorts. He would not show weakness. He was *not* weak, and someone was underestimating him quite badly if they thought he could be so easily overthrown. Still, he thought as he left the bright confines of Senate House behind, they would learn. He ignored a small group of laughing students who jostled past him, drunkenly hugging and winding round each other with all the joy and power and false glory of youth. They in turn ignored him as he stepped into the sleek black car and let it speed him away into what was shaping up to be a very long night.

Two hours later he was feeling mildly exasperated by the man tied securely to a chair in what he still thought of as Mr Solomon's office. Blood was splattered across the crimson carpet, but the mess was of no concern. Solomon had ripped a man apart in this room and his blood had been cleaned up easily enough. Scotchguarding, it would appear, really did work. Red's frenzied crying had finally diminished somewhat. He looked somewhat thinner and more pathetic without his crisp shirt and couture suit. There were burn marks on his chest and three of his teeth were missing. It hadn't been a pleasant process, Mr Bright was sure, but it had been necessary.

Mr Bright himself hadn't watched. He'd been sipping camomile tea and reading the papers in the cool calm of the lounge while the two professionals had briskly gone to work. He trusted them to do what they did best, and at the end of the day, he wasn't a monster. He'd lived too long and seen too much to relish watching a man being broken in order to speak the truth. As it turned out, Asher Red had taken very little breaking.

A vague sense of disgust washed over him as he waited for the man in the chair to collect himself. The windows were closed, as was the door, and an unpleasant tang hung in the room. The old saying was true: fear really did stink. Asher Red had always been so smooth and calm and contained, with an air of arrogance and superiority that few of his peers had ever dared challenge. Perhaps it was the contrast of that image with the pathetic husk of a man dribbling blood and saliva into his own stained lap that made the scent so sour.

Mr Solomon had always disliked Asher Red. He'd called him a man in denial of his own humanity: an overblown peacock. Perhaps Solomon had been right. Mr Bright had neither liked nor disliked the man, but he had put an element of faith in him. His father had served the Network well, and he'd always presumed the son to have the same qualities, but it would appear that was not the case. His terrible ambition had made a fool out of him; the pen-pusher had been around power so long, he clearly thought it belonged with him. But he had been stupid in too many ways, and he'd sold himself cheaply – perhaps not in terms of money, but certainly in terms of information. The Network had so many assets that money was of no value.

Information, on the other hand, was always a commodity.

'So, you never met them face to face?'

'No.' Asher Red's voice was barely recognisable through his swollen lips and bleeding mouth. 'It was all through emails and phone calls. They promised me a place in the Network. They said I had the *Glow.*' He looked up, his eyes pleading for some kind of understanding. 'They promised me that under the new regime I would have my own sector. I would be someone. One of *you.* They said I would live here.' He sobbed again, and Mr Bright thought it was well that he should. The man was a fool. Had it not occurred to him that if his secret partner felt he was so special, why had he never shown his face, or given him a name or two? Had Red really been that arrogant that he hadn't seen how expendable he was?

'What do you know about the women?' Mr Bright asked.

'I already told you.' Asher Red managed a small, helpless shrug. 'I had to set up a Hotmail account for each one. I contacted them with a precise message when I was told to. I met them at the Lathan Hilton.' He blubbed out fresh tears as the stupidity of what he'd done finally hit home. 'They'd told me there were no cameras, that I wouldn't be seen.' A thick line of mucus hung from his nose. 'I believed them. I kept each girl until I got a call saying a car was ready for them at the back of the hotel. I took them down and I didn't see them after that. They were strange, almost like they were sedated.' He sniffed, but the stream of snot refused to shift. 'And that's everything, I promise you. I haven't heard from him since.'

'I don't doubt it.' Mr Bright believed him. 'You were just a lackey, and you've done your task.' He let out a long breath. 'Your father would have been disappointed if he'd been here. He was an intelligent man. He understood loyalty. He was respected.' He let his voice linger over the last word, before moving over to the door. He needed some clean air, and perhaps a strong coffee.

'What are you going to do with me?' Asher Red asked so quietly that the tremulous words barely made it across the room.

Mr Bright didn't answer, but quietly closed the door behind him. Asher Red was in no place to be asking questions. His own office next door was a pleasant relief. There was no scent of fear staining the surfaces, and the temperature of the air was pleasant; neither too hot nor too cool. He poured himself a coffee from the freshly brewed pot and sat behind his large desk. The three women's folders were neatly lined in a row, their photos on top. He needed to look into their family backgrounds if he was to find out who was manipulating them.

A red light flashed on the large phone and he answered it on loudspeaker.

DeVore said, 'All three women *were* projected, fifteen years ago when they were teenagers. I fed their images in and searched the data stream. The results were one hundred per cent.'

Fifteen years ago these women were flagged up by the Interventionists? He looked down at the files again. What had made them so important? They had been to someone, however. And that someone had clearly spent the years since playing the long game. He felt a small flash of respect for his mystery opponent. 'Why? What questions were asked? Were they requested information, or just random data?'

'I don't know.' DeVore sounded tired, but Mr Bright didn't care. There had been a time when it had taken far more than several sleepless nights to bring on even the hint of fatigue. They'd grown soft. Maybe that's why death had finally come among them.

'But each woman was projected from one of the three who left their hard reflections behind and subsequently died,' DeVore added.

'I want to know why.' If they had come from the three dead Interventionists, then the display of their faces in the stream fifteen years ago would not be coincidental. They either projected them purposefully, or someone asked them a question which produced those women as the answer. But who?

'The only people who put questions to them are us: the Inner and First Cohort.'

'I know that.' Mr Bright tried to keep the impatience out of his voice, but didn't succeed. Perhaps some of their own were as intellectually challenged as Asher Red – or maybe they had just been here so long they'd forgotten who they really were. 'Go through the data again, and again if you have to, until you can give me something more.'

He ended the call and leaned back in the vast leather chair. He pushed a button under the desk and his computer rose up from within its surface. Another button turned on the slim TV on the wall, which was tuned to the 24-hour news channels. Anything else was unnecessary. He watched for a few moments. The leadership debate was now in full swing, with various Cabinet ministers coming out with their knives. On other channels images of the destruction caused by the recent spate of international bombings still raged out from the screen.

Everything was unsettled. The world was already financially on its knees and now *someone* – one of their own – was intent on unbalancing it further. Whoever it was wouldn't be working alone either. They'd invaded the House of Intervention and used those poor freaks to wreak havoc. The challenge was coming – but from where, and why? He looked again at the three women's files. Fifteen years of planning at least. He had been watching the Jones family for the greater good of all, but who had been watching these women? He needed to go through the X accounts and that was going to take some time. Asher Red was going to have to wait a while for his answer.

Chapter Twenty-Three

Cass got to the station just before eight, not too early and not too late. Despite trying to act as normally as possible, it felt as if everything he did was in some way conspicuous or slightly out of place. He hadn't slept much, and his dreams had been disturbed by the constant invasion of the dead and the feeling that at any moment someone would come knocking on his door asking about Powell's death. No one did, though, and when morning finally rolled around the ghosts retreated to wherever they went when daylight pushed them aside.

After parking in his normal space he took the stairs two at a time up to his office, nodding his usual hellos as he went. He paused to grab a coffee from the machine. The station was rarely empty, and even this early it was already buzzing with life, people firing up computers and sorting through the files of crimes – some they had a chance of solving, others so cold they'd all but frozen – and nearly all bland and dull and terrifyingly mundane. These days it sometimes felt like everyone was a criminal.

The coffee burned and he felt an invisible bubble form between him and the rest of the people working. Sure, a few of them had known about, and even in a small way been involved in, Bowman's drug syndicate, but yesterday he'd *tampered* with a crime scene – no, he thought as he walked towards his office, he'd tampered with a *murder* scene. He'd perverted the course of justice and left the scene of a murder with the death unreported. He might not have killed Powell himself, but he'd done enough to hang himself if anyone ever found out. In his mind he'd had just cause, but no one else would see it that way. What he'd done was criminal – there were no two ways about it. He turned his computer on and waited for the inbox to fill with people requesting various overdue reports as it did every day. Yes, what he'd done was criminal, but as long as he wasn't found out he could live with it. He lived with worse. Still, a cold sick feeling refused to release its grip on his guts and it took every bit of his willpower not to keep checking the doorway for unfamiliar coppers striding towards his office.

As it was, the next person to come in was Armstrong, just before nine.

'Where have you been?' Cass asked. 'Thought you were an early bird.'

'I am.' The sergeant held up some sheets of paper. 'The phone records boys get in at 8.30. I was waiting for them, and sat on them until they got us these.'

Armstrong was good. He was a career copper and a good detective, a rare combination. Cass had decided the young man was like a terrier; if he got something between his teeth, he wouldn't let go. 'Good. What have we got?'

'It is good. There's one number that comes up over and over on Angie Lane's records, for the best part of the last six months. Some calls and a lot of texts – I mean, hundreds in a month.'

'And? Who is it?'

'His name's Dr Anthony Cage.' Armstrong grinned. 'He's a lecturer in Business at South Bank University.'

Cass leaned back in his chair, all his own troubles forgotten for a moment.

'Do you think she was calling him about her schoolwork?' The heavy sarcasm in the young man's voice made clear what he thought about it.

'Let's go and find out.'

'He's at home. No lecture until this afternoon.'

'Got the address?'

'Of course.'

'Good.' Cass drained the last of his coffee. 'I'll drive.' He was glad to be getting away from the oppressive confines of the office, and in his own car he could smoke. Armstrong was just going to have to get used to that. 'Let's go and crawl through the rush hour.'

Rachel Honey's tea was almost cold by the time she remembered to drink it. She sipped it anyway, her mind elsewhere as she stared out of the window and onto the street. Sleep had evaded her; what she'd seen in the Uni car park had been niggling in the back of her mind. It was wrong, she knew it. And then there was the other thing. She sighed, and it felt like her flat sighed back at her in sympathy. Maybe she was making a big deal out of nothing. Maybe it could all be explained away. She didn't think so, though. The knot in her stomach was telling a different story.

She put the mug down before getting the policeman's card out. She stared at it for a moment, indecisive and hesitant. He *had* said to call if she thought of anything. But what if he thought she was just wasting police time? She chewed her bottom lip. There had been something slightly frightening about DI Jones – something hard in his eyes that she'd never seen in someone before. But there had been kindness there too, and he was clever – anyone could see that. She shook herself slightly and picked up the phone, her heart thumping nervously in her chest. The call rang out and clicked onto answerphone. She waited for the gruff voice to finish and then left her message. It wasn't what she'd planned to say, coming out all garbled and wrong, and she hung up, embarrassed. God, she could be such a moron at times. Still, hopefully he'd get what she meant, and anyway, she could always call back later.

She took the undrinkable tea into the kitchen and poured it away. She might not have spoken to the detective but she felt better already. She leaned against the sink. Why was she waiting for him to do all the work anyway? If she wanted to be a journalist, then why the hell didn't she start now?

Cass got out of the car and glanced at his phone before heading up the path to Dr Cage's house in Chiswick. Doctors were surrounding him these days, but at least this one was not a medical doctor but a PhD in Business, and he was still very much alive. He'd had two missed calls; one from Perry Jordan and one from a number he didn't recognise, and his message icon box was flashing.

'Turnham Green Tube Station is just round the corner from here,' Armstrong said. 'That came up on her Oyster card.'

A net curtain twitched in the approaching house and Cass put his phone back in his pocket. The messages would have to wait. He didn't want Armstrong overhearing anything Jordan might say, and if it was Mr Bright on the other number, that could wait for now too. He was here on the business of the innocent. Angie Lane's dead fingers had tightened their grip. The curtain dropped back suddenly and Cass almost smiled. He could smell the man's guilt from here. It was amazing what human behaviour gave away.

The front door hadn't opened before they reached it, even though Cage knew they were coming. Cass knocked hard. The man who opened the door stared impassively at them.

'Yes?'

'Detective Inspector Jones, and this is DS Armstrong. Murder Squad. We need to talk to you about Angie Lane.'

'You'd better come in.' The faux-casual expression slipped and the man swallowed. Cass could tell that this wasn't going to take long.

'Is your wife at home?' Cass asked.

'I don't have one.' Cage led them into the sitting room. 'Never been married. I like my own space.'

Cass was surprised. Why would Cage have killed Angie if it wasn't to protect his marriage? 'We've been looking through Angie's phone statements,' he said. 'She sent you a lot of texts. And it wasn't one-way traffic. What was going on with you two?'

Cage sat opposite him. Armstrong stayed standing. It was clear Cage wasn't lying about living alone; there were no soft touches or knickknacks dotted on the surfaces, and there was a distinct lack of family photographs.

'Does it matter? She's dead now.'

'It certainly matters if they were in any way relevant to her death,' Armstrong said.

'But Angie killed herself. One of those student suicides.' Cage's eyes flickered from one policeman to the other but didn't linger on either, falling to the floor instead. He wasn't a bad-looking man for someone in his fifties, but his skin was starting to sag around his jowls and when his shoulders slumped, the small pot belly was accentuated. Fear never made anyone pretty.

'I'm a busy man, so let's cut to the chase.' Cass leaned forward, forcing Cage's nervous eyes to meet his steady ones. 'We both know that Angie didn't kill herself. It just looks like she did. Now, why don't you tell me what went on with you two?'

'I didn't kill her,' Cage said. 'I didn't kill her.'

'You were sleeping with her. And giving her money. Don't deny it; we've seen the cash withdrawals.' Cass was jumping the gun on the bank account details, but it was a good hunch, and if it got a confession out of the man quicker, then Cass was all for that.

'I don't know how it started.' Cage shrugged slightly. 'Well, I do – a cliché. Extra help with assignments. Staying after class. That sort of thing.'

He hadn't denied the money, and Cass saw Armstrong scribbling down a note. He'd be getting the statements for the evidence file as soon as they were back at the station. Cass was learning that Armstrong was nothing if not efficient – maybe at last some of the endless paperwork would get done.

'A lot of the students like me.' Cage fiddled with his thinning hair. 'I try to make studying more interesting for them – you know, tell a few jokes, give them personal anecdotes. But although they like me, they're still lazy in the main. Angie wasn't, though. She really wanted to do well. She was maybe more grown-up than some of the rest.'

'So you started fucking her?'

Cass was crude deliberately, but it worked; Cage flinched.

'Yes,' he said, staring down at his hands. 'Yes, I did. She was young and pretty. I didn't think she'd fall in love with me, though.'

'You didn't feel the same way?' Armstrong asked.

'I was fond of her.' Cage smiled sadly. 'I was definitely flattered. Maybe for a little while I thought that was love.'

'Did you tell her you loved her?' Cass said.

Cage had the good grace to look away.

'I might have done. Once or twice. And then she started talking about us moving in together and starting a family and I knew then that I'd made a terrible mistake.'

'You thought it was just fun between consenting adults.' Cass snorted, derisively. 'But for her it wasn't just fun, because she wasn't really an adult. Not like you. She was just starting out, and she'd fallen in love. So what did you do? Break it off?'

'Yes.' Cage's trembling had spread up his body and he swallowed hard. He had the look of a man who had been wanting to talk for days. So much murder was mundane, and Cass could almost feel sorry for this man, if he hadn't so coldly dressed the murder as suicide.

'She didn't take it well. At first she texted constantly, telling me how much she loved me, and that she was sorry and she wouldn't push for the relationship to go further – all that stuff.'

'But you're old enough to know she didn't mean it, right? She was just saying whatever it would take to get you back.'

'I knew that the best thing I could do was to be firm about it. It would be better for her in the long run. I've got this far through my life without becoming a family man. I couldn't start now. Plus, well – she was a student.'

'It's not illegal to sleep with a university student, is it?' Armstrong asked.

'No, it's not, but it is frowned upon. And Angie knew it. Once she realised I meant what I'd said she started making threats – she was going to tell the Dean that I'd been giving her money for sex.' His face flushed. 'As you know, I *had* given her money. I even gave her a thousand pounds – a kind of goodbye gift. But the money wasn't anything to do with sex and never had been. She'd had a waitressing job in some restaurant that paid peanuts, and she was struggling to pay her rent. Her parents were having a hard time, I think, so she couldn't go to them. I wanted her to quit the job, so I said I'd help her with things.' He shook his head at his own stupidity. 'I think she read more into it than was there.'

'So you killed her?'

'God, no!' Cage looked up. 'No – I gave her more money. I thought maybe if I could just manage the situation until she calmed down then everything would be all right. She was a nice girl. I didn't think she would actually tell the Dean – but I did worry about who she had told. She always swore she'd kept us a secret, but she was upset and angry, and you know what girls are like when they get a glass of wine or two into them. They talk about men; whether they're twenty or forty, that doesn't change. If she told someone, then it would be back to the Dean in no time. He's a "no smoke without fire" man – "fire" being the operative word.' He looked over at Armstrong. 'It might not be illegal to sleep with a student, but I'm a man in my fifties and if I lost my job I wouldn't get another shot. I've got some savings, but I need to stay in employment to get the mortgage paid off. I don't have much of a private pension. I— I used to have a small gambling problem in my thirties, and I lost some equity that way, back when there was such a thing. There are plenty of younger lecturers out there who'd easily fill my place, and for a lot less money. One whiff of this and I'd be out on my ear – especially if anyone mentioned the cash.'

'No one ever wants to look like they're paying for it, do they?' Cass asked.

'And I wouldn't want Angie to look like a cheap whore,' Cage countered, showing a flash of inner fire, 'which she wasn't.'

'Your concern for her is touching. Right up until the point you killed her.'

'I didn't kill her! Oh Christ, this is such a mess.' He rested his head in his hands for a moment and composed himself before sitting up again. 'She called me, said she had to speak to me, it was urgent. I'd been teaching, but she was at home. She said her housemate was out and could I go round, so I did.' He took a shaky breath. 'She was in the kitchen cutting up vegetables when I got there. She was smiling and happy – it took me off-guard. I had been expecting tears and tantrums. She made me a coffee and we talked for a bit, just small talk, about work and the course. Then out of the blue she told me she was pregnant. Just like that, with a big smile on her face. She said wasn't it wonderful that we were going to have a family? She said we should get married; that she'd be the perfect lecturer's wife. I couldn't believe it – she was talking away, and all I could see in my head were the faces of my colleagues in the faculty office and how they'd sneer at me. I'd get the sack and then be stuck with a baby to support and a bitter woman. It was like seeing my entire life crumbling away because some silly little cow didn't realise that it had just been fun and friendship.'

'What happened?'

'Well, I told her she had to have an abortion. I told her I'd pay for it and then that would be it: everything had to stop – the money, the texts, everything. I'd had enough.'

'You hadn't used protection?' Cass asked. Clearly Cage was one of the deluded middle classes that believed the bug could never find them.

'She said she was on the pill, and I believed her. Anyway, when I told her enough was enough, she just snapped. She lunged at me with that stupid vegetable knife like she wanted to stab me in the throat. She was screaming and swearing at me, and I grabbed her wrists and just threw her back to defend myself. She was wild – I'd never see her like that. There was some water on the floor, maybe from where she'd been washing the veg in the sink, and she slipped. She banged her head on the corner of the breakfast bar and went down.'

'So you thought you'd help her along by slitting her wrists and leaving her to die?'

'No.' Cage swallowed hard. He'd paled with the memory. 'I told you. *I didn't kill her.*'

Cass frowned. He'd been locked in Cage's tale, but now a different image rose up in his head suddenly: two girls coming out of the lecture theatre, both going to their lockers to dump their books. But when he left them, one was still holding hers. The key hadn't worked.

'Someone else did,' Cage finished. 'And she scares me.'

'Oh fuck.' Cass was suddenly on his feet and heading to the front door.

'Where are you going?' Armstrong called after him.

'Call a panda to come and take you and him back to the station. I'll see you there.' Someone else could have the fun job of telling Cage it had all been for nothing. Angie Lane hadn't been pregnant – she'd just been desperate for him to want her back. There was nothing in the path report about a baby. It was all so fucking stupid.

As he unlocked the car, he played back the first message on his phone – the one from the number he didn't recognise. It wasn't Mr Bright. *Shit.*

'Hi, DI Jones? It's Rachel Honey. From South Bank?' Her voice was soft and hesitant. 'This is probably nothing. I mean, really probably, but I've just been thinking about Angie. You see, it doesn't make sense, what Amanda said – there's probably an explanation and I don't want to waste your time, it's just – well, Angie was on the caving trip, down to Cheddar Gorge. They did caving and pot-holing. Isn't it dark in those kind of things? Like I said, it really is just a stupid thing, but I just can't get it out of my head, not combined with seeing them in the car park. Not Angie— After Angie was dead. I'm not making sense, am I? Maybe you could call me back if you get a few minutes? Thanks.' The message cut off. Shit. He pressed redial and waited for her number to start ringing. It did. No one answered.

Rachel stood in the doorway for a long few minutes. Going through someone else's stuff felt wrong on every level, and her heart pounded and her ears buzzed as the seconds ticked silently away. Finally, she pushed herself away from the cool wooden door behind her. Amanda wouldn't be back from Uni for at least an hour – there was nothing to be nervous about. Still, a chill of fear bloomed in her stomach and sent bile burning up towards her throat and she took a deep breath.

The room had been the small dining room of the flat, but she'd converted it after what had happened to Angie. The table was now folded down against one wall and in the middle of the floor a single blow-up mattress was neatly covered with a pillow and duvet. They'd picked up a cheap second-hand chest of drawers and side table for her stuff, although the other girl had left quite a lot at the old place to be collected when the lease was up. Maybe what Rachel was looking for would still be there rather than here? What was she looking for anyway? A confession? A locker key? Love letters, maybe?

She slid open the small drawer of the side table, careful not to knock any of the face creams and odds and ends that were stacked up on top. There was very little in there: a couple of magazines, some A4 lined paper and a couple of Biros under a battered university textbook, as well as a small make-up bag. Rachel quickly rifled through it – various lipsticks, eye-liner and mascara, just what she'd expect to find. She closed the drawer, flinching slightly at the grating of wood on wood. She was hardly proving her mettle as a hard-ass journalist. She was terrified searching a room in her own flat – how would she ever manage to do anything seriously undercover if she couldn't even manage that?

On the other side of the small room the chest of drawers proved equally fruitless. Its surface might have been a mess of jewellery trees and bits and pieces, but inside, each layer was impeccably neat. Even her underwear was folded and allocated into a section of one drawer; knickers to the left, tights and socks in the middle and bras on the right, all further sorted in colour coding. Rachel carefully searched around and under them but there were no hidden treasures. There wasn't even anything remotely seductive about any of the items. That was odd after what she'd seen. What *had* she seen? Really? The two of them in a car, talking heatedly, and then Amanda getting out – after checking there was no one else close by to see them. It meant something, she was sure it did, and what else could it mean other than an affair? She looked back at the sensible underwear and its tidiness that was so at odds with the clutter on the top. Was all that jewellery and mess just for show? If someone sorted their knicker drawer into itemised piles, then surely their rings and necklaces would be equally organised?

She frowned and moved on to the remaining drawers, her hand sliding carefully between each folded top or sweater to check nothing unusual was hidden there. There wasn't. She sat back on her heels for a moment before crawling round to check the small space between the back of the wood and the wall. Nothing. Thus far *nothing* just about summed it up. There were just clothes and accessories – where was all her personal stuff? If it had been Rachel in Amanda's position, she knew she'd have brought photos and pictures, to make the new room feel a bit like home. So it looked like Amanda had either left those back at the place she'd shared with Angie, or she just didn't have any, both of which options would be weird. There *was* something here – there had to be.

Looking under the duvet proved fruitless, revealing nothing but a clean sheet pulled tight across the airbed. Rachel's own bed-making consisted of just casually straightening up the top layer before heading off to college, and that was on the days she was feeling particularly diligent. Judging by the tautness of the cotton, Amanda clearly made hers with hospital-corner efficiency every morning. She rearranged the duvet as perfectly as she could manage before slipping a hand between the mattress and the carpet and running it all along the length. After that she checked the pillowcases, but all they contained was soft foam.

The fear she'd felt when she started was gone, replaced by niggling frustration. Her hair had come loose from her ponytail and she pushed it out of her face as she looked around her for somewhere she might have missed. In the corner of the room, a TV sat on an upturned dark blue plastic storage box. Her heart picked up the pace as she carefully lifted the heavy monitor – God only knew where Amanda had got this relic – and put it down on the carpet. She sat beside it and tilted the box upwards. She smiled. A single shoe box was hidden there. She pulled the cardboard container out and carefully lifted the lid. If Dr Cage had sent Amanda love letters – which would make him an idiot, but then most men were – then this is where they'd be.

Her heart raced as she tipped the contents out, no longer concerned about order as her curiosity overwhelmed her.

A frown slowly crinkled her face as she spread the various pieces of paper out in front of her. These weren't love letters. One was a statement from a firm of accountants providing what looked like quarterly balances for a series of investments and fund accounts, many of which were held abroad – one even in the Cayman Islands. Amanda might plead student poverty like the rest of them, but she certainly wasn't broke. In another envelope was two hundred pounds in cash. That made no sense either. Why would she have that much money – and why hide it away?

The cash was immediately forgotten when she unfolded a battered letter dated almost ten years previously. It was from a Harley Street doctor's address. She didn't know the name, but whoever he was, he had a lot of letters after his name. A psychiatrist? She scanned the several short paragraphs that followed.

> **Amanda Kemble has been a difficult child to evaluate. She is remarkably composed and has moments of being charming and engaging. While the death of her father when she was so young seems to have had no lasting effect on her, I do believe that witnessing her mother's slow deterioration and ultimate death from cancer goes in some way to explain the psychotic episode she recently had. When questioned on her mother ...**

Psychotic episode? What the hell did that mean? What was all this? Who was the girl that she'd let into her flat? Had Angie Lane known anything about this? She read to the end, and turned over, looking for some clue to what the younger Amanda might have done, but the event was only alluded to, and never mentioned in detail. Whatever it was, the doctor thought Amanda should be re-evaluated in another year. She stared at the sheet. Why had she even kept this?

'I killed my mother's cat.'

Rachel almost yelped as the voice cut through the silence and her own thoughts. She looked up. Amanda stood cool and composed in the doorway.

'I remember it took a long time to die. Comparatively. My mother took longer. It seemed like she took for ever to die. The cat died in an afternoon. I cut bits off it, just like they had with my mother. And just like with my mother, the amputations didn't save the cat.' She paused. 'It was very messy and I really don't like mess. They didn't have to worry about me doing that again.'

Rachel sat on her heels and stared up at the other girl. The fear was back now, and her mouth had dried. She thought she should say something – something innocuous and innocent, but she could feel the weight of her own guilt in the paper in her hands.

'I could mention how rude it is to look through someone else's things. And aside from that, you never find anything you might like.' She held up one hand. 'Are you looking for this?'

Something silver glinted between her fingers. A locker key.

'Are you sleeping with Dr Cage?' Rachel finally found her voice as she left the papers where they were lying and got to her feet.

'Good God, no.' Amanda laughed, a short sharp bark of unpleasantness. 'What an absurd suggestion. It wasn't me, it was silly little Angie. She was in love with him.'

Rachel was about to ask another question when Amanda

pushed the door closed and brought her other hand out from behind her back. The bread knife.

Somewhere out in the hallway, her mobile phone began to ring.

Cass was almost halfway across London by the time the station called back with Rachel Honey's address and he swore and cursed at every unfortunate driver that couldn't get out of his way quite quick enough, despite often having nowhere to go but the pavement, regardless of how loudly he blared his horn. A team was headed to the University to see if Amanda Kemble was there, and back-up was following behind him to the girls' flat. Rachel Honey didn't have a lecture until this afternoon, so she would likely be at home. If Amanda was there too, and if Rachel decided to confront her, then God only knew what would happen. No, he corrected himself, he didn't need God to tell him: Amanda Kemble would fight back. What the hell did she have to lose?

Finally at the bridge, Cass managed to get some speed up. Ten minutes. That was all he needed, ten minutes to make sure Rachel Honey was safe. He slapped the steering wheel and willed the traffic forward. Whatever other shit was going on, he did not want another dead teenager on his hands. Rachel Honey would *not* die on his shift. She fucking well would not.

'Angie wasn't scared of the dark,' Rachel said, trying to keep her voice steady. *Don't look at the knife. Just keep talking.* The steel shone, teasing her, but she kept her eyes firmly on Amanda's face. 'She went on the caving trip.'

'*That* was what made you suspicious? That was it?' Amanda spat the words out and then her mouth twisted.

'Not that it matters now. I saw police cars heading towards the Uni, and Cage isn't answering his phone. It doesn't take a genius to figure out that he's blabbed to that stupid detective. He must have had a crisis of conscience.'

'Maybe they just figured it out,' Rachel said. 'Like me.'

'What, because she went *caving*? That's hardly going to get me locked up for life.'

'You couldn't get into your locker. I didn't think about it at the time. When the police came. You couldn't get into your locker, because you'd brought the wrong key. It was Angie's key, not yours – the one you'd stolen so you could write *Chaos in the darkness* on her locker door.'

'That was unfortunate – but I doubt he noticed.'

'I did.' Rachel's eyes widened as another thought dawned on her. 'That morning when we came out of the lecture – you wanted us to hang back and let the others out first, and you were going on about how people were calling Angie a slut and that she had a poor choice of boyfriend. You said people were so quick to believe rumours.' She gasped slightly. 'That was a threat, wasn't it? You kept us back on purpose so you could say that where Dr Cage could hear you, didn't you?'

'It's all been so much fun.' Amanda smiled. 'It really has.'

The envelope stuffed with cash sat at Rachel's feet. 'Were you blackmailing him?' she asked. 'Did he kill Angie?'

'Blackmail? Why would I do that?' Amanda flicked her wrist and the serrated knife pointed at the pile of papers on the ground. 'You've clearly seen that I'm not exactly short of cash. I inherited well. I found that cash in Angie's room afterwards. I thought I'd better take it so that it didn't raise any questions. I've been meaning to give it back to Anthony, but he's been so tetchy about even being seen with me.'

'Anthony?' Rachel asked. 'Doctor Cage?'

'Yes. After everything I did for him, he seems to want me just to disappear. It doesn't work like that though.'

Rachel felt a chill grip her guts. 'What did you do for him?'

'Angie, of course.' The thin girl took a step forward, gripping the knife more firmly, as if she'd suddenly remembered what she intended to do with it.

Rachel had always thought of Amanda as weak and fragile, but as she moved the sinews in her arms were clear. There was nothing fragile about her. Rachel had a weight advantage, but Amanda had a knife, and her own madness to drive her forward.

'What did you do?' she asked softly.

'They were in the kitchen when I came home. She was on the floor, all spaced out, bleeding from where she'd banged her head, but still whining at him about something. He was panicking and going on about how he hadn't meant it and he'd just pushed her away to protect himself.' She frowned slightly with the memory. 'I could see in that moment exactly what had been going on – it was like the whole affair was mapped out there on the kitchen floor. I'd lived in the house with her all that time and she'd never even told me. She was supposed to be my *friend*. We talked. And she *never told me*.'

'Did you tell her about all this?' Rachel pointed down at the papers.

'That's different.' The lips tightened again. 'That's completely different. This was girl stuff – housemate stuff – the sort of thing *friends* tell each other. She'd been laughing at me all that time and I hadn't even known.'

'She wouldn't have been laughing at you. She wasn't—'

'Shut up. You don't know anything.' Two more steps closer.

'What did you do, Amanda?' Rachel had an awful feeling she could see where this was going – this was a girl who'd tortured a cat. Poor Angie – and even stupid Mr Cage for that matter – hadn't stood a chance.

'I took care of it. Angie was trying to get to her feet so I went over to her, grabbed her by the hair and rammed the back of her skull against the corner of the worktop,' she said, sounding pleased with herself. 'She wasn't getting up after that. Cage just stood there, his eyes popping out of his head as if he'd never seen anything like it. I told him to pass me the knife from the side. I think I actually slit her wrists without even consciously realising what my plan was – it was obvious though; all those silly kids killing themselves, and here was little Angie with her stupid secret crush. Everyone was going to want to be my friend after that. Everyone wants to know about death. *Everyone.*'

'I never realised you were so lonely.'

'Oh, save your pity for yourself. Cage was blubbing by then. He kept asking what I was doing – even when it was completely bloody obvious! I could see he was relieved. She wouldn't be taking the piss out of him any more either. I sent him home then. I didn't want him getting blood all over himself and looking suspicious. I told him I'd write "Chaos in the darkness" in her locker and then when it had calmed down I'd be in touch.' She smiled. 'I didn't even know what I wanted from him then – I still don't think I do, but the power was quite something.' She pushed the door closed, sealing any possible escape route off.

'It was quiet in the house with just her and me. We didn't have a clock ticking to count her last seconds down, but I think I heard them all the same. Or maybe it was just the slowing of her heartbeat. It wasn't like Mum at all. It was so much quicker. I loved it,' she said, 'despite the mess. I think she looked right at me for a moment, and she was so confused. Imagine dying not knowing why. How terrible to die with a riddle in your head. At least you won't have that.'

'You're insane,' Rachel said, backing away slightly. 'What's the point of killing me if the police are already coming for you?'

'What's the point of not?'

Amanda lunged forward.

'Rachel?' Cass banged hard on the front door. 'Rachel, are you in there?' He stood back and looked over the front of the ground-floor flat. Neither of the young women owned a car, so there was no way he could know if one or both were inside. 'Amanda?' He banged again. No one came to the door.

'Shit.' He redialled Rachel's number, but didn't hold the phone to his ear. The ringing from the handset somewhere on the other side of the door was clear. He may have learned that he didn't know much about kids over the past couple of weeks, but he knew they never left the house without their mobiles.

'Rachel?' he shouted again. The answer came in the smashing of glass from somewhere inside. *Fuck it.* There was no time to wait for back-up. He kicked hard at the door, the effort sending shock waves vibrating up the rest of his body. The door didn't budge. He kicked again. It was a shitty little house conversion in a grotty street set up for students and those who wanted to rent by the room. The door would give – it had to. He grabbed the metal rubbish bin from the small front garden and tipped out the black bags of rubbish before using it as a battering ram against the wood. Something cracked at last and he threw it down before launching

343

himself shoulder first once again at the door. Finally he stumbled through into the hallway.

'Rachel? Amanda?'

No one answered, but he could hear sounds of a struggle coming from the second room along the small corridor. He ran inside, accompanied by the sound of sirens finally pulling up outside. The two girls were both on the mattress, Rachel trying valiantly to keep Amanda's hand with the large bread knife away from her throat and body, while the other girl clawed at her with her free hand. One of Rachel's arms was badly sliced and there was blood on her T-shirt that might have come from a second wound. Both girls were locked in battle and Cass didn't bother calling their names again. Instead, with his teeth gritted, he took a precise short run-up and delivered a kick to the side of Amanda Kemble's head, not too hard, but definitely not too soft. The girl let out a sharp yelp as she rolled away, her eyes wide and shocked. Rachel pulled herself away from the mattress as Cass grabbed the dropped knife. Behind him, the room suddenly filled with police.

'That's Amanda Kemble,' he said. 'Arrest the bitch. And where's the ambulance?'

He crouched by Rachel, both of them sweating and panting slightly, and looked at her arm. 'You okay? Is this the only place she got you?'

'I think she got my side too,' she said. 'But I've got a bit of padding there, so I think I'll be okay.' She was forcing a smile, despite the tears in her eyes, and Cass gave her a gentle hug. Something about her strength reminded him of Claire May – and just like Claire May, that internal strength and belief in right had led her into danger. But at least this young woman got out alive. Just.

'You did good, Rachel.'

As a dazed Amanda was hauled to her feet, safely cuffed, Rachel said, 'She's crazy, you know. Really crazy.'

'There's a lot of it about.' He got to his feet as two paramedics arrived. 'These two will take you to the hospital. I'll get a WPC to go with you. Is that okay?'

Rachel nodded. Her eyes were full of questions, and Cass wondered if that part of her nature was going to be a gift or a curse for the rest of her life. Maybe it would be both.

In the packed hallway he checked his other message. Perry Jordan had sent a work address for Dr Shearman: he was the Director of Research at a facility in Milford Lane in the centre of town. Cass ground his teeth. If he was going to have any chance of getting some information about the night Luke was taken, then he needed to go now. Gibbs and Powell were both dead – what if someone was going after Dr Shearman next? More importantly, what if someone decided to come after him for Powell's death, even after he'd cleaned the scene? His time on this trail was running out, one way or the other, and he needed to make the most of what he had left.

He told the back-up to make sure Rachel Honey's parents were contacted and she was looked after in hospital, and to sling Amanda in a cell until he got there. It wasn't as if they needed a confession from her anyway. Cage had told them everything they needed to know, and now she'd been caught red-handed in an attempted murder. She wasn't going anywhere.

He got into his car, lit a cigarette and headed back to the city. It was time to find out some personal history.

After crossing the river he had to go up to the Strand and along to get to Milford Lane to avoid the one-way system, and he left his siren attached to the top of the Audi when

345

slinging the car at the front of the discreetly plaqued entrance to Encore Facilities. The last thing he wanted was to get clamped.

He was about to head through the rotating door to the brightly lit reception area beyond, when something about the sign made him pause. He read it again. Encore Facilities was engraved in large bold letters, but underneath the small print read The Flush5 Group. He looked up at the road he'd just driven along to get here. The Strand. His blood fizzed. The Strand was very, very close to Temple Underground Station.

The smartly dressed young woman on the main reception told him he'd need the second floor for Dr Shearman, and once he'd filled in a visitor's badge and signed his presence on their register, she sent him towards the lift with a smile. His skin tingled and his heart thumped. He'd thought he was coming here to find out about Luke and suddenly his head was filled with other possibilities. At the second floor he stepped out to find himself in a small and very quiet reception area, elegantly dressed with white armchairs and a low white-painted glass-topped coffee table. Two doors led off from it, and both required swipe cards to get in.

'I'd like to speak to Doctor Shearman, please.' He smiled at the middle-aged woman behind the desk.

'I'm afraid Dr Shearman doesn't come in until six this evening. Did you have an appointment?'

'No.' Cass pulled out his police ID and showed it to her. It had its usual effect, and her smile fell and was replaced with an expression of hardened disgust. He didn't care, although it always darkly amused him that everyone wanted the police around when it suited them, as long as any trouble went to *other* people.

'It's really nothing to worry about,' he lied pleasantly. 'I wanted to speak to him about being an expert witness in a case. You do phobia research here, don't you?'

He watched the tension relax from the woman's shoulders. Of course it would; he'd given her something that made sense far more than suggesting the good doctor could be involved in anything untoward – like the theft of a baby, or something that caused several young students to take their own lives.

'Yes, it's something the doctor is an expert on. You'd have to ask him how it all works – I'm admin staff, not medical – but I think he uses a mixture of hypnosis and aversion therapies. He thinks that it's something to do with different people having different kinds of chemicals produced in their brains. We have a lot of brain scans around anyway. It's all quite fascinating really, isn't it? What makes us tick?'

'How far are you from Temple Underground Station here?' he asked.

'Oh, a two- or three-minute walk at the most. Why? Is that relevant?'

Cass ignored her question. Phobias, Temple tube and the good doctor only works in the evenings. Cass didn't believe in coincidences. Too much was adding up here. But could the man who had helped in the disappearance of his brother's child really be involved in the suicides? Surely that was a coincidence? His blood froze. *There are no such things as coincidences.* A man with silver hair had told him that.

'I need you to check some records for me. I want to know if any of the following students have been treated for their phobias here: James Busby is the first. Then Katie Dodds, Corey Denter and Jasmine Green.'

'I thought you wanted Dr Shearman to be an expert

347

witness.' The disdain was back, made worse by the knowledge that she'd unwittingly given information away.

'I do,' Cass said. 'A very expert witness.'

'I'm afraid I can't—'

'Let me explain. You can either let me know if those students were treated here, or I can go and get a warrant and then there will be police all over this facility before there has to be. I am also sure that if I take a look through the visitors' book downstairs I'll probably find evidence that each of them signed in to see Dr Shearman at some point. You seem like a civilised and decent human being, so let's keep this decent and civilised, shall we?' He smiled again. 'I'll also want Shearman's home address.'

'What were those names again, please?' she asked. Cass gave them to her.

In silence she searched the computer. She frowned and then typed some more. Eventually, she looked up. 'There seems to be some discrepancy in the system with regard to those test subjects.'

'Which is?'

'They were all treated here. I can print out the dates they signed in – that's all data transferred from downstairs, and their names are still in the cat scan directory, but their actual files have been deleted from the system.'

'You don't have hard copies?'

'Let me check.'

Cass came round to the side of the desk so he could see what she was doing in the small office at the side of her workstation. He didn't want her calling the doctor and giving him time to run. As it was, she was simply pulling open racks of files in a filing cabinet. Cass had a feeling this was a woman who had no intention of getting on the wrong side of the law, regardless of how much she might respect her boss.

'Nothing,' she said, coming back to her desk. 'It's very odd. Flush5 are very strict on filing and record-keeping.'

Cass said nothing to that. Flush5 wasn't an organisation he felt any trust in. It had shadows at the edges – the dark fingers of The Bank and the Network were hooked right into it.

'Print out what you've got for me. And can you ask the young woman downstairs to find those names in her visitors' book please? I'll be wanting to take that with me too.'

The woman nodded, her eyes alive. She didn't ask any more questions.

Cass moved across the room and then rang Armstrong.

'Where the hell are you?'

It seemed his sergeant had lost a little deference in the time they'd known each other.

'I've found where the students were going for their phobia treatments.'

'You've what? But—'

'Don't ask me questions now, Armstrong, just do what I'm telling you. I need you to get over to the home of a man called Dr Shearman and bring him in. As soon as I've got the documents I need from here I'll be back. Hold him there. I want to speak to him myself. You got that?'

'Got it,' Armstrong said. 'What's this bloke's address?'

Cass gave it to him. 'I also need you to send someone over here – I'm at Encore Facilities in Milford Lane just off the Strand. I figure we might need the names and addresses of everyone working here if we're going to get some idea of what was going on. We don't want them wiping their systems while we've got Shearman in the nick.'

'How did you find this place?'

'Let me know when someone's picked up Shearman and I'll head back,' Cass said, avoiding the question. He was going to have to figure out a way to answer that one. Encore didn't come up on any Internet searches when they'd tried finding suitable places in the area that the kids could have been too. It was clearly a deeply private listing. Still, as long as he had a result, Armstrong could ask as many questions as he liked; the DCI wouldn't be looking for too many answers. The brass never did.

It had been a long time since Mr Bright had studied the X accounts in such detail, and he'd forgotten what a web they were, linking forward and back to so many 'legitimate' accounts within The Bank. That he didn't entirely understand the complete flow of their funds was of no concern to him. This wasn't a nanny state, and had never been set up as one. They each managed their own affairs, and as long as the tithe was paid into X20, then all was well. There was always going to have to be an element of trust in these matters, and the truth was exactly what he'd pointed out to Asher Red – when people were this rich, they ceased to be greedy in terms of money; it was the power games that became interesting.

He'd found himself sidetracked into examining the finer details of all the smaller, more personal businesses that several of the Cohort had made their own. There were so many, and he was surprised at how much minutiae it took to keep this world of theirs turning, even now, when it was on its knees. Someone was moving money around somewhere. Whoever was planning to come against him had been preparing for fifteen years or more: they were playing the long game. And he knew better than most that the long game cost money – all the voided folders and the single current one in the Redemption files were proof of that. His opponent would be spending money too. He'd glanced once again at the women's folders and then it had dawned on him that he was taking the long way round. He had been looking at the trees instead of the wood, and that wasn't like him at all.

He went straight for the conglomerates after that, the ones that the girls' fathers had worked for, where they had 'coincidentally' risen rapidly through the ranks approximately fifteen years previously. Someone had wanted to make sure the teenagers had the best of opportunities. He tracked the ownership of each back further, through the web of accounts and worldwide investments, until he finally saw the trail.

He sat back and smiled. So there it was – he had the name. Someone wasn't as clever as he thought he was. They'd learn. He looked at his watch; time was moving along and he still had lots to get done. He made two swift phone calls, making it clear to each of the recipients that it was time to choose. He had the boy and he had the First – those facts wouldn't escape them. They'd choose wisely. Plus people invariably preferred the status quo, and even in these times of fear and change, he was very much the safer option.

The phone calls done, he returned to Mr Solomon's office, where he discovered to his dismay that the stench had worsened rather than abated. Still, he didn't intend to be in here long. He didn't approach the man in the chair but softly shut the door and observed him in the quiet. Red's eyes were wide and he was visibly trembling. His rapid breath was the only sound filling the opulent room in that moment. Castor Bright could almost see the fear rippling like heat from the man's body. Therein lay the source of the smell. Thankfully, not for much longer.

The brown eyes were filled with terror, but somewhere behind that there was still an echo of hope. That was unfortunate, for Mr Red at any rate. He was about to become very disappointed. It always astounded Mr Bright just how misplaced hope could be, and this was no exception. Perhaps it was part of being human; perhaps it was that hope that had garnered support for the one who thought he could come against him. Looking at the accounts showed that he had clearly appealed to those who believed they were dying. He shook the thought away. He had never been much of a philosopher, and he didn't intend to start now.

'I know who your mystery partner is. It doesn't take long to find these things out if you understand how to look.'

'Who? Who is it?'

'Oh no.' Mr Bright wiggled a manicured finger back and forth. 'I think that's probably quite irrelevant to you now. I also think it is just that you remain in the dark.' He smiled, but although his eyes twinkled, they lacked amusement.

'This does, however, leave me in a position where I no longer require your services. I think it's time to terminate your contract with us, Mr Asher Red. I'm sure you understand.'

Asher Red's mouth moved slightly, as if he were trying to force more words from somewhere amidst the broken teeth.

'I shall have to be quick about it,' Mr Bright continued, 'which I'm sure will be a relief to both of us. I have a meeting with the architects' – he allowed himself a little humour at his private pun – 'at the site of the new building in an hour or so and I wouldn't want to be late, so let's get started, shall we?'

In the chair, Asher Red made a mewling sound as whatever vain hope he'd had trickled away. After that the air stilled, as if time itself had held its breath. Castor Bright's eyes burned and he allowed himself to *become*. He laughed with the joy in liberation, and bright light filled the room, the gold turning to white and then something that shone beyond that. Asher Red began to scream, but Mr Bright barely noticed it. In the moments before the man died, Mr Bright shared his secrets with him – he showed all he was, all he ever had been, ever would be, and all the terrible power and glory that was held in the *Glow*.

Mr Bellew liked the cool of his new underground headquarters. He was hidden almost in plain sight. It had been a long time since any of the Network had visited the secondary tunnels and empty spaces they had once used as their headquarters. It had been a novelty when the Underground system had been new more than a hundred and fifty years ago, but that had soon worn off, as very few of their number liked the idea that they were occupying the bowels of a world that belonged to them, rather than rising above it. Mr Bellew had never been interested in metaphor, however, and the old headquarters suited his purpose now.

He watched the three women strapped down in the strange white pods that were identical to those so far away in the House of Intervention. There had been a lot of screaming from them during the course of the day, but he couldn't help that. He had had to push them; he had no time to nursemaid them through this. As it was, the changes were happening faster than he or any of the technicians had expected – but then, none of them, including Mr Bellew himself, had ever seen anything like this before. How could they have?

The physical transformation had come last with those who had passed their gifts on before they died: there was no reason to suspect it would be any different with these women, and he was happy about that. He needed them as they were for now, and as far as he could tell, the only outward sign of the chemical changes that were raging through their simple bodies was the unhealthy sweaty sheen on their skin.

All three had started projecting almost as soon as they'd been hooked up to the machinery, but it was the Porter girl's data-stream that was the most interesting. Where the other girls' screens were filled with random images that made no sense, thus far at least, Abigail Porter was projecting with purpose: the faces were all recognisable; politicians and figures in business, all influential, each driven by very different ambitions. He didn't need to put questions to her regarding many of these personalities – that information had already been taken at the House, when they all rose to – or were placed in – positions of prominence. The House had indicated who would create balance in this unstable world, and they had been duly elected in accordance with the findings. Mr Bellew intended to add a little unbalance, in order to support his cause – to bring a little chaos back. He smiled at his own joke with a touch of pride. Wit wasn't normally in his repertoire. Perhaps Mr Bright had taught him something after all.

It was the final image that Porter was projecting that caught his interest: a man he knew nothing and everything about: Cassius Jones. Over and over again, the dark-haired, angry-looking policeman flashed onto one or all of her screens, and she would start to hum some old piece of music he didn't quite recognise under her breath. As soon as she broke the silence, the others would join in tunelessly and their screens would blank out for a brief moment. The man's image bothered Mr Bellew. Mr Bright thought no one else had paid much attention to his tracing of the bloodlines, but they'd all paid attention when he brought the Jones family together. Both sides had been direct descendants.

This projection was the boy's uncle – the boy whose hidden presence – along with some lingering loyalty from days long gone by – had made it so hard for Mr Bellew to get support … at least until the Dying had come among them. That changed things. But still, many saw the boy as some kind of saviour. Mr Bellew sat on a fence. They all knew whose bloodline it was, and that one could go either way – cruel or kind, saviour or destroyer. As far as Mr Bellew was concerned, the boy and his family were just the joker in the pack: maybe they'd be something, and maybe they'd be nothing. The House of Intervention had always been silent on that one. Any questions had drawn a blank, ever since Castor Bright had brought Alan and Evelyn Jones together, and yet here was Cassius Jones, on Abigail Porter's screens. Still, he thought, the policeman was not his immediate concern. He needed to get these women ready for the tasks he had planned for them.

'Try again,' he said. The projecting was all well and good, but if they couldn't reflect, then it was all pointless. They had the potential to be the perfect assassins: they were each highly trained in self-defence and gun usage, and understood the top politicians in each of their home countries. They knew the layouts of buildings and the movements of leaders. If they could master reflection and be in several places at once, then he could cause more than enough unrest – not perhaps for what the sick expected from him, but for his own ends. The sick were dying anyway, and once he was done, then perhaps it would be best if they died more quickly.

The Russian girl spouted gibberish as the machines whirred around them, enhancing whatever abilities were coming naturally – or perhaps unnaturally – to them now that they were changing, and the American began to cry, whispering softly to her God. She needed to learn that he was her God now. He looked back at Porter. Why did he get the feeling she was fighting his commands? She could do better than this, he was sure of it.

'Try harder,' he growled at her, and nodded to one of the technicians. Three more lights came on down the side of her pod and the girl gasped. Her eyes glowed silver – and then it happened: a second Abigail Porter appeared beside Mr Bellew. He smiled. For someone who had been known simply as a general, a man of brute force, he was getting better at these games.

'It hurts,' both Abigail Porters said, 'oh God, it hurts!'

'Don't stop now.' Mr Bellew looked from one to the other. 'Now you just have to make the Reflection hard.'

A shimmery image of the American appeared on the other side of him. It wasn't as strong as Abigail's, but it was there, and he got her soft tears in stereo too. Mr Bellew laughed aloud as the Russian finally managed a brief flicker of herself on the other side of the room. He was Charlie, and these were his Angels.

Chapter Twenty-Four

Back at the station, energy hummed through the team filling the Incident Room. Everyone was *up*, everyone was *on*. Even through his own tiredness and jangling nerves he could feel it in himself: it was the hard buzz that was felt when getting a result on someone's death. They had Amanda Kemble in custody, and now Richard Shearman. Everything was wrapping up – as far as the team was concerned, anyway. For Cass there were still lots of answers he needed, and he intended to get them.

Armstrong was striding into an office further along from Cass's when he grabbed him. The sergeant almost jumped.

'Where's Dr Shearman?'

'Number 3. Look, the DCI wants to talk to you—'

'I'll go up in a second. I just need to check on the doctor.'

'Okay,' Armstrong said. His hand held the door to, leaving only nothing of the room visible through the small gap. Someone on the other side was on the phone. The words weren't clear, but Cass was sure whoever it was had an American accent. Ramsey? Was Ramsey here?

His heart tripped over its own beat and he stared at Armstrong, whose gaze slipped away as a voice called his name from behind them both.

A constable held up a receiver.

'Got Phone Records on the phone for you.' The constable smiled. 'No pun intended.'

'Phone Records?' Cass studied his sergeant.

'Yeah.' Toby Armstrong licked his lips. 'I thought I'd get Amanda Kemble's call details too – you know, make sure the case against her and Cage is watertight. She must have called him since Angie's death.'

'Good thinking,' Cass said, forcing himself to smile. Something was wrong here; he could feel it. Armstrong was nervous.

'I'll be back up in ten minutes, okay?'

'Sure.'

Cass walked away, heading down to the interview rooms. He did his best to keep his pace even. Whatever was going on, they weren't ready to ask him about it yet, and that suited him fine.

'Shouldn't there be two of you?' Dr Shearman was sweating despite the coolness of the bland interview room. He'd only been in there ten minutes or so and already large circles were visible around the armpits of his shirt. There was bravado in his voice, but his eyes were all puppy-dog soft and wanting to please. Cass had seen his sort before. Normally he pitied them; not this man, though – this one was too steeped in conspiracy for any sympathy. Two babies had been stolen and several students were dead. Somehow this man was involved in both cases.

'Don't believe everything you see on TV. We're busy today. And anyway, you see that bulb up there?' He pointed to a dead light on the wall. 'If I was recording this, that light would be on.' Of course he should have been recording it. The DCI would go ballistic if he knew Cass was alone with the suspect, but he had a feeling that this was going to be the least of his worries shortly. Inside his head, a clock ticked loudly. It had been Ramsey he'd heard upstairs, he was sure of it. What would the Chelsea DI be doing here, other than somehow tracking Dr Powell's death back to Cass? There were probably other cases on the go that crossed over between the two nicks, but for Ramsey to show up today about a different matter would be too much of a coincidence – and one thing that Mr Bright and Cass appeared to agree on was that such coincidences didn't exist. The world was shifting again, and Cass was very much on his own. He'd talk to Ramsey later. It hadn't been Cass on the CCTV image of Gibbs' killer. Ramsey would trust that someone was setting Cass up – they were friends. And after all, it had happened before and Ramsey had seen the truth. He looked at the sweating doctor whose face was hidden behind a curly beard.

'Let's think of this as more of an informal chat,' Cass said. 'Off the record.' He laid out the pictures of the dead students in front of him. 'James Busby. Katie Dodds. Cory Denter. Jasmine Green. Recognise them?'

Dr Shearman's eyes narrowed, confused. The tape wasn't running and this wasn't a proper interview. That information wasn't sitting with what he'd expected, and Cass hoped it would unsettle him enough to slip up.

'All I did was try and cure their phobias by hypnosis and exposure while under hypnosis. It was a six-week course. I did nothing to them that would make them self-harm. I was trying to help them.'

'But you didn't come forward when you saw them in the paper. Surely you must have realised that they had all been through your research facility.'

'I didn't think it was relevant. They'd all finished their courses with me well before they killed themselves. It wasn't because of me.' His words came out in hurried breaths. 'And I didn't want to lose my funding.'

'The funding that allowed you to pay them so well? In cash too. I'm sure we'll be contacting the tax office about that.'

'The cash came from the company that funds me. It's gifted money. They weren't doing a job.'

'All these kids did your programme, and yet none of them told any of their friends or even their families.' Cass looked up from the photos of the dead that smiled on paper but gripped at him with cold fingers in the dark night. 'Now I might not know much about kids, but I know they talk. So how come they were so secretive?'

Dr Shearman chewed his bottom lip for a moment and squirmed in his seat. This was no cool cucumber.

'Hypnosis,' he said eventually. 'When they came for the induction we tested them for their susceptibility. While they were under they were told not to talk about the programme. The funding company did it. They said they didn't want the students sharing what they were doing because we might then get inundated by applicants with false phobias just wanting to make some easy money.'

'Because you were paying so well.' Cass leaned forward. 'Why were you paying so well?'

'I paid what I was instructed to pay.'

'I thought you were in charge of your own research, but maybe you're just someone else's puppet. Who funded you?'

'A company called HMG Investments. They're part of The Bank.' Dr Shearman had started to peel skin from the edge of his thumbs with his fingernails. If he wasn't careful he'd start to bleed.

'Of course they are. Flush5 is owned by The Bank, isn't it? And yours is a Flush5 facility. But give me a name.'

'Look—' Dr Shearman eyes pleaded for some kind of clemency as he spoke. He clearly didn't know Cass Jones at all. 'I hadn't seen those students for weeks before they died. I barely remembered their faces, let alone their names. I don't actually do the treatments, I just supervise and look at the results. The only time I even think about the names is when he comes to see the brain scans.' He stopped abruptly, his eyes guilty.

'He?' Cass asked softly.

'No one. Nothing.'

'Someone other than you had an interest in their brain scans?'

'I'm saying nothing until my solicitor gets here.' Dr Shearman ran one hand over his curls. They shone with sweat. He wasn't holding together well.

'You've done all right for yourself, haven't you?' Cass kept his tone light. 'A very nice place of work right in the heart of town. No grotty hospital ward for you. None of that will stop five manslaughter charges being brought against you, though. You might not get a life sentence, but you will rot in prison for the rest of your miserable life.'

'But I didn't—'

'It doesn't matter that they finished your supposed fucking programme weeks before they died,' Cass growled. 'It'll be easy to say that something in your secretive research set them off because there are no other links, don't you understand? People will take answers where they can find them. Add into that the likelihood of the court finding out that a baby died in the your only shift at the first-ever Flush5 ward in the Portman Hospital all those years ago and you'll look like a total incompetent. Flush5 won't go anywhere near you – they'll find a way to hang you out to dry and distance themselves.' He watched Dr Shearman's eyes dart this way and that as if he could miraculously find an escape route from this situation, before adding, 'Especially as the baby didn't die, did he, Doctor?'

'How do you—?' Dr Shearman recoiled as if punched hard in the face. 'Oh Christ, I always knew it would get messy. I should have known.' He rested his head on his hands and took two deep breaths. Cass thought perhaps he was trying to stop himself crying. Weak people always thought the bad things they got involved in were somehow not their fault because they hadn't thought them through properly. It was an excuse that he never swallowed. No one thought anything through – they just made random selfish choices. Some people were just better at accepting the outcomes than others.

'Who looked at the brain scans?' he asked.

'A man called Bright. Mr Bright. Whatever happened to those kids it was to do with him – not me. Something about their scans interested him and he asked me for their addresses and files.' He shrugged, a helpless gesture in a helpless man. 'I gave them to him and that was it.'

As his head reeled, a small part of Cass wondered how his body could even be feeling surprise. It had to be Mr Bright. Of course it did – everything always came back to Castor Bright. He was everywhere Cass turned, and he always had been, even when Cass had been blissfully unaware himself.

'I never wanted to be in straight medicine,' Dr Shearman continued. 'I thought I did when I started out – it sounded romantic. But I didn't have the nerves for it. There were too many incidents, things that went slightly wrong. Not enough to cause any inquiries, but enough to raise eyebrows. I found the pressure of having people's lives in my hands just too much. I locumed for ages, and I thought that

I was probably going to end up as GP in some inner city surgery where they couldn't be too choosy. I'd never make partner. I knew then that I should have gone into research rather than general practice – I'd always been more interested in the workings of the mind rather than the body, but I figured it was too late. No one was giving out research grants any more, and certainly not to men like me.' His Adam's apple bobbed up and down. 'Then I was approached by Mr Bright. I should have trusted my first instinct and said no, but he was offering me my dreams – financial support through my retraining, a facility . . .'

'Stick to the story.'

'He said he needed me to do one small thing. I had to be available at short notice to work a shift at the maternity ward at the Portman in order to deliver a baby to the Gray family. It had to be born within a certain time frame and I'd probably have to do a C-section birth. When the boy was born I had to take him to the hospital administrator – a man called Powell – and then replace the Grays' child with a dead one, which would be delivered to me at the hospital. That's what I did.'

'I totally forgot all about it until Mr Bright came to Encore a while back. He asked me what my new research project was, and when I told him he said he wanted me to use students. Originally I had planned to use older adults whose phobias were far more ingrained. He told me to place ads on the noticeboards in the unions – just very small ones.'

Cass kicked himself for not thinking of checking the boards. Shit, he was getting old – that was basic textbook stuff, and neither he nor Armstrong had done it.

'Mr Bright wanted his people to do the initial test hypnosis' – now that Shearman had started talking, he was determined to unload his soul – 'and then every so often he would come along and look at the brain scans. Some interested him and some didn't – I don't know why. He didn't tell me, and I didn't ask. I just gave him their addresses and their files and told him when their six-week course would end. If something happened to those kids it was after they left me! He was my boss. He'd given me everything.'

'And all in exchange for stealing a baby.'

'How do you know about that?' Dr Shearman asked. He was lost and out of his depth. He always had been, but today was the day he was finally realising it.

'I know about a lot of things,' Cass said. 'I know you're about the only one involved in what happened that night who's still alive.'

Dr Shearman's eyes widened. He clearly hadn't paid attention to the news that day. But then, he probably hadn't known Dr Gibbs at all; he'd stayed home the night that Dr Shearman worked at the Portman.

'I also know,' Cass continued, 'that you should keep your mouth shut about Mr Bright – this whole conversation – or it's likely someone will kill you too.'

'But I can't.' Dr Shearman half-rose out of his chair. 'I can keep quiet about the baby, but if I don't say anything about Mr Bright, no one will believe those student suicides didn't have anything to do with me.'

'Nothing to do with you?' Cass snorted. 'You only procured them, right? Who cares what happened afterwards.'

'But I didn't do anything – and you know what he's like! He's not a man you say no to!'

'Tell it to the judge.' Cass had no more time for this man. He had his answers, and as far as he could tell, Dr Shearman's fate was sealed. There was no way Mr Bright would allow himself to be traced from Dr Shearman's research facility, and as soon as he heard that the doctor had been pulled in he'd shut down whatever it was he'd been doing anyway. Without saying another word, he pushed away from the desk and left Dr Shearman to sweat alone.

Back on his own floor, he paused at the coffee machine, as much to gather his thoughts as to get a drink. The coffee was shit anyway, but at least holding the hot cup stopped his hand shaking so much. Dr Shearman would take the flack for what happened to the teenagers, and Cass found that didn't much bother him, despite it being a miscarriage of justice. Dr Shearman was involved in giving Luke away. He could live with Dr Shearman in jail just for that.

He wandered back along the corridor, his slow pace at odds with the flurry of activity around him as officers chased warrants and typed confessions and smiled about potential bonuses. He felt completely apart from them all; he still had a mystery to solve, one that had been wrapping around him like a web since he was born. He stopped and frowned. His office door was open and there were people behind his desk, staring at his computer. One was Armstrong, but he needed to take two steps to his right before he could make out the other two – Ramsey and DCI Heddings. Fuck. None of the three were smiling, and none of them, even Ramsey, looked as if they were in any form of disagreement. Shit. What could they have on him? A trace left at Powell's house? What? He left the coffee on a desk and turned round, forcing his pace to stay naturally slow. If he was going to face those three, he needed a cigarette first. The fire escape on the floor below would do. He needed peace and quiet. He needed to think about what the fuck was going on here, and what the fuck he was going to say – not necessarily in that order.

*

Abigail hurt. It was the thought that fit best. She hurt in every cell of her being, and she felt each cell as if it was a universe of its own. She sank back into her body, becoming one again, and the agony dulled to a throbbing pain. This was wrong. However right the changes felt, what this golden man was doing to them was wrong. She should have known, but she was so absorbed in the emptiness, and the end to that, that she'd been blind. The pod had been around her for ever. There had been nothing else. Other thoughts fought those, the thoughts that had once been all of her. This was wrong. It needed putting right.

Behind her eyes and on the screen the policeman filled the space. The other screens crackled blank for a moment. She kept seeing him, over and over. He was connected in so many ways – he was connected to everything. He was golden, like the tall man, but he didn't know it. He didn't *want* it. The tall man made the Russian split and she screamed. Abigail could tell the man thought that the changing had made the Russian a little crazy, but Abigail thought that made her the sanest of them all – and anyway, the pain was enough to make anyone scream. She would like to make the tall man split and scream. It would be her turn again soon and she dreaded it. It hurt so much, opening up the new door in her mind and making her see too much of everything, and she couldn't control it. It tore at her soul. Still, she was better than the others at it, despite how hard she tried not to be. The tall man knew that, and he smiled at her a lot. She hated him.

The policeman. The policeman was the key to everything. Hayley was dead, she knew that, even though sometimes through that open door she was sure she could hear her screaming in the chaos of colours, and she was sure she would never see her parents again. Natural and unnatural –

she felt both. This tall man, however, he was wrong. He needed stopping. *This* needed stopping.

His mobile phone rang out and the noise of its call tone was so loud it filled her from head to toe, making her flinch. She wished her hands were free to press into her ears.

'Yes?' the tall man said. He spoke quietly, but she could hear everything, even the rush of each particle of air from his breath at it hit the handset.

'It's Mr Craven,' the voice at the other end answered. Abigail concentrated, ignoring the pain of such loudness in her head, blocking it out in order to hear the words.

'Mr Bright knows,' the caller continued. 'He called me and asked if you'd spoken to me. I said no, of course. He's definitely suspicious of you.'

'It's too soon.' The tall man cursed and paced for a second. 'I'm not ready to take him yet.'

'Maybe not, if you're planning a war,' Mr Craven said. 'However, if you want to take a more subtle approach ...?'

'What do you mean?'

There was a long pause. 'You do believe you can get us home, don't you, Mr Bellew?'

'Of course I do. That's my plan: to gain forgiveness for all of us.'

'He's got a meeting this afternoon,' Mr Craven continued, 'with the contractors at the new building. I don't know why he deals with these things himself, but I imagine once an architect, always an architect. I suppose he still finds it all fascinating.'

'What's your point, Mr Craven?'

'My point, Mr Bellew, is that you could ring the contractors and cancel the meeting and then meet him there yourself. Have it out. I thought you could go through the front, and I'd go through the back. There'd be two of us and one of him. And you've always been strong. The way I see it, it's either that, or he rallies the troops and comes after us.'

'How do I know I can trust you?'

'Easy. I faxed back permissions to access certain of my accounts to one of your solicitors' offices earlier. We both know Mr Bright will check to see who's been supporting you. My name will be on that list.'

It was Mr Bellew's turn to pause. 'What's the address of this building?

'Between Hanway Street and Oxford Street. You can't miss it. It's the only high-rise going up anywhere in London. They'll be meeting on the first floor.'

'How do you know that?'

'I rang the contractor under the guise of checking meeting times. They're scheduled for half an hour from now. Shall I call them back and cancel?'

'Yes,' Mr Bellew said. 'And I'll see you there.'

'Let's get this dealt with.'

The conversation ended. Abigail's heart thumped. Mr Bright. Another name that meant something, and for some reason the policeman rose up in her head again. Mr Bright and DI Jones.

The golden man stared down at his phone for a moment and then she felt his eyes rest on her.

'I want her hard reflection ready to take with me,' he said.

'Out of here? But—'

'In ten minutes. Do whatever it takes.'

He closed the door behind him and the technician scurried off to do whatever he did on the machines that made her able to do what he wanted. It was something that should come in time, this splitting, something that had to be learned slowly, not forced. He wasn't a patient man, though, and he had no care.

She thought of the policeman. She thought of the address. When she could see them both, she shut her eyes. She only had a minute or two.

Cass leaned over the edge of the railing and was about to flick the rest of his cigarette away when he realised there was a woman standing in the alleyway below looking up at him. He stared. It wasn't just any woman – it was Abigail Porter. What the fuck?

'Stop him,' she said. Her words carried clearly up to him, even though she wasn't shouting. 'You have to stop him. The new building between Hanway Street and Oxford Street. First floor. Stop him. Mr Bright will be there. Thirty minutes.' Her voice faded slightly. 'Stop him.'

'What are you doing here?' Cass dropped the cigarette and ran down to the next level, closer to the ground. When he got there, she was gone. He scanned the alley. How the fuck had she gone so quickly? What had she been doing here? Her words echoed in his head. *Mr Bright will be there.* Mr Bright was fucking everywhere. And now Abigail Porter had surfaced, albeit only briefly.

He pulled out his phone to call David Fletcher, but it was ringing already. He frowned as he looked at the name. Artie Mullins? He stared and almost didn't answer it. But Artie never rang him unless it was important. What had happened now?

'You at the nick, Jones?' The familiar gruff voice spoke.

'Sort of. On the fire escape smoking. It's a bit of a busy day here. Why do you ask?'

'Don't go back inside.'

Cass froze. 'Why?'

'A little birdie told me I should check up on you. My curiosity got the better of me and I did. Seems like you're in trouble, mate.'

'What kind of trouble?' Cass looked back up at the door he'd come out of. It was still closed. No one was looking for him yet.

'Do you remember a bloke called Adam Bradley?'

For a moment Cass almost said no, and then his memory threw up a picture – a dark-haired, skinny junkie on the other side of an interview table. Mr Bright had used Bradley to deliver the tape of the two boys' shootings during the Solomon/Man of Flies case.

'Vaguely.'

'He was wanted for the murder of two doctors yesterday,' Mullins said.

Suddenly, the man who disappeared over Powell's wall and the faceless man on the news at Gibbs's murder site merged into one in his head. It was Adam Bradley – healthier than he remembered, but Bradley nonetheless.

'He was found with his neck broken this morning,' Mullins continued.

'I don't see what that's got to do with me, though.' Cass was tired of the games – what was Artie driving at?

'Plenty, apparently. Police found his mobile phone in his flat. According to my inside sources, your number called it last. You've called him a few times over the past couple of days.'

'What?' For a moment, Mr Bright and Luke, and Ramsey waiting for him upstairs, all emptied from his head. He *hadn't* rung Bradley – he'd totally forgotten about the boy's existence until a few moments ago. What the fuck was this?

'Well, phone records say you did: one short call lasting a few minutes, and a couple of missed calls.' Artie paused.

'Maybe you didn't realise you were phoning him?'

Cass ran his mind over all the calls he'd made in the past few days. Finally, he got it. His blood chilled. Mr Bright. Always Mr Bright. What had the man said when he'd given him the card with that phone number on it? *Trace that number if you want, but your time would probably be better spent on other things. It won't give you any information on me.* The truth, hidden in a riddle – no, there was no information on Mr Bright in the number, but if he'd traced it, it would have come back to Adam Bradley.

'Fuck.' Cass kicked at the railings in frustration. He *should* have traced it; he shouldn't have been so damn sure that it would come back a blank. Mr Bright worked in hidden truths, he always had. Hidden truths. What a fucker.

'There's more. That PI you use? They've knobbled him. He's on your call records a lot. He's told them he gave you details for both dead doctors. Add to that that your fingerprints were on the outside of Powell's door and broken dining room window and the woman on reception at that hospital where Gibbs works remembers you visiting there the day he died, and you're pretty fucked.'

Memories rolled like film in his head. Cleaning down the inside of Powell's house but not thinking about how he touched the window frame on the outside to get in. The receptionist's face as he flashed his police ID at her through her screen. Shit.

'There's a team at your flat going through the rubbish on your street now. If they find a murder weapon you can kiss your arse goodbye.'

'Fuck,' Cass repeated.

'Someone's got it in for you, boy,' Mullins said, 'because I'm presuming you didn't kill anyone?'

'You're presuming right.' Once again it was someone on

the wrong side of the law, not bogged down by evidence and procedures, who saw the truth for what it was. 'Thanks for letting me know.'

'I've done you a small favour. There's a little present underneath the passenger seat of your car. Something to even up the sides a little. Good luck, Cass.'

The call clicked off. Cass let his blood rage and his eyes burn uncontained for a moment. Mr Bright had set him up. He'd known Cass would follow that trail for Luke – Christ, he'd even played with a warning by telling him it was a dangerous trail to follow – and used it to set him up. Did he even care where Abigail Porter was, or had that meeting just been a ruse to give Cass Bradley's number? Of course it had. Now it looked like Cass had used Bradley to kill the two doctors, and then Cass had killed Bradley himself. Jesus. He knew what they'd be thinking too: he'd gone crazy looking for his brother's son. Fuck. Once upon a time, Mr Bright had said he was Cass's guardian angel. The man had wrecked Cass's family, and now he was bent on destroying Cass himself.

Mr Bright will be there. That was what Abigail Porter had said. Well, it was time he took his fight to the silver-haired man. It wasn't as if he had very much left to lose. He quickly trotted down the fire-escape stairs and walked to his car. He ran his hand into the space under the passenger seat and smiled as his fingers felt the cold steel of the handgun. Good work, Artie, he thought as he pulled away and out of the station, good fucking work.

Arthur 'Artie' Mullins put the phone down and leaned back in his office chair, looking at the two strangers in front of him. He could get why Cass might know the girl, but the tramp? Jones was clearly mixing with some odd people. No wonder he was always in so much fucking trouble.

'So, little birdie,' he said, 'that's Jones warned. My contacts on the inside are going to want payment for that information, but I'll collect that from Cass when I see him. It'll make a change, him giving me money.' He smiled. 'I won't ask why you didn't want to tell him yourself, or in fact why you're so interested in him. That's none of my business.'

The truth was simpler than that: something about the pair unsettled him and he'd learned over the years to trust that instinct. He never had liked birds that knew more than they let on. Still, even if they weren't friends of Cass's exactly, it looked like they had his best interests in mind, and at least they'd chosen Artie to come to. Now he had the inside on what was happening. If they were all out looking for Cass, it might be a good evening to do a bit of business in Paddington.

'Now is there anything else I can do for you both before you fuck off?' he asked.

'Yes,' the red-headed girl said, and Artie had to admit she had a very fuckable smile. 'We need to borrow a car.'

The old tramp pulled a bundle of notes from the depths of his tatty coat pocket and put it on the desk. To Artie's expert eye it looked like about five grand.

'As a matter of urgency,' the girl added.

Artie gave her his most fetching grin. 'I think I can accommodate.'

DCI Heddings looked like his head was going to explode as he stared at the evidence laid out on the desk before him.

'We let him leave the building?' He looked up at the gathered men. 'Correct that – *you* let him leave the building?'

'I thought he was talking to Dr Shearman,' Armstrong said.

'He shouldn't have been near a bloody suspect! Not with all this' – he swept his hand through the air above his desk – 'going on.'

'We needed to lock his computer, and we were waiting for his phone records to come through. It seemed easier to have him down there than up here.'

'And now he's bloody out there?' Heddings sighed. 'Any idea where he's gone?'

'No.' Armstrong shook his head. 'Can we track him on his mobile?'

Heddings snorted. 'Who do you think we are, MI bloody 5?'

'You said he was working with the ATD? David Fletcher?' Inspector Ramsey looked at Armstrong.

'Yes.'

'We might not be able to follow his moving phone signal,' Ramsey said softly, 'but Fletcher will.'

For a moment there was silence, and then Heddings slapped hard on the desk. 'Well, get on with it then! I want him nicked and back here before he can cause any more bloody chaos! Jesus Christ, the tabloids are going to have a field day.'

Chapter Twenty-Five

Mr Bright looked down. At least he'd avoided getting too much mud on his soft Italian leather shoes. One day the track that ran between the two London streets would be paved and gated at both ends, but for now it was simply access to the remains of the building that had been knocked down to make way for his vision.

Up on the first floor, he allowed himself a small smile of satisfaction. Somewhere far above he could hear the sounds of labour, but the lower half of the building was empty of workmen today. His heels clicked on the grey concrete slabs. There was something satisfying about seeing the gritty shell of a building before all the sleek veneer of the outer skin hid it from view. It was the solid foundation – the shape of the thing that would be forgotten once shiny steel and glass took its place. Such a sight always reminded him of his best work.

He was less sure of what to make of the scene ahead of him, though. Mr Bellew was here, with Abigail Porter. Even from a distance he could see that Mr Bellew looked smug – well, that would probably fade, but the girl herself looked as if she was in agony. She hugged herself, small pants and mewling sounds escaping as her shoulders shook, and the pain shone in silver from her eyes. It was truly a pity, he concluded. She was interesting. He would have liked to have known her better.

'*Et tu*, Mr Bellew?' he asked with a smile. 'You're not the contractor I was expecting.'

'Your meeting is cancelled.'

'So it would appear.'

They stood at opposite ends of the floor that was yet to be filled with walls and rooms and lights, the air a gloomy blue, reflecting from the tarpaulins that covered the empty windows and crackled with every hint of breeze.

'I'm sorry it had to be this way,' Mr Bellew said, 'but it's time for a change.'

'Humour me before we do this.' Mr Bright took a few steps forward into the empty space between them. 'Why the bombs? Why the damage?'

'I have learned from you, Mr Bright. Even a humble general has to get to grips with politics. I wanted to make it look like you were losing your hold on all this. Plus, I told the dying that if we damaged our own work we'd be forgiven and that the walkways would open up for us.'

Mr Bright filled the space with a burst of good-humoured laughter. 'And they believed you? That's a speech I'd have liked to have heard.'

'There is persuasion in strength, and I've always been strong. And I had some Interventionists. I told the dying that they had projected us getting home.'

Mr Bellew slowly came forward, pulling the woman with him. She could barely stand. He was bragging now, but then, he had always been a bragger. It would be his downfall.

'What is it with these women and the Interventionists?'

'We've forgotten who the Interventionists were. We just see them as *things*, useful creatures with strange powers, but no sense of existence. They haven't forgotten, though.' Mr

Bellew smiled. 'And they want to die – which is ironic, really, given how much the rest of us are fighting against it.'

'If they're so keen on it, then why don't they?'

'They can't – not without passing on all that they've grown to do. I was there fifteen years ago when they projected the three girls, and I finally asked enough questions to see what they wanted me to understand. These were the women they could pass on to.'

'Of course.' Mr Bright nodded. 'They bred too, all those years ago. The blood will be out there somewhere.' He looked again at the silver agony on Abigail Porter's face. She must have had a little silver in her before all this started.

'I watched the women grow, ensured their families did well, put them into positions of access to important people.' Mr Bellew's grin spread. 'I have plans for them. They'll help me create my New World Order. Once they were ready, I told the Interventionists I needed something from each of them, and then I'd let them die. They performed magnificently, didn't they?'

Mr Bright was much closer. He tilted his head in Abigail's direction. 'It doesn't seem to have done her much good.'

'Ah, but she's not really here. She's hard reflecting. I've had to force the learning somewhat, but she's a natural. She's projecting back, just in case. I wouldn't want the other two getting into the wrong hands.'

Mr Bellew let the woman's arm go and she dropped to the floor with a yelp before crawling away towards the wall.

Mr Bright didn't look at her; she wasn't important. There were only a few feet between the two men, and they began to circle. He could see his own rising excitement in the other man's dark eyes – this was like the old days.

Footsteps came up the stairwell that Mr Bellew had used

and the tall man paused and looked back at the newcomer. His face was triumphant.

'Mr Craven,' he said.

'Mr Bellew.' Craven smiled.

'Well, well.' Mr Bright looked from one to the other.

'So will you come quietly?' Mr Bellew asked him.

Mr Bright raised a finger as more footsteps tapped up the concrete behind him. Mr Dublin appeared from the lower level. 'Am I late?'

'I think you might have misunderstood the situation, Mr Bellew,' Mr Bright said softly.

Mr Craven strolled out from behind Mr Bellew and stood the other side of Bright from Dublin. 'I may be sick, Mr Bellew, but I'm not a fool. You're going to get us *forgiven*? Find us *a way home*?' he snarled. 'I think not.'

'You betrayed me!' Mr Bellew's arrogance slipped away, anger taking its place.

'Oh come, come, Mr Bellew,' Bright said, 'we're all betrayers. Don't look so surprised. Now the question is—' and he smiled, '—are *you* going to come quietly?'

'Never.' The tall man drew himself up tall and his eyes sparkled with gold.

'I rather thought not.'

There was a moment of silence and then without warning all four *became*. Three flew at one, and their rage was terrible.

Cass abandoned his car in front of the skeleton building and ran in on the ground level. It was empty.

'Mr Bright?' The name tore loud from his lungs. He was past caring about safety. Whatever Mr Bright's plans for him were, the man seemed more intent on fucking him over than killing him. 'Mr Bright? I know you're here!' The empty space echoed ghosts of his words back to him and he headed to the stairs on his right: concrete blocks with no handrails stretching upwards. He took them two at a time as a sudden blast of wind raced down the other way. He leaned into it.

'Mr Bright?' he called again, rounding the corner and taking the last twenty steps or so to the next level. Lights danced down the stairs towards him and his heart chilled. *Solomon.* He hadn't seen light like that since Mr Solomon died. With sweat sticking his shirt to his back, he took the last few stairs slowly, but still he flinched as he emerged onto the first level and the full glory hit him and his breath ran free. He raised one arm to cover his eyes against the raging swirl that filled the vast space of the unfinished floor. Shades of gold and white and red and all the colours in between flashed this way and that, a tornado of colours that couldn't exist with such sharpness and clarity, and hiding within them were wings and teeth and sinews and blood. A wind raced through the building, beating Cass's body to the ground, and it was full of the angry roar of battle.

And then suddenly it stopped. The wind fell. Colour drained from the world and for a second all Cass could see were the shadows of the shapes in black spots in his vision. Everything was still. The tarpaulin behind him rustled slightly and he pulled himself up to his feet.

Four men stood in the centre of the room: one, a tall, broad, dark-haired man, had a deep gash down one cheek and blood soaked through his torn shirt. Two slim younger men stood on either side of him. Their suits were neat, but their faces were flushed. Gold still shone in their eyes. For the first time in a long time, Cass didn't think *there is no glow.* What was the point? To think that would be to lie to himself, and he was done with that.

'I'm afraid I can't stay long and chat.' Mr Bright smiled

at Cass, his teeth perfectly white in his composed face. 'I have to take care of this minor situation.'

'You set me up,' Cass growled. His face was burning.

'I set you *free*.' Somewhere in the distance a siren wailed. 'You weren't made to obey those rules. Now, if you'll excuse me, I have to go, and I think you have company coming.'

Cass raised his gun. The bastard wasn't going anywhere. Not yet.

'I think we both know it would take more than that.' Mr Bright's laugh was a cool stream on a summer's day.

'We had a deal. Where's Luke? Why did you steal him?'

'Oh yes, our deal. In all this excitement I'd almost forgotten. I didn't steal Luke. He was given to me.'

'You're lying.'

'I don't need to lie, Cass, and certainly not to you.' His eyes twinkled. 'Do you think you're the only Jones to do a deal with me?'

Cass frowned and his skin chilled. Jessica and Christian would not have given their baby away – they just wouldn't. They were too *good* for that. And if they had, why would Christian have left him that note? It didn't make sense.

'Do you think I just let people go, Cass? Do I strike you as that kind of man?' Mr Bright's voice was soft. Cass said nothing. He didn't know what to say. He wasn't sure that he wanted to hear what was coming next after all. That didn't stop Mr Bright speaking, though.

'It was your father: your father brought me the baby.'

'Bullshit.' Cass spat the word out through gritted teeth and his finger tightened involuntarily on the trigger. His *father*? The man who found all that faith? The one who kept trying to get Cass to forgive himself? Was it really Cass he wanted the forgiveness for after all? One child called Cassius, and one child called Christian. His father had run

380

away from Mr Bright, that's what Father Michael had said. Had he run – or had he bargained his way out?

'Your father showed so much promise in the early days; it was perfect when he and Evelyn fell in love. Everything was going to plan – we would create a new dynasty. And then he had a change of heart. Found God.' Mr Bright shook his head, as if talking about a child's foolishness. 'He wanted his freedom. I would have taken you, Cass, had he had this epiphany earlier. You were the first born; it would have made sense. But you were already born and they had bonded with you, and anyway, I don't think he would have agreed to give up any of his own children. He would have stayed against his will, and that would never have worked. So we made a deal.' He looked over at the other men. 'Take him to the car.'

'So you're Cassius Jones,' the man with ash-blond hair and delicate features said. His voice was cut-crystal. 'I hope we'll meet again.'

'I hope the fuck not.' Cass didn't care that the other man half-smiled at him before turning away. He didn't care that there was something close to affection in the expression. The Network would learn that if they were going to have any emotions for Cass, affection would not be one of them.

'You made a deal?' He didn't have much time. They would be coming for him, he was sure of that, and he needed to be gone before they got here.

'I gave him a choice: his freedom for a child, for the first-born son of his children. I hoped it would be your child, Cass. You were always more like us than Christian. He, however, was more malleable. You insisted on marrying Kate, and she would have weakened the blood. Jessica, however, she had the Glow. We'd been watching her family and it didn't take much to get her and Christian together.

Glow attracts Glow, I've noticed.' He glanced at his watch. 'On the night Luke was born, your father brought him to the hospital administrator's office and I gave him the replacement. I didn't want to hurt Christian. I'm not a monster.'

Cass stared at him. His own father had betrayed Christian. Was there anyone who hadn't betrayed his poor dead brother – the *good* brother?

'I'll be seeing you, Cassius Jones.' Mr Bright turned and walked away. 'You take care now.'

'Where's Luke now?' Cass shouted after him, running down towards the other end of the vast space where Mr Bright was heading for the back stairs.

'That wasn't part of our deal.' With a grin that bordered on mischievous, he disappeared into the stairwell.

'Help me.'

The desperate plea stopped Cass in his tracks and he turned. There was someone curled up against the wall. Abigail Porter. Had she been there the whole time?

'Help me,' she said again, the words barely more than a harsh whisper. Mr Bright was going to have to wait. Cass jogged over to her and crouched.

'Abigail? Are you hurt?'

'It hurts. I can't get back. *I can't get back.*' Her head was down, between her arms that were hugging her knees. Her shoulders shook. 'I don't want to see any more. I can't. I can't.'

'Jones?'

Cass looked up sharply as Fletcher's voice carried up from downstairs. Fuck.

'Jones? Where are you?' Ramsey that time. 'We need to talk.'

'We have to go, Abigail. Now.' There was no time. If he

didn't leave now, it would all be over. He reached down to grab her arm and haul her to her feet. She looked up.

'Jesus.' Cass recoiled as if punched in the face.

Blood from both her ears was dying her lank hair, but it was her eyes that stopped him in his tracks. There were no whites, no iris nor pupils, only pools of colour and black, marbling together. It was like looking deep into space. He could see everything and nothing.

'I fooled him,' she whispered. 'I left the reflection behind.' Silver tears rolled from her broken eyes. More voices drifted up at them, declaring the downstairs area clear.

'Give me the gun,' she barked, 'please. I'm torn in two, and in the spaces ... oh God, in the spaces ...'

'What are you going to do?' Cass asked. He thought he knew the answer. Abigail Porter was dying – whatever else was going on inside her body, she'd pushed it too far to survive. Watery crimson ran in the sweat from her scalp. Was her whole being starting to haemorrhage?

Footsteps clattered on the far stairs and he glanced towards them. There was no time for softness now. Abigail Porter had her fate, and he had his. He was damned if it was all going to end here. He released the safety and pressed the gun into her clammy hand and turned and ran for the second set of stairs. He didn't look back. He didn't want to look into those eyes again. If he did, he might find himself dragged to whatever hell her mind was in.

He was halfway down to the next level when the first gunshot cracked through the damp air.

'*Shit!*'

'*Put the gun down!*'

Cass pushed forward. More shots rang out, followed by more shouting, and then just as he reached the ground there was one final retort before the awful silence fell. His breathing was hard in his ears, and despite the chilly air he was sweating. Abigail had bought him some time, but how was he going to be able to use it? His car was round at the other side of the building, where Fletcher and Ramsey's cars must be – there was no way he could get to it. His best chance was to head to Oxford Street, and try and get lost in the crowds. It was thin, but it was all he had. He pushed his legs onwards into a sprint instead of a jog, ignoring the strain on unused muscles and relying on his adrenalin to keep him going. He would not get caught. He would not get caught.

'Cass, stop!' It was Fletcher's voice, its disembodied form chasing him up the gritty track, and without slowing, he glanced over one shoulder. The head of the ATD was coming up behind him, his gun raised.

'I mean it, Cass. Stop or I'll shoot!'

Despite the burn in his legs, Cass fought the urge to laugh: a hysterical laugh, but one all the same. *Stop or I'll shoot.* In all his years on the force he never thought he'd hear that cliché aloud. He weaved slightly.

'Fuck.' Fletcher's curse carried towards him. He'd stopped running. That meant only one thing. His heart thumping, Cass swerved from side to side, his eyes almost closed as he waited for the bullet. *He wasn't going to make it. He should just give up. He wasn't going to make it.* Still his legs powered forward.

Two things happened at once. The first was that a car screeched to a halt in the street in front of him and the back door flew open. The second was that Cass felt as if he'd been thumped hard in the back of his right shoulder.

'Get in!' a woman's voice screamed from the driver's seat of the car. She had a voice like honey, Cass thought, as his body spun slightly and stumbled. His ears echoed with the rumble of thunder. Not thunder. Gunshot. As he clumsily righted himself, one side of his body listing madly, he caught a glimpse of Fletcher, raising his gun again. Beyond him, a fair distance behind, were Ramsey and Armstrong. They were shouting something that Cass couldn't make out. He hoped to fuck it was 'Don't shoot!'

'Quickly!' the woman shouted again, and if Cass could have got his breath he would have screamed back, 'What the fuck do you think I'm trying to do?' but instead he just ploughed his feet through the mud and flung himself into the back of the car. She was driving away before his last leg was in, and that was fine with him.

The tramp leaned across him and pulled the door shut. Cass looked down at the bloody mess of his body. His shoulder felt like it was freezing and his eyes burned like ice. His breathing was rapid. So this was what it felt like to be shot. The world was getting dark at the edges and a wave of nausea made a lazy attempt to flood his system. The girl weaved the car expertly through the traffic. He wondered about asking where the fuck they were going, but couldn't get the words out. Still, anywhere was better than Paddington Green nick.

'They weren't lying about you, son.' The tramp beside him let out a hearty laugh. 'You really do have *the glow.*'

'*Fuck the glow,*' Cass was pleased to hear himself say. It seemed like a good alternative to *there is no glow.* The sense of self-satisfaction didn't last long. Barely a moment later the darkness claimed him and he passed out. It came as something of a relief.

Mr Bright liked the corridors at night, when it was quiet. He'd smoked a cigarette on the roof – it wasn't a cigar kind of evening – and then sat with the First for a while. Presently he'd go back to The Bank and carry on his paper trail from Mr Bellew's accounts. Most of his followers had been the sick, and were no immediate threat now that their leader was, to all intents and purposes, gone. He'd decide what to do with them later.

It had been two days since they'd brought Mr Bellew in, and things were slowly calming down. They always did. He'd read about Jones' escape in the papers and on the news, and then got the first-hand events from his various connections. He hadn't had any doubt that Cass would get himself out of the situation, but he was curious about that car and who was driving it. It was no matter – he'd find out in due time. Jones was injured and would need to recover before he came after Mr Bright, which he surely would. In fact, he was banking on it.

He stopped outside one heavy door and slid open the panel on it. Mr Bellew sat curled up against the wall, strapped into a straitjacket. The restraint was unfortunate, but it stopped him scratching at his eyes. The big man's mouth hung open slightly and a long strand of drool hung from it. At least he wasn't screaming.

A brief wave of sadness washed over Mr Bright. Mr Bellew had been one of the finest: arrogant to the last, even as they strapped him down and told him to try for the walkways, he had smiled and laughed and told them he'd make it. As always, however, Mr Bellew had overstated his own abilities, and now here he was, with empty eyes and no *Glow*. He'd had a small last laugh, though. His facility in the old Underground tunnels had been found, but abandoned. According to the papers, Abigail Porter had died in the shootout – it amused him that she'd managed to fool Mr Bellew – but there were still two more out there, programmed to do whatever it was Mr Bellew had wanted of them. Still, they couldn't stay hidden for ever.

He slid the hatch shut, leaving Mr Bellew to his madness, and headed for the lift. Thus far, he concluded, most things were going according to plan. Yes, there had been the odd, unexpected mishap, but all things considered, there had been no harm done.

Epilogue

Elroy Peterson couldn't sleep. He couldn't sleep and he couldn't eat and he couldn't do anything except see the colours behind his eyes. Terrible colours. He'd left the house earlier, and found himself standing by the tube station, totally confused and looking down at his Oyster card as if it could somehow tell him where he should be going. He should be going somewhere, he was sure of that. But where? It hurt to think.

He cried a lot when the house was empty. He hadn't been to Uni for two days. What was the point? What could possibly be the point of all of this? He was crying now, standing in the bathroom at two in the morning, just staring at his reflection as if it could somehow tell him who he was. As if it could somehow fill the empty space inside him. Something had broken him; a part of him was missing. Sometimes he could hear himself screaming and the only way to stop it was to scream himself.

He lifted the knife and, looking down, slowly carved the only words that made sense into his naked chest. It didn't hurt. Nothing could hurt compared with what was going on behind his eyes. He wondered about going back to his bedroom, but instead he lowered the lid on the toilet and sat down. He didn't want to get blood on the carpet. He didn't want to make a mess. He cut his wrists with no thought whatsoever, an absent gesture of an absent mind, and then leaned his head back against the cistern. It was cold as space. He didn't cry any more after that.

When they broke the door down in the morning, despite his wishes not to, Elroy Peterson's death had made quite a mess. The words clumsily carved into his chest were still legible though. They, not the blood that covered the pale and cracked tiles around his drained body, were what made his housemate scream.

Chaos in the darkness.

THE END

Acknowledgements

As always, a huge thank you to my editor Jo Fletcher and my agent Veronique Baxter for their continued support. You both rock. I also owe thanks this year to Ray and Matt Marshall at Festival Film for loving the first book enough to want to make television out of it. Best of luck with that, chaps! The longer that I write full-time the more I realise the importance of my writery friends – they're a network of support I just couldn't be without. As for all the real-life friends, thanks for making me take time out from the work to have some fun. You're all the best. And a final thanks very much to whoever invented the Internet for making research so much easier. We writers all salute you.

SP